THE PARTY'S J

The French lieutenant looked like a visitor from another world as he stepped onto *Torbay*'s shattered deck. He came aft in his immaculate uniform and, enemy or no, he could not hide the shock behind his eyes as he saw the huge bloodstains on the deck, the dead and the heap of amputated limbs piled beside the main hatch for later disposal, the dismounted guns and shattered masts.

"Lieutenant de Vaisseau Joubert of the *Ville de Paris*," he introduced himself. His graceful, hat-flourishing bow would have done credit to Versailles, but Captain Paul had lost his own hat to another French marksman sometime during the terrible afternoon, and he merely bobbed his head in a curt nod.

"Captain Sir John Paul," he replied. "How may I help you, Monsieur?"

"My admiral 'as sent me to request your surrender, Capitaine."

"Indeed?" Paul looked the young Frenchman up and down. Joubert returned his gaze levelly, then made a small gesture at the broken ship about them.

"You 'ave fought magnificently, Capitaine, but you cannot win. We need break through your defenses at only one point. Once we are be'ind you—" He shrugged delicately. "You 'ave cost us many ships, and you may cost us more. In the end, 'owever, you must lose. Surely you must see that you 'ave done all brave men can do."

"Not yet, Lieutenant," Paul said flatly, drawing himself to his full height.

"You will not surrender?" Joubert seemed unable to believe it, and Paul barked a laugh.

"Surrender?" I have not yet *begun* to fight, Lieutenant!" John Paul replied. "Go back and inform your admiral that he will enter this bay only with the permission of the King's Navy!"

—from "The Captain from Kirkbean" by David M. Weber

ALTERNATE GENERALS

EDITED BY
HARRY TURTLEDOVE

With editorial assistance
by Roland Green

BAEN

A Baen Books Original

Baen Publishing Enterprises
P.O. Box 1403
Riverdale, NY 10471

ISBN: 0-671-87886-7

Cover art by Charles Keegan

First printing, August 1998
Second printing, January 2000

Distributed by Simon & Schuster
1230 Avenue of the Americas
New York, NY 10020

Printed in the United States of America

CONTENTS

THE TEST OF GOLD
Lillian Stewart Carl

The old man lowered himself carefully onto the couch. Every day the pain in his belly grew worse. By winter he'd be at rest in the tomb of his ancestors beside the Appian Way. He'd had a long life, as soldier and merchant, and if Mars, Mercury, and Mithras called him, so be it. But there was something he had to finish first.

Through the opening of the atrium he could just see Caligula's old bridge between the Palatine and the Capitoline, a hard marble angle against the glare of the summer sky. A beam of sunlight touched the door of the room. The air was warm and still. Even so he felt cool, as though the rectangular porphyry panels and columns of his home exuded a chill.

Unless it was simply the memory of chill. He leaned closer to his table, spread out the scroll, and started to read what he'd already written.

Ave. I was named C. Marcus Valerius after my father and tutored by the best Greek slaves. At the age of twenty, in the sixth year of the reign of Nero Augustus, I was made a military tribune and assigned to the staff of Catus Decianus, procurator of the province of Britannia. My mother and sisters wept to see me off to the very edge of the earth, but my father reminded me I was now beginning a brilliant career.

The road through Gaul was long. The farther north I went the colder the wind grew and the more sullen the rain. But the coarse humor of my little band of legionaries never faltered. One auxiliary from Iberia, called Ebro after his native river, jested even with me. At first I took offense. Then I realized that Ebro had many campaigns beneath his corselet, while I had none, and I learned to return gibe for gibe.

By the time we took ship across a rough gray sea and landed in Britannia I was wet through, unshaven, muddied from boot to helmet. And yet I could do no less than to press on, doing my duty, with that Roman honor which brought us not only an empire but the will to rule it.

In Londinium I presented myself to Catus Decianus. He had the small sleek head and obsidian eyes of a snake, and barely gave me time to bathe before he assigned me a task. "The king of one of the British tribes," he explained, "has lately died. He bequeathed half his property to the Emperor. As well he should, after all the trouble he caused us ten years ago. These barbarians are a stubborn lot. All we intended was to disarm them, and they had the gall to rebel."

I nodded as sagely as I could.

"The king's name was Prasutagus," Catus went on. "Of the Iceni, beyond Camulodunum. He has no male heir, so there's no question of the kingdom continuing. You're to make an accounting of the Emperor's property. I intend to deliver it to the governor when he returns from his campaign against the Druids."

Thanks to Ebro's stories I knew what he was talking about. "The Druids are the priestly class. They have great power, no Gaulish or British ruler will make a move without consulting with one."

If Catus was impressed with my knowledge, he showed no sign of it. "So it's in our best interests to stamp them out. Suetonius has them bottled up on some island in the northwest, and their women with them."

"I'd like to pay my respects to Gaius Suetonius Paulinus. And my father's. They campaigned together in Mauretania."

"Then you'd better get on with it, Tribune. Suetonius will be back before summer, his eagles draped with Druid gold. You don't want to still be mucking about in a barbarian village by then, do you?"

"No sir." I saluted. "Until I return, then, sir."

Catus was already unrolling a scroll, and dismissed me with a wave of his hand. I reminded myself I needed his good will to advance my career and set out on the next stage of my journey.

Londinium was little more than a cluster of merchant's wood and wattle houses around a bridge over the Tamesis, although I could tell from the new roads being driven outward in every direction that Suetonius intended the city to be a hub of commerce. The road north cut through marshland.

When I think of Britannia I think of water—the great river, the marshes, heavy clouds like sopping fleeces, unrelenting rain. There trees grow thick and forests thicker. But just as I decided Britannia was the soggy frontier of Hades itself, the rain ended and a warm wind rolled up the clouds. For the first time I saw the British spring, so many shades of green I couldn't count them and a sky of such rich blue as to put lapis lazuli to shame.

Camulodunum, an old tribal capital, had been made into a colonia for retired legionaries. This part of the country was pacified, and all the building work had gone into a vast temple to Roma and Claudius Augustus. Just completed, it stood square and proud—and, I had to admit, pretentious—among the mounds of the native huts. The natives themselves cleared away leftover stones, casting resentful glances toward the old soldiers who lounged on the steps.

Ebro spat onto the paving stones. He could say more with a glob of spit than most men with words. But, as befitted my dignity, I didn't ask whether he was reproving the native workers or our own veterans.

At last Venta Icenorum rose before us. Black birds swooped and croaked above huge circular earthworks. Human skulls grinned from recesses in the gateposts. The guards were tall blond men sporting fierce moustaches, hair swept back like horses' manes, and massive embossed shields. They greeted me civilly enough in their strange tongue, although there was a certain amount of sword and spear rattling as they conducted me through the town. By standing as straight as I could I made myself as tall as the shortest of them.

Women and children dropped their tasks and looked at me. Even the dark eyes of the cows and horses turned my way. My escort strolled along casually, but one sharp look from Ebro and my legionaries marched in good order.

The buildings were also circular, of wood pilings with conical thatched roofs. Inside the largest was a vast hall ringed with wooden pillars. A ray of sunlight struck through a vent hole in the roof. In the dimness beyond stood several more warriors. The king's guard, I assumed, now at loose ends.

But the warriors seemed more haughty than uncertain. Turning, they deferred to a figure who stepped through a curtained doorway. A woman. I waited a moment, but no one else appeared.

She was tall as the men, a full handsbreadth taller than me. She wore a dress and a cloak woven in squares of different colors. Holding the cloak was a gold brooch cunningly wrought in swirls of gold, decorated with enamel chips. About her neck lay a gold torc, strands of braided wire with animal-headed knobs resting against her white throat. Even her hair was gold, a startling golden red, braided and ornamented with beads. Her eyes were as blue as the British sky. They fixed on my face, looking me up and down in the same manner I'd inspect a horse, although I've never been quite so amused by an animal.

Everyone was looking at me. They expected me to deal with a woman. I made a show of removing my helmet and tucking it under my arm. "Ave. I am C. Marcus Valerius. I bring greetings from the Senate and the people of Roma."

"I am Boudica, queen of the Iceni. My husband was your ally."

Ally, not client, I noted. But I'd heard that these Britons were a proud people. "I'm tribune to Catus Decianus, procurator. I've come to make an accounting of your husband's legacy."

"I've never known a Roman," she said, "who'd let anything of value slip through his fingers."

I took her statement as a jest. Unless—well, no, her Latin was impeccable, she meant what she said.

She went on, in a low vibrant voice, "He left you half his property. The other half I hold in trust for my daughter, heir to the rule of the Iceni."

I glanced at the assembled warriors. But they couldn't understand what she was saying, no wonder they didn't seem unsettled by it.

"We'll hold a feast tonight, in your honor," concluded Boudica. "My men will show you and your men to your own house."

I realized I was standing there with my tongue stuck to the roof of my mouth. "Ah—thank you. We'd like a bath, after the long road. . . ."

She smiled so broadly crescent lines cleft her cheeks. "I'll have the servants bring you basins of water."

"Thank you," I said again, as though I were the client.

Boudica turned and went out through the curtain. Beyond it stood a brown-bearded man wearing a white robe and a collar of gold. Her head tilted toward his and she spoke. The curtain fell.

I made a neat about-face and strode back down the length of the building. My task here, I thought, wasn't going to be as simple as I'd first assumed. If Boudica's jewelry were any indication, the Iceni had more than a few trinkets worthy of Nero's coffers. And delivering such an accounting would certainly grease my path to advancement.

The old man put down the scroll. Someone was shouting in the street, and a wheeled vehicle rattled by, but the house itself was silent.

His belly hurt. He considered calling for his wife to rub his back, but no, she'd be in her garden, gathering the herbs for this afternoon's banquet. She'd prepare his porridge and soft meats with her own hands, as she usually did, but beneath her keen eye the cooks would make ready a sumptuous meal for a very special guest. Already a spicy odor hung in the air, but his appetite had deserted him long ago.

"Rufus!" the old man called in his reedy voice.

The servant materialized in the doorway.

"Let me know the moment my son arrives."

"Yes, master." The servant vanished again. A good man, Rufus. Marcus had left instructions in his will that he be freed. . . .

Not that the instructions in a will were always followed, were they? With a groan he picked up the scroll again.

Warriors and their women sat down together at the feast, ranged in a circle around a blazing fire in the center of the great hall. Servants passed meats, breads, herbs, and a Falernian wine as fine as any my father ever served at his table in Roma. I'd heard that the chief god of the Britons was Mercury, the patron of merchants. I began to see why.

Through the smoky gloom I caught again and again the gleam of gold, electrum, and gilded bronze. Everyone wore ornaments, brooches, necklaces—outside I'd seen even their splendid horses adorned with metalwork.

Every ornament was designed in the living lines of plants, of horses' tails, of serpents. Our own utilitarian items seemed dull and flat.

Tonight Boudica's brooch held a cloak of green silk stitched with sinuous designs in gold thread. It rustled faintly as she motioned me to sit beside her and her daughters. They were lissome, red-headed girls of about fifteen and twelve, introduced as Brighid and Maeve. When I asked if Prasutagus had arranged marriages for them before his death the girls looked faintly shocked, but Boudica smiled.

She herself was perhaps five and thirty, past her youth but not beyond remarriage. I expected every tribal monarch across Britannia was vying for her hand. Even half the wealth of the Iceni would be a prize.

Every now and then one of the warriors hurled some boast at me, which Boudica translated, erring on the side of courtesy, I imagine. She made no move to reprove the mens' boisterousness. Her rule was probably only courtesy to their king's widow, I thought. She had no real power.

The white-robed man sat behind us. More than once I felt his eyes on the back of my neck, but every time I looked around his bearded face was bland. At last I asked Boudica who he was, thinking he was perhaps her brother and guardian.

"He is Lovernios," she replied. "My advisor."

The man himself nodded, with an amused smile identical to Boudica's. I'd never before found myself the butt of such a subtle joke. Was Lovernios a druid who'd escaped Suetonius's nets? Between my ignorance of the Iceni's customs and the delectable wine I was no doubt playing quite the fool. I made a note to pay closer attention.

The fire burned down and the faces of the Iceni grew red as Boudica's hair. But their taunts and the occasional gnawed bone were aimed more at each other than at my men, who sat to one side watching the scuffles as they'd watch a gladiatorial combat.

Boudica exchanged a look with Lovernios. He slipped out. Another man entered, raised an instrument like a lyre, and began to sing. "It's the story of a boar hunt," Boudica murmured, her breath piquant with wine and herbs. "He'll sing of bulls and horses and the deeds of our ancestors."

As a follower of Mithras, I understood the bull, and nodded.

The girls rose from their seats. "Good night, Tribune," said Brighid gravely, and little Maeve blushed and said, "Good night."

"Young ladies," I returned with a slight bow.

Boudica stood up, draping her cloak about her shoulders. "Come with me, Tribune, and I'll show you one of our temples."

"Very good, Lady." I managed to stand without stumbling. The cool night air, even with its hint of manure, tasted delicious after the close, smoky hall. I expected Boudica to bring me to a building, but no, we walked down into a dell in the side of the embankment. Above us a sentry stood outlined against the star-strewn sky, a glint of gold at his neck.

In the bottom of the dell burned a fire, illuminating a tree so large all I could see of it were a few limbs curving toward the earth and rising again. A semicircle of gold was embedded in one thick limb. Above the fire a small bronze cauldron hung from a tripod, steaming gently. Nearby a spring issued from a rock grotto and rippled away into the darkness.

With one twist of her hands Boudica removed her torc. It must have been almost pure gold to bend so easily. She held it up, so that it shone red-gold in the firelight. Then she threw it into the water. I started forward, appalled and confused in equal measure. But it was gone.

She laughed. "Gold belongs to the gods. They send it

to us, we work it into shapes which honor them, and then we give it back."

"Oh." I could hear Catus's voice quizzing me—how many springs and wells contained gold offerings? Where did the gold come from?

"This is the shrine of Andrasta, my patron goddess," Boudica went on. "Victoria in your tongue."

"Minerva," I translated.

"Not necessarily." She pulled what I now saw was a golden sickle from the tree, and from a branch cut a bunch of small white berries. She sprinkled them into the cauldron. "Mistletoe, which grows on the sacred oak. Vervain, henbane with its purple flowers, the early fruit of the elder."

The odor filled my head, flowers and herbs both sweet and bitter.

"And what accounting will you give to Catus?" she asked.

I wondered if she intended to offer me a bribe. "The truth."

"Well then, Tribune Marcus, the truth is that my late husband left his property to your emperor hoping to buy respect. But respect can't be bought."

"Why not? I know freed slaves who've made themselves into successful merchants and become quite respectable."

"Wealth makes one respectable, does it? But our wealth is our freedom. And that's what we would keep." She swept the sickle through the liquid in the cauldron, throwing several drops onto my forearm. My flesh burned. Instinctively I lifted my arm to my lips. The hot liquid scalded my tongue. First a foul taste, and then a honeyed one, swelled into my mouth and nose. Boudica smiled.

The wind whispered in the branches of the tree. The water laughed. The embers of the fire made a rosy glow among the shadows. In the distance men shouted and sang. Boudica was murmuring something in her own tongue, something which tickled the edges of my mind. She unbraided her hair. It flowed thick and golden red down her back.

She, too, was a druid, a priestess, a magician. . . . I felt myself shrinking, smaller and smaller, until I squatted on the grass looking up at her. My long ears twitched. My paws were velvet soft. I was a hare, lolloping about the dell. And she was a gray hound, running after me like a swirl of smoke. I bounded across the grass and she was on me, her teeth closing on my puff of a tail.

I dived into the spring. The chill made me shiver. I was a fish, sleek and cold, looking up through the surface of the water at the distorted shapes of fire and tree. And she was an otter, her smooth body knifing through the water, so that whichever way I darted she was on me.

I launched myself upward, into the air, wings beating, beak open to draw in more breath. Into the tree I flew. The budding leaves brushed my face. And she was a hawk, gliding among the branches with swift, sure strokes, talons striking feathers from my tail.

I fell to the ground a tiny grain of wheat and lay immobile, gazing at the tree, the fire, the water, the sky. She came toward me, a black hen pecking and clawing. She grasped me in her beak. I cracked open, seed and chaff, and scattered into the night. Scattered into the morning, and the golden sun rising in Boudica's blue eyes.

Her cloak billowed into hills, valleys, mountains, groves. Mistletoe sparkled like dewdrops among the branches of mighty oaks. The turf rang to the beat of horses' hooves and then parted, revealing the white chalk beneath, making figures of gods and men which not only lay across the land but which were the land itself.

The brooch on the cloak became an embroidery of wells, streams, and rivers lacing sky to earth, land to sea, a green glass sea swelling and falling to the slow spirals of sun and moon. Roads were golden threads stitching together grove and field, hill and shore, strung with temples like fine beadwork. Hibernia in the far west was sewn to Britannia was sewn to Gaul and on into the east, Galatia, Sarmatia . . . The fine golden embroidery ripped, cut by the iron weapons of Roma, weapons sharp and greedy not for gods but for gold.

Boudica's hands gathered me up. I blinked, returned to my body. She was not sharp and hard as a hen's beak, but warm, soft, moist, a fully-fleshed woman leaning over me, her hair a gleaming curtain around us. My mouth was filled by the taste of honey.

Her draught had addled my wits. It had opened my eyes. It had not sabotaged my capabilities. I'd known only courtesans, and to be made free of a high-born woman, Briton or no, was both intimidating and stimulating. . . . She made free with me, not playing the wanton for my pleasure so much as she expected my pleasure to please her. Which it did, if I do say so myself.

I woke from the dream, from the vision, in Boudica's bed. I was knocking my fists against my forehead, trying to awaken my wits, when the door of the house opened and Boudica entered. Her hair was tidily braided. She wore a simple woven cloak. "Good morning."

"What did you do to me?" I demanded.

"I laid a *geas* upon you. A fate. To know the truth and to speak it."

"I would do that in any event. Truth and honor go hand in hand."

"Do they?" She picked up my tunic from the floor, shook it out, and handed it to me. "Is truth golden? Or is gold truth?"

"Gold is gold." I dressed, glancing warily over my shoulder.

"Then you'd better get on with counting that gold which is yours," she said, and shooed me out the door.

I walked back to the house she'd assigned to me, trying not to catch anyone's eye. If the warriors found out what had happened they'd slay me on the spot. They took insult easily, these men, and what greater insult could I hand them than to make free with one of their women? Even worse, with one of their priestesses? I remembered a straying vestal virgin and her lover buried alive, and shuddered.

Not one warrior paid me any attention at all, even though a couple of Boudica's serving women glanced at me and giggled. I ducked into my house and saw my pack of tablets and pens. That was it. Boudica had sacrificed her honor in order to influence my accounting. But my duty was to make an honest count . . . Wondering if yet again I was somehow playing the fool, I gathered up my supplies and set about my business.

The next five days passed from sunlight to soft rain to night and back again. It seemed as though I'd never before noticed the burgeoning of spring, the waxing of the moon, the intricate patterns of wind, water, and wood.

My men went hunting with Boudica's warriors and acquitted themselves honorably, even as Ebro muttered about undisciplined Iceni hooligans. He drilled my small command every afternoon, to the amusement of Maeve and the younger children. But drill can be learned, while courage cannot; with proper training, I noted, the Iceni would make fine auxiliaries, serving the eagles as well as Ebro and his kind.

One afternoon wagons rolled up the ramp to the gate, bearing treasure from the northwest. Suetonius was campaigning in the northwest, I remembered, and made a note in my margins.

Lovernios worked with me, translating records cut on strips of wood. I had to trust he was giving me a fair accounting, but I didn't catch him out once. They used writing only for the tallying of goods and stock, I learned. When it came to the epics of beasts, gods, and heroes, Lovernios and the bard could recite for hours without faltering.

I finished my task. The night before I left, Boudica took me back to the sylvan temple below the embankment. This was the first time we'd been alone together since I'd waked in her bed. I was both relieved and disappointed to see no fire and no cauldron beside the stream, only a charred circle in the grass. The golden sickle was gone.

But still the branches of the great tree creaked, and water droplets danced above the mossy rocks. Boudica removed a gold torc from her throat and fitted it around mine. "You like gold, don't you? Then try this for size."

The torc was heavy, pulling my collarbones down, elongating my neck. All this time I'd seen her and the warriors wearing such ornaments, and I'd never realized just how uncomfortable they were.

She grasped the knobs at the ends of the coil and pressed them together, choking me. "Gold belongs to the gods. It devotes us to the gods. They can take us at any time. The braided strands are the rope around the throat and the tree limb above. They're the sword which separates head from body. Death takes only a moment, but the next life goes on forever. Do you love me?"

Startled, I opened my mouth to utter some flattery, but my lips and tongue said, "No."

Laughing, she released the torc and teased my short, dark hair. "Good. I wouldn't want you to think our hour together was—personal. I only wanted to taste exotic meat. As you did."

Fair enough, I thought, and was surprised at myself for thinking it. "And this—*geas*?"

"You will know the truth and you will speak it. Whether that will be a blessing or a curse remains to be seen."

I didn't follow her meaning. I twisted the torc from my neck and held it out to her.

"No," she said. "Keep it. As a gift from Andrasta."

Still puzzled, I looked one last time around the dell, and, concealing the torc in my cloak, returned to my tablets and my pens.

The next morning I took my leave of Boudica, Brighid, and Maeve. And of Lovernios, even as I wondered what Suetonius would think of my courtesy. At the eaves of the forest I looked back at Venta Icenorum, at the dark soil of the fields awaiting the plow and the blue arch of sky. So our ancestors must have lived, wild and free, before submitting to the rule of law. . . . I remembered the skulls decorating the gate, and chilled, rode away.

When I made my report to Catus Decianus I thought briefly of minimizing not only the wealth of the Iceni, but their position at the knot of the golden thread of trade. My tongue, however, couldn't shade the truth, let alone utter a lie. I found myself telling him even of Boudica herself, of her strength and beauty and determination to hold the Iceni for her daughter.

His chin went up. His brows rose. "So tell me then, Tribune, how is this barbarian village defended?"

My heart sinking, I told him that, too.

The old man let the scroll roll shut. He shut his eyes and touched his lips with his fingertips. From the atrium came the sounds of voices, footsteps, and furniture sliding across the tile floor.

"Are you in pain?" asked his wife's voice.

"Yes, as always," he replied, looking up. "But mostly I'm tired."

"Why are you writing it down? It was so long ago." She walked to his side and began stroking his shoulders.

"It's my *geas*. I know the truth and I must speak it."

She sighed. "The memories are harsher for you than they are for me."

"You were guiltless. I was not." He captured her hand and held it to his face. It was scented with rosemary, thyme, and coriander, the hot herbs of a hot climate. "What will you do when I've gone to Mars and Mithras? Is there comfort in your secret new god, the crucified one?"

"He reminds me of the gods I knew as a child, who taught that death was not an end."

"As Mithras teaches, too."

They leaned together in companionable silence, as they had for almost forty years now. From the corner of his eye Marcus saw her dangling braid, its red-gold faded to gray. Which was just as well—her hair color no longer drew comment in the streets, although her height always would.

Through the atrium he could see the flat, pale sky. "Thank you, my love," he said, releasing her hand, and spread open the scroll.

The next time I saw Venta Icenorum, it was burning. The damp thatch of the roofs singed slowly, sending billows of gray smoke to mingle with a gray sky. Men lay dead beside their plows in the muddy fields. Birds both black and white wheeled overhead.

A blond warrior was pinned by a javelin to one of the gateposts. Inside the town women screamed and arms clashed. But Catus's legionaries had taken the Iceni by surprise. Why should they suspect an attack by an ally?

I urged my horse toward the Great Hall, Ebro jogging at my knee, sword drawn. But already the sounds of battle were dying. I wondered how many of the bodies we passed were of men I'd lately heard boasting. But perhaps they were the fortunate ones, to go so swiftly to their gods. . . . There were very few bodies, I noted, and wondered whether Catus had been fortunate enough to attack when most of the warriors were out hunting.

I couldn't believe my eyes. Catus himself stood atop a small platform hastily assembled from logs, the standard bearers ranged behind him. Before him Boudica was lashed to an upright pole. Two legionaries crouched nearby, clasping themselves, red-faced. She'd not gone without fighting, then.

Catus signaled. Two centurions stepped forward, ripped

Boudica's dress open, and began applying their rods. The slap of leather against her back made my gorge rise. "Catus!"

He ignored me. Obviously he meant not only to bring the Iceni under Roman rule here and now, but to punish Boudica for her presumption. But she was hardly presumptuous in following her own customs. . . . High-pitched screams made me look around.

Several legionaries were dragging Brighid and Maeve away, tearing at their dresses and shouting coarse wagers at each other. Horrified, I swarmed down from my horse and came face to face with Ebro. His laconic expression didn't change, but his meaning was obvious. The legionaries were following orders. By interfering I'd only call censure upon myself.

I spun around and shot the sharpest look of which I was capable at Catus. He was inspecting Boudica's brooch, turning it back and forth to catch the light. Nothing personal, just business, Roma's virility making an example of the proud women of a proud tribe.

The girls' screams turned to sobs. Boudica never screamed. Her eyes blazing, she spat quick painful gasps—curses, no doubt—toward Catus and toward me.

Again I started forward, again I stopped. Tightening my jaw, I climbed back on my horse. She dealt honorably with me, I shouted, and swallowed every word until my gut knotted with them. What of my honor? I made my accounting, as was my duty—should I have said the Iceni were a poor people, not worth the conquest? But I couldn't lie, Boudica's *geas* had seen to that.

I saw her face twisted in pain and rage and the blood running down the white flesh of her back, dabbling her braids with crimson. I heard the cries of her dishonored daughters. What of Roma's honor, to treat a free-born people like disobedient slaves?

Overcome with horror and shame I fled, and supervised the squads who were already loading gold ornaments into carts and rounding up the horses and cows. That evening when we left the ruins of Venta Icenorum I didn't look back.

Within a day wild rumors filled the shops and taverns of Camulodunum—screams had been heard in the theatre, ghosts had been seen along the seashore. The Romans began glancing warily behind them. The Britons exchanged furtive smiles—except for the women married to our veterans.

I knew their dread, and told Catus, "The Iceni will respond to this insult with war."

"Let them," he returned. "A disorganized rabble will make a good drill for our soldiers."

He went trotting back to Londinium with his booty. Despite the pleas of the settlers, he left only two hundred legionaries to man the nonexistent defenses. And he left me, telling me this was my chance to further my career in the service of Nero Augustus.

In truth, I was no longer certain I wanted to serve Nero. But I thought of my family, and their ambitions for me, and steeled myself to die.

Not only the Iceni went to war, but their cousins the Trinovantes. It was noon when the warriors fell upon Camulodunum, tens of thousands of them screaming their battle cries, their maned hair flying behind them, utterly disdainful of us and of death.

My little squad fought well, but for every warrior we brought down ten others came behind. By evening only Ebro and I were left, standing back to back on the steps of the temple while the city burned around us.

Several warriors ringed us, while others sprinted up the steps. A moment later the great bronze statue of Claudius came rolling down, with a clattering crash loud enough to wake the senators back in Roma. They tore the emperor's effigy apart. They fired the temple. They dragged Roman and Briton alike into the streets and cut them to pieces. The gutters ran with blood.

They didn't advance on Ebro and me until the ceiling of the temple caved in and a gust of hot black smoke almost knocked us over. Ebro took down two, and I might have stabbed one, but their long swords overcame our short ones. We were brought in chains before Boudica.

She stood in a light wicker chariot, her face glowing, her red hair fluttering like leaping flames. A gold torc shone at her throat. Behind her stood Brighid, trembling with rage, and hollow-eyed Maeve, pale even in the light of the fires. Lovernios stood next to them, holding a staff, a golden sickle tucked into his belt. At their feet rose a gory pile of severed heads, steaming in the cool of the evening. Among them I recognized the misshapen faces of men who'd done their duty.

"Shall I add your head to my trophies, Marcus?" Boudica asked, her voice grating, her scowl like a slap across my face.

I forced myself to stand tall, wearing my chains like a torc, and met her eyes. "I am once again in your hands, Lady."

"I knew that dog Catus would come for the gold. I planned that. I never in my worst nightmares thought he would come for me and mine. What did you tell him?"

"The truth."

She stared at me. And then she laughed, humorlessly. Her daughters looked up at her, more fearful than curious. Lovernios stared down at the blood pooled at his feet.

"Here's another truth for you," Boudica went on. "We've just had word from the northwest, as Catus has no doubt had word in Londonium. Suetonius took the sacred island of Mona and destroyed the druid college there. My plan is twisted and bent back upon itself. But I shall go on to victory despite all, in Andrasta's name."

One of the warriors dragged Ebro's head back and raised his sword. "No!" I shouted. "If you crave more blood, take mine."

Boudica looked me up and down, as she had the first time we met. A ghost of her amusement moved deep in her eyes and vanished. "Very well, then. I'll show your man more mercy than you showed my daughters." She jerked her head. The warrior released Ebro, but not without pushing him into the dirt.

"Thank you," I said, and bent my head for the blow.

"Oh, don't be so noble, Marcus. You know what your life is worth." The horses stamped and neighed. Turning, Boudica flicked the reins. The chariot moved off across the battlefield that had this morning been a peaceful colonia. Her warriors saluted her and went back to plundering the town.

Yes, in that moment I knew what my life was worth. Boudica had planned all along to revolt, perhaps even before her husband's death. Lovernios and his druid colleagues had drawn Suetonius and his legions away to the northwest. And then Boudica had dangled the lure, gold and horses and power, before Catus and before me.

Of course Lovernios and most of the warriors hadn't been in Venta Icenorum the day of Catus's raid. Boudica had sacrificed her own town in order to enrage all the Britons and lead them into rebellion. That Suetonius had won his battle added fuel to the fire. That Boudica and her daughters suffered such dishonor fed the fire to a white heat.

And as for me? It was my honor that had been in peril that night in the dell, not hers. Oh I'd played the fool, all right. She'd knotted me into her plot like an iron thread drawn through the midst of her gold embroidery.

"Marcus," said Lovernios, drawing my eyes to him. "Poenus Postumus in Glevum is occupied with our cousins the Silures, and won't be able to reinforce Suetonius. But I'd like to know how many men are garrisoned at Lindum, and the disposition of Petillius Cerialis, their legate."

Boudica had intended all along to capture me once the rebellion began. Because I knew the truth, and had to speak it. And so I did, halting and stammering as the blood drained from my face and sickened in my gut.

Ebro stared at me, his long face growing longer, but said nothing.

The old man bent over the scroll, not knowing whether it was the pain in his belly which drew a chill sweat to his forehead, or the memory. Even today he couldn't smell damp straw burning without growing queasy.

"Master," said Rufus's voice. "Your son is here. He sends his respects, and has gone to the bath house."

Marcus glanced up. "Thank you."

The shaft of sunlight inched closer to his couch, dust motes spiraling in its golden glow. It was time to make an end. He picked up his pen, moistened it in the pot of ink, and continued to write.

The Britons left Camulodunum, its white temple blackened, the bodies of its citizens worried by wolves and crows. Their army spread far beyond the road, warriors, horses, wagons laden with plunder sauntering across the untilled fields not just in poor order, but in no order at all.

Not that I offered any criticism. I trudged along behind Boudica's chariot in a black melancholy which lay heavier on me than the chains they'd removed. Ebro, too, walked unencumbered, sometimes at my side, sometimes behind me, his eyes darting to and fro.

But if we'd tried to escape our captors would've made short work of us. Don't think I wasn't tempted—if I couldn't throw myself on my own sword, then that of a British warrior would do. But a stubborn spark of life kept me on my feet. And the *geas* kept my tongue wagging.

Boudica glanced in my direction every so often, as

did Maeve, but Brighid made a point of presenting me with her back. None of them spoke to me. It was Lovernios who told me that Petillius Cerialis had come south from Lindum with a detachment of the Ninth Legion and met with a larger detachment of the Iceni. Petillius escaped the slaughter with only his cavalry, and was now walled up in Lindum licking his wounds.

I saw the conquest of Verulamium with my own eyes. The Britons were drunk on blood and booty, and spared no one. The baggage train grew longer—longer by far than Catus's. Boudica turned toward Londinium.

Lovernios came to me yet again. By this time I was as filthy outside as I felt inside. Even so, I rose to my feet and offered him a place by the tiny fire Ebro had kindled.

"No, thank you," he said. "I must ask your advice."

I smiled thinly at our mock courtesies.

"Suetonius arrived in Londinium with his cavalry last night, far ahead of his legions. They're making forced marches down Watling Street, and will arrive in good order, I daresay, but too late."

I nodded. "Londinium has no defenses. Suetonius knows he can't hold it."

"He's already taken what battle-ready men he could find and headed back to the northwest. Londinium is ours for the taking."

"For the destruction," I said.

Lovernios didn't contradict me. He waited.

If only, I thought, I could bite out my own tongue and lay it at Boudica's feet. I spoke through my teeth. "You have to strike Suetonius now, before he rejoins his legions. If you can wean your warriors from their plunder."

"I can't," Lovernios replied. "But she can." He turned away from the fire into the darkness, then looked back around. "By the way, Catus Decianus has fled to the continent."

I sat back down, indulging myself in a vision of Catus's

ship sinking, his British gold plunging into the watery grasp of the British gods. Ebro spat into the fire. Around us, beyond the trees, other campfires blazed, and the sounds of men singing filtered through the night.

The next night the army ranged itself from bank to bank of the Tamesis, trapping the city between fire and water. Boudica called me to her own bonfire, and gestured silently toward a gleaming pile of arms and armor. Roman arms, and finely-wrought armor. In the midst of the pile stood a javelin, and upon it was spiked Suetonius's head. I recognized him, if not his shocked expression—he'd dined with my family more than once, and he and my father had reminisced about old times. . . .

For once my tongue was still. I said all I needed to say in a look at Boudica.

The bones of her face had grown sharper, and her blue eyes were clouded by gray like a noon sky overcome by storm clouds. Her mouth was tight, as though it'd forgotten how to smile. She was beyond sated, I think, sick on her own vengeance. But to stop the war before total victory would mean retribution. "I hold no grudge against you, Marcus," she said. "When this is over, you'll be free."

"I'll never be free of you, Lady." As I squared my shoulders and turned toward my own little fire I saw Maeve peeking from the flaps of Boudica's tent. Somehow I managed to summon a wink for her. Her eyes widened and she disappeared inside.

Ebro and I sat against the massive trunk of an oak tree, a warrior nearby, and watched the destruction of Londinium. Even at such a distance our faces burned in the heat of the fires, and the screams of the tortured came clearly to our ears. A stream to the west of the city was dammed by severed heads. The waters of the mighty Tamesis were stained with blood. The smoke rose thick and black into the sky, so that the sun looked like an open sore.

I fingered the braided gold of the torc, wrapped around

my upper arm beneath my cloak. Its weight kept me off balance, but I couldn't bring myself to throw it away.

Two nights later Lovernios came to me again, told me the two legions were a day's march away, and asked me for advice.

"They're better trained and better disciplined," I told him dully. "But you outnumber them ten to one. Choose your field so as to give them little room to maneuver and you can defeat them."

We discussed tactics and the disposition of troops until he at last turned to go. "Thank you."

"Lovernios," I called. "You tell me. How many other tribes have joined your war?"

"The Atrebates have refused to rise," he answered, "as have the other tribes in the south. And Cartimandua, queen of the Brigantes in the north, is still your ally."

I didn't need to drive home the point. I sat back down and prayed for an end, for any end.

Boudica met the legions on Watling Street, between the Roman fort at Manduessum and the British temple at Vernemeton, at a place where the road ran into a narrow defile. Her warriors seethed over the field, beyond counting. They were so confident of victory they brought their families, in wagons at the rear of the field.

The legions divided into three columns, flanked by cavalry and auxiliaries. From our perch on a rocky hillside Ebro spotted the cluster of standards. Beside them I recognized the compact body of Agricola, Suetonius's most able lieutenant, striding up and down delivering a speech. The legions were in good hands. They would die with honor, and with them the Roman rule of Britannia. How Boudica would then deal with her own cousins, I couldn't imagine.

She harangued her warriors, her daughters displayed at her side, no doubt pouring scorn on Roma and its men and calling for even more blood. Her voice had become hoarse and shrill, like a crow's.

At last she released a hare from her cloak, which scurried away toward the Roman line. The Britons clashed their weapons and shouted taunts. I turned away, remembering the night I'd been a hare to Boudica's hound. But that had been a long time ago, in my youth.

All day the battle raged. The Britons broke like waves against the Roman shore. But at last the sheer weight of numbers began to bottle the legions in the defile.

I was so enrapt I didn't notice Ebro slip away. We had no guards—no warrior would have missed the battle to watch two such impotent prisoners—so I hurried after him across the bloody ground, past the contorted bodies of Roman and Briton alike.

Boudica leaned forward in her chariot, her hands upraised as though casting a spell. Her hair fell in red waves down her back. Her green cloak billowed behind her. Brighid's hands were raised in imitation, her own hair flowing free. Behind them slumped Maeve, like a tired schoolgirl wanting nothing more than for the lesson to end.

Several warriors ran by, their long swords mottled with blood. And then I saw Ebro, with a long sword of his own—he'd found it on the field, no doubt. He ran at the chariot, brandishing his weapon, shouting in a deep voice I'd never before heard him use, "Death to the witch! Death to the enemy of Roma!"

He struck at Boudica and her daughters, once, twice, three times, the sword flaring in the red light of the westering sun. Maeve screamed. Brighid gasped and fell against her mother. Clutching her breast, Boudica stared with cold, empty eyes at her attacker. Blood drowned her green cloak and its golden stitches. The startled horses jerked forward. I seized their bridles and stopped them.

Five Iceni warriors fell upon Ebro, cut him down, and kept on hacking long after he was dead. Then they turned to me.

"No," said Boudica. She sank to her knees, clasping

Brighid to her side. Maeve sat down with a thump behind them. "Take me away, Marcus. Now."

I led the horses and the chariot away, expecting a spear in my back at any moment. But as the rumor of Boudica's wound swept the field the Britons were maddened. Some threw themselves on the Roman swords. Some threw down their weapons and fled. As I gained the hillside and the dappled shadow of an oak tree Agricola began to drive forward, pinning the Britons between the defile and their own wagons.

Boudica, Brighid, and Maeve huddled in the bottom of the chariot, the discolored cloak spread over them. Ebro hadn't seen the cloak become Britannia. He'd never tasted the liquid from the cauldron. All he knew was that Boudica had enspelled me to betray my duty, and it was his duty to deliver me. I sent Mithras a quick prayer for Ebro. I didn't know which god to address for the women, as Andrasta seemed to have deserted them.

Brighid's cheeks were chalk-white. She was dead, I realized. Maeve cried. In her bloodstained hand Boudica held a vial made of finest Roman glass. She caught the irony in my glance and tried to smile. But her smile was only a feeble grimace.

Behind me someone moved. I spun around. It was Lovernios. "We are lost," he said.

"You can still rally your warriors," I told him.

"No. The queen's body is our own. If she isn't strong and sound, then neither are we."

I'd heard of such a superstition. Had Ebro? That was something I'd never know. I turned back to her.

"Do you hate me?" Boudica asked.

My tongue said, "No. You did your duty, as I did mine. A pity, that my ambition and your freedom couldn't be coiled into the same pattern."

"Duty makes as intricate a pattern as truth. Perhaps there's a greater truth, that in time will receive us both. I'll know, in just a few moments." With her teeth she pulled the stopper from the vial, spat it out, and drank.

I glanced up at Lovernios.

"Wolfsbane," he said. "Poison. You don't think she'd let herself be taken by your people, do you?"

Boudica offered the vial to Maeve. The child shook her head. "I don't want to know, not yet."

I realized by the strength of her voice that she hadn't been wounded. Ebro might not even have struck at her, but twice at Boudica. I leaped forward and pulled Maeve from the back of the chariot. She stiffened at my touch, but didn't fight me as I wrapped her and her stubborn spark of life in my tattered cloak.

Boudica choked, gasped, and died. Maeve's slender body shuddered with hers, and then was still. She turned to Lovernios. "Here is my first and only order as queen of the Iceni. Take them away, and sink them in some deep pool, so that they're lost forever to the sight of men."

"And you?" Lovernios asked. One tear fell from his eye and traced a path into his beard.

"I'll protect her," I said. And that was the first thing I'd said in days that was clean and fresh.

Maeve and I sat together beneath the tree as Lovernios led the chariot and the bodies of the two queens into the green and gold afternoon. Neither of us spoke. Boudica had made a magnificent gamble, worthy of a magnificent woman, and she had lost.

The legions marched over the demoralized Britons, until the bodies of men, women, children, animals lay sprawled as far as the eye could see. At last a centurion ran up the hillside, recognized my clothing and, despite the dark stubble on my face, my origins. He escorted us through the merciful shade of dusk to Agricola. Overwhelmed by detail as any commander would be after such a victory, he barely asked who I was, and paid no attention to Maeve.

I'd wondered many times that spring if I'd ever see

Roma again. Returning was like waking from a dream. But it was no dream, for Maeve was with me, first as my ward, then as my wife. It was a year before she smiled again, but smile she did. As did I.

More than once over the years I've stood on the Gaulish shore and glimpsed the white cliffs of Dubris, but I've never again set foot on the island itself. In Maeve's eyes, though, I see every day the clear lapis skies of Britannia.

Ave atque vale.

The old man laid down his pen. His gut cramped and a cold sweat trickled down his face. The gods had waited long years before taking him as they had taken Boudica, with a bellyful of poison.

His family's delight at his return had become displeasure when he told them his ambition was burned to ashes. But his knowledge of Britannia and the trading of gold made him a successful merchant, so that he sacrificed to Mercury as often as to Mars and Mithras. For truth didn't run in straight lines, but made spirals, and braids, and intricate golden embroideries.

"Good evening, Father," said his son from the doorway.

Marcus looked up. "We've a few moments before the guests arrive. Sit beside me, Artorius, and let me tell you once again that while I was a disappointment to my father, you are not to me."

"How could I disappoint you, when you've taught me so much?" Artorius's even-tempered smile was his mother's, and yet his grandmother's humor, bright and sharp as a golden sickle, lurked at the corners of his mouth. At one and thirty he was in the prime of life, a tall, clean-limbed man with a glint of red in his brown hair. He'd already served as quaestor and curator in Dacia and Macedonia. Now he was going to the province of Britannia as procurator. Which, Marcus thought, seemed only fair.

Maeve walked into the room and handed Marcus the torc. "Here it is."

It was almost too heavy for him. He would've dropped it if Artorius's strong hands hadn't caught it. Marcus passed it gladly to his son. "I know now why I carried this through fire and blood. For you to throw into the Tamesis, in the name of the goddess Andrasta and of peace."

"As you wish," Artorius said, his doubt tempered with respect.

Marcus handed him the scroll, too. "And this is for you to read on your journey north. To remind you that every truth and every duty has many different braided strands. To remind you of Seneca's aphorism: Fire is the test of gold, adversity, of strong men."

"In your veins runs the blood of both Roma and Britannia," Maeve told him. "May you found a new race. May your name and the names of your descendants be long remembered, in Britannia and beyond its borders."

The gleam of the torc was reflected in Artorius's indigo blue eyes. "I'll bring honor to my name and my blood, I swear it."

Marcus smiled through his pain, content.

TRADITION
Elizabeth Moon

July 31, 1914. Durazzo, Albania

Rear Admiral Sir Christopher George Francis Maurice
Cradock strode briskly along the deck of his flagship,
H.M.S. *Defence*, walking off the effects of last night's
dinner with the officers of the S.M.S. *Breslau*. Despite
the political tension of the past few weeks, it had been
a pleasant evening of good food and good talk, punctuated
by the clink of silver on china and the gurgle of wine
into glasses as the mess stewards kept them filled.

Only once had Commander Kettner revealed any hint
of that German confidence which so nearly approached
arrogance. "You English—" he had said, his voice rising.
Then he had chuckled affably. "You have so much invested
in tradition," he had continued, more relaxed. "We
Germans have a tradition to make. It is always so for
vigorous youth, is it not?" The clear implication that the
Royal Navy was superannuated had rankled, but Cradock
had passed it off graciously. Time enough to compare
traditions when the young eagle actually flew and dared
its talons against Britannia's experience. He had no doubt
that rashness would be well reproved.

Cradock took a deep breath and eyed the steep tile
roofs, bright in morning sunlight, that stepped down to

the harbor, its still water perfectly reflecting both ships and buildings. Behind them rose the mountains in which—in happier years—he had hunted boar. No foxhunting here, but a sportsman could find some game anywhere.

He glanced over at *Breslau*, admitting to himself that the Germans had certainly reached a high standard of seamanship. Every detail he had seen the day before had been correct. Several of the officers had read his books; they had asked him to expand on some of the points he'd made. Only courtesy, of course, but he could not help being pleased.

A thicker ooze of smoke from *Breslau*'s funnels stained the morning air. Cradock slowed. On her decks a subdued flurry of movement he recognized at once. Astern, the smooth reflection of the mountains shattered like a dropped mirror as her screws churned. He turned to his flag lieutenant.

"What do we know of Admiral Souchon and the *Goeben*?" Cradock asked.

"At last report, sir, the *Goeben* had made port in Trieste, then gone to sea for gunnery practice."

A cold chill ran down Cradock's back. Gunnery practice? If the Germans were intending to declare war first, only they would know when. The Japanese had given no warning to the Russians at Port Arthur in 1904.

"When *Breslau* weighs anchor, send word to Admiral Milne," Cradock said. "And inform Captain Wray that we will be returning to Corfu immediately."

"Sir."

In short order, the German light cruiser was moving out of the anchorage, a demure curl of white at her bow that would, Cradock was sure, lengthen to a streak when she was out of sight.

August 6, 1914. Early morning off Corfu

Admiral Cradock considered, as he took several rashers of bacon onto his plate, at what point his duty to His

Majesty might require disobedience to his superior, Admiral Sir Berkeley Milne. It was not a dilemma in which he had ever expected to find himself.

When he raised his flag in H.M.S. *Defence*, a British admiral in command of a cruiser squadron in the Mediterranean could expect a constant round of visits to attractive ports, dinners with dignitaries who all wanted some concession, meetings with other naval officials, all conducted with the utmost ceremony. Here were the smartest ships in the Royal Navy, and the most favored officers.

Now he commanded a squadron at war, a situation calling for very different talents than the ability to dance with a prime minister's daughter or make polite conversation with French magistrates and Turkish pashas. And—more to the point—a situation in which mistakes would imperil not merely an officer's reputation and future career, but the very survival of the Empire.

Cradock knew himself to be an old-fashioned sailor. Seamanship was his passion, correct and accurate handling of ships in all weathers, placing them where they could best effect strategy. Seamanship required comprehensive knowledge of exact details: how to organize coaling, how to coil ropes, how to turn a ship in formation precisely where she should turn. Most important, it required naval discipline, on which both naval tradition and the whole towering edifice of empire depended. Lack of discipline led to slovenly seamanship, and that, in the end, to disaster.

His responsibility, therefore, was to do what his commander told him. Therein lay the rub.

Admiral Sir Berkeley Milne, Commander in Chief of the Mediterranean Fleet, had in the past few days revealed himself no Nelson. For three days, Milne had thrashed around the Mediterranean in vain pursuit of the German ships, shifting Cradock's own squadron about in useless dashes, a waste of coal and energy. Now, on the second full day of war, when the German ships were in Messina and could have been bottled up by placing adequate force at either end of the Strait of Messina, Milne had instead taken his battle cruisers off to coal in Bizerte—all the way to North Africa. He had ordered Cradock to stay at the mouth of the Adriatic, and placed only little *Gloucester* to watch the exit to the eastern Mediterranean, because he was sure the Germans would try to go west.

Cradock was not so sure of that. What he knew, with absolute certainty, was that the *Goeben* would cause the Royal Navy immense trouble if she were not sunk, and that the Admiralty wanted her sunk. And he could not sink her from here, sitting idly off Corfu waiting for Milne to give sensible orders. That fox Souchon had plans of his own.

As a technical problem of naval tactics, it came down to speed and guns. The German ships were faster, especially the turbine-powered *Goeben*, and *Goeben* had bigger guns that outranged his by several nautical miles. Thus the *Goeben* could, in theory, stand off at a distance where her great shells could pound the cruisers, and their shots would all fall short.

He could think of ways to trap such a ship, ways to neutralize her superior speed and gunpower. What he could not imagine was any way to do it within the confines of his duty as a subordinate to Admiral Sir Berkeley Milne. This latter problem, one more of strategy than tactics, had occupied his mind the day before, disturbed his sleep, and—this hot August morning—it affected his appetite.

He stroked his beard. He could understand why Milne had not followed the German ships into the Strait of Messina. England had gone to war because the Germans violated Belgian neutrality; she could hardly, in such circumstances, violate neutral Italy's territorial waters. In terms of strategy, as well, Italy's unexpected neutrality was a precious gift, freeing the British and French fleets from the threat they had most feared.

But to leave the strait unguarded, except by ships too small to engage the Germans—that was folly indeed. Should he, even in the face of Milne's contrary orders, move his squadron over to back up Kelly in *Gloucester*? No, because all that dashing about had left his destroyers short of coal, and in a fight with *Goeben* he would need their help. Coaling had to come first.

He finished his breakfast without really noticing the taste and smell, mechanically downing bite after bite, and put his mind to the easier problem.

He would need every ship under his command, cruisers and destroyers alike. If he could have ordered the weather, a storm at night would have been ideal, but this was the season of burning blue days, one after another, and bright moonlight made night attack in the open sea as dangerous as in daylight. Not in the open sea, then. Wherever the Germans went, after Messina, they would have to run to earth eventually. For all her speed, the *Goeben* devoured coal; that meant coming into harbors. Close to the intricate coastline of Greece or Albania, her speed and her range would be of less use, and he could—if he guessed where she was headed— be in position to intercept her, appear at his range, not hers.

But only if he was free to do so. The solution of one problem doubled back to the insoluble greater one: Milne's refusal to let him act as he thought best. Cradock felt like a horse reined in by a timid rider, unable to run freely down to his fences. And he knew he would be blamed for any failure, as a horse is blamed for a fall by the very rider who caused the problem.

He pushed that thought aside—it did no good—and in order to place himself ahead of Souchon considered where in the Mediterranean he might go. West to harry the French, or escape via Gibraltar into the Atlantic? Not with three battle cruisers who outgunned the *Goeben*, not to mention the French fleet, awaiting her there. North to the Austrians at Pola, their allies? No, because the Adriatic was a trap, and Souchon too smart a fox to run to an earth with only one door. Southeast to harry Port Said and the Suez, or Alexandria? Possibly, but where would he resupply? Or northeast, to Constantinople, with exits to both the Black Sea and the Mediterranean, exits easily mined and guarded by forts on land?

If Souchon had reason to believe that the Turks would let him in, that they were thinking of allying with the Germans . . . that is where he would go. Of course the Turks should do no such thing—they had declared themselves neutral. But . . . *were* they?

That was the question. Cradock spread marmalade on his toast and considered. Turks were Orientals, with who knew what logical processes. The British had been advising their navy, but the Admiralty had just seized two Turkish dreadnoughts under construction in British yards. The British had helped defend the Turks against the Russians, but they had also helped Greece gain her independence from the Turks. Which, at this juncture, would sway those devious pashas?

A tap heralded the arrival of his captains for the morning conference. It began with a situation report from his flag lieutenant that located each ship in the Mediterranean, so far as was known. Cradock suppressed the comment he wanted to make. Milne was only just around the northwest corner of Sicily, and proceeding with measured pace back toward the Strait of Messina.

"Where's *Indomitable*?" one of the others asked.

"Back in Bizerte, coaling," Fawcett Wray, his flag captain said. "There was some problem with requisitions . . ."

Cradock said nothing. He had done his small best to improve the coaling efficiency of his squadron, but Milne's insistence on personally approving every detail made it almost impossible. He seemed to think initiative more dangerous than any enemy.

"Requisitions!" That was Coode, captain of destroyers.

Cradock had heard him on other occasions; now he cocked an eyebrow at the young man, who subsided like a kettle moved off the fire, steam almost visibly puffing from his ears.

"Gentlemen, the German ships will have to emerge today, or face internship." That got their attention. "Let me explain what I expect them to do." Quickly he retraced his reasoning on the possible courses of action open to the Germans.

"The Turks would not dare harbor them," Wray said. "They must know it would turn us against them. We are their naval advisors; they asked for an alliance with us only last year—"

"Which was refused," Cradock pointed out. "The government did not want to inflame the Russians or the Germans with a formal alliance there . . . but I daresay the Turks took it differently. In addition, on our most recent visit to Turkey, I heard from the locals that Admiral Souchon was a great man. When I asked why, they told me about his having sent the crew of the *Goeben* to help fight a fire in a Turkish barracks in Constantinople, back in May. Several of the Germans died; the Turks—you know how emotional they are—got up a celebration of some kind."

"But . . . the Turks are neutrals. Even if they admire Souchon—"

"They're Turks. Intrigue is their nature, along with theft and pillage. They have as well that touchy Oriental vanity, which a trifling matter like assistance in a barracks fire would flatter. For Orientals, this is enough. It does not occur to them that any British captain would have done the same."

"But you don't seriously believe they would come into the war as German allies? Not after all we've done for them—"

"I doubt very much they would ally with Germany . . . but I can imagine them giving sanctuary to the *Goeben* and then finding Souchon more than a match for them. With those guns leveled at the city, can you imagine the pashas refusing his demands?"

"Well, sir," Coode said, "if this is what you think the Germans are going to do, then why aren't we blockading the southern end of the Strait of Messina, instead of sitting over here watching for Austrians?"

"Admiral Milne's orders," Cradock said. "I intend to ask Admiral Milne for permission to position the squadron where we can engage the *Goeben* under more favorable terms. We will need to move south to do so. Therefore, we must attend to coaling the destroyers at once."

Cradock took a turn on the deck, observing every detail of his squadron, the sea, the signs of weather in the sky, trying to avert his mind from the signs of weather— heavy weather—ahead in his relationship with his commander. Across the blue water, Corfu rose in terraces of gold and green; the mingled scents of lemon groves, thyme, and roses on the breeze competed with the nearer whiff of coal, oil, metal polish, and the freshly holystoned deck. Westward, beyond the blue morning shadows, sunlight burned on the lapis sea, and in the distant haze Italy's heel formed a vague smudge on the horizon. In this second day of war, peace lingered here, where nothing but his own ships seemed warlike.

When Milne finally answered his signal, it was to refuse permission to reinforce *Gloucester* at the western exit of the Strait of Messina.

Cradock did not tell Milne he had sent the destroyers to coal at Ithaca. Half-formed in his mind, a plan grew, like a stormcloud on a summer's day, hidden in wreaths of haze. If the *Goeben* broke free and ran east, as he expected, where and how could he catch her, given that his ships were slower? Not by a stern chase—she had outpaced even the big battle cruisers. Not by an interception—she could spot his smoke as far away as he could spot hers, and with her speed easily avoid him. No—he had to decide where she was going to be, and surprise her.

Which he could not do if he waited to ask Milne's permission. Like a thundercloud suddenly revealed, his dilemma stood clear. Was he seriously considering ignoring his orders to guard the Adriatic, making an independent decision to anticipate Souchon's movements and engage the enemy ships? Without informing Milne, in direct contravention of custom and naval law?

The very thought made him wince. He had had it drummed into him, and he had drummed it into others: commanders command, and juniors obey. To act on his thoughts risked not only his ships and his men, but the very foundations of naval discipline. Even if he was right, even if he caught and sank the *Goeben*, he might well be court-martialed; he would certainly not be given another command. Milne would never forgive the insult; Beattie, Jellicoe . . . he winced again, imagining the astonishment and anger of men he respected, whose respect he desired. He was appalled himself. It was like a member of the field intervening in place of the M.F.H. and giving orders to the huntsmen.

Yet—he remembered the cold day when he'd first seen the bumptious red-headed young officer of hussars who was now First Lord of the Admiralty. For a moment he warmed himself in the glow of that infectious grin, that intensity so akin to his own. Stirrup to stirrup they had faced stone walls, sunken lanes, hedges that in memory seemed as much larger as last year's salmon. Bold, free-going, young Churchill's mistakes would be those of confidence and high courage; he might fall, but he would never shirk a fence. *He* would approve.

Yet again—Churchill was a civilian now, and had never been in the Navy. He had never been the model of an obedient young officer, even in a service as lenient as the cavalry. Moreover, he had a reputation as a weathercock, changing parties for profit. Cradock dared not trust that memory.

His mind strayed to the First Sea Lord, Prince Louis Battenburg. An able man, who had earned his rank and position, but—would he understand the dilemma in which Cradock found himself? If only Jacky Fisher were still First Sea Lord! There was a fire eater who would approve anything, were the *Goeben* destroyed.

He took a long breath of Corfu's aromatic air, and reminded himself that, after all, he might be wrong. Souchon might run for the Adriatic. Or even Gibraltar. He might not have to make that choice.

Cradock ate a lunch that had no more flavor, in his distraction, than his breakfast. His destroyers had had to search all the way into the Gulf of Corinth for their collier, whose foreign captain had somehow gone to the wrong Port Vathi. Now they were coaling. Milne had finally reached the western exit of the Strait of Messina, with battle cruisers who could surely defeat *Goeben* if Souchon were stupid enough to go that way. His own rebellious thoughts spurred him toward bigger obstacles.

He could not wait until a crisis to decide what his priorities were, just as a foxhunter could not wait until the last few strides before a fence to decide whether to jump. That way lay shies and refusals. No, the bold rider sent his horse at every fence resolved to clear it. His officers and men needed his direction, his resolution.

Nelson had been blind to a stupid order at Copenhagen— could he not be deaf to a stupid order in Greece?

Who was he, to compare himself to Nelson?

Should not every English admiral compare himself to Nelson, and strive to match his stature? Would Nelson be more afraid of displeasing a senior, or letting an enemy escape?

But Nelson had not had a wireless to pass on every whim of commanders far away. How would a Nelson have dealt with that distraction? Again he thought of Copenhagen, of Nelson putting the telescope to his blind eye.

He had one advantage surely more valuable than speed or guns: a depth of knowledge of the Mediterranean which neither Milne nor Souchon could match. He knew it in all seasons, all weathers, in more detail than Souchon could possibly have acquired in only ten months. His mind held not only chart data, but mental images of bays and inlets and passages apt for coaling, for unseen passage from one island to another. Shingle beaches, sand beaches, steep cliffs dropping straight into deep water, sea caves . . . like familiar fields long hunted over, whose every hedge and fence and gate is known to members of the hunt, he could bring it all to mind.

August 6, 2030 hours.

On the broad breast of the sea, the moonlight shone, as it had for thousands of years, lighting sailors home. Now it lit dark billows of coal smoke against a sea like hammered pewter. Two long, lean shapes slid through the quiet sea, menacing even as they fled. Behind them, a third, much smaller: H.M.S. *Gloucester* trailing the German ships *Goeben* and *Breslau*, and by her own smoke they knew she was shadowing them. To port, the coast of Italy, opening northward into the Gulf of Otranto; far ahead, on this course, the boot heel of Taranto, aimed in a backward kick at the narrow strait that led into the Adriatic.

On *Defence*, south of Corfu, Cradock stared at the charts and finally shook his head. *Gloucester* had reported the German ships leaving the Strait of Messina just after 1700 GMT, 1800 local time. Now, over two hours later, the German ships were still steaming ENE, as if aiming for the Adriatic. If that was where they were going, it was time to move the squadron north to intercept them. Cradock did not believe it.

"He must turn, and turn soon," he said.

"If they go north . . ." Captain Wray glanced at him. The other cruiser captains said nothing; they would let the flag captain do the talking, for now. "Our orders said keep them out of the Adriatic."

"He is a fox; he will not run into that trap." He felt a prickle of annoyance; he had explained this before. He sensed in Wray less enthusiasm for the chase than he would have wished in his flag captain. Weeks before, during a discussion of the German ship, Wray had kept harping on the German battle cruiser's strength, the range of its guns. Now he repeated himself.

"But . . . even if you're right, sir . . . the *Goeben* is far too powerful for us to engage without at least one of the battle cruisers to assist."

Cradock smiled at Wray, trying to hearten him. "She has bigger guns, certainly. And more armor. And more speed. But she is only one—no—" He put up his hand to forestall the younger man's correction. "I know, she has *Breslau*. But we easily overmatch *Breslau*. At night, along the coast of Greece . . . the *Goeben*'s advantages lessen markedly."

"Ah." Wray's face lightened. "You intend a night engagement in navigation waters? With the destroyers . . ."

"Yes. Pity it's so clear. But if we position ourselves where I am convinced she is likely to go, we can pick our best location, where the *Goeben*'s speed and range cannot help her. Then our numbers must count. I expect she will pick up her pace after her turn—she is only luring *Gloucester* on, loafing along at eighteen knots or so, hoping her lookouts will slack off."

"Not Captain Kelly's lookouts," Wray said, grinning.

"Quite so. So when she turns, I expect her to pick up speed, to twenty-four knots or more, and be off the southern capes of Greece before dawn. Now—this is what I propose—" He spread the chart back out and explained in more detail.

2130 hours.

Cradock was dozing in his cabin, taking what rest he could, when Captain Wray called him. "Signal's just in from *Gloucester*, Admiral," he said. "The Germans have turned, just as you thought. They were trying to jam the signal, but *Gloucester* kept sending. I took the liberty of informing Admiral Milne, but have received no reply yet."

Milne, Cradock thought, would be sure it was a trick. Luckily Milne would still be at dinner, and unlikely to give a return signal until he had finished. Cradock didn't want to talk to Milne about what he planned, and be told not to do it. "What's her speed?" he asked.

"Nineteen knots," Wray said.

"Odd," Cradock said. "I expected a spurt. Souchon must want to evade *Gloucester*; that would have been the ideal time to do so."

"She just turned."

"Mm. Ask *Gloucester* to inform us instantly of any change in her course or speed. And set the squadron's course to take us south to Sapienza behind Cephalonia and Zante." If the German ships kept that speed, his ships could easily arrive at Sapienza well before them, and choose their best place to engage.

Within minutes, he felt the cruiser thrust into the gentle swell with more urgency. Far below, sweating stokers would be shoveling coal into the furnaces . . . coal he would have to replenish. His mind ranged ahead, to the location of colliers.

It was near midnight when Captain Wray tapped at his door. Cradock woke instantly, the quick response of the seaman.

"Another report from *Gloucester*, sir. The German ships have separated; Captain Kelly's following the *Goeben*, and she is on the same course, at 17 knots. *Dublin's* trying to find them; she has two destroyers with her, *Bulldog* and *Beagle*."

"Seventeen knots." Cradock ran a hand through his hair. Why was such an admiral, with such a ship, crawling across the Mediterranean at a mere 17 knots when he could have outpaced the *Gloucester* and been free of her surveillance? "He has some problem," Cradock said. "He didn't get coal—no, we know he got some coal. He didn't get enough to go where he wants to go—he's moving at his most economical speed to conserve it until he meets a collier somewhere. Or . . . he has boiler trouble."

"You can't know that, sir."

He didn't know it. He knew only that no man with a ship fast enough to shake a shadower would fail to do so unless something had gone wrong. And *Goeben* had been snugged away at the Austrian naval base of Pola for weeks before the war started. She could have been undergoing repairs . . . and those repairs could have been interrupted by the outbreak of war, just as his own ships' repairs had been.

"And our position?"

"About eight miles off Santa Maura, sir, here . . ." Wray pointed out their position on the chart. "We'll be entering the channel between Santa Maura and Cephalonia in the next hour. Oh—and Admiral Milne wants to know your dispositions."

"I'm sure he does," Cradock said, stretching. "So do the Germans. Signal Admiral Milne that we are patrolling. I'm going up on deck for a while." Wray looked as he himself might have looked, had his admiral ever told him to send a false signal. But they were, he thought, following the orders Milne would have given—that the Admiralty wanted him to give—if Milne had but the wits to give them. *They don't pay me to think*, Milne had said once . . . but they might pay a high price because Milne didn't.

The moon swung high overhead. To either side, the other cruisers knifed through the water, pewter ships on a pewter sea, blackening the starry sky with smoke. Behind them, sea-fire flared and coiled from their passage. Ahead, he could see the signal cones of the destroyers, and the white churn of their wakes, the phosphorescence spreading to either side. To port, Santa Maura, Leucas to most Greeks, rose from the sea in a tumble of jet and silver, the moon picking out white stone like a searchlight. Southward, the complicated shapes of Cephalonia and Ithaca, with the narrow straight passage between them.

"Have the squadron fall into line astern," he told Wray. The signal passed from ship to ship; the cruisers dropped smartly into line at four cables . . . his drills had accomplished that much. He hoped the gunnery drills had done as well. He noticed that the cones were all correctly hung. "Reduce speed if necessary, but not below fifteen knots."

He thought of little *Dublin*, with her two destroyers, desperately trying to find the Germans by their smoke. She might be lucky, but she surely could not sneak up on *Goeben* in this clear moonlit night. The Germans could not fail to see her any more than he could fail to see the ships of his squadron. Perhaps he should send her to guard the Adriatic gate which he had left wide open? That made sense, but so did another plan. Let her go to Crete, where the Germans might have another collier standing by. At dawn, when he hoped to spring his trap on the Germans near the Peloponnese, the smoke of *Dublin* and her destroyers might make the Germans swing closer to the Greek capes.

He gave these instructions, and eventually—atmospherics, the radioman explained—*Dublin* acknowledged them.

August 7, 0230.

He had dozed again, his body registering every slight change of course, every variation in speed, while the squadron passed Santa Maura, Ithaca, the rugged heights of southern Cephalonia, the northern part of Zante. The tap at his door roused him instantly. It was Wray.

"Sir . . . I have to say I don't like it."

"What?" Cradock yawned as he checked the time. Two-thirty.

"At the speed *Goeben* is making, sir, she will not be at the Greek coast until late morning. We cannot bring her to battle in daylight; you said so yourself." Wray stood there like someone who expected a vice admiral to have the sun at his command. Cradock yawned again and shook his head to clear it.

"Where is she now?"

Wray moved to the table and pointed out *Gloucester*'s most recent position on the chart. Cradock smoothed his beard, thinking. "It's inconvenient," he murmured.

"It's impossible," Wray said.

Cradock looked at him. Surely he could not mean what that sounded like. "Explain, Captain."

"It's what I said before, sir. She's too fast, and her guns outrange ours. She can circle outside our range, picking off the cruisers one by one before they can get a shot." Cradock frowned; was Wray seriously suggesting they abandon the attempt?

"And you propose?"

"To preserve the squadron for action in which it can have an effect," Wray said. "We cannot possibly sink the Germans . . ."

"I think you're missing something," Cradock said, smiling.

"Sir?"

"If the Germans do not appear until late morning—as it now appears—then we have time to entrap them where their greater speed will do them no good."

"But sir—she will see us if we're in the Messinian Gulf. She can stand off Sapienza far enough—in fact it would be prudent to do so. We cannot fight her there."

"That is not the only place, not with the lead we seem

to have. But it will require a new plan. Signal the squadron
and the destroyers: we will heave to while I decide what
to do."

"Yes, sir." Wray left for the bridge; Cradock leaned
over the charts.

"Is it cleverness, or some difficulty?" Cradock said,
to himself. Souchon had the reputation of a bold man.
He had thrust all the way to Bone and Phillipeville, and
made it safely back to Messina. Clever of him to leave
Messina in daylight, clever to attempt that feint to the
north. If he anticipated trouble in navigation waters, it
was clever of him to slow, to arrive when he had the
best visibility, when he could see a waiting collier, or
British warships.

He felt *Defence* shiver successively, like a horse shaking
a fly from its skin, as the revolutions slowed and her
speed dropped. Deliberately, he did not go on deck to
see how the following cruisers obeyed the signals. *Defence*
shuddered through her secondary period of vibration
and steadied again.

How many hours ahead were they? If they pressed
on as quickly as possible and *Goeben* did not speed up,
they would be a clear eight hours ahead . . . she could
not possibly spot them. What then? His fingers traced
the familiar contours of the Morean coast. If *Goeben*
held on the shortest course for the east, she would pass
between Cythera and Elafonisi. But that provided the
obvious place for a trap, and if she chose to go south of
Cythera—or worse, south of Cerigotto—his ships could
not catch her. He must not head his fox; he trusted that
Gloucester's pressure would keep Souchon running a
straight course.

Behind the rocky coast of the Peloponnese, the rosy
fingered dawn broadened in classical design over a
wine-dark sea. Westward, day's arch ran to a distant
horizon unblemished by German smoke. They had passed

Navarino, where almost ninety years before the British had—with grudging help from their French and Russian allies—scotched a Turkish fleet. Under the cliffs to the east, little villages hugged narrow beaches. Spears of sunlight probed between the rough summits, alive with swallows' wings.

As they cleared the point of Sapienza, the squadron came out of the shadows of the heights, and into a sea spangled with early sun. To port, the Gulf of Messenia opened, long golden beaches between rocky headlands; the old Venetian fort at Korona pushed into the water like a beached ship. Ahead, the longer finger of Cape Matapan reached even farther south. Water more green than blue planed aside from the bows; Cradock felt his heart lift to the change in the air, the light, the old magic of the Aegean reaching even this far west.

He glanced aloft at the lookout searching for the smoke of German ships. One of the destroyers had already peeled off to investigate the gulf for a German collier in concealment; another had gone ahead to investigate the Gulf of Kolokythia. Here he could have ambushed *Goeben* in the dark, but in daylight these gulfs were traps for slower ships.

"You must signal Admiral Milne," Wray said.

"And let the *Goeben* hear how close we are? I think not," Cradock said. "Admiral Milne is . . . cruising somewhere around Sicily. He will follow when he thinks it convenient, when he feels certain of events." Cradock smiled, that wry smile which had won other captains' loyalties. "We are the events. We will sink *Goeben*—or, failing that, we will turn her back toward him, and the 12-inch guns of the battle cruisers."

"But if we don't—" Wray was clearly prepared to argue the whole thing again.

"I had a hunter once," Cradock said, meditatively. He gazed at the cliffs rising out of the sea as if he had no interest in anything but his story. "A decent enough horse, plenty of scope. But—he didn't like big fences. Every time out, the same thing . . . you know the feeling, I suppose, the way a reluctant hunter backs off before a jump."

"I don't hunt," Wray said, repressively.

"Ah. I thought perhaps you didn't." Cradock smiled to himself. "Well, there was only one thing to do, you see, if I didn't want to spend all day searching for gaps and gates."

"And what was that, sir?" asked Wray, in the tone of one clearly humoring a superior.

Cradock turned and looked at him full face. "Put the spurs to him," he said. "Convince him he had more to fear from me than any fence." Wray reddened. "I thought you'd understand," Cradock said, and turned away. He hoped that would be enough.

By 0730, they were clearing Cape Matapan; Cythera lay clear on the starboard bow. Cradock peered up at the cliffs of the Mani, at the narrow white stone towers like fangs . . . still full of brigands and fleas, he supposed. Some of the brigands might even be spying for the Germans. They would do anything for gold, except, possibly, spy for the Turks.

The German ships were likely to pass Matapan fairly close, if they wanted to take the passage north of Cythera . . . plenty of places along that coast to hide his cruisers. But none of them were close enough, especially if the Germans went south. He dared not enter those gulfs, to be trapped by the longer reach of the German guns.

No. The simplest plan was the best, and he had time for it. Ahead now was the meeting of the Aegean, the white sea with its wind-whipped waters, and the deeper blue Ionian. This early on a fair summer's day, the passage went smoothly; the treacherous currents hardly affected the warships on their steady progress past Elafonisi's beaches, the fishing village of Neapolis, and the steep coast of Cythera, that the Venetians had called Cerigo.

Around the tip of Cape Malea, he found the first proof that Souchon intended to use that northern passage. Off the port bow, a smallish steamer rocked uneasily in the Aegean chop.

"Greek flag, sir," the lookout reported. "The *Polymytis*."

"If I were Souchon," Cradock said, "this is where I would want to find a collier. I would want one very badly."

"But it's Greek."

"Souchon flew a Russian flag at Phillipeville," Cradock said. "And our destroyers could use more coal." He sipped his tea. "I think we will have a word with this collier. An honest Greek collier—if that is not a contradiction in terms—should be willing to sell the Royal Navy coal, in consideration of all the English did to free Greece . . ." He peered at the ship. Something tickled his memory . . . something about the way her derrick was rigged, her lines. The German ship *General* had appeared in Messina tarted up like a Rotterdam-Lloyd mail steamer, though she belonged to the German East Africa Line.

"From where, and where bound?" he asked; Wray passed on his questions.

The dark-haired man answered in some foreign gibberish that sounded vaguely Turkish or Arabic, not Greek.

"He says he doesn't understand," he heard bawled up from below.

"He understands," Cradock said quietly. His eye roved over the steamer again. Ignore the paint (too new for such a ship), the unseamanlike jumble of gear on the deck, the derrick . . . and she looked very much like a ship he had seen less than a year before putting out from Alexandria, when she had flown the German ensign. He even thought he could put a name to her.

"We'll have a look at her," he said to Wray.

Wray swallowed. "Yes, sir, but—if I may—she is flying a neutral flag."

"She's a German Levant Line ship—imagine her in the right colors. She's no more neutral than *Goeben*. She is most likely old *Bogadir* with her face made up. If, as I suspect, she's carrying coal, then—one of our problems is solved. Possibly two."

Under the guns of the secondary battery, *Polymytis's* captain submitted to a search.

"She's not a very *good* collier," the sublieutenant remarked when he came back aboard, much smudged. "Her bunkers are even harder to get at than ours . . . but she's bung full of coal, and her engineering crew is German, I'd swear. White men, anyway."

"Take her crew into custody, and put a prize crew aboard." Collecting the collier might be enough. But it might not. The *Goeben* still might have enough coal to reach the Dardanelles, and she would surely be able to call on other colliers. Even a lame fox could kill chickens. He would have to bring her to battle.

The sea was near calm, but that wouldn't last, not here at the meeting of the two seas. Already he could see the glitter off the water that meant the Aegean was about to live up to its name. The Etesian wind off Asia Minor crisped little waves toward him . . . and at day's end it would blow stronger.

Unfortunately, it would blow his smoke to the south; if he stayed here, off Cape Malea, that black banner across the channel would reveal his presence to the Germans. How could he make them come *this* way, the only place where he could be sure his guns would reach them?

They must see nothing to alarm them. He would position three cruisers south of the passage, behind the crook of Cythera's northeast corner, where the smoke would blow away behind that tall island, invisible. The other, with the destroyers, would wait well around the tip of Cape Malea, far enough north that their smoke would be dispersed up its steep slopes. He would put parties ashore who could signal when the Germans were well into the channel.

The signal flashed, and flashed again. Cradock smiled at the charts, and then at his flag captain. Souchon was as bold and resolute as his reputation. He had chosen the direct route, after shaking off *Gloucester* back at Matapan. Cradock had fretted over the signals from above that told of exchange of shots between *Gloucester* and *Breslau*; the minutes when the *Goeben* turned back to support *Breslau*—when he feared she might turn away from the northern passage altogether—had racked his nerves, the more so as he could not see for himself what was going on.

But the Germans had gone straight on when *Gloucester* turned away, and now—now they were well into the passage.

Defence grumbled beneath him, power held in check like a horse before the start of a run. Below, stokers shoveled more coal into the maws of the furnaces; boilers hissed as the pressure rose. Thicker smoke oozed from the funnels, whirled away in dark tendrils by the wind. Cradock could almost see the engineering officers and engine crew, alert for every overheated bearing, every doubtful boiler tube. Gun crews were at their stations, the first rounds already loaded and primed, awaiting only the gunlayers' signals.

But ships could not reach racing speed as fast as horses; he had to guess, from the positions signalled to him, the moment to begin the run-up. He wanted the cruisers to be moving fast when they cleared the island. So much depended on things he could not know—how fast the *Goeben* was, how fast she could still go, how Souchon would react to the sudden appearance of hostile ships in front of him.

Signals flashed down, translated quickly into *Goeben's* position on the chart in front of him. She was not racing through; she was up to nineteen knots now, but keeping a steady course, well out from either side of the channel, *Breslau* trailing her. When . . . when . . . ? He felt it, more than saw it in the figures on the chart. *Now*.

Defence surged forward, behind *Black Prince*, and ahead of *Warrior*. Cradock squinted up at the lookout. The Germans would be watching carefully; they had the sun over their shoulders, perfect viewing. But surprise should still gain *Black Prince* the first shot. She had won her vanguard position on the basis of an extra knot of speed and her gunnery record. He put into his ears the little glass plugs the Admiralty provided.

Across the passage, fourteen sea miles, he saw dark smoke gush from the funnels of the *Duke of Edinburgh* and the destroyers. In minutes, it would drift out across the passage, but by then they would be visible anyway.

For an instant, the beauty of the scene caught him: on a fair summer afternoon, the trim ships steaming in order under the rugged cliffs. Then his vision exploded in fire and smoke, as *Black Prince* fired her port 9.2-inch guns; the smoke blew down upon *Defence* coming along behind, and obscured his vision for an instant. Then *Defence* was clear of the point, and at that moment he saw the raw fire of *Goeben*'s forward turrets, just as *Defense* rocked to the recoil of her own. White spouts of water near *Goeben* showed that *Black Prince*'s gunners had almost found her range.

Too late now for fear or anxiety; his heart lifted to the raw savagery of the guns, shaking every fiber, the heart-stopping stink of cordite smoke, chocolate in the afternoon sun, blowing over him. *Black Prince*'s port guns fired again, and behind, he heard the bellow of *Warrior*'s, as she too cleared the point. The shells screamed on their way like harpies out of Greek legend.

The *Goeben*'s first shots rocked the sea nearby, sending up spouts of white. Had she picked out the *Defence*?

She would surely try to sink the flagship, but he trusted his captains to carry on. His orders had been clear enough: "Our objective is to sink the *Goeben*, first, and the *Breslau* second."

The German ship's guns belched again; she could bring six of her ten 11-inch guns to bear on any of the three ships on her starboard bow. Cradock hoped her gun crews were not as good as he had been told.

White flashes of water, and then an explosion that was surely on the *Goeben* herself. She steamed on, but another hit exploded along her starboard side, even as her guns belched flame. Then a curtain of water stood between him and the German ships, and *Defence* rocked on her side, screws shuddering.

"Very close, sir," Wray said. He looked pinched and angry. Cradock looked away.

"Yes, excellent shooting." But his own crews were doing well, maintaining a steady round per minute per gun. Where were the destroyers in all this? They were supposed to have raced around the tip of Malea, laying smoke that would blow into the battle area and confuse the *Goeben*—he hoped. He looked ahead, to find dark coils of smoke already rolling over the afternoon sea, and the flash of *Duke of Edinburgh*'s guns . . . she was finally out from behind Malea, moving more slowly than his own ships. They had not wanted Souchon to see all that smoke until he was well into the trap.

Defence bucked a little as the sea erupted behind her, another near miss that dumped a fountain over *Warrior*'s bows. The guns rocked the ship again. Cradock looked at the chart, and his stopwatch. *Black Prince* should be near the point at which she was to start her turn, bringing her end on to the *Goeben*. He had worried over that point, on which so much depended. For three of his ships, it reduced by one the 9.2-inch guns that could bear on the *Goeben* . . . but it reduced the range more quickly, and that would, he hoped, be sufficient advantage.

Black Prince's stern yawed starboard as her bow swung into the turn. Cradock felt *Defence* heel to the same evolution. Then, just as he glanced aft to look at *Warrior*, he saw the aft 9.2 turret erupt in flame, like a column of fire. *Defence* bucked and slewed, like a horse losing its grip on slick ground. Black smoke poured from the turret. If they had not turned—he was sure that salvo would have hit *Defence* amidships.

Even as he watched, *Warrior's* forward turret exploded in a gout of flame—seconds later, the starboard turret blew, and then the next . . . as if some demon artificer had laid a fuze from one to the other. In his mind's eye, he saw what had happened, the flash along the passages. Another vast explosion that showered *Defence* and the sea around with debris, and the *Warrior* disappeared forever beneath the restless sea.

"I told you," Wray was saying, fists clenched, when he could hear again. They watched as shell after shell struck the *Goeben* without apparent effect. "We don't have the weight of guns to damage her even this close; she'll sink one after another . . . the whole squadron lost to no purpose."

"He's slowing," Cradock said, peering through the curls and streamers of smoke. The only possible reply to what Wray had said would disrupt his command. He concentrated instead on the battle. If he had been Souchon, in that ship, and if she could still make twenty-seven knots, he would have tried to run the gauntlet. Was Souchon, instead, turning to run away westward? Or had he suffered damage? No ship, however armored, could withstand a steady barrage of 380-pound shells forever. One of them would have to hit something vital. Enough of them, and she must, eventually, go under.

Minute by minute, the ships converged through a hell of smoke and fire and spouting water, battered and battering with every gun that might possibly bear. Despite the blown turret, *Defence*'s boilers and engines drove her forward at twenty knots, a nautical mile every three minutes, and the interception became a matter of interlocking curves, the *Goeben* weaving to bring her undamaged guns to bear, the British responding as they could. From fourteen thousand yards to twelve, to ten, to eight. Destroyers darted in and out, zigging wildly from *Goeben*'s secondary batteries. Three were gone already, blown from the water by shells too small to hole the cruisers.

Cradock, eyes burning with smoke and sweat, struggled to keep his gaze on the *Goeben*, to distinguish her smoke from the rest. A stronger gust of wind lifted the smoke, and there she was. One funnel blown askew, and the smoke from its opening unhealthily pallid with escaping steam, most of her secondary guns on this side dismounted . . . but the big guns still swung on their mounts to aim directly at *Defence*. His mouth dried. Below him, *Defence* fired, and he saw the flare from *Goeben*'s guns just as someone jerked him off his feet and flung him down. The bridge exploded around him; he felt as if he had been thrown from a horse at high speed into timber, and then nothing.

He could not catch his breath; his sight had gone dark. Voices overhead . . . a weight lifted off him, and someone said, "Here's the admiral!" How much time had gone by? What had happened? He struggled to open his eyes, and someone said, "Easy, sir . . ." More weight came off; he could breathe but the first breath stabbed him. Ribs, no doubt. Wetness on his face, stinging fiercely, then he got his eyes open to see a confusion of bundles he knew for bodies, blood, steel twisted like paper.

"*Goeben*," he managed to say.

They didn't answer, struggling with something that still pinned his legs. He couldn't feel it, really, but he could see a mass of metal. Shouts in the distance, something about boats away. His mind put that together. Was the ship sinking?

"Is—?" he started to ask, but a sudden explosive roar drowned out his words. He felt the tilt of the deck beneath him. No need to ask. "You'd better go," he said instead, to the faces that hovered around him.

"No sir," said one, in the filthy rags of what had been a Royal Marine uniform. "We're not leaving you, Admiral."

He didn't have the strength to argue. He couldn't focus on what they were saying, what they were doing; his vision darkened again. Then he felt himself lifted, carried, and eased into a boat that rocked in the choppy water. He could see *Defence*'s stern lifting into the sky.

"*Goeben*?" he asked again. The men in his boat looked at each other.

"She's still making for the Aegean, sir. Slow, but so far she's not sunk."

"Captain Wray?" he asked.

"Got off in another boat, sir."

For the first time in years, the motion of the sea made him feel sick. He asked one of the men to hold his head up, and over the gunwale saw the *Goeben* in the distance, battered, listing a little, but still whole, limping eastward almost to the tip of Cape Malea. Behind her, hanging on like bulldogs, were two destroyers. Somewhere, big guns still roared; he saw one shell explode on the cliff face, spouts of water.

He could not see the torpedo that, after so many misses, exploded under the *Goeben*'s stern and jammed one of her rudders. But he saw the sag of her bow toward the Cape, and he knew what that meant.

"Dear God," he said softly. "She's going to hit the rocks."

"Admiral?" The face bent over his looked worried; Cradock tried to point and managed only a weak flap of his hand. But they looked . . . as the *Goeben* yawed in the current, her bow swinging more and more to port, into the rocks that had claimed, over thousands of years, that many ships and more.

Another half mile and she would have been well beyond Cape Malea, with sea room to recover from steering problems. Instead, her remaining steam and the current dragged her abraded hull along the rocks, and the destroyers fired their last torpedoes into her. With a vast exhalation of steam, like the last breath of a dying whale, the *Goeben* settled uneasily, rolling onto her side.

August 8, aboard H.M.S. *Black Prince*

Cradock lay sweating in his bandages in the captain's cabin, more than a little amazed that he was alive. Too many were not. *Warrior* gone with all hands. *Defence* sunk, and only 117 of her crew recovered. Six of eight destroyers . . . *Scorpion* and *Racoon* were still afloat, but of the others only a very few hands had survived. Only 83 of the Germans, Admiral Souchon not among them. *Black Prince* and *Duke of Edinburgh* were both in need of major repairs, unable to do more than limp back to Malta. Admiral Milne had already expressed his displeasure with the loss of so many ships and men, and, as he had put it, "reckless disregard of his duty to his superior." He foresaw that Milne would take credit for the success, and condemn the method by which it had been achieved. Like Codrington at Navarino, he would be censured for having exceeded his orders, while the Admiralty shed no tears over the vanquished enemy. Well, they would have retired a one-legged admiral anyway.

A tap at his door introduced yet another problem.

"Sir." Wray stood before him like a small boy before a headmaster.

"Captain Wray," Cradock said mildly.

"I was . . . wrong, sir."

"It happens to all of us," Cradock said. "I've been wrong many times."

"But—"

But he wanted to know what Cradock would say about him, in his official reports.

"Captain Wray, I never finished telling you the story of that hunter," he said. A long pause; Wray looked haggard, a *What now?* expression. "I sold him," Cradock said. "To a man who wanted a good hack." Wray seemed to shrink within his uniform. "Have some tea," Cradock offered, seeing that the message had been received.

"Nothing can change the nature born in its blood," he said, quoting a Greek poet, most apt for this ocean. "Neither cunning fox, nor loud lion." Nor coward, though he would not say that. He could take no pleasure in Wray's humiliation, but in the Navy there were no excuses. That was the great tradition.

AND TO THE REPUBLIC FOR WHICH IT STANDS
Brad Linaweaver

"He that once enters at a tyrant's door
Becomes a slave, though he were free before."
— Sophocles

Even Caesar dreams. There is no surprise in this. Perhaps the surprise is that ordinary people dream, or can dream at all—hoping for a better life that never comes. Only nightmares tell the truth.

Caesar's dreams are usually rehearsals. The general, the politician, must always plan, even when consciousness sneaks away like a harlot in the dark. Alone with his visions, he sees the land and sea and people as the gods must see them. Early in life he learned that free will exists, but only for leaders. Once a choice is made, free will becomes a phantom as inexorable law grinds out its verdict. What is true in the blood-drenched mud of the battlefield is true for the white marble sarcophagus of the Roman senate.

He wakes in the hot night and turns in bed to see his wife still asleep. Calphurnia is not as beautiful as his first two wives but he loves her more. Her breasts are perfect, smooth hills rising and falling like legions marching over countless landscapes of countless campaigns. He touches them, touches her, and feels a force less terrifying than love. Her sigh reassures him that in her arms, he is accepted; he is at peace.

Love demands more—as does his love for Rome. Love demands the spilling of blood, the conquest of peoples, even the agony of civil war. Love requires constant proof of devotion.

He has a sour taste in his mouth that can only be removed by wine. He can't sleep anyway so he carefully leaves the bed. No need to wake his wife if the stroking of her breasts failed to rouse her. He needs to walk, to think. This night of March the fourteenth there is much to think about.

When he gets in this sort of mood he envies his soldiers. Their souls are pure because their worries are, if not small, at least manageable—getting laid, getting drunk, not being a coward. Whether the battle is won or lost, they are judged by how they behaved as men. Only men. They are not judged by the standards of a god.

He pours himself good, red wine and drinks deep. He never drinks to escape himself but only to relax the tension that is his constant companion, nagging him on to greatness. The moon observes him through his doorway and he thinks how cool it looks, as if made of ice. The night is so still and humid that he wishes he could cool off.

He remembers an evening like this when he was held by the pirates of Pharmacusa. They were simple men, simpler than his legionnaires. When they ransomed him at twenty talents he laughed at their conservatism and recommended they raise it to fifty. They enjoyed his company and believed he was joking when he promised that one day he'd see them crucified.

His pleasant manner confused them. His lack of fear disarmed them. In his heart he did not wish them dead and this they could sense. But they did not reckon with his devotion to Rome. She must be served. Her enemies must be punished. This is the force driving him to war upon the republic. Nothing else makes him stand up to the senators and the aristocratic families they represent. Fighting their corruption is the whip driving him on to greater glories, taking what he learned as a general and applying it more generally—the *sine qua non* of a dictator.

A soft voice whispers his name in the dark. He returns to his wife. She wants to ask what keeps him awake this night, but they both know the answer. He has called the senate into session on the morrow. The word is out that he will use the opportunity to declare war against the Parthians. There is another rumor as well: that he will use the opportunity to force the issue of kingship. Even some who accept him as dictator will balk at the final, logical step.

He wants to speak, to set her mind at ease . . . but no words are worthy of the moment. Instead he makes love to her with a passion he hasn't felt in years. She is pleasantly surprised. She adores him still. It is good to be conquered yet again by the general who won in Gaul, Greece, Egypt, Asia Minor, Africa, and most recently Spain. Part warrior, part diplomat, he distracts her attention with fingers and tongue and breath, before accepting her surrender.

Then she watches him rise from the moist sheets and neatly arrange his hair as if an audience awaited him in the darkness of their bedchamber. She is almost happy. For some reason, she remembers the controversy surrounding the funeral oration he gave for the death of his first wife—a young and lovely girl. Only older women had been so honored before. Caesar was accused of self love. Calphurnia has spent her married life wishing her husband to be guilty of more of this self adoration, expecting that such a surfeit will leave some for her.

"I had a dream," she hears herself say.

"What?" he asks, distracted by an insect buzzing in the warm darkness.

"Must you go to the senate tomorrow?"

He sits on the edge of the bed and brushes her hair with the same attention he lavishes on his own. "I must not disappoint them."

An ocean of meaning is contained in those few words. They are his motto. Although born of a patrician family, financial problems have dogged him from the start. Early on he realized his aptitude for the military and learned that being a general requires more than skill in warfare. Statecraft is the extension of war by other means.

Make many promises but know which ones to keep. Don't be known as a man of thousands of virtuous words—such as his severest critic, Cicero—who never performs a single worthy action. Never devalue the currency except for a good cause. And there is no better cause than putting on spectacular entertainments for the people, be it a triumphal procession or a new series of gladiatorial contests. Always strive to be what the people expect of you, and, failing that, settle for the appearance. Forgive enemies when you think you can get away with it.

"You never disappoint . . . them," says Calphurnia, as if reading his mind. "But beware of daggers from those who lack your gifts."

"Your dream?" he demands, his voice suddenly loud, the orator bursting forth.

"Yes."

"Dear one, we know better than to believe in omens. The gods reward intelligence and punish stupidity."

This is a night of truth between them. She lets it out: "Sometimes I think the gods allowed there to be one Alexander the Great to torment all great men ever after with visions of the impossible."

Caesar laughs—a rare sound. "Put aside your fears," he tells her. "I have decided to do what is best for Rome, and the only question is who will resist the more, my friends or foes?"

He heads for the door, her voice following: "Where are you going?"

"I must take some of the night air. Probably won't be much cooler than in here, but I remain an optimist."

She remembers how to laugh.

The moon and stars are his companions—along with one thin, black cat, part of its side a red ruin from recent battle. Caesar doesn't intend to walk very far. But he must be alone with his decision.

Ever since his defeat of Pompey, he has realized the power that has come into his hands. Ever since the first night of passion with Cleopatra, he has realized how the world perceives him—his potential to be as great as Alexander. Perhaps even greater.

Again and again, he has told himself there is no turning back. That is what he said to himself when he crossed the Rubicon. When he shared power with Pompey he knew that one day he would have to destroy this rival general. When the foolish senators feared Pompey more than Caesar (because the man was a popular general from a non-aristocratic family) the future dictator realized the odds were in his favor from then on. No one is as dangerous as an aristocrat without money.

Poor Pompey. Assassinated in Egypt. Poor Egypt. Poor everyone who is not Rome.

And yet there is nothing inevitable about the decision *not yet taken*. His staunchest allies are ready to support him for king, complete with hereditary succession. He has been prepared to take that final step. A century of corruption, of aristocrats looting the state, cannot be undone by half measures.

So he has told himself.

But of late he has been troubled by dreams that sound like his hated critics with one important difference: instead of the whining voices of privilege he hears voices so deep and true that they must emanate from the gods. Their style is even more direct and clean than his proud soldier's memoirs. There is no dissembling, no circumlocutions, no bad analogies. They ask him why he loves Rome.

Why? His life has had no time for why. Only where and when. Why does he love Rome? As this troublesome question has taken root in his soul, as if a spear has been driven there, he doesn't like the answer. The rule of law, even if only for some, is better than the superstitions and traditions of the barbarians they conquer. He hates the republicans for how they have damaged good order, without which there is no trade, no prosperity. His decrees have already improved matters.

He's been telling himself that a rotten republic is only good for growing an empire. The State's will be done.

But the dreams, the voices, won't give him peace. They are different from the dreams of his past, maps guiding him to this summit. They ask if his empire might not cause the same problems as the republic, only on a greater scale that could never be corrected. What if his triumph starts a series of events leading to the destruction of the greatest civilization in history, handing over the world to emotion-guided children and their primitive taboos? A world of low prejudice and cunning with no room for nobility. The West become carrion for the East.

It is a terrifying thought.

Tomorrow Rome will listen to him. He will enjoy an opportunity few men in history have ever enjoyed. He will turn down the crown, any crown. He will . . .

A voice speaks to him from the dark. It is not his wife's, but almost as soft. It is a man's voice that he recognizes instantly. Brutus. One of Pompey's followers whom he pardoned.

"I have come to warn you," says the man from the shadows.

"Step out into the moonlight," Caesar bids him.

The man is nervous and sweating. But in this hot night, everyone sweats, even great Julius Caesar. The general's eyes see that Brutus's right hand hovers near a place where it would be expedient to conceal a weapon.

"What have you to tell me?" he asks the man.

"Of a plot against your life."

Despite what he told his wife about omens, the sudden appearance of this man gives Caesar pause. He recalls that Brutus believes himself descended from Lucius Junius Brutus, who overthrew King Tarquin and established the Roman republic. Not a family eager for royalty to pollute the public baths.

"Tonight I broke with Cassius," says Brutus. "I fear the death of the republic more than I fear one man. A martyr's death is fertile soil for other would-be kings. Cassius doesn't understand how some on your side could benefit from your assassination."

Caesar laughs, the second time in one night; the first time ever in a public place. Brutus is astonished.

"We think along similar lines, Brutus, although starting from very different camps. Tomorrow I will announce that I reject kingship. There is more."

"More?" asks the astonished man.

"I will announce that if my reforms are seen through, I will step down by a certain predetermined date. Then I will ask for the commons and the aristocrats to cease their endless squabbling and put Rome first in their hearts."

"By all the gods . . ." Brutus begins to speak, but his words die as his imagination collapses, vanquished by a man he cannot begin to fathom.

"Cassius must be told," Brutus says, half to himself. "He'd envisioned an even broader scheme than your death. He would have included your closest friends and allies, appendages of yourself. The others in the conspiracy wouldn't go along with that, but only I stood away from spilling your blood."

"I thought you hated me."

"I do. I did."

Caesar places his hand on the shorter man's shoulder. "You were a political friend."

Now it is Brutus's turn to smile.

The two men part and Caesar turns his head to the moon. He wonders how superstitious men would imagine this evening's events. How many portents would fill the sky? Would the moon turn to blood? Would its face be darkened? Would the stars wink out, leaving the sky as black as the soul of Cassius?

These are the musings of a battlefield general, already weary of statecraft as his life becomes a thing of politics where nothing is ever really decided. But the speech he will give tomorrow is written in his head, waiting behind his proud brow to spring forth as from the brow of Jupiter. That much is decided.

As he walks home he wonders if Calphurnia will be awake. Perhaps they can make love again. He'd like this to be a night for her to remember.

Before he reaches his door, another man steps out from the shadows. Caesar wonders how many people are near his house tonight. For a moment he thinks that it might have been a mistake not to keep soldiers on guard until dawn. At first, he thinks it is Brutus returned but this is a larger man.

And then he recognizes the proud face.

"What brings you here at this hour?" asks Caesar.

Mark Antony does not conceal his weapon, which glints white in the lunar light. He speaks only once: "I have come to bury you."

THE CHARGE OF LEE'S BRIGADE
S.M. Stirling

Brigadier General Sir Robert E. Lee, Bart., had decided that the Crimea was even more detestable than Mexico; even more than Texas, and that was going very far indeed. In all his twenty years of service as a professional soldier, he couldn't recall any place he'd been sent that even rivalled the Crimea—only Minnesota came close, and that only in winter. Even in Minnesota, he'd only had the Sioux to contend with, and not General Lord Raglan, the commander-in-chief of the Imperial expeditionary force.

He sighed, signed the last of the quartermaster's receipts, and ducked out of his tent, settling his sword belt as he did so, and tucking his gauntlets through it. It could have been worse; he might have persisted with his original plan to become a military engineer, and then he'd have been stuck trying to move supplies through the Crimean mud. There were scattered clouds above, casting shadows over the huge grassy landscape about him, with hardly a tree in sight. It reminded him of West Texas, come to that. Although Cossacks and Tatars were more of a nuisance than the Commanche had ever been. Not for want of trying, of course.

I wonder if Father spent as much time on paperwork as I do? he thought. Probably not; "Light Horse Harry" Lee had never commanded more than a regiment in the Peninsula, although he'd added considerable luster to the Lee name there, earned a baronet's title and along the way saved the family estate at Stratford Hall from ruin and bankruptcy. Perhaps the world had been a simpler place then, too, and an officer hadn't had to spend an hour before breakfast catching up on the damned forms and requisitions. Certainly the Iron Duke would never have let a campaign bog down the way Raglan had.

He sat down to breakfast with his aides, and the half hour he allowed himself for personal correspondence. The coffee was strong—Turkish, in fact—and there was a peculiar taste to the local bacon, but his Negro orderly Percy was a wonder as a forager, even when he didn't speak the local languages. The first letter was from Mary. Her joints were still annoying her; he frowned at the news. She was young for arthritis, and the news fanned his disquiet at being so much away; Mary rarely said a word about it, but he knew she'd been much happier when he was stationed near home as colonel of the 1st Virginia. And young Mary had the whooping cough ... Enclosed was the latest from Sitwell, the overseer. There was a certain pleasure to the homely, workaday details of Stratford Hall's operations; so much for guano, an experiment with the new superphosphate, the steam thresher working well, and excellent prices for this year's wheat crop. His brows went up at the figures; a bushel was fetching five shillings sixpence FOB Richmond! Although the harvest wages the freedmen were demanding ate up a good deal of it; the competition from the factories of Richmond and Petersburg was driving wages to ridiculous levels. Unlike many he'd never complained about the Emancipation Act of 1833 (and the compensation had been very welcome in clearing the last of his father's debts) but it did complicate a planter's life. Perhaps he should look into buying the contracts of a few Mexican or Chinese indentured laborers, they were popular in Texas and California these days. With these prices, he could afford to experiment.

War always went with inflation, and the Californian gold wasn't hurting either.

He must have said that aloud. Captain Byrd, the youngest of his aides, replied, "Not only California, sir," and passed over a copy of the Times.

"Ah," he said. The story waxed enthusiastic about the new gold discoveries in ... *Transvaal?* he thought. Then: *Yes—in the South African viceroyalty, far in the interior.*

"Truly we live in an age of progress," he said. What would his father have thought of great cities and mines springing up even in the heart of the Dark Continent, of railways transporting whole armies a hundred miles in a day? He skimmed another article, this one dealing with the siege of Vladivostock and the progress of the Far Eastern front in the war against Russia. *That might have been more interesting,* he thought. Certainly more mobile; but that part of the conflict was largely Indian troops, and the new Chinese Sepoy regiments. Reading between the lines he suspected that the Queen—God bless her—would be adding another to her list of titles at the conclusion of this war.

"Victoria, by the Grace of God Queen of Great Britain, Empress of North America, Empress of India and the Further East Indies, Sultana-Protectress of the Ottomans, Empress of Japan ... and soon, Empress of China?" he murmured.

"Persia too, I shouldn't wonder," Byrd said with a grin. "Queen of France, for that matter, except in theory."

Lee gave the younger man a frown; the French were touchy about that, and this army did include a large contingent from the Empire's continental satellite kingdom. Not that their sentiments mattered much— they hadn't since Wellington crushed the Revolutionaries and took Paris in '08—but it was ungentlemanly to provoke them. Father, he recalled, had done very well out of the sack of Paris. The Crimea was unlikely to yield any such returns, and in any case, standards of behavior had changed since the raffish days of George III and the Prince Regent. War in the new era—the Victorian, they were calling it, after the Queen-Empress—was a more staid, methodical, and altogether more respectable affair, as befitted an age of prosperity and progress.

"To business, gentlemen," he said, rising and blotting his lips. He carefully tucked the letter from home into the breast of his uniform tunic.

The regimental commanders of the 1st North American Light Cavalry Brigade waited, as did his orderly with another cup of coffee. "Thank you, Percy," he said, taking it and stepping over to the map table. "Gentlemen," he went on, nodding to the men in the forest-green uniforms of the Royal North American Army.

They stood silent or conversed in low murmurs as he brooded over the positions shown. Balaclava to the south, in Imperial hands now. The Russians were still in force on the rising ground to the north, the Causeway Heights and the Fedoukine Heights beyond the shallow North Valley. More low ground lay to the west, and then the British headquarters on the Sapoune Heights.

The Americans were separately encamped to the south of Sapoune; they were comparatively recent arrivals, and besides that were anxious to avoid the camp fever that was ravaging the rest of the Imperial Army. He looked around at the orderly rows of canvas tents, the picket lines for the horses, the horse-artillery park. Everything as it should be, smoke from the campfires, the smell of coffee and bacon and johnnycake, the strong familiar scent of horses. The 1st Virginia—Black Horse Cavalry, his own old regiment, now in Stuart's capable hands—the Lexington Hussars from Kentucky, the 22nd Maryland Lights, and the Charleston Dragoons. All Southerners, and he was glad of it; Yankees made fine infantry or gunners, but even their farmers just didn't ride enough to make first-rate cavalry, in his opinion. If a man still had to be trained to keep the saddle when he enlisted, it was ten years too late to make him into a horse soldier. Most of his troopers were from small planter or well-to-do yeoman families, with enough money to keep a stable and enough leisure to hunt the fox.

Most of them had seen service in Mexico too, apart from some recruits they'd picked up in Norfolk while waiting to be shipped across the Atlantic.

"For the present, the situation is static," he said. His finger traced the upper, eastern end of North Valley. "Those people are in strength here, and on the Causeway and Fedoukine Heights to either side. The French and elements of the British light cavalry are further north, skirmishing."

"No more Cardigan, thank God," someone muttered.

Lee looked up sharply, then decided to let the matter pass. Since 1832 Viceroy's Commissions in the forces of British North America had been theoretically equal to Queen's Commissions in the British army proper, but Lord Cardigan apparently hadn't heard the news and had a vocal contempt for all colonials. So had a number of his officers, and there had been unpleasant incidents, a few duels . . .

Of course, the man's a snob of the first water. He looked down on all *British* officers who weren't blue-blooded amateurs as well. *A living example of why the British have such superb sergeant-majors.* With officers like Cardigan, you *needed* first-rate NCO's. There were times when he wondered how the Mother Country had managed to conquer half the world.

"Our latest orders are to move up *here,*" he went on, putting his finger on a spot in the lowlands where the Causeway Heights most nearly approached Sapoune. "We're to be ready to move in support if the Imperial troops outside Balaclava need us. Any questions?" More silence.

"Please bear in mind, gentlemen, that the reputation of our regiments, our brigade, and the Royal North American Army rests in our hands. I expect brisk work today if those people bestir themselves. Let us all conduct ourselves in accordance with our duties, and our friends and kindred at home shall hear nothing to our discredit."

Stuart looked north, stroking his young beard and tilting the brim of his plumed hat forward for shade. "Can't be worse than Monterrey or Puebla, General," he said.

"Boots and saddles then, gentlemen."

The four regiments of American cavalry made a brave show as they trotted in column of fours past Lee's position; he saluted the flags at the head of each column, the Union Jack, the regimental banners, the starry blue of the Viceroyalty of British North America with its twenty-seven stars and Jack in the upper corner. The men looked fit for service, he thought; not as polished as the British cavalry units with their rainbow of uniforms and plumed headgear, but sound and ready to fight. Every man had an Adams revolver at his belt, a new Swegart breech-loading carbine in a scabbard at his right knee, and a curved slashing-sword tucked under the saddle flap on his left. Better gear than the British horse; the Americans had stuck with the '97 pattern saber and kept them razor-sharp in wood-lined scabbards. The '43 Universal Pattern sword the British used was neither fish nor fowl in his opinion, and their steel scabbards dulled the blade. Many of the English troopers were still carrying muzzle-loading Enfield carbines or even, God help them, lances.

Even the horses had gotten their condition back, and the commissariat had finally got a supply of decent remounts coming in, Arabs and barbs from Syria—wastage among the horses had been shocking at first.

Lee's head tossed. *I have become a true professional*, he thought. *Logistics have become my preoccupation, and glory a tale for children.*

He stood in the stirrups and trained his binoculars on the Sapoune Heights. The figures of the Russian infantry were still doll-tiny, as they labored to drag away the heavy guns the British had lost to yesterday's assault— the position had been foolishly exposed, in any event. Their gray uniforms were lost against the dry grass and earth of the redoubts; the men were calling the enemy soldiers *graybacks*, in reference to the color of their coats and also to the ubiquitous Crimean lice. He could see one of the steam traction engines as well, bogged down and three-quarters toppled over. They did well on firm ground, but anything softer stopped them cold. *Horses will have to bear with the warlike habits of men awhile longer*, he thought, slapping Journeyman on the neck. The gelding tossed his head and snorted, ready for the day's work, as he might be on a crisp Virginia morning in fox-hunting season.

"Cavalry," he murmured, as morning light broke off lanceheads. "Cossacks, and regulars as well—a regiment at least, in addition to the gunners and infantry. Captain Byrd, what was the Intelligence assessment?"

"Several *stanitsa* of Kuban and Black Sea Cossacks, sir, Vingetieff's Hussars, the Bug Lancers, and an overstrength regiment of the Czar's Guard cavalry," he said. "Do you think they will attack, sir?"

"The matter is in doubt. I would assume that those people have been given the task of covering the withdrawal of the captured guns, but I am informed that Russian behavior can be somewhat baffling—the Oriental influence, no doubt. Dismount and stand the men easy, Captain, but keep the girths tight."

He steadied a map across his saddle horn and pondered as the orders went out to the regimental commanders; behind there was a long rattle of saddles, boots and stirrup irons. *That will keep the horses fresh*, he thought.

"Sir."

He looked around. A lone figure was galloping towards

the Brigade's position, riding neck-for-nothing over irregular ground. A little closer and he recognized the tight crimson trousers of the Cherrypickers, Cardigan's own lancer regiment. The stiffness of his back relaxed slightly as he realized that it wasn't one of the regiment's regular officers. He recognized the man: one of Raglan's staff gallopers, a colonel. The man had an excellent reputation as a soldier in India—during the conquest of Afghanistan, and in the Sikh War, both of them prolonged and bloody affairs. Queen's Medal and the thanks of Parliament, but Lee thought him a rather flashy and raffish figure, for all his bluff John Bull airs and dashing cavalry muttonchop whiskers. *But he can ride*, Lee acknowledged grudgingly. Even by Virginian standards.

"Sir Robert," the man drawled as he reined in and saluted—public-school accent. *Rugby*, Lee remembered, and some faint whiff of scandal. "Lord Raglan commends your prompt movement, and wishes you to demonstrate before the heights in order to delay the enemy's removal of the guns."

Lee's eyebrows rose, and he tossed his head again. "Demonstrate, colonel? Am I ordered to attack, or not?"

"You are requested to use your initiative, Sir Robert," the staff officer said. "I might add that Lord Raglan is disturbed by the loss of the guns—Wellington never lost a gun, you know."

Lee scanned the written orders. As ambiguous as usual; he was becoming unpleasantly familiar with Raglan's style, and it was no wonder this campaign had taken a year. *We are very fortunate indeed that the Russians are not an efficient people*, he thought.

"Very well," he murmured, looking up at the Russian position again. The terrain and forces ran through his mind, much as a chess game might—except that here both players could move at once, and a piece once taken was unlikely to return to this or any other board.

"You will accompany me, Colonel. We will endeavor to satisfy Lord Raglan."

He cut the man's protests off with a gesture. An eyewitness with Raglan's ear would be able to give a more accurate picture than a written message afterwards.

"Captain Byrd," he went on. "My compliments to Colonel Stuart, and he is to report immediately."

The Black Horse rode forward in jaunty style, taking their cue from their commander's plumed hat and fluttering crimson-lined cape. Stuart pulled out ahead and cantered down the ordered rows of men, waving his hat as they cheered.

"If you want some fun, jine the cavalry!" one of the troopers called out as Stuart rejoined the colors.

"Walk-march, *trot*," he said, and the buglers relayed it. Not the intoxicating crescendo of the *charge*, the most exciting sound a cavalryman could hope to hear, but good enough. The two years since the Mexican campaign ended had been boring, and chasing guerrillas through the deserts of Sonora was more like being a constable than real soldiering anyway.

The six hundred men and horses stretched out on either side of the regimental banner, pounding along at an in-hand trot. Clods of dark mud flew up where the horses' ironshod hooves broke the thick turf of the steppe, adding a yeasty smell of turned earth to the odors of human and equine sweat, leather and oil. Stuart stood slightly in the stirrups. They were stirring around up there, all right. The hive was active. Closer, closer—four hundred yards, and he could see the crossed chest-belts of uniforms, and the dangling string caps of the Kuban Cossacks.

"Now to sting 'em," he said, and gestured.

The bugle sang, and the whole regiment came to a smooth stop in line abreast; he felt a surge of pride—it took professionals with years of practice to do that under field conditions. Another call and in every second company the men drew the carbines from the saddle scabbards before their right knees and dismounted. One trooper in five took the reins of the others' horses; the other four went forward six paces and sank to one knee.

Stuart listened to the company officers and noncoms: *"Load!"* Each man worked the lever of his Swaggart and the breechblock dropped down. Hands went back to the pouches at their belts, dropped a brass cartridge into the groove atop the block, thumbed it home. A long *click-clank* as the levers were worked again to close the actions.

"Adjust your sights, pick your targets. Aim low. Five rounds, independent fire. Ready . . . fire!"

BAAAMM. Dirty-white smoke shot out from two hundred and fifty muzzles. Then a steady crackling ripple, experts taking their time and making each shot count. Up among the thick-packed Russians milling among the redoubts, men fell and lay silent or sprattled, screaming. The soft-nosed .45 slugs of the Swaggarts did terrible damage, he'd seen that in Mexico. A round blue hole in your forehead, and the back blown out of your head— exit wounds the size of saucers.

"Remount," Stuart said, as muzzle flashes and powder smoke showed all along the line of the Russian position. *Might as well be shooting at the moon*, he thought. Nine-tenths of the Russian forces were still equipped with percussion smoothbores, muzzle loaders that were lucky to get off two shots a minute and *very* lucky to hit what they were aiming at if it was a hundred yards off. On the other hand, they had artillery up there, and as soon as they got it working . . .

A long whirring moan overhead, then a crash not far ahead of the line. A poplar of black dirt and smoke grew and collapsed before him. A few horses reared, to be slugged down by their riders' ungentle pressure on the reins. The troopers were swinging back into the saddles, resheathing their carbines, many of then grinning.

"Regiment will retire," Stuart said, smiling himself. Bobby Lee had told him to sting the Russians, and from the noise and confusion up there he'd done that, in spades. "Walk-march, *trot.*"

Every horse wheeled to the left, a hundred and eighty degrees. *That'll give those Englishmen something to think about,* he thought. *Show them some modern soldiering.* The British cavalry reminded him of things he'd read about the Hundred Years War—only they seemed to have taken the French cavalry as their model.

"Most impressive, Sir Robert," the English colonel said. "Ah . . . what do you expect Brother Ivan to do?"

"Nothing for a little while," Lee replied, keeping the binoculars to his eyes. "They rarely act in haste, I find. Nor do they coordinate the different arms of their forces well; however, they are formidable on the defense."

That was why he intended to provoke them into an attack, of course. In the next half hour or so the realization that he could sting the Russians any time he chose was going to seep through the thick Slavic skull of the Czarist commander up there. They couldn't leave his force in their front.

Time passed, and the Englishman fidgeted, rubbing at his stomach. Well, half the army had bowel complaints, with the foul water and worse food here—one of the common inglorious realities of soldiering. They'd called it "Montezuma's Revenge" or the "Puebla Quickstep" in Mexico. The ant swarm atop the heights shook itself down into some sort of order, and he could see teams sweating to turn the guns around; heavy guns, four-inch Armstrong rifles for the most part. That could be awkward, and would require him to retire. And . . . yes. The enemy cavalry were forming up in blocks by regiments—the blue and red of the regulars to the center, the formless gray of the Cossacks to either side. Six or seven thousand men, possibly more. Light broke off the lanceheads in a continuous rippling, and then the sabers of the hussars came out in a single bright flash, coming back to rest on their shoulders.

"Here they come, gentlemen," he said, and began giving orders in a quiet, unhurried voice, aware of the crackling excitement of his aides. *But then, they're young men.* He'd stopped feeling exhilarated at the sound of bullets about his ears well before the first gray appeared in his beard.

"Ah . . . will you retire, or dismount your men to receive them?" the English staff officer said.

Lee glanced at him. The man's fine English face was red with what looked like anger, but had that been a quaver in his voice? Lee dismissed the thought; the man had been in far worse situations in Afghanistan.

"Neither, colonel," he said, looking to left and right. "Momentum is all, in these affairs. Prepare to charge," he added in a louder tone.

"But Sir Robert—it's *uphill*!"

A roar came from upslope as the Russian cavalry rolled downward, a mile-long line of blades and glaring bearded faces and red-rimmed horses' nostrils. Hooves drummed like the Four Horsemen riding out on mankind.

Lee smiled. "A good cavalry mount is always part jackrabbit," he said. "And we take care to select the best." He drew his own saber, holding it loosely down by his side.

"Charge!"

The buglers took up the call along the American line, a sweet insistent song. The twenty-five hundred men of the Brigade went forward up the gentle swelling of the hill, building swiftly to a hard pounding gallop. They cheered, not the deep-chested *hurrah* of the British but a wild wailing shriek that rose and fell like nails grating over slate.

You always expect a crash, but you never get it, Lee thought, as the formations met. *Horses have more sense than men; they won't run into an obstacle.*

Instead there was a blurring passage at the combined speed of both formations, enlivened by the tooth-grating steel-on-steel skirl of sabers meeting, the cracking of pistols, the shouting of men and the unbearable shrieking of wounded horses.

A Cossack burst, lumbering, through the screen of men ahead of Lee, roaring through a beard like a stomach-length mattress that had burst its cover. The little stiff-maned steppe pony beneath him looked almost comically small, but it was fast enough to propel the lance head with frightening speed. Lee had been subliminally aware of the Englishman beside him; then the man was gone. The Virginian spared a moment's glance that almost cost him his life, and saw the British colonel hanging off one side of his horse with a heel around the horn, firing from under its belly, for all the world like a Commanche except for his glaring red face. A soldier's reflexes turned him as much as the shout of the standard bearer beside him, and he beat the lance aside with a convulsive slash. The Cossack went by; then there was another Russian ahead of him, a dragoon drawing back for a cut. Lee thrust, and the point went home. The momentum carried him past and he let it tug the steel free. Then the way ahead was clear, only the rest of the heights and the Russian infantry to face.

A quick glance right and left. The Russians had been rocked back on their heels and split, hundreds dismounted or wounded or dead; the Americans were still in formation, despite a scattering of empty saddles. *Time, ask me for anything but time*, Napoleon had said.

"Rally, left wheel, and *charge*," Lee said.

The trumpets sang again, and the whole Brigade began to pivot as if it was a baulk of timber and Lee and his staff the pivot. The officers were shouting to their men: the Marylanders in particular were a little ragged.

"Rally by the Virginians!" he heard, and allowed himself a little glow of Provincial pride.

"Charge!"

This time the path was downhill, and the Russian horse was caught in mid-wheel, caught in the flank and rear, nearly stationary. They broke, and he saw dozens going down under hooves and blades. Another halt-and-wheel brought the colonial regiments back to their starting place; he stood in the stirrups to make sure. If the enemy rallied quickly . . .

"They're skedaddlin'," his aide said exultantly.

"That they are, Captain," Lee agreed, nodding soberly and cleaning his saber before resheathing it. The fragments of the Russian force were withdrawing—not even directly north towards the heights, but in clots and clusters and dribbles of men clustering around an officer or a banner. Behind them trailed horses running wild with empty saddles, and a thick scattering of men on foot, running or hobbling or crawling after them.

"Oh, most satisfactory," he said softly, then spurred out in front of the Brigade's ranks. "Well done!" he called. "Splendidly done!"

More cheers came. *"We'll whip 'em for you agin, Marse Bob!"*

"There, you see, Colonel," he said, as he reined in once more. "No harm done—to us, at least."

"No bloody thanks to you!" the man cried.

Lee frowned. *Ungentlemanly*, he thought.

"Guns?" Lee said. "Which guns, if you please, sir?"

The new galloper from Lord Raglan seemed to be having a hard time holding his temper. Lee wasn't surprised; the staff around the supreme commander was riddled with faction and quarrels, and Raglan wasn't doing much to control it. The Virginian controlled his own irritation with an effort. He wished Raglan would compose the difficulties among his subordinates; he wished Raglan would take a firmer direction of the campaign. His wishes, however, had little or nothing to do with what Lord Raglan would actually do.

"Lord Raglan requests and desires that you seize the guns, Sir Robert," the galloper said. "Immediately."

Lee's brows rose. At least the order was decisive—ambiguous, but not vague. "I repeat, sir: *which* guns? The enemy has a good many batteries in this vicinity."

The messenger flung out a hand. "*There*, sir. *There* are your guns."

Lee's face settled into a mask of marbled politeness. "Very well, Captain. You may assure Lord Raglan that the Brigade will endeavour to fulfill his command."

Whatever it means, he added to himself. He looked north. Up the valley, with massive batteries on either side of it swarming with Russian troops, more guns and earthworks at the head of it, and huge formations of Russian cavalry and infantry in support. Then his eyes swung back to the Sapone Heights before him, running east and west from the mouth of the valley.

"Messenger," he snapped, scribbling on his order pad as he gave the verbal equivalent. "Here. To Sir Colin, with the Highland Brigade: I request that he be ready to move rapidly in support." The man saluted and spurred his mount into a gallop. "Captain Byrd, the Brigade will deploy in line, with the 22nd Maryland in reserve. Immediately, if you please. The horse artillery battery will accompany us this time."

The regiments shook out to either side of him; he reached out, trying to feel their temper. It reassured him. The men had beaten a superior force that morning; they had a tradition of victory. *If men believe they will conquer, they are more than halfway to doing so.*

This time they were going to *need* every scrap of confidence they could wring out of their souls. He looked left and right, drew his saber again, and sloped it back against his shoulder.

"Brigade will advance at the trot," he said quietly.

Bugles rang, shrill and brassy. The long line of the formation broke into movement, shaking itself out with the long ripple of adjustment that marked veteran troops. Ahead lay the long valley, and the first ranging shots from the Russian batteries on either side came through the air with a ripping-canvas sound—old-fashioned guns, but heavy, twenty-four and thirty-two pounders. Shot ploughed the turf, and shells burst in puffs of dirty-black smoke with a vicious red snap at their hearts. One landed not twenty yards to his right, and a section of the orderly front rank of the 1st Virginia was smashed into a bubble of chaos: writhing, thrashing horses screaming like women in labor but heartrendingly loud; men down, one staggering on foot with his face a mask of red and an arm dangling by a shred.

"Steady there, steady."

The voice of a troop commander, sounding so very young. The troopers opened their files to pass the obstacle and then closed again, adjusting their dressing to the regulation arm's length.

"Not up the valley, for Christ's sake!" That was the British colonel.

"Of course not," Lee snapped, letting his irritation out for a moment. Did the man think he was a complete idiot?

"Brigade will wheel to the right," Lee went on. Gallopers fanned out, and bugles sounded. That was a complex maneuver, with so many men in motion. "Right, wheel."

To his left, the 1st Virginia and the Lexington Hussars rocked into a canter. To his right, the Charleston Dragoons reined in, checking their pace. Smooth and swift, the whole formation pivoted until it was facing the junction of the valley with the Sapone Heights— where neither the Russian batteries nor the captured British guns could fully bear on the North Americans.

Not fully was a long way from not bearing at all, and as the Russian gunners perceived their target he could see muzzle flashes from the heights ahead, and from the batteries behind him came the wailing screech of shells fired at extreme range. *Time to get us across the killing field*, he thought, consciously relaxing his shoulders and keeping his spine straight and easy in the saddle.

"Charge!" he said.

The bugles cried it, high and shrill. This time there would be no retreat, and every man in the Brigade knew it. The troopers were raising their screeching cheer again, a savage saw-edged ululation through the rising thunder of thousands of hooves and the continuous rolling bellow of the Russian barrage. Men leaned forward with their sabers poised, or gripped the reins in their teeth and readied a revolver in either hand. The enemy were closer now; he could see the figures of men as they sweated at their guns. Closer, and they were loading with grapeshot. His face was impassive as he steadied Journeyman with knees and hands; the iron rain would not turn aside if he crouched or screamed. A riderless horse went by, eyes wild and blood on its neck from a graze that had cut the reins.

The grape blasted great swaths through the attackers, and the long war-scream took on an edge that was pain and fear and fury combined. Blades and glaring faces edge up around him, and then they were among the guns. Lee saw a man splash away from the very muzzle of a fieldpiece, and then he was urging his mount up and over in a fox hunter's leap, over the limber of a cannon. A gunner struck at him with a long ramrod, glaring, an Orthodox cross hanging on his naked hairy chest. He threw up his arms with a yell as Lee cut backhanded at him, and then the commander was through. He reined in sharply, wheeling the horse in its own length. Byrd and his other aides drew up around him . . . no, Carter was gone, and Rolfe was white-faced and clutching a shattered arm.

"See to him," Lee said. The wind was blowing the smoke of the barrage away. "To the regimental commanders—" *or their successors*, he thought, the losses apparent as the struggle around the guns died down tore at him "—dismount the 1st Virginia, the Hussars, the Dragoons and prepare to hold this position until relieved. I expect a counterattack soon. The Maryland Lights to remain mounted in reserve. At once, gentlemen!"

This was a good position. If the Highlanders arrived in time . . .

The Englishman beside him began to speak. There was a *crack*, and under it a distinct thudding sound. "By God, sir, I think I've been killed," he said with wonder in his voice, pressing his hand over a welling redness on his chest.

"By God, sir, I think you have," Lee blurted. The British colonel slumped to the ground.

Too many good men have died today, Lee thought grimly, and began to position his dismounted troopers. *I hope there was a reason why.*

"Get those guns set up," he snapped. "You"—he pointed at the captain in charge of the field guns—"split up your crews, use volunteers, and see if you can turn some of these pieces around. We can expect a counterattack far too soon."

"By God, Sir Robert," the white-bearded man in the kilt said, removing his bearskin in awe. "Ye've held harrrd, nae doot o' it."

Dead men gaped around smashed cannon; fallen horses were bloating already, adding to the sulfur stink of gunpowder.

"We are most heartily glad to see you, Sir Colin," Lee said hoarsely. He looked northward. The Russians were streaming back as the thin red line of the Highland Brigade advanced. What was left of the 1st North Americans stood about, too stunned to react as yet. Stretcher bearers were carrying men back towards the waiting horse-drawn ambulances.

"Aye, we'll no have trouble takin' the valley now. We

enfilade their whole position, d'ye see. 'Twould hae been nae possible if ye'r men hadna taken an' held this position. A direct attack—" He nodded to the open V of the valley. " 'Twould hae been a Valley of Death."

The bagpipes squealed out; the sound of glory and of tears.

"It is well that war is so terrible," Lee whispered. "Or we would grow too fond of it."

THE CRAFT OF WAR
Lois Tilton

—So, Alkibiades, was that your voice I heard last night, singing bawdy love songs in the street outside my door?

—In truth, Sokrates, I can't quite remember everything about last night. I think I was looking for the courtesan Artemisia's house. But I'm sure you won't begrudge me this celebration when I tell you what the occasion was. I leave tomorrow for Susa, for the Great King's court!

—Oh, to seek high office, I assume?

—Indeed so! I've decided it's time for me to follow in the family tradition. Wasn't my father a general? And my uncle Perikles was almost governor, before he was exiled—and you know those charges were false.

—Judging from last night, the only troops I'd consider you qualified to lead would be a company of naked dancing girls, or an army of satyrs with phalluses for spears.

—Why do you always have to be so critical, Sokrates? Haven't you been telling me for years that I should be more responsible to my civic duties instead of wasting all my time in drinking and debauchery? Now when I'm finally trying to get an important post, you say I'm not qualified. It's really not fair, you know.

—But what makes you think you're qualified to be a general? Why should the Great King appoint you to lead his Athenian troops? I mean, apart from the bribes you plan to spend.

—Why, my heritage, of course! You know my father was one of the generals in command of the invasion of Sicily, when we conquered Syracuse. And I'm an Alkmainoid on my mother's side, and no other family has more illustrious ancestors. Why should I do any less than they did?

—Well, then, suppose your father was a physician, and his father a physician before him. Would this family tradition qualify you to treat illness? Or would you first have to study the craft of medicine before patients could entrust themselves to your care?

—Please, Sokrates! None of your tricky questions, not after last night! My head is aching enough already, without dialectic.

—Then you tell me, my young friend, just how is being a general different from being a physician? Isn't a general responsible for the lives of the men under his command, just as a physician is responsible for the lives of his patients? Isn't victory in battle the proper object of his skill, just as health is the proper object of the physician's craft?

—Yes, but the state has never expected every man to be a physician. Traditionally, though, every citizen is supposed to serve in time of war: either as a hoplite on the battlefield or a rower in the fleet. When the Spartans revolted after the great earthquake, why, didn't you answer the governor's summons, didn't you buckle on your armor and pick up your shield to go put down the insurrection? But if I recall correctly, your real trade is cutting stone, as your father's was.

Besides, you know quite well that generals have always been chosen from the best families in the state. My father never had any particular training in the craft of war, and the governor never had any complaints about his service. And in the time of his father and yours, all Athens' generals were chosen by the Assembly on the basis of their family connections.

Just consider as an example the great general Miltiades, who repulsed the first Persian invasion at Marathon! Most of the Athenians wanted to hide and wait behind the city walls, but not Miltiades! He led the entire army out to meet the Persians on the battlefield, and he pushed them back into the sea! But wasn't Miltiades simply chosen as the representative of his family and tribe? So why should you think I would do any worse?

—If arrogance were the only qualification for leadership, Alkibiades, my young friend, then I'd have every confidence in your success!

But I think your own example will serve to demonstrate my point, after all. For in the first place, if the victory at Marathon proved Miltiades was such a great general, what did his failure at the siege of Paros demonstrate? You can't have it both ways. You'd hardly choose a physician who kills one of his patients for each one he cures, would you?

—I don't think that's really a fair argument, Sokrates. In a war, you have to consider not only your own general's skill, but the opposing commander's as well.

—Indeed you should! But again, your example serves only to illustrate my own point. At Marathon, Miltiades managed to defeat an enemy commander no more skilled than himself. But ten years later, when the Persians invaded again, he and all the rest of the Greek commanders were defeated in turn by a general who was a real expert in the craft of war.

—No, Sokrates, I think your example serves to prove my point, instead! Because I'll agree with you that Mardonios was an able general. Yet why was he chosen for his command? For his family connections! Because he was both a nephew and a son-in-law of the Great King.

—Ah, but you see, it isn't Mardonios I refer to at all.

—What do you mean, Sokrates? Is this one of your tricks again? Every schoolboy with his pedagogue wiping his nose can tell you that Mardonios was the Persian general who led the invasion of Hellas.

—Oh, it was Mardonios up on the white horse where every man could see him, I grant you that much. But the real credit should have gone to another general, a stranger—a barbarian, in fact—who was no more a part of the Great King's family than you are. But I see you doubt me. Would you care to hear the story as I heard it, myself?

—If it means no more of your questions, I certainly do.

—Well, then, have you heard of a man named Dikaios, son of Theokydes?

—That's another question, I'll point out. But wasn't he a traitor?

—An Athenian exile, yes, who turned informer. He came back after the war, to reclaim his property. I knew him then, when he was an old man and I was a young one. I'll say this for Dikaios—he'd become a man of importance among the Persian King's advisors, but still he returned to claim his ancestral house and land in Athens. By the way, you might meet his sons when you go to the court at Susa—Dikaios had a Persian wife and his sons hold high office now.

Be that as it may, this is what he told me:

After his first invasion force was defeated so soundly by Athens at Marathon, the Great King Dareios was more determined than ever to subjugate all Hellas to his rule. He knew that if he didn't, the men of all nations in his empire would consider him weak and plot more insurrections against him. So he began to assemble a great army for the purpose, but as we know, he died before his preparations could be completed.

Now, at about the time his heir Xerxes succeeded to the throne, a stranger from the land of Sind in the east came to the court at Susa, who claimed to be a general and an expert on the craft of war. His name, as far as anyone could make it out, was Sontseus. According to Dikaios, he never really learned the Persian language; an interpreter always had to speak for him, a man from Hind.

His story was that he'd been the general commanding the armies of a king in his own country—he called the kingdom Wu. But the king of Wu became jealous of his success in war and started to worry that Sontseus was plotting to take the throne for himself, and he was exiled, on pain of death. So he came to the court at Susa and offered his services to the Great King, because, as he said, he was a general and he wished to practice his craft.

At first, of course, no one there took him seriously. Besides his outlandish speech he always wore a long robe, not trousers like the Persians, and he couldn't ride a horse or drive a chariot. But Sontseus insisted he could prove he was a better general than any other commander in the King's service. Finally Xerxes was curious and asked him how he thought he could prove such a thing. And Sontseus answered: let the King give each general a hundred men each to train in his own way. Or a thousand men, or ten thousand—any equal number. Then pit them against each other in battle, and whoever was the losing commander would have his head cut off, and whoever won would be made general over all the King's armies.

Now, this was the kind of wager Xerxes enjoyed. Nothing he loved better than cutting off men's heads or noses if they failed him. So he agreed, and he called all his officers together and asked them which one would take the stranger's challenge. Now Artaphernes had been one of the losing commanders at Marathon, and he considered this a chance to recover from that disgrace and win the confidence of the King. So he accepted the challenge, and Xerxes allotted each of them one hundred men. Artaphernes picked his from the first ranks of the Immortals, all expert cavalrymen. But Sontseus chose untrained levies, and he exercised them in secret.

When the time came for the contest, Sontseus drew up his troops on foot in close order, much like our phalanx, but they were on open ground where they were vulnerable to a cavalry attack. So Artaphernes ordered his horsemen to charge and attack them on both flanks. Just as expected, Sontseus's troops broke and ran for their lives, throwing down their pikes like cowards. But as the horsemen charged after them in pursuit, the fleeing spearmen threw down caltrops they'd concealed underneath their cloaks: sharp, three-pronged spikes that pierced the horses' hooves and crippled them. And when the horses were down and the cavalry all in disorder, then Sontseus's company fell on them with swords and took the field in triumph.

—In other words, he only won by using a trick, a ruse!

—Indeed, that was one of the first maxims of his *Craft of War*, as Dikaios recalled it: "All warfare is based on deception."

But consider this: is what Sontseus did any different from the ruse that "wily Odysseus" used against the Trojans—the wooden horse? The important thing is this: Sontseus knew his opponent was arrogant and overconfident, and therefore his men would be, as well. His plans took advantage of that.

At any rate, Xerxes fulfilled his part of the bargain and cut off Artaphernes' head, even though he was part of his own family, as all his high-ranking generals were. But when it came to appointing Sontseus as commander of all his armies, it was another matter, because he didn't speak the Persian language. It had been difficult enough, apparently, for him to give orders to just one hundred men, even with his interpreter. To command a vast force in the field would have been impossible. So this is why we remember Mardonios the conqueror on his white horse and not Sontseus, although he had riches and honors enough for all that he accomplished.

Now, to understand what he did, you have to know

how the Great King's armies had been organized in those days, which is quite different from the way they are now, and that is all owing to Sontseus. Because if the battle of Marathon had proved one thing, it was the relative superiority of our Greek hoplites to even the best of the Persian troops, so that the Athenians could push twice the number of the enemy back into the sea. But the Persians had always relied on superiority of numbers to overcome this deficiency.

At that time, the Great King had a standing army of no more than ten thousand men, all of Persian blood, who were called the Immortals. Like the Spartans, they had no other occupation than preparing for war, and they had the best armor and equipment and training. But when the King went to war, then he would call on his levies, and every nation under his rule would have to send their soldiers for the campaign. At the time of Darius's death, he was planning to muster as many as three hundred thousand men under arms for the invasion of Hellas.

—So many men would strip the countryside bare as they marched through it!

—Precisely what Sontseus told the King. It was one of his maxims that "Advantage of numbers alone is no advantage."

But there were other problems with an army that size that he pointed out, as well. The soldiers came from all different parts of the empire, all with different weapons and equipment. They couldn't all speak the same language. And so many of them were conscripts, they had to be driven into battle under the lash.

But certainly your pedagogue did more than just wipe your nose. You must know how the poet described the Persian host.

> —And all the nations born of Asia
> Brought their swords from their own
> lands—

Ranks of them behind the banners
Of the King of Kings.

—Very good, my young friend!

So Sontseus reviewed the levies, one nation at a time, and from each of them he chose the best men, then sent the others back to their homes until he had an army of one hundred thousand remaining. Then he made sure each man was furnished with the best weapons and armor, although of course the equipment was in the Persian style, not hoplite armor such as our soldiers use. And he trained them all to march in step to the drum, and retreat to the sound of the gong, and he introduced large banners for signals, and flares for signaling at night, and so he built the army that conquered Hellas.

When Xerxes questioned the cost of equipping so many soldiers and keeping them all under arms, Sontseus replied:

First, that an army of paid volunteers, instead of conscript levies, would always be more eager to fight.

Second, that the King could request additional tribute in exchange for those men who were sent back to their own countries, and this would help defray the expenses.

And finally that a smaller, more efficient army was less of an expense, since there would be fewer men to feed and transport. For example, it would have taken a thousand additional ships to transport all the levies Darius had originally meant to assemble, along with all their equipment and supplies.

—It sounds like dull work, counting bags of beans and ships. More like an estate manager than a soldier.

—Ah, but part of the general's craft is the same as the estate manager's. This is precisely my point.

And Sontseus was a master of strategy, too, not just training and logistics. Another one of his maxims was: "Separate your enemy from his allies. First divide them, then plot against them both."

—Now that sounds like politics, not war!

—And is there a difference? Lies and deception are one of a state's best weapons in war. Unfortunately for Hellas, Sontseus was a master of deception, and dividing our states was too easy to accomplish. More than one city was willing to join the Great King's forces, either for gain or for revenge against their old enemies. But his principal enemies, the cities he most wished to defeat, were two: Athens, for what our hoplites did to the Persian troops at Marathon. And Sparta.

—Do you suppose that story is true, Sokrates, that the Spartans threw the Persian heralds into a well?

—I have no doubt of it. Too many other cities were sending Xerxes the tokens of submission to his rule. Telling his envoys to get their earth and water from the well was really sending a message to the other states of Hellas: to hold fast or they would have the Spartans to deal with.

But, as I was saying, Sontseus realized that his first goal must be to separate Athens from Sparta, for in those days they weren't enemies. What most people remember now is that Sparta refused to come to the aid of Athens at Marathon, because Persian agents spread the rumor that the Great King had bribed the Spartans to hold their army back, and most Athenians believed them.

—Because, of course, they would have done the same themselves!

—Alas, you're probably right. But this was the real origin of the hatred between Athens and Sparta. In fact, the Spartans did send an army, after all: two thousand hoplites, with the excuse that a religious festival had made them late.

—As if anyone would believe that!

—Well, many Athenians didn't. And from that time on, they were mistrustful of Sparta. However—this is my point—they were still nominally allies against the Persian king. So that when Hellas learned of the threatened invasion—as all the world must have known, from the

scope of Xerxes' preparations—the states all met at Korinth
to decide what they must do to defend themselves. The
larger party, the cities of the Peloponnese, all favored
making a stand at the Isthmus of Korinth. Since this would
have meant abandoning all Attika to the Persians, naturally
the Athenians opposed any such plan, and there was more
talk that once again the Spartans were going to sell them
out. But even the Spartans were aware that they could
never win the war without the Athenian fleet, which was
the strongest in all Hellas, and our general Themistokles
vowed that he would never commit the fleet if his allies
abandoned Attika to the enemy.

So the Greek states were all undecided on their strategy,
and they did nothing but quarrel, while all the time the
Persian preparations were well under way. Now of course
the Great King had always had his spies and agents among
us, and so this debate was no secret. But Sontseus made
the outcome inevitable when he divided the Persian force
and sent five hundred ships to invest the island of Kythera,
just across the straits from Lakonia. With this threat at
their rear, so close to home, the Spartans abandoned
all thought of sending their hoplites to the defense of
Attika, and without them there was no hope for Athens,
standing alone.

Sontseus by this one stroke accomplished his goal and
won the war, for he not only deprived Athens of all allies,
he deprived the rest of Hellas of the Athenian fleet. So
you see, Alkibiades, if you do become a general, you owe
it to him. Because Athens is still standing and our citizens
weren't carried off as slaves, while the only Spartan generals
now are barefoot, herding goats on Mount Ithome.

> *Well-watered Lakonia they ruled*
> *And Messenia's rich plowlands*
> *By the strength of their arms*
> *And their thirsty spears.*
> *But now bowed down in defeat*
> *Overcome by Persian might.*

—Yes, but Sokrates, you claim this Sontseus won the war before he fought a single battle?

—Indeed I do. And this was another one of his maxims: "To defeat the enemy without fighting is better than to win a hundred victories in a hundred battles."

—But if he never fought a battle, Sokrates, how can you claim he was so skilled at the craft of war? I mean, doesn't the essence of war lie in fighting?

—Well, he was too old a man to stand in the front ranks with a pike, if that's what you mean. And of course it's true that Mardonios gave the actual orders. But according to Dikaios, Sontseus was always there to plan the strategy and tactics, which were based on his maxims.

For example, he said: "Never let an enemy know where you intend to give battle. If he prepares in the front, attack in the rear where he is weak." Now, you know what happened when the Peloponnesian allies had concentrated their force behind the Isthmian Wall, expecting the Persians would have to attack them there. Instead, they turned the Isthmus into a trap, bringing up their forces from the rear, through the Argolid where there was no opposition.

And because another of his rules was: "Never attack an enemy at bay," he didn't waste his own troops in a futile frontal assault. He simply waited until they were so desperate they tried to break through to Korinth, and ambushed them on the road. "Show a surrounded enemy a way out, and he will take it."

> Raise your voices in lament
> For the Spartan dead!
> Raise a cry of mourning
> For the host destroyed!

—All right, Sokrates! I'm convinced! But what about all these maxims? Did Sontseus write them down? Because it's clear that all I have to do is study them, and I'll be the greatest general in history!

—He did write them down, according to Dikaios. He

called the book *The Craft of War*. Unfortunately, it was in his own language, which no one in the entire empire can read. His name is almost forgotten now, and a few of his maxims are all anyone remembers.

But his story does show that knowledge is at least as important in war as in any other activity, and that a general has to learn his craft exactly as a physician does.

—You know, Sokrates, it occurs to me that it's too bad our own generals didn't have this book. Or if this Sontseus had come over to the side of the Greeks instead of the Persian King's. If he was such a great general, we might have won the war and sent Xerxes back to his court in defeat.

—Well, my young friend, I'll just say this: if you can imagine Athens and Sparta—and all the rest of the Greek states—operating together against a common enemy, then you can imagine almost anything!

QUEEN OF THE AMAZONS
Jody Lynn Nye

Eleanor, Queen of France, fumed within the sumptuous hangings of her wagon. Her prison. How impossibly humiliating for a queen and a duchess. To be swept up and carried off like a loaf of bread by a common thief! Her husband had much to answer for.

The day was hot. They had been on the road from Antioch to Jerusalem since midnight. Louis had allowed the women to alight for refreshment only twice, and Eleanor had begun to feel every splinter, every grain of dust, as though they had become part of her body. She was tall for a woman, and slim, so that her bones were too long for the box, and she had too little padding to protect her from the bumping and swaying of her litter. Her thoughts were as uncomfortable as her body. She thought of the last coherent conversation she had had with Louis, in the regal hall in her uncle Raymond's palace in Antioch.

There she had folded her hands together on the embroidered silk tablecloth and looked up patiently at her sovereign lord. Louis was a thin young man made even thinner and more ascetic looking by the privations suffered by his army since they had left Paris eight months before.

"Louis, I will stay here in Antioch with my uncle. There is no earthly reason for us to go on so soon. Jerusalem

97

has waited these four years. It can wait another month until we're at proper strength."

"We are at the strength we will be," he had said, shaking his head sadly but with an air of resolve. "Our infantry has been absorbed by the infidel at Satalia. They will not be coming to our aid."

"Leaving you with what?" Eleanor had asked, quickly calculating what remained when one subtracted the largest part of the forces that had followed them from France. "The barons and knights? That is not enough to throw against the walls of Jerusalem."

"It will be, with the aid of the other kings and princes," Louis had insisted. "To free the Holy City at last!"

When that dreamy light burned in his eyes, Eleanor knew that nothing she said would sink in properly, but she tried all the same.

"Louis, you could have the strength of my uncle Raymond's Poitevins behind you, if you but delayed for a short time. Edessa is here, on the very border of Antioch. It guards the northern reaches of the Holy Land. Raymond will throw his armies in with yours, once the Turk has been driven away from the borders. Otherwise, he cannot leave here to aid Jerusalem. Help Uncle Raymond. Once his concerns are dealt with, he will help you with yours. It will be for the greater glory of God if all of the Holy Land is free and Frankish once again."

Louis frowned, and the dreamy light became one of anger. "Uncle me no uncles, madam!" he snapped, and she remembered how his temper, never well tethered, could range from peace to fury in a moment. "It seems more for the glory of Poitou than God that your uncle asks you to intercede with me."

"He did not ask me! It seems only good sense, if you will look at the greater scope of things."

"My dear one, what could be greater than to free the most sacred sites from the ravages of the infidel? It could be for the good of your soul, if only you would show the proper attitude," Louis protested.

"My soul shows considerable respect for the Holy Land. If you recall, I took the cross myself, from the very hands of our dear Pope Eugenius, but Louis, one thing at a time. Jerusalem is not in immediate peril; Edessa is! If you allow the Turk to come in, you will find it hard to get him out again. You can't turn your back on an open border."

"It seems to me that if Prince Raymond's motives were pure," Louis had said acidly, "then he would be eager to restore the county to Joscelin or his heirs, but my counselors say that once the principal towns of Edessa are recovered, they will be added to Antioch. I am not interested in enlarging his holdings. He has plenty of land—far beyond what his expectations could have brought him as a younger son."

"If you have been listening to the gossip, my husband, you will have heard that Joscelin is no fit steward," Eleanor had said. "He left the citadel unguarded. My Amazons and I could have done a better job myself. I would have ordered . . ."

Louis's eyebrows had lowered briefly. Eleanor had stopped and bit her tongue. Her last order, in February, had resulted in the deaths of many good men, and a night of terror for Louis and his knights. She had insisted that the advance guard and her ladies, highborn women called the Amazons as a tribute to their bravery in coming along on crusade with their queen, be moved from an arid tableland in Paphlagonia where Louis had ordered that they spend the night, to a comfortable and green valley within sight of the plateau. Because their forces had become separated in the course of the day, and Eleanor had not thought to have a scout remain behind, Louis came upon an empty encampment. While he cast around in confusion for the Queen and her party, the Frankish forces were set upon by Turks. Louis had climbed a tree and fought at bay until daylight, not knowing the fate of his Queen. The whisperers had held her fully responsible.

Louis had forgiven her, but not forgotten. He was angry with her, as angry as he had been frightened for her. Eleanor knew she was only partly to blame. She had since heard good counsel that the Turks had been watching them for some time, and only awaited their chance to attack the weakened Franks when their attention was elsewhere. God knew that the army, let alone the women, needed an oasis after the hard mountain passes. Only Louis would insist upon sleeping on a rock when there was soft grass within sight. She was sure he felt that if he mortified himself and them all in His name, God would eventually turn a loving face upon him again. Not that one could see much under the layers of dust he wore. Perhaps it kept off the fleas; but Eleanor was inclined to believe that his behavior was more of the self-imposed penance he was serving for the sack of the small town of Vitry. He had gone from an insecure, unworldly man-child to a king and general too soon. He had not learned moderation, of action or temper, until it was too late. Now he was as full of regrets as he had been of rage. It made him more uninteresting as a husband than he had been when they had married. At least Eleanor had had the well-being of her people in mind when she had acted. But the incident had devalued her currency with Louis, and he no longer listened to her. She tried her best arguments on her uncle's behalf, and all in vain.

She had feared her insistence would do little good. He was not interested in the periphery of the Holy Land, but its heart. In addition, Louis insisted his self-imposed penance for the sack of the town of Vitry and the burning of its cathedral with a thousand souls trapped inside could not be fulfilled in Antioch. It was the proper action of any Christian to defend the seat of the faith, as the Holy

Father had asked. He must save Jerusalem itself to save his soul.

That was Louis all over, Eleanor thought. He always went for the core, never seeing what was on the outside of things. But she did not have to go with him to Jerusalem. Her Amazons, out of favor with the army, were becoming fractious, openly lamenting having come on crusade. Eleanor, who never gave up unless she was bested, was feeling weary herself. Her uncle Raymond was a kindred spirit, loving luxury and beauty. He invited her to stay in his realm and rest as long as she liked. Louis had other plans.

Louis disapproved of Antioch, filled with pagan gods alongside the trappings of the holy church. It seemed too prosperous, when it should have been more godly, as it was close to Jerusalem. He was jealous of Raymond, and openly scorned the mercantile air of a place so close to the holiest of holies. But they had had to leave their infantry behind in Satalia, and the most recent news told them that it would not be coming to their aid. It was incredible that Louis would still think he had the strength to aid Jerusalem. Only the barons, knights, and clergy had been able to afford to take ship with them. It seemed as though God had refined the army step by step, first depriving them of the German forces, then paring away more men in the disaster of Paphlagonia, then stripping them of all the common men-at-arms, leaving only the pure soul, of which Louis was the heart. Eleanor was reluctant, after starvation, hardship, and utter discomfort, to leave Antioch so soon.

She had wanted to come along because she was bored in Paris. It was not as beautiful or as cheerful as her duchy of Aquitaine. Her musicians and troubadours had been driven away from the palace, leaving her without the familiar sounds she had loved since childhood. Her brain was rotting away in her head from ennui. Danger, discomfort, hunger and heat, or no, riding on crusade was far more interesting than remaining behind on the Ile. Every hill, every river, every rock was new to her. Each day was a gift. She was never meant to be shut away in a box, like the other treasures of the crown, and she would not be. Sometimes she thought she was more of a man than Louis. She bit her tongue from ever voicing this even to the closest confidants among her ladies. Her Amazons, Eleanor thought with pride. How brave they had been to come with her, never turning back in the face of hardship—although she suspected that some came because they were as bored as she. Danger was more exciting than routine. And they were not without amusements; on the road she had troubadours and minstrels and acrobats, and everyone was happy. Constantinople had been eye-opening, giving her many ideas for improving the dreary and ancient royal palace. She would tell all to Abbe Suger, whom they had left behind as regent, a good friend of Eleanor's, who appreciated beauty, and would find joy in the refinements and culture of the East.

Her uncle had given them great gifts, fed them, restored them, and put at their service all the comforts and honors that Emperor Manuel had denied them of Constantinople. Eleanor's Amazons had shown amazing fortitude, but they were tired. And she had no wish to go back to dull Paris, not before she had seen all there was to see here.

Antioch was paradise with a French flavor. The gardens were astonishing, trade brought treasures from every corner of the world, culture if not in the same extravagant fashion as at the court of Byzantium, then still impressive. And Edessa was on the doorstep. Its fall threatened Antioch, which guarded the northern borders of the Holy Land. Jerusalem would still be at peril—its king had been calling for help for four years and more. It could wait until Damascus was rescued. The crusade had in fact been called to restore Edessa to Frankish rule. She tried to insist, even suggesting that she and her Poitevins and Aquitainians would stay to help Raymond. She would leave the dull Louis and his tedious kingdom and his hopeless crusade for a cause that would do some good. The Poitevins were her vassals, and would stay with her. That was when Louis acted.

At midnight the night before, Louis had come to her rooms, ordered her to pack her goods, and set his men-at-arms to watch and make certain she did no more. Her things were loaded in total disarray on the sumpter mule trains. They sneaked out of the city before Prince Raymond could be alerted. Eleanor had been awake ever since, angry, hurt, and plotting. Louis would not have had the intelligence to plan a lightning raid like that. She blamed Brother Odo, Louis's confessor, and the eunuch Thierry, who hated all women.

"Ho-oo!" A cry from outside her curtains startled her, and her litter swung to an uncomfortable halt. Louis's face, well-begrimed with soil and sweat, appeared between the drapes. His eyes wore that dreamy look again that told Eleanor he felt the salvation of his soul within grasp.

"We are within sight of Jerusalem, lady. You have time to make your toilet before we enter the Holy City."

Eleanor roused herself, feeling the sting of cramped muscles as she climbed out of the wooden litter. She shook out her long skirts. The dull blue was made duller by the ochre haze that floated everywhere, and her gold embroideries had faded to tan.

The road dust was settling around them in a great cloud as Eleanor alighted. She took a deep breath. Polluted as it was, the air was still sweeter than inside the little box that was her prison. Around them, the sweet, heavy scent of dark green olive trees and that perfume that she could only identify as the odor of the Orient swam, raising her naturally buoyant spirits from the depths to which they had fallen.

"Are you all right, your majesty?" Berthe, one of her

ladies-in-waiting, ran to her side. The girl's face was moist with sweat, and her clothes were crumpled. It was for love of her queen that she had come along. Only Eleanor was forced to come.

"I am well now," Eleanor said, straightening her back. "Like any other living thing, I need sunlight to thrive." Two by two from the other litters, the rest of the Amazons came out, stretching sore backs and legs: Sybille, Countess of Flanders; Faydide of Toulouse; Torqueri of Bouillon, daughter of one of the most famous knights who had fought in the first crusade. They looked weary but excited.

"We are here, mesdames!" Faydide said. She was younger than Eleanor, and still had a girl's high spirits. "We have accomplished our journey to the Holy City! The salvation of our souls is assured."

"Praise be to God," said Sybille. She was the half-sister of the late King of Jerusalem.

The Amazons mustered themselves to enter Jerusalem in style. Escorted by the Knights Templar, they rode through the ancient walls wearing their white plumes and gold-painted boots, backs straight and chins held proudly. One would never know they had ridden a thousand miles in the most terrifying conditions. In contrast, Louis came into the city wearing a simple sackcloth robe and bearing his palmer's staff. The Frankish army was welcomed by the Queen Melisende and the Patriarch of Jerusalem. Eleanor instantly sensed a kindred spirit in the Queen of Jerusalem. She was a brave woman who had held the kingdom after her husband's death in regency for her small son, Baldwin. Melisende admired Eleanor and her women for their fortitude. They bid fair to become good friends.

Eleanor was interested in all new sights. After taking refreshment with the queen, she rode through the Holy City with her women, soaking up the atmosphere with a sense of deep accomplishment. No other woman could do what she had done.

Yet, she was still a prisoner. That night, her door was locked from the outside, and she heard the clank of mail of the guards set to keep her within. The following day, she donned her Amazon's garb once again for the meeting of princes that had been called at Louis's request. She wore her plumes partly to keep up her spirits, partly to see if she could start a new fashion, and lastly to see if she could get a response from Louis, who had ignored her since they arrived in Jerusalem the day before. Her spirits had revived somewhat in the sanctified air of the city, and she had no intention of being left out of negotiations that involved her vassals.

"Then we are agreed?" said Emperor Conrad of Hohenstaufen. "We shall move to reconquer Damascus at once, in the name of God and this most holy crusade."

"Agreed," said King Louis. The other princes and kings around the table nodded. "This shall prove our devotion to the cause. If we recover Damascus, it shuts off an open door through which the Turks and Egyptians pass freely, to the detriment of the Latin kingdom."

"It also benefits us all equally, with none the loser," said Queen Melisende. Eleanor, present but silent at the conference, understood that fact had much to do with Louis's agreement. After treating her uncle so shamefully, Louis had no intention to support any one who was enriching himself.

"We shall muster our knights at once," said the Grand Master of the Temple of Jerusalem.

And I shall remain here, Eleanor thought, making my own plans for escape. She smiled at Melisende, queen to queen.

But she had reckoned without the machinations of Thierry and Odo. On the morning that the Frankish army left Jerusalem, Eleanor and the Amazons were in its van. Louis's observers had seen how well his wife had gotten

on with the Queen of Jerusalem, and voiced their
suspicions to the king. Louis did not dare to leave her
behind, for fear that she would make good her threat
to leave him and return to the Aquitaine with her
liegemen. As a result, he had ordered her to accompany
them to Damascus.

Eleanor was angry to have her plans thwarted, but
she retaliated by mustering her own troops. No matter.
She would make the procession a pageant. The Amazons
put on their finest feathers and gold-embroidered tunics,
and polished their bronze shields to mirror brightness.
On her braided golden hair was a gilded helm adorned
with swan's wings and down, and on her feet were gilded
buskins laced up to her knee. She and her women wore
at their sides lightweight swords with golden hilts, meant
more to inspire than to wage battle. When they joined
the van, she heard more than one admiring whisper from
the assembled knights. Her cousins of Poitou were openly
complimentary. Eleanor sat at the head of her army with
her head high.

The weather was absolutely beautiful. Not a drop of
rain fell in all the long march across the Outremer from
Galilee to Damascus. The dust didn't trouble the Amazons
greatly because they rode at the front of the vast army,
with only guardian knights and scouts ahead. The sky
was almost the color of lapis lazuli, with the most
occasional white curd of cloud drifting by. The May sun
turned the ochre land to gold. Splashes of color on the
dry landscape were mud-brick houses, gardens of bright
flowers, and pagan temples of stone as beautiful as a poem.
How evil could the infidel be, Eleanor wondered, if they
raised such lovely and graceful houses to their god Allah?

As they drew closer to Damascus, Eleanor could not
believe her eyes. Cultivated crops and gardens had been
despoiled. Mature fruit trees, half-grown fruit still upon
them, had been cut down.

"So as not to feed us," snapped a knight.

"Did they do this themselves?" asked Sybille.

"Yes," Eleanor said. "They want to leave nothing of benefit for any of us. They've done more damage to their future than to ours."

"They've cut us off from water, too," said one of Eleanor's cousins, pointing to a damp, muddy ditch that ran along the side of the road into the ravaged orchard. "This was done almost before we arrived here."

"They fear us so greatly," Eleanor said, thoughtfully.

They arrived nearly within sight of Damascus without seeing a single soldier. As they passed through the orchards that surrounded the city, they were set upon by the defenders who lay in wait for them.

"To me, defenders of the faith!" Louis cried, and spurred his horse forward. Fifty thousand men followed in his wake.

The Franks fought through the forests and fields surrounding the city until they came within bowshot of the walls. Eleanor's bodyguard herded the Amazons away from the fighting, and brought them carefully to a place of safety near the ruins of a warehouse that lay at a distance from the city. From there, she could see Damascus well. Where was everyone? Eleanor scanned the walls of the city, empty of even a single soul. Damascus was by no means as large as Jerusalem, or even Antioch, but handsome and prosperous. Her gaze lit upon an overturned bucket beside a stone wellhead. The ground was still wet beside it. The gates, at the end of a well-worn road, were sealed shut. Between her and those gates bloody war raged.

Conrad and Louis fought like tigers, so said the pages and messengers who reported back to the queen and her bodyguard. They had won their way to the very gates, and were employing the ram. Eleanor knew the truth of it, for she could hear the repeated thud of the heavy metal face on wood and stone.

"The infidel fears us greatly," one young man reported, with a smug face. "Rumor has it that the city will surrender to us."

Towards nightfall, the enemy withdrew, and the Frankish army paused to regroup. Tents were raised at a short distance from the city, well outside the gates and away from any cover that would shelter raiders, and they spent the night in conference. The field in which they camped was dry, with crumbly clay soil. The watercourses that irrigated it had been dammed from inside the city. The parched troops muttered about the lack of resources, but Louis had insisted on this campsite.

"Better a thirsty night than a midnight rout," he said.

"You ought to know the efficacy of that," Eleanor said. Louis looked surprised, then abashed and angry at having their private quarrel brought up. "We should be better defended out here. There will be water enough when you have broken through the walls."

"True enough," Louis said. "Tomorrow, with God's help, we shall win this fight, in His name."

"The Damascenes are ready to surrender," said Conrad. His tunic was well stained with blood, none of it his own, and he looked weary. Rumor said that he had killed a dozen men, including one he had split in two with a single blow of his sword. "We should press our advantage, and win through."

False dawn broke behind them, and the army was on the move before the sun peeped over the horizon. Eleanor rose with the army. She and her women had arrayed themselves in their gorgeous Amazon dress, and ranged themselves in marching lines. Louis, in full battle dress, rode up on his war-horse, and spoke directly to his queen.

"You will stay here," he said, leaning out of his saddle to put his face close to hers. "You will not endanger yourself, nor anyone else."

"Yes, my lord," Eleanor said, with a steady voice, but inside she was furious. How dare he treat her like an idiot! Louis turned to his guard.

"Stay with the queen at all times. Protect her life with your own."

"Yes, your majesty," the knights chorused.

"The sun is rising!" cried Thierry of Flanders.

And with it came the defenders of Damascus. The Franks rode forth to meet them.

Eleanor and the Amazons were kept well back from the fighting. She had heard many more tales during the night. The Emir of Damascus, who had expected that the boy king Baldwin would continue to be tolerant of his holdings after the fashion of his father, King Folques, was reported to be in terror that the Franks were advancing. The city was weak. It would fall.

The battle, fought upon the blood of yesterday's fallen, was fierce. The guardians of the city fought with a terror that made them dangerous but erratic. Eleanor sat proudly upon her horse to watch the whole thing, eschewing the shelter of the wains into which her ladies had retreated in the heat of the day.

Louis was right in the thick of things, laying about him with his great sword. He looked alive and vital, almost a man, Eleanor thought.

The Franks brought forth the battering ram. They hammered at the high stone wall, knocking away pieces of stucco and exposing the cemented blocks beneath. Men fell as the defenders rained arrows upon them, but more took their place. Some of the stones began to crumble and shift.

"They are almost through," Eleanor cried.

More Damascene horsemen came charging in, and the Franks turned to defend their flank. The ram battered on. Suddenly, the army shifted, withdrawing the ram, moving company by company off toward the north. Louis and his men followed.

"Where are they going?" Eleanor demanded, disbelievingly. "Stop them! They are almost through the wall!"

But the fighting was moving, moved. Eleanor watched them go. When the troops were out of the way, she got a look at the wall they had been attacking. It was ready to fall! Louis as usual had gone to the core of things, and missed the bigger picture. There were hardly any defenders at the top. The Damascenes were as tired as the Franks. If they broke through here, Damascus would surrender.

"By heaven, look at that!" Eleanor exclaimed. "We must finish the job."

"Who must?" asked Sybille, suspiciously.

"We will!"

"Don't be foolish, sister!"

"No!" Eleanor insisted. "Damascus is ready to topple. If we go in, they will surrender. A woman could do it." She sat up high in her saddle and drew the sword at her side.

"To me, Poitevins! To me, Aquitaine! Amazons, follow me!"

She spurred her horse forward toward the fallen ram. Her cousins and bodyguards were so surprised it took a moment before they followed her. She galloped a dozen yards before they caught up with her. Behind, the other Amazons charged, shrilling a high-pitched war cry that split the air. Soldiers from a dozen princes' armies turned to run to their aid.

Louis's force of knights had withdrawn almost out of sight until they heard the Amazons scream. The men wheeled to intercept and defend them, but Eleanor's troops reached the walls first.

"Pick up the ram!" she cried. "We will win through here. Now!"

Her horse danced nervously out of the way as the willing hands of a hundred Poitevin and Frankish soldiers seized the heavy wood, and pounded it into the gate.

As she had thought, wood and stone fell apart after only a few blows. A cry of triumph rose from every throat as a hole appeared. More men sprang forward to pull at the stones and enlarge the hole. The Franks poured into the city of Damascus.

Eleanor could see no more for a time, as Louis's knights arrived and surrounded her with a protective ring of steel. The Damascenes surrounded them, but the faces she could see in flashes through the threshing blades and shields were frightened. They knew the Amazons had come again.

When the battle died away, the defenders of the city were surrendering in droves. Eleanor sat in the circle of her bodyguard with her women, and felt pleased with herself. The other Amazons were thrilled to have actually aided in the holy Crusade.

"I'd thought it a game until now," Faydide confided, fanning herself with her handkerchief. Her cheeks were pink and glossy with sweat. "But no longer! If you had told me we would charge the paynim, I would have died of fright!"

"We have earned the cross given us by the Holy Father," the sturdier Sybille said, kissing Eleanor. "Now my nephew's patrimony is secure." The king returned, wheeling his horse into the midst of them, scattering horsemen like chaff.

"What could you have been thinking of, madam?" Louis asked, as angry as she had ever seen him. "I warned you. Do you think you are a general, to order my men to their doom?"

"I won!" Eleanor said, opening wide and unbelieving eyes at him. "Where you withdrew, I pressed. I am a descendant of Charlemagne, Louis. Just because I am a woman does not mean I lack strategy or intelligence. Louis, we have won this day! Damascus is ours!"

Louis was not appeased. "Eleanor, you are my vassal and my wife. You will no longer behave in this fashion. What if you had failed?" Eleanor remembered Paphlagonia, and subdued her triumphant feelings. But surely that was paid for, now. The soldiers acclaimed her in the streets of the conquered city. She had hoped that with victory would come Louis's respect. No. He only loved her. His eyes were still turned only toward God. She was angry with him, and very tired of being Queen of France. Louis did not deserve her or her men or her lands. The thought of going home to the Ile depressed her mightily. She would make Louis pay for his treatment of her, but not now.

The Emir appeared in his silk robes, and formally offered the city to the Frankish princes.

"No man," he said, "no man could have conquered us so." He bowed deeply to them, and then to Eleanor. He straightened up and his dark eyes, like the sharp eyes of an eagle, looked straight into Eleanor's.

"You have broken our homes, Frankish queen, and cast us like Ismael into the desert. For that, I lay a curse upon you. You will have no peace for the rest of your days."

Eleanor smiled at him from her horse, resplendent in plumes and gold. "Anything would be better than wasting away, my lord."

And she never did have a peaceful life. But she much preferred it that way.

THE PHANTOM TOLBUKHIN
Harry Turtledove

General Fedor Tolbukhin turned to his political commissar. "Is everything in your area of responsibility in readiness for the assault, Nikita Sergeyevich?"

"Fedor Ivanovich, it is," Nikita Khrushchev replied. "There can be no doubt that the Fourth Ukrainian Front will win another smashing victory against the fascist lice who suck the blood from the motherland."

Tolbukhin's mouth tightened. Khrushchev should have addressed him as *Comrade General*, not by his first name and patronymic. Political commissars had a way of thinking they were as important as real soldiers. But Khrushchev, unlike some—unlike most—political commissars Tolbukhin knew, was not afraid to get gun oil on his hands, or even to take a PPSh41 submachine gun up to the front line and personally pot a few fascists.

"Will you inspect the troops before ordering them to the assault against Zaporozhye?" Khrushchev asked.

"I will, and gladly," Tolbukhin replied.

Not all of Tolbukhin's forces were drawn up for inspection, of course: too great a danger of marauding *Luftwaffe* fighters spotting such an assemblage and shooting it up. But representatives from each of the units the Soviet general had welded into a solid fighting force were there, lined up behind the red banners that symbolized their proud records. Yes, they were all there:

113

the flags of the First Guards Army, the Second Guards, the Eighth Guards, the Fifth Shock Army, the Thirty-eighth Army, and the Fifty-first.

"Comrade Standard Bearer!" Tolbukhin said to the young soldier who carried the flag of the Eighth Guards Army, which bore the images of Marx and Lenin and Stalin.

"I serve the Soviet Union, Comrade General!" the standard bearer barked. But for his lips, he was utterly motionless. By his wide Slavic face, he might have come from anywhere in the USSR; his mouth proved him a native Ukrainian, for he turned the Great Russian *G* into an *H*.

"We all serve the Soviet Union," Tolbukhin said. "How may we best serve the motherland?"

"By expelling from her soil the German invaders," the young soldier replied. "Only then can we take back what is ours. Only then can we begin to build true Communism. It surely will come in my lifetime."

"It surely will," Tolbukhin said. He nodded to Khrushchev, who marched one pace to his left, one pace to the rear. "If all the men are as well indoctrinated as this one, the Fourth Ukrainian Front cannot fail."

After inspecting the detachments, he conferred with the army commanders—and, inevitably, with their political commissars. They crowded a tumbledown barn to overflowing. By the light of a kerosene lantern, Tolbukhin bent over the map, pointing out the avenues of approach the forces would use. Lieutenant General Yuri Kuznetsov, commander of the Eighth Guards Army, grinned wide enough to show a couple of missing teeth. "It is a good plan, Comrade General," he said. "The invaders will regret ever setting foot in the Soviet Union."

"I thank you, Yuri Nikolaievich," Tolbukhin said. "Your knowledge of the approach roads to the city will help the attack succeed."

"The fascist invaders *already* regret ever setting foot in the Soviet Union," Khrushchev said loudly.

Lieutenant General Kuznetsov dipped his head,

accepting the rebuke. "I serve the Soviet Union!" he said, as if he were a raw recruit rather than a veteran of years of struggle against the Hitlerites.

"You have the proper Soviet spirit," Tolbukhin said, and even the lanternlight was enough to show how Kuznetsov flushed with pleasure.

Lieutenant General Ivanov of the First Guards Army turned to Major General Rudzikovich, who had recently assumed command of the Fifth Shock Army, and murmured, "Sure as the devil's grandmother, the Phantom will make the Nazis pay."

Tolbukhin didn't think he was supposed to hear. But he was young for his rank—only fifty-three—and his ears were keen. The nickname warmed him. He'd earned it earlier in the war—the seemingly endless war—against the madmen and ruffians and murderers who followed the swastika. He'd always had a knack for hitting the enemies of the peasants and workers of the Soviet Union where they least expected it, then fading away before they could strike back at his forces.

"Has anyone any questions about the plan before we continue the war for the liberation of Zaporozhye and all the territory of the Soviet Union now groaning under the oppressor's heel?" he asked.

He thought no one would answer, but Rudzikovich spoke up: "Comrade General, are we truly wise to attack the city from the northeast and southeast at the same time? Would we not be better off concentrating our forces for a single strong blow?"

"This is the plan the council of the Fourth Ukrainian Front has made, and this is the plan we shall follow," Khrushchev said angrily.

"Gently, gently," Tolbukhin told his political commissar. He turned back to Rudzikovich. "When we hit the Germans straight on, that is where we run into trouble. Is it not so, Anatoly Pavlovich? We will surprise them instead, and see how they like that."

"I hope it won't be too expensive, that's all," Major General Rudzikovich said. "We have to watch that we spend our brave Soviet soldiers with care these days."

"I know," Tolbukhin answered. "Sooner or later, though, the Nazis have to run out of men." Soviet strategists had been saying that ever since the Germans, callously disregarding the treaty von Ribbentrop had signed with Foreign Commissar Molotov, invaded the USSR. General Tolbukhin pointed to the evidence: "See how many Hungarian and Romanian and Italian soldiers they have here in the Ukraine to pad out their own forces."

"And they cannot even station the Hungarians and Romanians next to one another, lest they fight," Khrushchev added—like any political commissar, if he couldn't score points off Rudzikovich one way, he'd try another. "Thieves fall out. It is only one more proof that the dialectic assures our victory. So long as we labor like Stakhanovites, over and above the norm, that victory will be ours."

"Anatoly Pavlovich, we have been over the plan a great many times," Tolbukhin said, almost pleadingly. "If you seek to alter it now, just before the attack goes in, you will need a better reason than 'I hope.' "

Anatoly Rudzikovich shrugged. "I hope you are right, Comrade General," he said, bearing down heavily on the start of the sentence. He shrugged again. "Well, *nichevo.*" *It can't be helped* was a Russian foundation old as time.

Tolbukhin said, "Collect your detachments, Comrades, and rejoin your main forces. The attack *will* go in on time. And we shall strike the fascists a heavy blow at Zaporozhye. For Stalin and the motherland!"

"For Stalin and the motherland!" his lieutenants chorused. They left the barn with their political commissars—all but Lieutenant General Yuri Kuznetsov, whose Eighth Guards Army was based at Collective Farm 122 nearby.

"This attack *must* succeed, Fedor Ivanovich," Khrushchev

said quietly. "The situation in the Ukraine requires it."

"I understand that, Nikita Sergeyevich," Tolbukhin answered, as quietly. "To make sure the attack succeeds, I intend to go in with the leading wave of troops. Will you fight at my side?"

In the dim light, he watched Khrushchev. Most political commissars would have looked for the nearest bed under which to hide at a request like that. Khrushchev only nodded. "Of course I will."

"Stout fellow." Tolbukhin slapped him on the back. He gathered up Kuznetsov and his political commissar by eye. "Let's go."

The night was very black. The moon, nearly new, would not rise till just before sunup. Only starlight shone down on Tolbukhin and his comrades. He nodded to himself. The armies grouped together into the Fourth Ukrainian Front would be all the harder for German planes to spot before they struck Zaporozhye. Dispersing them would help there, too.

He wished for air cover, then shrugged. He'd wished for a great many things in life he'd ended up not receiving. He remained alive to do more wishing. *One day*, he thought, *and one day soon, may we see more airplanes blazoned with the red star*. He was too well indoctrinated a Marxist-Leninist to recognize that as a prayer.

Waiting outside Collective Farm 122 stood the men of the Eighth Guards Army. Lieutenant General Kuznetsov spoke to them: "General Tolbukhin not only sends us into battle against the Hitlerite oppressors and bandits, he leads us into battle against them. Let us cheer the Comrade General!"

"Urra!" The cheer burst from the soldiers' throats, but softly, cautiously. Most of the men were veterans of many fights against the Nazis. They knew better than to give themselves away too soon.

However soft those cheers, they heartened Tolbukhin. "We shall win tonight," he said, as if no other alternative were even imaginable. "We shall win for Comrade Stalin, we shall win for the memory of the great Lenin, we shall win for the motherland."

"We serve the Soviet Union!" the soldiers chorused. Beside Tolbukhin, Khrushchev's broad peasant face showed a broad peasant grin. These were indeed well-indoctrinated men.

They were also devilishly good fighters. To Tolbukhin's mind, that counted for more. He spoke one word: "*Vryed!*" Obedient to his order, the soldiers of the Eighth Guards Army trotted forward.

Tolbukhin trotted along with them. So did Khrushchev. Both the general and the political commissar were older and rounder than the soldiers they commanded. They would not have lost much face had they failed to keep up. Tolbukhin intended to lose no face whatever. His heart pounded. His lungs burned. His legs began to ache. He kept on nonetheless. So did Khrushchev, grimly slogging along beside him.

He expected the first brush with the *Wehrmacht* to take place outside of Zaporozhye, and so it did. The Germans patrolled east of the city: no denying they were technically competent soldiers. Tolbukhin wished they were less able; that would have spared the USSR endless grief.

A voice came out of the night: "*Wer geht hier?*" A hail of rifle and submachine-gun bullets answered that German hail. Tolbukhin hoped his men wiped out the patrol before the Nazis could use their wireless set. When the Germans stopped shooting back, which took only moments, the Eighth Guards Army rolled on.

Less than ten minutes later, planes rolled out of the west. Along with the soldiers in the first ranks, Tolbukhin threw himself flat. He ground his teeth and cursed under his breath. Had that patrol got a signal out after all? He hoped it was not so. Had prayer been part of his ideology, he would have prayed it was not so. If the Germans learned of the assault too soon, they could blunt it with artillery and rockets at minimal cost to themselves.

The planes—Tolbukhin recognized the silhouettes of Focke-Wulf 190's—zoomed away. They dropped neither bombs nor flares, and did not strafe the men of the Fourth Ukrainian Front. Tolbukhin scrambled to his feet. "Onward!" he called.

Onward the men went. Tolbukhin felt a glow of pride. After so much war, after so much heartbreak, they still retained their revolutionary spirit. "Truly, these are the New Soviet Men," he called to Khrushchev.

A middle-aged Soviet man, the political commissar nodded. "We shall never rest until we drive the last of the German invaders from our soil. As Comrade Stalin said, 'Not one step back!' Once the fascists are gone, we shall rebuild this land to our hearts' desire."

Tolbukhin's heart's desire was piles of dead Germans in field-gray uniforms, clouds of flies swarming over their stinking bodies. And he had achieved his heart's desire many times. But however many Nazis the men under his command killed, more kept coming out of the west. It hardly seemed fair.

Ahead loomed the apartment blocks and factories of Zaporozhye, black against the dark night sky. German patrols enforced their blackout by shooting into lighted windows. If they hit a Russian mother or a sleeping child . . . it bothered them not in the least. Maybe they won promotion for it.

"Kuznetsov," Tolbukhin called through the night.

"Yes, Comrade General?" the commander of the Eighth Guards Army asked.

"Lead the First and Second Divisions by way of Tregubenko Boulevard," Tolbukhin said. "I will take the Fifth and Ninth Divisions farther south, by way of Metallurgov Street. Thus we will converge upon the objective."

"I serve the Soviet Union!" Kuznetsov said.

Zaporozhye had already been fought over a good many times. As Tolbukhin got into the outskirts of the Ukrainian city, he saw the gaps bombs and shellfire had torn in the buildings. People still lived in those battered blocks of flats and still labored in those factories under German guns.

In the doorway to one of those apartment blocks, a tall, thin man in the field-gray tunic and trousers of the *Wehrmacht* was kissing and feeling up a blond woman whose overalls said she was a factory worker. *A factory worker supplementing her income as a Nazi whore,* Tolbukhin thought coldly.

At the sound of booted feet running on Metallurgov Street, the German soldier broke away from the Ukrainian woman. He shouted something. Submachine-gun fire from the advancing Soviet troops cut him down. The woman fell, too, fell and fell screaming. Khrushchev stopped beside her and shot her in the back of the neck. The screams cut off.

"Well done, Nikita Sergeyevich," Tolbukhin said.

"I've given plenty of traitors what they deserve," Khrushchev answered. "I know how. And it's always a pleasure."

"Yes," Tolbukhin said: of course a commissar would see a traitor where he saw a whore. "We'll have to move faster now, though; the racket will draw the fascists. *Nichevo.* We'd have bumped into another Nazi patrol in a minute or two, anyway."

One thing the racket did not do was bring people out of their flats to join the Eighth Guards Army in the fight against the fascist occupiers. As the soldiers ran, they shouted, "Citizens of Zaporozhye, the hour of liberation is at hand!" But the city had seen a lot of war. Civilians left here were no doubt cowering under their beds, hoping no stray bullets from either Soviet or German guns would find them.

"Scouts forward!" Tolbukhin shouted as his men turned

south from Metallurgov onto Pravdy Street. They were getting close to their objective. The fascists surely had guards in the area—but where? Finding them before they set eyes on the men of the Eighth Guards Army could make the difference between triumph and disaster.

Then the hammering of gunfire broke out to the south. Khrushchev laughed out loud. "The Nazis will think they are engaging the whole of our force, Fedor Ivanovich," he said joyfully. "For who would think even the Phantom dared divide his men so?"

Tolbukhin ran on behind the scouts. The Nazis were indeed pulling soldiers to the south to fight the fire there, and didn't discover they were between two fires till the Eighth Guards Army and, moments later, the men of the Fifth Shock Army and the Fifty-first Army opened up on them as well. How the Hitlerites howled!

Ahead of him, a German machine gun snarled death— till grenades put the men handling it out of action. Then, a moment later, it started up again, this time with Red Army soldiers feeding it and handling the trigger. Tolbukhin whooped with glee. An MG-42 was a powerful weapon. Turning it on its makers carried the sweetness of poetic justice.

One of his soldiers pointed and shouted: "The objective! The armory! And look, Comrade General! Some of our men are already inside. We have succeeded."

"We have not succeeded yet," Tolbukhin answered. "We will have succeeded only when we have done what we came here to do." He raised his voice to a great shout: "Form a perimeter around the building. Exploitation teams, forward! You know your assignments."

"Remember, soldiers of the Soviet Union, the motherland depends on your courage and discipline," Khrushchev added.

As Tolbukhin had planned, the perimeter force around the Nazi armory was as small as possible; the exploitation force, made up of teams from each army of the Fourth

Ukrainian Front, as large. Tolbukhin went into the armory with the exploitation force. Its mission here was by far the most important for the strike against Zaporozhye.

Inside the armory, German efficiency came to the aid of the Soviet Union. The Nazis had arranged weapons and ammunition so their own troops could lay hold of whatever they needed as quickly as possible. The men of the Red Army happily seized rifles and submachine guns and the ammunition that went with each. They also laid hands on a couple of more MG-42's. If they could get those out of the city, the fascists would regret it whenever they tried driving down a road for a hundred kilometers around.

"When you're loaded up, get out!" Tolbukhin shouted. "Pretty soon, the Nazis will hit us with everything they've got." He did not disdain slinging a German rifle on his back and loading his pockets with clips of ammunition.

"We have routed them, Fedor Ivanovich," Khrushchev said. When Tolbukhin did not reply, the political commissar added, "A million rubles for your thoughts, Comrade General."

Before the war, the equivalent sum would have been a kopeck. Of course, before the war Tolbukhin would not have called the understrength regiment he led a front. Companies would not have been styled armies, nor sections divisions. "Inflation is everywhere," he murmured, and then spoke to Khrushchev: "Since you've come in, Nikita Sergeyevich, load up, and then we'll break away if we can, if the Germans let us."

Khrushchev affected an injured look. "Am I then only a beast of burden, Fedor Ivanovich?"

"We are all only beasts of burden in the building of true Communism," Tolbukhin replied, relishing the chance to get off one of those sententious bromides at the political commissar's expense. He went on, "I am not too proud to load myself like a beast of burden. Why should you be?"

Khrushchev flushed and glared furiously. In earlier days—in happier days, though Tolbukhin would not have thought so at the time—upbraiding a political commissar would sure have caused a denunciation to go winging its way up through the Party hierarchy, perhaps all the way to Stalin himself. So many good men had disappeared in the purges that turned the USSR upside down and inside out between 1936 and 1938: Tukhashevsky and Koniev, Yegorov and Blyukher, Zhukov and Uborevich, Gamarnik and Fedko. Was it any wonder the Red Army had fallen to pieces when the Nazis attacked in May 1941?

And now, in 1947, Khrushchev was as high-ranking a political commissar as remained among the living. To whom could he denounce Tolbukhin? No one, and he knew it. However furious he was, he started filling his pockets with magazines of Mauser and Schmeisser rounds.

Sometimes, Tolbukhin wondered why he persisted in the fight against the fascists when the system he served, even in its tattered remnants, was so onerous. The answer was not hard to find. For one thing, he understood the difference between bad and worse. And, for another, he'd been of general's rank when the Hitlerites invaded the motherland. If they caught him, they would liquidate him—their methods in the Soviet Union made even Stalin's seem mild by comparison. If he kept fighting, he might possibly—just possibly—succeed.

Khrushchev clanked when turning back to him. The tubby little political commissar was still glaring. "I am ready, Fedor Ivanovich," he said. "I hope you are satisfied."

"*Da*," Tolbukhin said. He hadn't been satisfied since Moscow and Leningrad fell, but Khrushchev couldn't do anything about that. Tolbukhin pulled from his pocket an officer's whistle and blew a long, furious blast. "Soldiers of the Red Army, we have achieved our objective!" he shouted in a great voice. "Now we complete the mission by making our departure!"

He was none too soon. Outside, the fascists were striking heavy blows against his perimeter teams. But the fresh men coming out of the armory gave the Soviets new strength and let them blast open a corridor to the east and escape.

Now it was every section—every division, in the grandiose language of what passed for the Red Army in the southern Ukraine these days—for itself. Inevitably, men fell as the units made their way out of Zaporozhye and onto the steppe. Tolbukhin's heart sobbed within him each time he saw a Soviet soldier go down. Recruits were so hard to come by these days. The booty he'd gained from this raid would help there, and would also help bring some of the bandit bands prowling the steppe under the operational control of the Red Army. With more men, with more guns, he'd be able to hurt the Nazis more the next time.

But if, before he got out of Zaporozhye, he lost all the men he had now . . . *What then, Comrade General?* he jeered at himself.

Bullets cracked around him, spattering off concrete and striking blue sparks when they ricocheted from metal. He lacked the time to be afraid. He had to keep moving, keep shouting orders, keep turning back and sending another burst of submachine-gun fire at the pursuing Hitlerites.

Then his booted feet thudded on dirt, not on asphalt or concrete any more. "Out of the city!" he cried exultantly.

And there, not far away, Khrushchev doggedly pounded along. He had grit, did the political commissar. "Scatter!" he called to the men within the sound of his voice. "Scatter and hide your booty in the secure places. Resume the *maskirovka* that keeps us all alive."

Without camouflage, the Red Army would long since

have become extinct in this part of the USSR. As things were, Tolbukhin's raiders swam like fish through the water of the Soviet peasantry, as Mao's Red Chinese did in their long guerrilla struggle against the imperialists of Japan.

But Tolbukhin had little time to think about Mao, for the Germans were going fishing. Nazis on foot, Nazis in armored cars and personnel carriers, and even a couple of panzers came forth from Zaporozhye. At night, Tolbukhin feared the German foot soldiers more than the men in machines. Machines were easy to elude in the darkness. The infantry would be the ones who knew what they were doing.

Still, this was not the first raid Tolbukhin had led against the Germans, nor the tenth, nor the fiftieth, either. What he did not know about rear guards and ambushes wasn't worth knowing. His men stung the Germans again and again, stung them and then crept away. They understood the art of making many men seem few, few seem many. Little by little, they shook off pursuit.

Tolbukhin scrambled down into a *balka* with Khrushchev and half a dozen men from the Eighth Guards Army, then struggled up the other side of the dry wash. They started back toward Collective Farm 122, where, when they were not raiding, they labored for their Nazi masters as they had formerly labored for their Soviet masters.

"Wait," Tolbukhin called to them, his voice low but urgent. "I think we still have Germans on our tail. This is the best place I can think of to make them regret it."

"We serve the Soviet Union!" one of the soldiers said. They returned and took cover behind bushes and stones. So did Tolbukhin. He could not have told anyone how or why he believed the fascists remained in pursuit of this little band, but he did. *Instinct of the hunted*, he thought.

And the instinct did not fail him. Inside a quarter of an hour, men in coal-scuttle helmets began going down into the *balka*. One of them tripped, stumbled, and fell with a thud. "Those God-damned stinking Russian pigdogs," he growled in guttural German. "They'll pay for this. Screw me out of sack time, will they?"

"*Ja*, better we should screw their women than they should screw us out of sack time," another trooper said. "That Natasha in the soldiers' brothel, she's limber like she doesn't have any bones at all."

"Heinrich, Klaus, *shut up!*" another voice hissed. "You've got to play the game like those Red bastards are waiting for us on the far side of this miserable gully. You don't, your family gets a *Fallen for Führer and Fatherland* telegram one fine day." By the way the other two men fell silent, Tolbukhin concluded that fellow was a corporal or sergeant. From his hiding place, he kept an eye on the sensible Nazi. *I'll shoot you first*, he thought.

Grunting and cursing—but cursing in whispers now— the Germans started making their way up the side of the *balka*. Yes, there was the one who kept his mind on business. Kill enough of that kind and the rest grew less efficient. The Germans got rid of Soviet officers and commissars on the same brutal logic.

Closer, closer . . . A submachine gun spat a great number of bullets, but was hardly a weapon of finesse or accuracy. "Fire!" Tolbukhin shouted, and blazed away. The Nazi noncom tumbled down the steep side of the wash. Some of those bullets had surely bitten him. The rest of the German squad lasted only moments longer. One of the Hitlerites lay groaning till a Red Army man went down and cut his throat. Who could guess how long he might last otherwise? Too long, maybe.

"*Now* we go on home," Tolbukhin said.

They had practiced withdrawal from such raids many times before, and *maskirovka* came naturally to Soviet soldiers. They took an indirect route back to the collective farm, concealing their tracks as best they could. The Hitlerites sometimes hunted them with dogs. They knew how to deal with that, too. Whenever they came to rivulets running through the steppe, they trampled along in them for a couple of hundred meters, now going one way, now the other. A couple of them also had their canteens filled with fiery pepper-flavored vodka. They poured some on their trail every now and then; it drove the hounds frantic.

"Waste of good vodka," one of the soldiers grumbled.

"If it keeps us alive, it isn't wasted," Tolbukhin said. "If it keeps us alive, we can always get outside of more later."

"The Comrade General is right," Khrushchev said. Where he was often too familiar with Tolbukhin, he was too formal with the men.

This time, though, it turned out not to matter. One of the other soldiers gave the fellow who'd complained a shot in the ribs with his elbow. "*Da*, Volya, the Phantom is right," he said. "The Phantom's been right a lot of times, and he hasn't hardly been wrong yet. Let's give a cheer for the Phantom."

It was another soft cheer, because they weren't quite safe yet, but a cheer nonetheless: "*Urra* for the Phantom Tolbukhin!"

Maybe, Tolbukhin thought as a grin stretched itself across his face, *maybe we'll lick the Hitlerites yet, in spite of everything*. He didn't know whether he believed that or not. He knew he'd keep trying. He trotted on. Collective Farm 122 wasn't far now.

AN OLD MAN'S SUMMER
Esther Friesner

The sun casts waves of shimmering heat over the Pennsylvania farmland, but he feels only cold. It is July. It might as well still be November. He tries to recall whether or not he was brought to the table for the Thanksgiving dinner, but he finds himself wandering through places in his mind where nothing dwells, not even light, where the walls of countless cells have been scrubbed slick and bare as hollow bones.

The question of Thanksgiving nags at him, senselessly, like an old dog that refuses to give up its tattered rag of a chew toy. Mamie isn't here to answer; perhaps she's gone to town, perhaps she's visiting the grandchildren, perhaps he's only lost in the false impression that she's gone at all when she's really still somewhere quite close, inside the house. He would ask her about Thanksgiving if he could, if he were only certain that one Thanksgiving is all that he's lost, if he could have some sense of self-assurance that his lips would respond to his desires well enough to form the proper words.

In the end, what does it matter, whether he can frame the stubborn question, whether he truly needs to have the answer? Even if he had the power to ask it, there is no one he can turn to for an answer. He is alone. The young male nurse who left him here, in this chair, within the safety of the glassed-in porch, is worse than absent.

He brings too much with him when he tends the old man. He has yet to learn how to hold back the play of fear and pity over his face when he looks his patient in the eye.

The old man sees the nurse's thoughts as clearly as if they were set before him on his desk back in the White House: *You are our President and you are dying. Don't do it on my shift; don't leave the blame for your death with me.* And the old man also sees, as if it were a battle plan unrolled before him, the way his keeper's mind shifts the little metal figures on the mat, picking up the piece that is Eisenhower and tossing it away without a second thought, moving up to the front lines the piece that is Nixon.

Not yet, young man, not yet. I'm incapable of performing my duties as before, but is that all it takes to be cast aside? Helpless isn't dead, he thinks behind the dull, expressionless sanctuary of his eyes. *I'm still in here, you know.* He wants to do something, raise a fist, a hand, no more than the tip of a finger, call up some short, sharp word to startle the nurse out of his comfortable assumptions about the old man's condition. But even if he could hold onto the little spark of will still raging bright within him, he lacks the power to direct it held. It dances just beyond the reach of his fast-fading strength, defiant, elusive, indifferent to his history of command.

So he lets it go. Why bother to try ensnaring it, taming it, sending it here or there? The effort is too much for him to direct, much less maintain. Letting go is easier, he's found. Peace always follows surrender: Who should know that better than he, even if the surrender wasn't his until now?

Peace . . .

When the first stroke laid its cold finger across his brain, he was in his office, working on correspondence at his desk. There was to be a state dinner that night, and his mind was racing ahead to the preparations he would have to make for it as soon as he got all those papers before him cleared away. So much to do! So many places to be! So many questions demanding his immediate answer, all of them vital! How could one man manage it all without—?

No warning shot heralded the moment when the world spun itself out from under him, papers scattering, pen tumbling from a hand suddenly gone slack. His every anchor was sucked away, chains slipping through limp fingers, pulled inexorably far and farther from his grasp in the great outrunning tide. He'd held on then for as long as he could, fought the damned thing, called for aid only when he realized there was no wise choice but to summon other souls to back him against this strongest, strangest, subtlest of foes. His secretary Ann Whitman hurried in, stood there stunned for just a moment when she saw him collapsed in his chair, gabbling, half-formed words sliding off his tongue. Ann, who could share the bounty of his laughter, bear the eruption of his rages . . . to have her see him like this! But what choice did he have? What choice?

Ann, the good soldier: Loyal as any man in his command, she put aside her shock, snapped back into full capability, as always ready to serve him, save him. She got Goodpaster from the next office, he was the one who got the old man to bed. There was no pain, then. As he lay where Goodpaster had left him, still smarting from the shame of Ann having been the first to see him brought low, he heard the call go out for a medic. Dr. Snyder came at once, summoned other doctors, a council of war that promptly shut its doors against him while they conferred, just as if he were only a stretch of disputed terrain.

By God, let them try it!

His anger is as fresh now as it was the instant he realized they'd changed him from their President to their ward.

Time finds no place to hook its ordered days into his mind. All times are one to him, events a tumble of bright crystals in the barrel of a brass kaleidoscope, unchanged themselves, changing only in the falling out of their eternally disordered patterns. He sits on the glassed-in porch at Gettysburg and lies in the White House bedroom and it is *then* for him just as it is *now*. His hands are in his lap, resting palms upward, the fingers slightly curled, but at the fierceness of his indignant memory he almost calls up enough power to force them closed. Almost. They tremble and release and that is all.

It was different then, when the doctors and their private confabulations were more than just shards of memory careening through his jumbled thoughts. *Then* he found his strength again soon enough to get up from the bed where they'd beached him, present himself in robe and slippers before the startled eyes of the doctors and Mamie and their son John, and grin to see the look of horror on their faces to see him standing there just as if nothing had happened at all.

Nothing. There was the joke of it, the laughter that crumbled to cold ash in his throat. When he tried to speak, to tell them that he was well, that he had a state dinner to attend, that there was no need to send Nixon in his place, nothing came out of his mouth but gibberish, a scramble of sound that finally choked to a halt in silence. And in the red rage that flamed up inside him at the body's treason, that flung itself against the cold bars of his mind's captivity, something happened, something as small as the snap of a twig. Something stole past the sentries of his senses without the honest, piercing pain of the heart attack that had struck him just over a year ago. It whispered softly in his ear: *Enough. Rest.* Anger and indignation stood with him only for a breath as his body swayed crazily in a black wind no one but himself could feel, then they were torn away into the gale's shrieking heart and he fell into the dark.

Now here he sits, a bead on a wire, a little counter marking off his place in the strands of hours and days and weeks. They pass over him as they will, differing only as far as their patterns of light and shadow, heat and cold, the austere white of winter sometimes spattered with the clownish colors of Christmastime, the gold of summer stained with the gray of rain. How many years? How many lost?

If I cannot attend to my duties, I am simply going to give up this job. Now that is all there is to it.

Whose words were those and where had they come from? Are they his? Yes, his. But they were words that were more than thoughts, words spoken aloud, strong and clear, before the second stroke cut off his command of speech. *Aloud!*

Aloud? He tries to speak. He cannot even whisper. He's been so long without the sound of his own voice that it's become no more to him than a doubtful memory. Did he ever truly hand down that calm, well-considered decision between the attack of one stroke and the next? Or had his assailant even given him that much time to speak? Were those words uttered only in a dream— waking or sleeping, no difference there for him any more, no matter—afterwards?

I should have resigned.

The thought is there with a frightful clarity, bright as any light from heaven on the Damascus road. It is almost like a revelation of the old days, when there were no ghosts or winding paths or cold and empty places in his skull. Its vigor dismays him; he is not used to the vitality of his thoughts as they were before.

He lets his head bow forward, looks down at his hands. Shadows from the tree outside the porch pour through the glass, stain the palms with unmoving shadows. There is no wind, not even the prayer of a breeze to stir the branches, shift the shadows, and yet he hears the rush of air across a great water and sees the chop of Channel whitecaps cupped in his hands. The sky rumbles with planes, earth creaks and moans like an old house under the burden of falling shells, bursts into a bitter roar of grief where they strike. Men's eyes surround him, waiting for a word, and he gives it, and they go out across the water to take the beach because he says it must be so.

Beyond the walls of glass the bees are hovering above the flowerbeds Mamie planted, little dots of black and gold diving into the scented, honeyed heart of the blossoms. Even from here he can see the frilled petals tremble, white and yellow, pink and red. He thinks he hears the cattle lowing in the pasture, the herd of purebred Angus that is still his pride.

He is walking in the pasture now, a flower in his hand. His mind is clear of any desire to question how he comes to be walking, after so long confined to the bed, the chair, the capable strength of his several nurses. He accepts this change without question because his world no longer holds fast to *then* and *now* and *someday*. Sometimes a man must act without looking anywhere but straight on. A general must look ahead and choose the path he'll send others to tread. If he looks back, what will he see? Boys at study, boys at play, mothers holding their infant sons close to the breast, fathers smiling down into the cradle.

I should have resigned.

The pasture is a minefield, every crater in it holds an empty cradle. If he goes on, he knows that he will see worse sights than these.

He goes on.

They are waiting for him on the hillside, a gathering of tall men in fine wool uniforms with shining, polished boots and the bearing of kings. He strokes his naked cheeks, feeling somewhat ill at ease to come clean-shaven into the midst of so many lush beards and noble sets of whiskers. Their eyes meet his with kindness, but their lips remain small, untouched by smiles. He knows that he is welcome, even if they welcome him to a place and time that can hold nothing but duty and death.

There is a stand of trees on the hill; he thinks they might be oak even as he knows that it doesn't matter. The words that cherish differences between tree and tree, man and man, have no place here. The sheltering oak that draped the poet's house in shade, its trunk the trysting place where he first kissed his lost sweetheart, that tree is now nothing more than an objective, a target against which the generals must hurl men. The boy who fished the backwoods stream with string and pin at only six years old, who brought fat trout home to the black cast iron frypan and his mother's praises, her scrubwater-chapped hands stroking the smoothness of his dark hair, that boy is now a man who will try to take the objectives of the generals' field and—perhaps, likely, at a hazarded guess—die.

I should have resigned.

He is shaking hands with the generals on the hillside, nodding greetings to those who remain higher up, on the hill's crest, too rapt in what they see in the lowland farther away to bother with the social niceties. Their uniforms are dark blue with bright buttons, snipped from a midnight sky, stars and all. There are keen, solid swords or the dashing sweep of sabers at their belts. Some wear hats that shade their eyes from the summer sun, others break with dignity to remove them and wipe the sweat from their brows. One holds a tattered leatherbound Bible in his hand.

The old man can smell their sweat even over the more pleasing reek of manure in the cow pasture. How can the smell of cowpats remain when the pasture itself is gone? Before he can begin to seek the answer, his sense of smell is hit hard by the sharp invasion of burned black powder, the tang of hot iron as clouds of gray smoke rise up from the unseen lands beyond the hill.

He starts forward, drawn by the smoke's voluptuously

rising cloud as if it were a siren's song made visible. The ground beneath his feet is firm, yet he hears the deep boom of artillery passing through both air and earth, and he knows that by rights he should feel the guns' impact as well as hear it. Wildly he thinks, *It's my age. My illness. The senses play tricks on me, turn traitors, all of them. And yet . . . here I am, on my feet once more, alert. No. Illusion. Impossible.*

Yet knowing how impossible it all is, he still goes on.

A hand grasps him by the arm. The gentle slope beneath his feet turns sharply up to form a wave of turf that blocks his view of smoke and sky and sun. For a dozen breaths he stares at the ragged green grass of summer inches from his eyes, the soil that teems with life in the teeth of the guns, then slowly turns around.

It's one of the blue-coated generals who has detained him. The man is an imposing figure despite the thinning of his steel-gray hair. His silver-shot beard is neatly trimmed, but in a way that tells of military precision rather than worldly vanity, and the eyes that shine behind the wire-rimmed glasses burn an icy blue. He has the sort of nose that would look well in profile on an ancient Roman coin, though his eyes hold too much melancholy to serve him as a Caesar.

Hope, the old man thinks, regarding the bearded general's dour face critically. *Where's the look of hope you owe your troops, the optimism? We've got to have it, hold it for their sake. It's our obligation as their leaders, the least we can give them when we're asking them for so much. Hope against hope, but with the reality of the situation tight in our grasp, that's what we've got to give them, that's what command is all about. Showing a face that tells the boys* We can win! *and holding back a face like yours with a look that tells them outright what they already suspect, fear, flee:* You're bound to die. *But who here'd have the guts to tell you as much to your face? If I could speak— But you would never listen, would you,*

General Meade? No, not you. And he stands once more on the rocks and stony ridges of this very battlefield and hears Montgomery's elegantly accented, supremely arrogant voice pronouncing the hindsight judgment without appeal that Meade ought to have been sacked, and Lee along with him.

But Monty's gone, and this is not the Gettysburg where two former commanders of another war strolled at leisure among the monuments, blind to the dead. The old man realizes that he's slipped somehow into the hairline fissures that snake along the boundaries of world and world. He's never had much use for such notions. Vision and imagination that allow a general to guide a battle yet to be fought don't necessarily impose the presence of dreams on him as well. The old man comes from a long line of pragmatists, honest, solid citizens, men who knew their business, and yet . . .

The general is speaking to him. "Don't go over the hill," Meade says, and it's not a request at all. The cold blue eyes can flash from gloom to wrath at a word. "Your place is here, with us: Command, not combat."

The old man hears him, sees his lips move, but the words don't seem to reach his ears as anything but sound without true meaning. He feels himself slipping back into the shell of skin he left behind him on the glassed-in porch. Another face is inches from his own, another mask than Meade's. The male nurse is smiling, asking him if he'll be wanting his lunch soon, not expecting any answer. The nurse talks to him the way he'd talk to a goldfish. The old man doesn't blame him; men need to talk, and men on solitary duty need to hear the sound of their own voices if only because noise has always kept the demons at bay. But talk to yourself and they'll lock you up, even when you desperately need to get the words out before they burn away your soul.

The nurse's face retreats, melting away General Meade's with it. Montgomery's outspoken ghost lingers awhile in the wake of their departure but the wind that blows across the Channel soon sweeps it off as well. Foam washes over the old man's feet in their leather bedroom slippers. He feels the water's chill, though summer has come to France. He stares into the pearly foam, surveys the pale sand that still awaits the first bloody assault out of the sea, and foam and sand blend pallors until they form the sheet of slick white paper under his hand.

He is writing again, his fingers steady around the pen. He sits alone at a table, a terrible burden of unsaid words bowing his back, all of them born out of thoughts that don't bear thinking. He lets them escape the only sane way, as ink on paper. He has made the decision that will be D-Day. Now he is writing an apology.

I should have resigned.

He looks up from the blank sheet before him and his eyes see only darkness. So many decisions made, so many paths rejected, so many possibilities still to be sorted through. But when shadows conspire to conceal every way your feet might carry you, when you're left as good as blind, then how can you choose any path at all? He's given an order conceived according to the best of his knowledge. What does he really know? Too much. Too little. His own power combined with the burden of harm his ignorance might do is an insight that threatens to break him.

What did Meade know for sure before he came to Gettysburg? What did Lee know, or Pickett, or any man who came to stand at the top of a hill somewhere at a distance from the sound of cannon, the smoke of guns, the flash of swords? Easy for Monty to condemn them, in afterthought, when the battle was reduced to little dots and bars of red and blue on a map, troop movements become the sleek, imperious, sweeping black arrows that once were countless young faces, all the lost legions of someone's sons.

He is writing an apology that accepts full blame for

every pale, death-startled soldier boy's face if D-Day fails. Hope. Hope against hope, a general's faith in what is sometimes little more than a well-considered gamble. Where was Meade's faith? Where is his? Tomorrow's assault on the beaches of Normandy will succeed because it must, and yet he knows that if he doesn't put down these words now—just on the chance of failure, purely for his own soul's sake—he will face tomorrow as less than the general his boys will need.

The screams of horses tear the pen from his hand, wrench him back to the hillside, back to where a sheet of paper covered with words has become again an upraised wall of earth that bars him from the battle. Meade's hand is still on his arm; he shakes it off in spite of the general's angry remonstrations, turns to the wall, thrusts his fist deep into it, through grass and soil and rock, until the barrier before him crumbles and he sees the lands beyond.

Rifle shots crack. Cavalry steeds dash pell-mell against the guns. Other horses bound in harness haul artillery upslope, flanks foamed, hides striped red with the marks of whip and spurs. He watches them struggle, strive, stumble into one of the field's uncountable, invisible pitfalls of sudden panic, founder in the whirlpool and go down. He has never seen anything so white as their madly rolling eyes.

The concussion of an exploding shell behind him throws him from his feet. He sprawls at full length in the mud, in his bathrobe and pajamas and scuffed leather slippers, his outflung hands falling across the shattered chest of a dead man.

This is his first time in the heart of combat, down on the lines, out where he hasn't got an entourage of warm bodies to trim away and smooth over the jagged edges of recent battle so that he can survey the ground his commands have conquered. It's not his fault, it's timing: He should have seen this sort of service in the Great

War, but the war itself went out like a blown candle flame by the time he got his orders to go over. Even now he's not sure how deeply he regrets this lost chance, or whether he's only telling himself he's sorry things turned out as they did because that's how he thinks a soldier *should* feel.

And how should he feel now, face to face with what's left of a man? He has never been in combat but he has seen combat's harvest. How could he avoid the dead? He looks into the corpse's face and meets eyes that have fixed their clouding gaze on heaven, though only a heaven of common sky, untroubled by any presence more divine than birds, clouds, the winds that race across the world.

This was how they lay that day at Normandy. This was the rest you gave them, their service to you rewarded. He knows that voice, although it belongs to nothing human. It is the same presence he felt stealing into his skull as he stood there in the doorway facing Mamie and the doctors, trying to smile away the first stroke's damage before the second came to claim its share.

Enough, it whispered then; *Rest*, as if he were a wakeful child too overtired to sleep, too cross and willful to find comfort in his mother's arms.

He shakes his head like a dog just come in out of the rain, tries to shake away the words and the ghosts of the words which that presence in his head keeps whispering. Foolishly, wildly he looks to the dead man for help, but the dead man is only a boy, unused to being asked for anything at all except obedience, compliance, faith in the commands of those whose superior years must make them his betters.

The old man knows he doesn't dare to stay here. The voice is gone, for now, but he knows that if he lingers here, it will be back. Like the single, stubborn housefly that's circling the glassed-in porch, lighting on the old man's hands again and again because he lacks strength enough to drive it decisively away, the voice will return.

So he pushes himself to his feet, his bathrobe gummed with mud that's made of blood and dirt, and he runs. His leather slippers slap over the hard ground, skid in places where the rush and retreat of men and horses and iron-sheathed wheels haven't chewed the grass away. A shot-torn banner flaps across his face like the passing of a ghost, the caress of a shroud. White stars and blue bars on a field of faded red twist and unfurl before his eyes. The stars all fall down, points jabbed into the earth like bayonets, taking root, springing up again in rows of plain white markers at his feet, some crosses, some themselves a different kind of star.

The tip of one slipper catches on the marble base of the only cross that stands out of military true to its neighbors. He falls a second time as he fell before, when the bombshell hit, and all that was there to break his fall was that poor boy's body. But this field has already taken its dead deep into the shadows, hiding them away under sweet green grass as if their shaken, broken bodies had always been things too torn and horrible to bear remembering. Like this—plain markers standing in their precise and proper rows—like this they're numbers, printed blocks of red and blue, black arrows on a map, acceptable.

"Is that so? Acceptable?" A hand reaches down to him and he takes it, using it to help himself regain his feet. The gentleman who has come to his aid wears gray. "No more acceptable to you, sir, if truth be told, than it ever was to me."

He stares at the man who speaks and can't help but feel diminished in the face of such bearing, confidence that isn't cockiness, a self-possessed air of command that still makes place for humility. For the first time since the cracks between worlds opened for him, the old man feels himself to be woefully underdressed. His slippers are in a sorry state, his robe thoroughly stained from all the tumbles he's taken while wearing it. Mamie will be fit to be tied when she sees what he's done, but wherever she is, Mamie isn't here, and that's a pity. He thinks of the fine impression a lady of breeding like his wife would make on a born gentleman like General Lee.

He makes a perfunctory adjustment to the fit of his bathrobe belt and clears his throat to speak, but the words are still trapped at an appalling distance. He stands there tongue-tied and knows he's blushing, but General Lee knows the art of setting a man at ease and pretends not to notice.

"When did you first start thinking about their numbers, sir?" the general asks, and when the old man's face creases in protest he is quick to add: "I don't mean when did you first think of them *as* numbers. That's a trick we all try, when their faces get to be too much for us, and may God have mercy on those of us who do succeed." He raises his eyes and surveys the horizon where seabirds soar and dip and cry into emptiness. "So many of them, so very many . . ." The graves only seem to go on forever. They end, as they must, at a road, a fence, the sea. Somewhere beyond the point that Lee's eyes have found there is a green field where cattle wander, and past that there are clouds drifting across the sky.

"There's many things that become too hard to think of head on," Lee tells him. "Still, I don't believe I ever thought that way when I was young. A war was a history book to me then, battles were chapters—that much I always accepted—but the hour I realized that some day I would have to write them all with men . . ." He shakes his head and takes the old man by the arm. "The morning is very fine. I enjoy the smell of the sea. Walk with me now, and for a while—just for a little while—let's neither one of us face a single thought that doesn't bear thinking."

They are walking together between the rows of graves. Absurdly the old man wishes that all this would flicker itself away and change into the rolling greens of a golf course. The thought of himself in his favorite golf togs,

Lee still splendid in the uniform of the Confederacy, makes him laugh. It's the first real sound he's been able to force out of his frozen throat and it breaks over the field like a thousand thunderclaps.

Lee's mouth smiles, though his eyes have lost the knack. "That's a start back, anyway," he says.

The old man stares at him: A start back? Back to where, to what? Not to the battlefield, surely? Not to the dead boy's broken body, and the terrified horses, and the generals rooted among the oaks on the hill, moving blocks of blue against blocks of red?

Not back to the voice he's fled.

"Why not?" asks Lee. "Go back and find it again, the voice, the promises it made to you. It's what you've wanted, what you've sought: Enough. Rest. Surrender. Peace. Peace . . . or was it only silence? You're afraid, General. After all these years, you're finally afraid. What you commanded then, at Normandy, was nothing to the power one word of yours carries now." Lee's eyes turn to the skies above the empty fields where something terrible flashes. A single cloud boils up and spreads its churning crown into a shape that's become an icon of more dread than one poor scythe-bearing skeleton ever was.

The old man can't take his eyes from the mushroom cloud. He thinks that if he gazes at it long enough he'll see it bloom with faces. That is when he knows—though he's told himself over and over again that surrender isn't something he can swallow—that surrender is precisely what he seeks. Let someone else give the word, change the world with yes or no. Let someone else see the faces of mothers, fathers, sisters, brothers, children in his every memory of all the boys he's sent beyond the brink. And now—! Now, when it's become so easy to command so much—!

He looks into the cloud. He doesn't dream, being a practical man, but he can imagine. He knows that if ever a thought didn't bear the thinking . . .

"Daddy?"

A hand, very small and warm, grabs his clumsily. He looks down and his heart cracks open wide. His son is there—not John, not his second-born, but Doud, the baby boy they baby-named Icky.

Icky's body lies in Fairmont Cemetery in Denver; Icky, not even four years old when scarlet fever touched him and he died.

Icky is here, among the graves.

The old man stoops and takes his son into his arms. The boy laughs and lays his soft cheek against his father's aged face. *When I looked at you in your cradle, I never dreamed I'd see you in your grave.* The old man begins to cry and Icky frowns, confused, tries to brush away each teardrop as it falls.

"Daddy? Dad? It's all right."

The old man's arms are empty. Icky is standing before him, a man grown. His uniform is strictly Army, his boots are caked with mud, he's shifted his helmet so that his father can see the red mark that it's left on his child's brow. His free hand reaches out to pat his father's shoulder. He can't embrace the old man now; his other hand cups the butt of a rifle. "It's all right," he says one last time before he turns away and jogs off to join the line of young men marching up the road to Paris, to Berlin, to Gettysburg.

"*Icky!*" The name breaks itself against the sky, driving back the spreading poison of the cloud. The old man stands with arms outstretched after a dream and hardly knows he's found his voice again.

Others know. General Lee's hand claps him on the back. "Enough," he says. "You've rested long enough. You'll find your peace in time, but not like this. Let them hear you speak again, all of your sons."

The old man's head bows. He looks into his hands, now brimming with the flowers he once laid on Icky's grave. "Speak," he repeats as if he's only talking to the flowers. "With what a word, a single word of mine now has the power to do?" The cloud is gone, but its ghost has come to linger on his face.

"With what a single word of yours can stop." Lee takes the flowers from him, one by one, and scatters them over the grass. They are walking again, this time over a silent battlefield strewn with the dead. A mist is rising. Men scuttle here and there, setting up their boxy cameras that perch like spiders on spindly legs. They do not notice the generals as they pass.

"Look at that," the old man says with sorrow. He points to where one photographer is dragging a young man's corpse from where it's fallen so that it catches a better angle of the light. "As if that poor boy were just another of his studio props, a bolster, a chair."

"A number," says Lee. "A counter. But not to you. Never to you. Now do you know? Now can't you see why this— this peace you think you've gained by your surrender— can't be, can't last?"

"If I don't come back, someone else will do my job for me."

"Yes." Lee takes the last flower from the old man's hands and casts the petals into the wind, but they are tiny toy soldiers by the time they fall to earth. The old man knows that you can buy a box of them for a dollar, then buy another easily when the first lot's all broken or crushed or gone missing. So why then does he bother to kneel in the mud of the battlefield and pick them up carefully, tenderly, one by one?

"Someone else will do my job for me," he tells them as he cleans the dirt from their faces and lays them down in rows. He stands at last. "If I let him."

Lee is gone. The old man has no time to spend on wondering where he's vanished. So much to do! And if he doesn't do it, who will? The thought chills him.

But summer swiftly drives the chill out of his bones. His fingers curl, his hands are fists again before he knows it. He is standing in the sunlight and the bees are swarming so drunkenly over Mamie's flowerbed that they're dive-bombing the glass that screens the porch. His eyes dance nimbly, following their crazy flight, his blood hums with the furious beating of their wings. He feels the life in them and laughs because he feels it in himself as well, at last, at last!

Then a sharp gasp. A crash of something heavy to the floor. The male nurse stands there gawping, empty hands shaking over the wreck of the lunch tray he's let fall.

"Well?" The general snaps even as he smiles. "What are you staring at, son?" And he fills his lungs with the joyous laughter that greets each soldier who's finally come home.

THE LAST CRUSADER
Bill Fawcett

The lay brother set aside the small glass of brandy he had accepted after being seated. It was apparent to him that everyone else in the large room had consumed far more before he had arrived. Berthier wished he had drunk more himself. His journey through the camp of the defeated Prussian and Russian armies had been traumatic. He had not seen so many wounded men, such broken spirit since their defeat by Soult and Davout in 1805. A week ago these men had chased the Grande Armee out of Prussia and into Belgium. But the revolutionaries had turned and dealt them a mauling.

A Frenchman was a strange spokesman for the Royal Alliance's most famous churchman, but no one doubted his devotion after over a decade of service. The small, slight man seemed almost lost among the glittering nobility and general officers that surrounded the well-padded chair he reclined in. His simple, dark clothes seemed almost monastic among the gaudy uniforms.

A bit amused by the attention he was attracting, Berthier smiled meekly in what he hoped was a way befitting the personal secretary of the greatest man of his age. The man whom Europe called the Last Crusader. Two men present were possible heirs to the throne of Russia, one distantly to that of England and Hanover, half a dozen were lesser kings, even a gaudily robed

146

representative of the Ottoman Empire sat in a corner quietly amused at the chaos surrounding the churchman's assistant. In one corner of the inn stood a group of Russian officers. They had hurried forward with only one corps, mostly cavalry, and so lent more moral than real support of the battle. But no nation wanted to not have some presence at what had been expected to be the final campaign against the revolutionaries. Prince Bagration was among them and could be counted as a friend. The rest had stopped murmuring over their maps because they were simply curious to hear tales about the man who had done more than any other in Europe to defend Christianity and Divine Rule. Even the Orthodox Christian Russians were obviously anxious to learn more though the man they were hearing about was not only a papist, but likely to be the next pope. Berthier began talking quietly. He was nervous, but didn't want to show it. His Cardinal was ambitious and wanted the support of the men here. He'd begin with a story familiar to everyone. The famous "whiff of brimstone" in Toulon.

The city of Toulon had been under siege by the godless Directorate for months. Sustained by the British fleet the city had been barely affected by the siege itself. They had invited the British fleet to anchor there and the money gained from supplying that fleet had brought a return of prosperity to a trading center that had been hard hit by the war between France and her neighbors. The fact that no one was collecting any taxes had been a giddy addition to the feeling after years of forced penury from supporting the Directorate's wars. With thousands of British soldiers and sailors present there had been little the Paris government could do until recently. But, after three years, Davout had fought the Austrians to a standstill in the Piedmont and like a reverse Hannibal he had made a dash over the Alps to besiege the city with the two best corps in his army.

"When the Holy Father heard of the withdrawal of

so much of the Revolutionary army," Berthier warmed to his story, "he had suspected Toulon was its target. There was little he could do. The army of the papal states was in no condition to venture an offensive and the British, caught in a bleeding war against irregular Spanish forces after their invasion of Spain from Portugal, had no men to spare. What he could do was send priests to replace those who had been slaughtered by the revolutionaries. To head this delegation, perhaps mostly to remove him from Vatican politics, the pope had chosen Monsignor Buonaparte, promoting him to bishop of Toulon." To still his protests Berthier finished the thought to himself. The pope had little to lose. If the city held, them the church had contributed. If it fell, it was unlikely that the irritating young Corsican would return to his never ending machinations within the Vatican hierarchy. This priest was, of course, Napoleon Buonaparte, though then he still used the Corsican form of his name, Bonaparte.

The expatriate hesitated and looked at his audience. There were rumbles of conversation from the Russians and the clink of glasses being refilled everywhere. He was losing them. After the beating they had received the day before, Buonaparte had explained to Berthier in detail why it was vital that their mood be uplifted. The decisions they made tonight could end or even lose the war for the Christian forces. Many of them were near drunk, and all were too nervous to listen to a long story.

"So let me cut to the moment that won the battle." That had them. "Bishop Buonaparte was near the docks when the French assault began. The shelling was horrible, destroying homes and families. There was a panic and the streets filled with mobs seeking only safety. The British couldn't help but react. Even as their regiments were throwing back Davout's columns, their admirals were hurrying to their ships. Roundshot, aimed at the ships, occasionally overshot into those trying to board. As the admirals approached the docks each had to fight their way through thousands of panicky citizens demanding a place on their ships. Each admiral was trailed by servants and wagons full of goods. It was apparent they were planning to leave.

"Buonaparte confronted them, but they pointed to the mob. There was nothing, they explained, that they could do to defend a mob. They would be calling the regiments in within the hour. Every time the bishop tried to argue, they gestured toward the mob, which had by now begun looting the dockside warehouses. I was, I must admit, among this mob, having been in the employ of the city fathers and so was in fear for my life should the city fall. The guillotine may be merciful, but it is not appealing.

"At this crucial point a battery of Royal Horse Artillery arrived at the dock, called back to allow time to load its guns. By grace of His power it was commanded, not by an Englishman, but by a devout Catholic from Ireland. The short bishop hurried over to that officer and spoke with him for some minutes. From their gestures it was apparent that at first the artillery officer refused the Buonaparte's demands. Then, as they continued, he succumbed as so many have, to the young Corsican's determination. Finally he gave the order and his men unlimbered their guns at the edge of the docks. It is a pity this brave man died later that day in the battle to drive the French off the hills overlooking the harbor.

"A red-coated colonel strode over to protest, his opinion obvious from his expression. The young bishop dashed across the dock, literally flinging men out of his path. He intercepted the colonel, and a short time later the man retreated without ever speaking to the artillerists.

"The blast of all six guns was stunning, even among the shot and shell landing among the fleet. There was a brief moment of increased panic which ended in a stunned silence as the mob realized none had been hurt."

Berthier threw up his arms as he had seen Napoleon Buonaparte do there on the dockside. Surprisingly, the gesture once more demanded silence and got it. The clerical secretary continued in a quieter tone.

"Into that silence rose the voice of one man, Bishop Buonaparte. His speech is too familiar to everyone who can read for me to repeat here. He spoke of how the brimstone of Hell, even worse than that which came from the barrel of those cannon, awaited those who betrayed their king and faith. He appealed to the mob as the heroes they would in fact soon be. I recorded that speech, jotting it down in a notebook I carried, even then. His voice resounded and even the sailors on board the British ships, at least those who had his words translated to them, cheered themselves hoarse when his sermon ended.

"The rest, as you know, is history. The mob cheered and rushed to the defense of the city. They arrived just as Davout's troops were breaking through the British lines and threw the revolutionaries back. Bishop Buonaparte continued around the city, beginning each of his fiery sermons with that famous whiff of brimstone, until over half the city's population was pressing outward and only cowards remained behind. My transcription of that sermon was turned to pamphlets that fired the Vendee and brought me to the Cardinal's service.

"The British admirals saw that the situation had changed and ordered their regiments to hold their ground and, finally, attack. Toulon was saved for Louis and the faith. Bishop Buonaparte became Cardinal Buonaparte, the pope's appointed Chaplain to the Armies of Europe and defender of the faith."

There was a general murmur of approval from which Berthier took heart. He had been sent to give heart to these men and prepare for the Cardinal's appearance. It appeared he was doing so. Even the two British liaisons were beaming with approval, forgetting their admirals had been panicking along with the mob.

It was less than an hour before dawn. They would make the decision soon: to send their armies back toward the safety of Berlin and Vienna or join with their allies and revenge the beating they had taken the day before. Cardinal Buonaparte would arrive, as he always did, at just the right moment. There was time for one more sermon. Raising his voice, he smiled at Bagration and received a knowing nod in reply. The prince was one of the few sober men in the room. Blücher had been wounded and sat propped in the corner. It was hard to tell if he was awake or not. None of the Prussian officers had the energy left to investigate and it made no difference. Their defeat at Ligny had been hard on all of them.

Raising his voice to gain everyone's attention, Berthier began.

"It was after Moreau and Davout had joined forces and taken Vienna." The secretary hesitated here. He needed the Austrian's assistance, so he had better not dwell on how they had bungled three battles with the fast marching revolutionary armies.

"Things were quick to change even after Prince Charles' failed attempt to counterattack across Lobau Island and save the city.

"From the Pratzen Heights it was apparent that the French had exposed their flank, or so it seemed. Most credit their plan, if indeed the brilliant deception was planned, to Davout, not old Moreau. The same commanders you faced yesterday at Ligny. The crisis came, as you will remember when Cardinal Buonaparte was completing a mass for the Russian guards on the Pratzen Heights. From his elevated position he may even have been the first to see the blue columns climbing up the hill toward the almost empty plateau. He had just called the battle to stop the godless Directorate a divine crusade for the first time.

"Few who were there will forget the sight of Cardinal Napoleon leading the guard down the hillside on the back of a hussar's borrowed horse and the gold thread of his vestments and cardinal's mitre glowing as the bright sun emerged for the first time that day. The Cardinal's mad dash into the face of the enemy with the colonels of the Russian Guard Infantry and Cavalry regiments to either side has since, as you must have noticed, been the subject of hundreds of paintings and engravings."

Privately Berthier recalled not only how many of those paintings Napoleon Buonaparte had himself subscribed, but how excited the Cardinal had been after his only real experience with combat. Even wounded, he had only left the battle when a young aide to Kutusov led the Cardinal's horse back up the heights over his protests. For some time the Corsican had even considered leaving the church to accept a command in the Austrian army. But eventually Berthier and the others were able to convince him of the folly of his choosing the likely obscurity of a military career over his successful clerical calling.

"The guard, streaming down the hill, fought as madmen, or as the nobles of a noble nation should. The columns halted in confusion, and while the guard was shattered, it took nearly two hours for the revolutionaries to reform."

Cardinal Buonaparte would arrive soon. It was time to end on a note that prepared for that. Standing, raising his glass in salute, Berthier bellowed out, "To Buonaparte and the Sun of Austerlitz," then turning to face the Russians the secretary added, "and Prince Bagration, who saw the danger and met the next French attack on the Heights with his own!"

"To the Sun of Austerlitz," everyone rose and bellowed the traditional toast.

As if he had been waiting for just such an opportunity, and Berthier suspected he had, the Cardinal swept into the room to start a renewed round of cheers. His speech, though he always referred to them as "saddle sermons," roused the gathered generals even further. Finally, a hushed silence descended. Shorter than any other man there, Buonaparte was lost for a moment as he extended his arms outward for silence and strode toward the man who had to decide whether to support Wellington or put the safety of his twice-invaded nation first.

Evidently Blücher had not been asleep, or the recent commotion had awakened him. He looked up, his clear eyes gave no sign of the copious wine he had swilled to soothe pain from his torn back and leg.

"What shall it be, General?" Cardinal Buonaparte asked in a quiet voice. "Victory or Safety?"

No one would fault the elderly commander if he chose to protect his capital. The entire Prussian army was here, having pushed the revolutionaries back from Saxony. If this army broke, and it nearly had the day before, no one would blame him. The spirited Marshall Ney was pressing hard at its rear and the rumble of cannon could be heard now that silence reigned. If the army was caught between the two French forces and Wellington fell before they arrived, everyone knew that the approaching Russians would retreat as before and all of Prussia would be open to another occupation by revolutionary armies.

The silence continued as Blücher met the eyes of his staff. Many had advised retreat. They could await the Russians. Wellington had been unable to even occupy Spain, how could they count on him to face the two greatest generals of their age?

Cardinal Napoleon Buonaparte, special Envoy of His Holiness in Rome and appointed Chaplain to the Armies of Europe, could see the resolve beginning to fade from the old man's face. He was tired, injured, and had been fighting this was for over a decade. Leaning forward he spoke in a low voice that only Blücher could hear.

The old general shook his head, then smiled. He

reached up and the small churchman helped him to rise. The pain this cost the Prussian was apparent.

Pulling himself to his feet, Blücher smiled through the pain.

"*Vorwarts!*" he announced in a loud voice. Forward, attack, it was his favorite command in battle. "*Vorwarts to . . .*" The general hesitated and stumbled to the maps spread on the room's one large table. Stabbing a grimy finger at the map which contained the best estimate of where Wellington would stand he announced once more, "*Vorwarts* to Quatre Bras."

The cheers were deafening as the corp commanders gathered at the maps to plan their movement. Quietly, almost as if he knew he had finally accomplished his goal, Cardinal Buonaparte withdrew from the inn. The time for chaplains was past. Now was the time for soldiers. But he knew that history would record that he had had his finest hour at Waterloo.

BILLY MITCHELL'S OVERT ACT
William Sanders

I believe, therefore, that should Japan decide upon the reduction or seizure of the Hawaiian Islands the following procedure would be adopted . . . Attack to be made on Ford Island at 7:30 A.M. . . . Group to move in column of flights in V. Each ship will drop projectiles on the targets. . . .
— Brig. Gen. William Mitchell, Report of
    Inspection of U.S. Possessions in the Pacific,
    Oct. 24, 1924

General Mitchell in Near Fatal Aeroplane Crash

General William "Billy" Mitchell is reported in critical condition following a crash at Fort Sam Houston, Texas, on Monday. According to unofficial sources, the General's engine failed upon takeoff from a new flying field which he was inspecting. Details of his injuries have not yet been released.

General Mitchell had been assigned to Fort Sam Houston in March, after his dismissal as Assistant Chief of the Air Service. The removal was generally seen as a response by the present Administration to the General's public criticisms of its policies on national defense, particularly aviation.

The General has gained wide public notice with his controversial writings and statements on air power, including the claim that aeroplanes can sink warships, which he demonstrated in 1921 in tests off the Virginia coast.

—Kansas City *Star*, Tuesday, Sept. 1, 1925

Well, the Army finally found a way to fix Billy Mitchell—they let him fly one of their airplanes. The Germans couldn't bring him down but the U.S. brass and Calvin Coolidge did it. These worn-out old kites that the boys have to use, why, it's a scandal. Black Jack Pershing had better ships down on the border in '17, chasing Pancho Villa—and not catching him.

—Will Rogers, syndicated column, Sept. 4, 1925

At first I felt as if my whole world had crashed with him. We had been married only a couple of years, and I had just had our first child. It all seemed too much to bear.

But now, looking back, I know that crash was a blessing. By that time Billy was really out of control, just spoiling for a big fight with his bosses. Pretty soon, they'd have given it to him—and they'd have won.

They would have forced him out of the service, and that would have killed him. Billy wouldn't admit it, but the army was his whole life. He might have lived another dozen years or so, but he'd have been dying of a broken heart all the while.

—Elizabeth Mitchell, letter to Burke Davis, quoted in *Billy Mitchell*

Near summer's end I received word that my old friend Billy Mitchell had been seriously hurt in a crash in Texas. Naturally I went to visit him as soon as my duties permitted.

I found him bearing his physical suffering with Spartan fortitude. Much worse, for him, was the frustration of helplessness. He talked wildly of calling reporters to his bedside to denounce what he regarded as the negligence and incompetence of his superiors, and of writing yet more inflammatory books and articles. I saw that he was still bent on the same foolhardy course, which could only end in a court-martial and the ruination of his military career.

I reminded him sharply that his first duty was to our country, which could ill afford to lose an officer of genius at a critical time in her history. I pointed out that publicity-seeking tactics were beneath a general officer's dignity. And I told him that for a military man to directly challenge lawful authority—even that of the President—as he was doing, could never be tolerated in a democracy such as ours.

My words must have taken effect, for from that time forward he began to moderate his tone, and to cultivate self-discipline and diplomacy. Thus was General Mitchell preserved for his unique destiny. Little did I suspect the part I had played in history.

—General Douglas MacArthur, *Reminiscences*

MacArthur claimed to have been responsible for Billy Mitchell's "conversion." Well, MacArthur always did give himself full credit, that was his way. My own view is that Billy just thought things over and came to his own conclusions, because that was *his* way.

He had plenty of time to think. Smashed up as he was, there wasn't much else he could do. He told me once that the nights were the worst. The pain kept him awake, and he wouldn't take any drugs no matter how bad it got. You can call that guts or just Billy Mitchell being contrary as usual.

—Capt. Eddie Rickenbacker, *Between Wars*

Since my body was out of action, I decided to use the time to improve my mind. I began to study the history, language, and culture of Japan, believing as I did that

Americans would one day have to deal with this astute, aggressive race.

In my reading I came across the term *gaishin-shotan*. Literally, this translates "to sleep on firewood and lick gall." To the Japanese, however, it means the acceptance of hardship and ignominy in order to take a future revenge, as in their tale of the forty-seven samurai who deliberately subject themselves to disgrace in a secret plan to vindicate their honor.

For the next decade and a half I slept many nights on firewood, and I cultivated a connoisseur's taste for gall. . . .
—Brig. Gen. William Mitchell, unpublished
memoirs

When he returned to duty in the fall of 1927, he seemed a different man. No one was sure how seriously to take the metamorphosis. After all, this was General Billy Mitchell.

Even that was not strictly true. When he was removed as Assistant Chief of the Air Service, he also forfeited the "temporary" star he had worn since 1918. At the time of the crash, technically, he was a colonel. The press, however, always call him "General Mitchell," to the chagrin of certain persons.

But then those persons would always go livid at the mention of Billy Mitchell, in whatever context. He had stepped on too many toes; not everyone was willing to forgive and forget.

So he spent the next fifteen years at a series of obscure posts where nothing had happened since the Indian Wars, at jobs a competent sergeant could have handled, under senile or alcoholic commanders who knew nothing about aviation but did know that powerful figures in Washington would be grateful to the man who found a way to tie the can to Colonel Mitchell.

And through it all, through all the frustrations and petty humiliations that only a peacetime army can inflict on a man, he kept his head down and his mouth shut and soldiered on, till at last even the diehard Mitchell-haters had to admit that he had indeed changed.

They were wrong, of course. Billy Mitchell had never for a minute stopped being Billy Mitchell. He was merely borrowing a technique from the only navy people he had any use for—the submariners. He was running silent and submerged.

—Ladislas Farago, *The Ordeal of Billy Mitchell*

When we heard who our new wing commander would be, we all went a little nuts. To an army aviator of my generation, Billy Mitchell was close to God Almighty. We all knew the story, how he'd gone to the wall for aviation back in the Twenties, and the price he'd paid. And now he was going to command the Eighteenth! They'd even given him back his brigadier's star.

Then I thought about it and I said, "Oh, Lord! Whose bright idea was this?"

You see, the Hawaiian Department in the spring of '41 was a very strange, unreal little world, very insulated and pleased with itself. The Germans were very far away and the Japs were known to be too backward to be a serious threat, so there was very little attempt at real soldiering. Having a smart-looking turnout of the guard, or a solid lineup of jockstrappers—everybody was absolutely obsessed with sports—was much more important than trivial details like teaching men to load and fire their rifles.

Sending a man like Billy Mitchell to a place like that was like hiring Jack the Ripper to play the piano in a whore house.

—Col. George Stamps, *The 18th Bombardment Wing: An Oral History*

The decision to assign General Mitchell to Hawaii was my own. General Marshall approved it. Contrary to certain published reports, President Roosevelt was not involved.

We were faced with a growing threat of war in the Pacific. The Hawaiian Islands were obviously of vital strategic importance. It seemed to me that a recognized expert on air power would be more usefully employed there than running an artillery observation training school in Georgia, which was what he was doing at the time.

In the military we speak of the principle of calculated risk. In sending General Mitchell to command the 18th Bombardment Wind, I took such a risk. I accept full responsibility for the consequences.

—Gen. Henry H. Arnold, statement to the Joint Congressional Committee on the North Pacific Incident

The Flying Fortress at that time was the glamor ship of the Air Corps and there still weren't that many in service. The guys who flew them thought we were pretty hot stuff.

Mitchell knocked that out of us in a hurry. He worked us like a bunch of cadets. We trained as we had never trained before, doing things they had never taught us at flight school. In fact he had us doing things that would have gotten us busted down to permanent latrine orderlies anywhere else in the Air Corps.

The big thing then was high-level precision bombing. We had been taught that our function was to fly high above the enemy in a ladylike manner and drop our bombs, using the fancy new Norden bombsight which was supposed to let you put a bomb into a pickle barrel from 20,000 feet.

The Old Man said there was a time and a place for that and then there was a time to get down and get dirty. "Come in low," he would say, "get on top of the enemy before he knows you're coming, and stuff the bomb load up his backside."

One fool tried to argue that a low level attack made you a bigger target. The Old Man drilled him with that fifty-caliber stare of his and said, "Any man who goes to war and thinks of himself as a target should have stayed home and knitted socks for the Red Cross. The point is to kill the bastards before they can make you *any* kind of target."

There was a rumor that Roosevelt had sent him to the Islands in the hope that his presence would deter Japan from starting trouble in the Pacific. I don't know whether he scared the Japs any but he sure as hell scared us.

—Lt. Col. Mark Rucker, "Billy's Boys," *Wings*, Feb. 1971

HONOLULU—Hawaii is one of the world's last proud bastions of peacetime complacency. Europe may be vibrating under Wehrmacht boots, London and Chungking may be smoking from the latest air raids, the panzers may be driving across Russia slowed only by bad roads; but people here regard these things the way residents of an exclusive neighborhood regard the news of a gang shootout down on the docks. Every weekend the battleships tie up in pairs at their moorings in Pearl Harbor, while the sailors go on liberty and the officers attend important social functions. And the grass at Schofield Barracks is said to be the most neatly-trimmed grass in the U.S. Army.

Certainly no one believes war will ever come to the Islands. The only potential enemy in the Pacific is Japan and Japan is not taken seriously. The local view of the Japanese is wholly contemptuous and will astonish anyone who has seen, as I did in China, the professional abilities of the Japanese military.

One exception to the whimsical atmosphere can be found at Hickam Field, where General Billy Mitchell has a bunch of big Flying Fortress bombers. I had a chance to watch them work over the old battleship *Utah*, which is used as a target ship. They came in low and fast and they planted their practice bombs with the precision of top banderilleros. They were as good as anyone the Germans had in Spain and that is saying a good deal.

I was told that General Mitchell personally flew the lead plane. Clearly he is not one of those generals who die in bed.

> —Ernest Hemingway, "Fishing Off Diamond
> Head," *Esquire*, July 1941

To: Commanding General, Dept. of Hawaii
From: Commander, 18th Bombardment Wing
Subject: Reconnaissance

1. Current international developments suggest the possibility of armed hostilities between the United States and the Empire of Japan at some point in the near future. In the event of such hostilities, the Hawaiian Islands would be a prime target for an enemy attack using carrier-borne aircraft.

2. The history of the Japanese Empire indicates that such an attack would not necessarily be preceded by a formal declaration of war.

3. Surprise being essential in such an operation, the attacking force would most likely approach from the north or northwest, this part of the Pacific Ocean being virtually empty of naval and merchant shipping.

4. In keeping with the principle of surprise, the attack would probably be launched at dawn, perhaps on a Saturday or Sunday.

5. The period through mid-December will be the time of maximum risk. After this the seas of the North Pacific are usually too rough for carrier operations.

6. It is therefore recommended that a schedule of reconnaissance flights be instituted immediately, using all available aircraft and concentrating on the north and northwest sectors. Cooperation with naval air units will be essential.

7. Aircraft should carry full defensive armament. If detected by an approaching carrier force, it is likely they will be attacked.

> William Mitchell
> Brig. Gen. USAAF

Of course everybody thought he was crazy. The navy fliers had a joke that Billy Mitchell had put in too many hours at high altitude without his oxygen mask. General Short would probably have thought that was a good one, except I don't think he knew what an oxygen mask was.

Short was the commanding general of the Hawaiian Department. He was an old infantryman with so little grasp of aviation that he wanted to take away our ground crews and train them as infantry. Still, Mitchell was obviously keeping his people hard at work, and Short was old-school enough to approve of that.

So Short let Mitchell have a fairly free hand in training his people. He listened to Mitchell's frequent warnings and predictions, though, with the amused indulgence you might give an otherwise gifted friend who happens to belong to some extremely weird religious cult. And he made it plain that there would be no nonsense about long-range recon flights, searching the northern seas for, as he put it, "imaginary Japanese bogeymen."

—Maj. Gen. Richard Shilling, *Pacific Command*

5 November 1941
To: Commander in Chief, Combined Fleet, Isoroku Yamamoto
Via: Chief of Naval General Staff, Osami Nagano
By Imperial Order:

1. The Empire has resolved on war measures in early December, expecting to be forced to go to war with the United States, Britain, and the Netherlands for self-preservation and self-defense.

2. The Commander in Chief, Combined Fleet, will execute the necessary operational preparations.
3. Detailed instructions will be given by the Chief of the Naval General Staff.

SENATOR TRUMAN: General Short, tell the committee your opinion of General Mitchell prior to December nineteen forty-one.

GENERAL SHORT: I considered him an outstanding and dedicated officer. Some of his ideas struck me as rather fanciful, but on the whole I regarded him as an asset to my command.

TRUMAN: Would you say there was friction between the two of you?

SHORT: Not at all. He did have a tendency to push a bit beyond appropriate limits, to try and bypass chains of command. But I put that down to a commendable zeal.

TRUMAN: What about the matter of reconnaissance patrols? Was that an example of, as you put it, fanciful ideas?

SHORT: More an example of his impatience with proper procedures. General Mitchell was preoccupied with the idea of an air attack on Hawaii. He wanted to conduct aerial patrols over the waters surrounding the Islands, particularly to the north. As I explained to him—more than once—offshore patrolling was the navy's responsibility.

TRUMAN: Was the navy in fact flying patrols to the north?

SHORT: I assumed they were. Later I learned otherwise.

TRUMAN: General, are you familiar with the old army saying, "When you assume…"?

SHORT: I beg your pardon?

TRUMAN: Never mind. Weren't you aware of the international situation? Did you in fact take any measures at all to protect your command in case of trouble with Japan?

SHORT: Certainly. I instituted a major anti-sabotage program.

TRUMAN: Sabotage? You were worried about sabotage?

SHORT: Hawaii had—has—a large Japanese population.

TRUMAN: Were there ever any cases of sabotage by these people?

SHORT: None. Obviously my security measures were effective.

TRUMAN: So you authorized no patrol flights by General Mitchell? And you had no knowledge that he was making them on his own?

SHORT: None whatever. Naturally I knew his aircraft were going off on long flights every day, but according to him these were merely training operations, meant to give the crews experience in long-range over-water navigation. It was only later that I learned that he and his officers had been falsifying their reports and flight logs. Since the beginning of November they had been flying regular patrols over the northwest sector to a radius of as much as eight hundred miles.

TRUMAN: And this was in violation of your orders.

SHORT: Direct and flagrant violation, sir. I was appalled.

—Hearings of the Joint Congressional Committee on the North Pacific Incident, March 3, 1947

Captain Mark Rucker was just about ready to call it a day. It was getting late and he was a long way from home.

He was, in fact, about 800 miles northwest of Oahu. That was much further out than the book said he should be; but Rucker's boss had spent his life rewriting the book.

Brigadier General Billy Mitchell had come a long way since the stormy days of the 1920's, but he was still a man obsessed. He was by no means alone in believing war with Japan to be imminent, but he thought he knew exactly where and how it would begin. Any morning now, a Japanese carrier force would come pounding down out of the North Pacific and launch a surprise strike against the U.S. bases in Hawaii. If history was any guide, they wouldn't bother to declare war first.

He had even worked out the route they would take: across the emptiest part of the sea, between the 40th and 45th parallels, out of range of patrol planes from Midway and the Aleutians. East of the International Date Line, they would swing southeast and make directly for Hawaii.

He was so sure he was right that, once again, he was laying his military neck on the line. For over a month, under various pretexts and subterfuges, his B-17 pilots of the 18th Bombardment Wing had been flying regular patrols over the northwest sector. There were too few planes for proper coverage, but Mitchell felt anything was better than simply sitting blind, waiting for the enemy to attack.

He hadn't been entirely dishonest, though, in writing the flights up as long-distance training missions. In the course of these patrols, his airmen had developed a whole bag of tricks for extending the B-17's range. Captain Rucker wasn't seriously worried about getting home. He had been farther out than this, many times.

All the same, Rucker was relieved to see that he was reaching the end of his ten-degree patrolling arc. Time to head for the barn . . . but then his copilot, Lieutenant Ray Agostini, began shouting and pointing off to the north. A moment later Rucker saw it too, a great gray blur against the darkening sea.

My God, he thought. We've got somebody's whole navy up here.

—Walter Lord, *Day of Battle*

Admiral Yamaguchi argued that we should maintain air patrols while en route to Hawaii. I opposed this on grounds of security. Should a scout plane encounter an enemy or neutral vessel, the ship might radio news of the sighting, thus warning the Americans of the presence of a carrier force in the North Pacific.

Admiral Nagumo agreed. No planes would be launched until the morning of the attack. However, each carrier would keep six fighters in readiness during the daylight hours.

Late on the afternoon of 5 December, the cruiser *Abukuma* signaled that her lookouts had spotted an airplane off to the south. No one else could see anything in that direction, the sky being quite cloudy. Admiral Nagumo ordered the *Akagi* to launch her ready fighters. The six Zeroes searched the area but found nothing and had to return in the gathering dusk. Meanwhile our radiomen reported no transmission anywhere in the vicinity.

After some discussion it was decided that the alarm had been false. We would proceed as planned. But the incident obviously worried Admiral Nagumo. Later that evening I saw him on the bridge, staring unhappily at the southern sky.

—Capt. Minoru Genda, *I Flew For The Emperor*

Captain Rucker was already climbing through the clouds, heading for home, by the time the Zeroes took off. He never even realized they were after him. But he had something else to worry about: the B-17's radio, which had been acting up for hours, was now refusing to transmit at all. He would have to wait till he got back to Hawaii to make his report.

At 2215 the wheels of the B-17 finally touched down at Hickam Field. Rucker's long day, however, was far from over. General Mitchell was waiting at the control tower, as he often did—there was a rumor that the "Old Man" hadn't slept since 1925—and when he heard Rucker's report he fairly exploded. Within minutes, the unfortunate pilot was hustled into Mitchell's car for a wild high-speed run up to Fort Shafter.

Mitchell's ballistic driving style was legendary, and Rucker found the ride even more terrifying than his recent brush with the Japanese. But nothing was as scary as the experience that followed. Less than an hour later the young captain, still in his sweaty flight suit and needing a shave, found himself in a room full of generals and admirals and lesser brass, all of them firing questions at Rucker and arguing among themselves.

Under the grilling, Rucker had to admit that he hadn't gotten a very good look at the mystery ships. He was sure that he had seen at least three carriers and a couple of battleships, with various other unidentified vessels; he believed they were heading southeast.

Admiral Kimmel was frankly skeptical. So was Admiral Bellinger, the navy air commander. Army fliers were notoriously imaginative when it came to ship sightings. If Rucker had seen anything at all, it was probably a Russian freighter. For that matter, Japanese fishing fleets often turned up in those waters, raising questions as to what they were up to.

General Short appeared confused; he was an elderly man and he had been awakened from a sound sleep. He seemed less interested in what Rucker had seen than in what the airman had been doing up there in the first place. That Mitchell had been running a regular system of unauthorized reconnaissance flights, deliberately contravening Short's orders, was far more upsetting than any ship movements. As he later testified, only the lateness of the hour and the uncertainty of the situation stopped him from placing Mitchell under arrest.

Some time after midnight a consensus was reached. At dawn Bellinger's big PBY patrol seaplanes would go check the northwest sector in a proper manner. Just in case they found something, the fleet would go on alert. There was no point bothering Washington until more was known.

As the meeting broke up, Rucker overheard an exchange between a couple of naval officers:

"Well, it's finally going to happen."

"War, you mean?"

"No, no. I mean Billy Mitchell's court-martial. I can't believe it's taken this long."

—Gordon Prange, *Resort to Arms*

It was never clear just how the thing was managed. Later accounts and recollections were contradictory and vague. Pilots remembered being awakened in the middle of the night and given a hurried, rather cryptic briefing; air and ground crewmen had the usual enlisted man's memories of working frantically and being shouted at. The one thing everybody recalled was an atmosphere of great urgency and secrecy. Whatever was happening, it was big.

No one questioned for a moment the legitimacy of what they were doing. Even instructions to load the B-17's with live bombs went unchallenged. The armorers were draftees, with a few career NCOs; none were in the habit of questioning direct orders from generals.

As for the pilots, they testified later that it never occurred to them that General Mitchell might be acting without authority. Off the record, most agreed that it would have made little difference. They would, they said, have followed the Old Man to bomb Hell with water balloons.

(Mark Rucker, the only one who knew the truth, was lost in the sleep of the utterly exhausted. Mitchell had ordered him to "go get some rest" and he had been only too glad to oblige.)

The men labored on through the night, swarming over the hulking olive-green bombers by the glare of floodlights, filling the long-range tanks with high-octane fuel, hoisting the ugly fat bombs into the yawning bays, passing up belts of gleaming .50 caliber ammunition. Meanwhile the rest of the Hawaiian command, from General Short to the soldiers at Schofield Barracks, slumbered unaware.

At four in the morning the first B-17 rolled down the

floodlit runway and climbed away, its exhausts flaring blue-white against the night sky. It was Rucker's plane; but it hardly needs saying that this time Billy Mitchell was at the controls.

—Martin Caidin, *The Glory Birds*

Just before sunrise a radio message was received from Admiral Yamamoto relating the wish of the Emperor that the Combined Fleet should destroy all enemy forces. Officers and men listened joyfully to the reading of the Imperial Rescript. We were filled with firm resolve to justify His Majesty's trust and set his mind at ease by doing our utmost duty in the attack on Pearl Harbor.

After this the fleet began final refueling operation. This was hard and tricky business and very dangerous. Close attention was required to prevent collisions. Also, we were deeply unsafe from attack. Normally our carriers proceeded in double column, first the *Akagi* and *Kaga*, then the *Soryu* and *Hiryu*, lastly the *Shokaku* and *Zuikaku*. Thus all ships could give good mutual protection fire. But during our refueling all ships sailed over a wide surface making room for the tankers to come amongst us. All maneuver was impossible including turning the carriers into the wind to launch planes.

I was standing on the flight deck of the *Shokaku* watching the refueling with Lt. Watanabe. The sky was very cloudy and the wind brisk but the sea was not very rough. Lt. Watanabe said, "This is a sign that Heaven favors our mission."

Just at that time the cruiser *Chikuma* began firing her guns rapidly toward the south. I looked forward and saw twelve large airplanes emerge through the clouds, flying directly towards us in a graceful and resolute manner.

"On the other hand," Lt. Watanabe said, "I could be wrong."

—Lt. Cdr. Kazuo Sakamoto, *Zero Pilot*

✧   ✧   ✧

It was eight-thirty when we found the Japanese. We had been in the air for *hours*—not to mention being up most of the night before *that*—and we were feeling, shall we say, a bit tuckered. But when we broke through the clouds and saw what was waiting for us, everyone became remarkably *alert*.

I mean, I hadn't realized the Japanese even *owned* so many carriers. All those lovely great wooden flight decks down there below us—I had the *strangest* thought that they could have made the most marvelous dance floor, right on top of the Pacific Ocean.

However, there was no time for *that* sort of thing. The ships were already opening fire and huge dirty puffs of smoke appeared all about us, unreasonably close and making the most *ghastly* noise. I reached for the bomb release, while up in the cockpit Major Stamps announced: "Okay, guys, stick your heads between your legs and kiss your asses goodbye. Here we go."

—Capt. Basil Crispus, unpublished manuscript

Mitchell's B-17's had arrived at the worst possible time. Slowed to a nine-knot crawl for refueling, their usual tight defensive formation in disarray, Nagumo's ships were wide open.

The Japanese gunners put up a withering storm of AA fire, all the same. Flak chopped the port wing clean off Lt. Jack Devlin's Fortress, sending it spinning into the sea. Capt. Roy Earle's bomber simply vanished in a great blinding explosion.

By now everyone was being hit. Great holes appeared in wings and fuselages; controls went mushy as flying surfaces shredded away. Fires broke out and engines began to smoke. Yet the ten remaining planes roared on; as would be proved again and again over the next few years, the B-17 was an almighty hard airplane to shoot down.

The human body was less durable. Already the Fortresses

were becoming flying abattoirs where wounded men screamed in pain and rage and copilots wrestled the controls from dead pilots.

Then they were over the target.

—Edward Jablonski, *Flying Fortress*

Watching from *Akagi*'s bridge, Captain Genda was professionally impressed. The big bombers were faster than they looked and their pilots obviously knew their business. Brave men, too, to attack at such a low altitude; Genda felt an impulse to salute.

A stick of bombs exploded off *Akagi*'s port bow. *Kaga* and *Soryu* vanished for a moment behind towering columns of water, only to reappear a moment later, untouched. It seemed the combined fleet might escape harm after all.

Then a B-17 roared close overhead, through a wall of fire from *Akagi*'s guns. Genda looked up and saw a number of black objects dropping out of the bomber's belly, like a sow giving birth to a littler of pigs. A second later *Akagi*'s flight deck erupted in flame and smoke and Genda was knocked off his feet. As he hit the deck Admiral Nagumo landed on top of him.

At about the same time *Soryu* took a bomb through her flight deck, starting fires on the hanger deck below. *Zuikaku*, turning sharply to dodge the bombs, plowed into the tanker *Shinkoku Maru*, tearing a huge hole in the tanker's side and crumpling the brand-new carrier's bow. The destroyer *Akigumo* took a stick of bombs amidships that broke her in two.

Then the bombers were gone, climbing sharply away into the clouds. All, that is, but one.

On *Akagi*'s shattered bridge, supporting a dazed Nagumo, Genda watched in amazement as a single Fortress came circling back, trailing smoke. Every ship in the fleet was firing at it, even the mortally wounded *Akagi*, but it bored through the flak in a shallow dive, heading straight for *Kaga*. Genda realized suddenly what the American was doing.

—John Toland, *Rising Sun*

Our plane was the last one in the formation and we were still hauling ass out of there, Lt. Martinez pouring on the gas, trying to get up into the clouds before those Zeroes could take off. I was manning the port waist gun, watching to see if anything was after us. So I saw the whole thing.

You could see the Old Man's plane was hit bad. Smoke was trailing out behind and it looked like part of his port wing was gone. There was no way to know about the crew, of course, but I think they must have all been dead by then. There's just no other way the Old Man would have done what he did.

He hit that Jap carrier square in the middle of her flight deck, right next to the bridge island. For a second you could see the tail of his plane sticking up there like part of a big dead bird. Then there was this huge explosion, like nothing I'd ever seen before. It must have been like the end of the world for those poor damn Japs.

I felt like I ought to say a prayer or something. But I just wasn't up to it. I had a piece of shrapnel through my leg and it was really starting to hurt like a son of a bitch.

—M/Sgt. Darrell Hatfield, interviewed by Quentin Reynolds, *They Called It North Pacific*

The President had called a meeting in the Oval Office at 3 P.M. to discuss the deteriorating situation in the Pacific. He was just telling us how he still hoped to avoid war with Japan—at least until Hitler was defeated—but that if war did come, he wanted the Japanese to commit the first overt act. Then a naval officer came in with a message from Hawaii.

"My God," the President said upon hearing the news.

"This is terrible. I was afraid of something like this."

Secretary Knox said, "Mr. President, they were clearly on their way to attack Pearl Harbor. There's just no other explanation. Surely that justified a preemptive strike."

The President shook his head. "Frank," he said, "you know that and I know that, but I've got to sell this to the American people. And they've all grown up on cowboy movies. They still think the good guy never draws first."

Secretary Hull said, "What will you do now, sir?"

"Ask Congress to declare war," the President said. "There's no choice now. We're committed."

He turned to me. "Find out if Mitchell is still alive, Henry. I'd like to have the crazy bastard shot, but I suppose I'm going to have to give him the Medal of Honor. He's started the war and he may as well be its first hero."

—Secretary of War Henry Stimson, private diaries

By midmorning *Kaga* had sunk and *Akagi* was a blazing hulk. *Soryu* was still seaworthy but unable to fly planes, and *Zuikaku*, her bow damaged, was having trouble keeping up. But Nagumo, now flying his flag in *Shokaku*, refused even to consider turning back. He had never believed they would take the Americans by surprise; he had always expected to have to fight his way in. His losses so far had been heavy, but not unacceptable.

The Combined Fleet pushed onward, shadowed at a discreet distance by Bellinger's seaplanes but otherwise unmolested. The tankers had been left behind and the warships were now making almost thirty knots. Now some pilots begged to be allowed to launch an attack; their planes lacked the range for a round trip, but they were ready to make a one-way suicide raid. Nagumo vetoed the idea. He had lost too many planes and pilots already.

In Hawaii, despite great and general confusion about what had happened, it was realized that there was now no choice but to finish was Mitchell had begun. A message when out to Admiral Newton, just outbound for Midway with *Lexington* and a stout escort force: forget Midway, turn north, find the Japanese and attack when in range.

Only eight B-17s had made it back, none in remotely flyable condition. Hickam Field still had a dozen new A-20 attack bombers and thirty obsolete B-18s. Late in the afternoon, when a PBY reported the carrier group only 500 miles from Oahu, the decision was made to strike with what was at hand.

The A-20s were very fast, too quick even for the nimble Zeroes; they hit and ran without loss. But their small bomb loads were inadequate against warships, and their pilots green; they damaged a couple of destroyers, nothing more.

The B-18s arrived an hour later. They had no business there at all. Essentially little more than modified DC-3 transports, they could barely make 120 mph. They carried only two machine guns and no armor. They were slaughtered. None survived; none even got near the target.

But the massacre left the Zeroes low on ammunition. They began landing to reload, while Nagumo watched the sky. Soon it would be dark and he would have all night to run toward Hawaii, to get in range for a dawn attack.

That was when the *Lexington*'s planes appeared overhead. One of the fastest carriers in the world, "Lady Lex" had been powering northeast all day with a bone in her teeth. Now her scout bombers fell out of the clouds in near-vertical dives against Nagumo's carriers. *Hiryu* was ripped apart, then the lame *Zuikaku*, while bombs again mauled *Soryu*. In the twilight, *Shokaku*'s pilots tailed the victorious SBDs back to *Lexington* and put two torpedoes into her, but she managed to limp into Pearl Harbor the next day.

That morning, when he had read the Imperial Rescript to his officers, Nagumo had commanded the biggest carrier force ever assembled. Now, a short December day later, he was down to two carriers, one a helpless cripple. And there was no telling what other American forces might be out there.

It was time to quit. As darkness fell, the remains of the Pearl Harbor attack force turned and headed back toward Japan. Meanwhile Kimmel's battleships, which had finally sortied from Pearl Harbor, waddled slowly northward, striving doggedly to reach the scene of the fight that had, like history, already left them behind.

—Fletcher Pratt, *Battles That Changed History*

On Saturday, December 6—a day which will live in infamy—air and naval forces of the Empire of Japan attempted to launch an attack against American forces in Hawaii.

Fortunately, the approaching force was detected and destroyed by American military and naval aircraft. A great airman, General Mitchell, gave his life in the battle, as did many other brave men.

I ask that Congress declare that since the unprovoked and dastardly attempt by Japan on Saturday, December 6, a state of war has existed between the United States and the Japanese Empire.

—President Franklin D. Roosevelt to Congress, Dec. 8, 1941

Billy Mitchell died as he had lived, an outrageous and incorrigible spirit; a loose cannon on the deck of history, and an annoying problem for those who argue, as is now fashionable, that individuals cannot affect the course of great events. Since the day in 1914 when Gavrilo Princip gunned down the Archduke Ferdinand in Sarajevo, no single act by a single man has had such enormous consequences.

Unquestionably, Mitchell had handed Japan a calamitous defeat. A priceless asset, the finest carrier force in the world, had virtually ceased to exist even before the war was properly begun. Even worse was the loss of so many expert pilots and seamen, who could never be replaced in time to meet the American counterattack.

And the ambitious plan of conquest had been thrown fatally off schedule. Everything—the landings in Malaya and Luzon, even the delivery of the formal declaration of war—had been timed to the projected December 7 attack on Pearl Harbor. Like the Germans they admired so much, the Japanese militarists were good at devising highly complex schemes of war; unlike their allies, however, they seemed unable to think on their feet, to react quickly and improvise when things failed to go as planned. The Japanese blitz, which was supposed to conquer all of Southeast Asia in three months, never quite recovered its balance.

On the debit side, the quick victory had made the Americans dangerously overconfident. The image of the Japanese as myopic buck-toothed buffoons had been reinforced; all that was needed was to "slap the little yellow bastards down" and teach them not to trifle with their racial superiors. Reality would come soon enough, during the bloody campaign to relieve the Philippines— where the U.S. Navy would lose more ships than had been present at Pearl Harbor that morning—and the shock and disillusionment would do much to turn the American public against the war.

But all that was in the future. For now, America had a hero.

—William Manchester, *Pacific Crucible*

> *There was smoke on the water, there was fire*
>   *upon the sea,*
> *When General Billy Mitchell flew against the*
>   *enemy—*
> —"Smoke on the Water," copyright 1942 by Woody
>   Guthrie

❖   ❖   ❖

A hero! Why would anyone call that son of a bitch a hero? The only thing I can say for him, he had the decency to get killed.

So he stopped a Japanese attack on Pearl Harbor. Look, our people in Hawaii weren't helpless, you know. They had radar, so they'd have spotted the Japs coming and been ready for them. And then after beating off the attack we could still have gone after their carriers and sunk them. We'd have kicked their asses, you better believe it.

And if the Japs had fired the first shots, then the American people would have gotten together behind the President, and we'd have stayed in there and won the war properly.

As it was, thanks to Mr. Hero Billy Mitchell, we never did have a unified war effort against Japan, the way we did against Hitler. The isolationists ran around calling the President a warmonger, claiming Mitchell had secret orders from the White House, all that crap. Of course the Republicans were glad to have an excuse to oppose the President on any question, while the liberals were never comfortable about going to war to protect white colonialism in Asia. And John Q. Public, poor bastard, just didn't want to fight any wars anywhere if it could be avoided.

So the war in the Pacific dragged on indecisively, year after year, and the opposition grew—my God, we even had people marching against the war, right in front of the White House! Young punks were writing, "Hell, no, I won't go!" on draft-office walls, enough to make you puke. Till finally it got so bad the President just gave up and announced he wouldn't run again in '44.

I always thought it was a mercy that FDR died right after the election. At least he didn't have to watch Dewey making that half-assed peace with Tokyo—and we wouldn't even have gotten that, only Hitler was finished and Stalin's troops were massing on the Chinese border and the Japs realized they'd get a better deal with us than they would from Moscow.

And FDR didn't live to see the Communists overrun Asia, even obscure places like Korea and Indochina, and the U.S. not doing a goddamn thing about it because by that time the public was so sour on the Far East that it was political suicide even to talk about getting involved in anything west of Hawaii. Thousands of American boys died relieving the Philippines, after that prancing tinhorn MacArthur managed to get himself trapped there—listen, don't get me started on MacArthur—and ten years later when the Hukbalahaps marched into Manila and proclaimed the People's Republic of the Philippines, you had senior congressmen telling the press that the U.S. had no vital interests in the region! Why, that shifty-eyed little weasel Richard Nixon stood up in the House and said there was nothing in Southeast Asia worth the loss of a single American life!

That, by God, was Mitchell's legacy. He was just a goddamn cowboy.

> —Senator Harry S. Truman, interviewed by Merle Miller, 1961

They must have made a mighty noise, those twelve B-17s, as they swept northward across the island of Oahu in the darkest hours of Saturday morning. Surely some of the men at Schofield Barracks heard them—men in all-night craps games, or standing guard, or down in the latrine putting an extra shine on a pair of boots against the morning's inspection. Most of us, though, were sound asleep.

Maybe we did hear, at some level. Maybe the roar of those forty-eight Wright Cyclone engines vibrated its way down to where we lay in our bunks, into our sleeping consciousness, so that we stirred briefly before returning to the lonely dreams of soldiers.

Whether we heard or not, it is certain that none of us had any idea at all that our world was about to be altered forever, in ways we could never imagine or understand.

—James Jones, "The Day It Happened," *Saturday Evening Post,* December 9, 1961

A CASE FOR JUSTICE
Janet Berliner

I was not quite eleven and living in Cape Town, South Africa, when Jan Christian Smuts, "Oom Jannie" (Uncle John) as we called him, died. As his son wrote, "The gallant mountaineer had crossed his last Great Range."

That day—September 11th, 1950—was a sad one for every liberal, every Jew, every South African concerned about the future of what was then my country. We all felt that we knew him personally. I was too young then to fully comprehend the sadness that surrounded his passing, but as I grew older, as I began to understand more and rebelled against the system, I developed a reasoned fondness for the Oubaas, the Old Master.

Fondness became respect when I found myself at school in Stellenbosch, walking the riverside paths that he and Isie—his wife-to-be—had walked in their salad days, talking of the Shelleys, Percy and Mary, and properly avoiding physical contact. Being a dreamer, I often imagined myself to be Sybella Margaretha Krige (Isie), blue eyes sparkling, curly brown hair lifting on the breeze, wandering with Jannie beneath Simon van der Stel's magnificent oaks. I imagined sharing a passion for Shelley and for Shakespeare's tragedies, and I swear I heard him say, "You are less idealistic than I, but more human," as he compared me to ". . . the spirit of poetry in Goethe."

What I do know, with the wisdom born of hindsight, is that he said of me—of Isie—later, ". . . (she) recalled me from my intellectual isolation and made me return to my fellows."

General Jan Christian Smuts, founder of the League of Nations, proponent of freedom, Prime Minister of South Africa, lived a long and statesmanlike life. Though he kept journals, and wrote speeches and even books, he refused to write an autobiography. He would, he said, live life and create memories, leaving to his family and to history the task of writing about the events that shaped his life and about the events he helped to shape.

As the years passed, those books were written. The best of them, or at least the one which closest captures the spirit of the Old Master, is by his son, Jan Christian Smuts II. However, since he was not present to hear all of his father's conversations, since he could not enter his father's mind or body, the General's personal history remains incomplete and open to speculation by historians and writers of fiction alike.

The *events* as written here are historical fact. The details, the embellishments, the links between the events—the texture and the metaphysics—are, for the most part, mine. I offer them into the record as my view and mine alone of the unrecorded—the alternate—history of Jan Christian Smuts.

Cheeks glowing from a climb he, not that long ago, would have made without effort, the spare near-octogenarian stared down at Pretoria. The seat of government of the country he had served for the better part of his life was ablaze with jacaranda blossoms and he would willingly have sworn that he could smell their sweet scent even this many miles away. Gazing upward, he saw mountains he would never again climb, though once he would have considered them little more than hills.

". . . The mountain represents the ladder of life, of the soul. I see it as the source of religion, of the religion of joy, of the soul's release from all that signifies drudgery and defeat," he said, repeating with equal conviction the speech he had given at the top of Table Mountain more than a quarter of a century ago at the unveiling of the memorial to South Africa's WWI heroes.

This, he thought, is what it's really all about. The hills, the mountains, the veld, the flowers. He was at heart a farmer, a botanist and a student. Not that he didn't take pride in being Jan Christian Smuts—General, Prime Minister, Statesman—but his place in history was of less importance to him than the fact that any day— any hour—which passed without event, without the making of a memory, was a waste of God-given life. The only time he did not feel that pressure was when he communed with nature or when, in the wee small hours, too tired to rise, he fed upon those memories he had already made. During those hours, having as usual retired early, he awakened and contemplated his life, envying his friend Winston who used those hours to their fullest for writing his diaries or for dealing with leftover affairs of state.

He breathed deeply, exhaled, and swung his thin arms in windmill circles to energize himself for the rest of the walk home. Stooping every now and again to examine a plant or a bloom with his trained botanist's eye, he continued walking, downhill now toward Doornkloof and the small Irene farming community where he lived whenever he could escape from the official government residences in Pretoria and Cape Town. It was a walk he had taken so often that his feet moved through the short spring grass of their own accord, stopping only when his mind insisted upon breathing deeply of the perfumed September air.

How deeply he loved this country of his, he thought,

this South Africa, with all of its diversity. And this would always be his favorite time of the year, when thoughts of enemies were occasionally diverted by the insistent growth and renewal that surrounded him.

His mind wandered to his next political battle—the clearly anti-British citizenship change that the Nationalists wanted to implement. In his opinion, anyone who came to South Africa with the intent of staying deserved full citizenship after two years. The Nats felt differently. The fact was that most of the people who would be affected by a change in the rules were British.

Anger for Malan, his chief opponent, sent adrenaline rushing through Smuts' body and he increased his pace. Failing to watch properly the rude path he was following, he did not see the thorn that the day-witch had placed among the grasses.

He held onto his foot and hopped about, resisting the urge to curse—aloud or silently. In his mind's eye, he saw the Modjadji, heard her voice and, too late, recalled the Rain-Queen's warning: "Watch the paths you walk. The day-witch will place a medicated thorn in a familiar path. At first you will feel only pain in your foot, but eventually there will be pain in the leg. As the medication passes into the rest of the body, *Hu fa*. You will die."

The throbbing in his foot interrupted the flow of Smuts' memory. Sitting down upon the ground, using great care so as to be certain that he removed all of the thorn, he rid himself of the offender. His foot continued to throb. He contemplated walking home barefooted, but deciding it would be neither sensible nor seemly, he retied the leather sandals he'd been wearing for thirty-four years, the ones Mohandas Karamchad Gandhi—Indian barrister and South Africa's nuisance number one—had made for him by hand while he was in jail before his final departure for India in 1914. A sign of respect, not love, since they had spent so many years at loggerheads. Gandhi's work on the sandals had apparently delighted his fellow prisoners, for it temporarily stopped his continual fiddling at Western music, for which he apparently had no ear at all.

The pain having reduced itself to a dull throb, Smuts searched the area for a makeshift walking stick and limped his way down and around the last hill. As a diversion, he returned to his replaying of his visit with the Rain-Queen, doing it right this time and transporting himself back into her presence in the way she had taught him—

"So you are the one they call Oubaas, the famous Old Master," Modjadji said in excellent English. "I met your daughter not so long ago. She is a charming young woman, well-mannered and well-schooled."

"I thank you, Modjadji," Smuts responded. "My wife and I are most grateful for the hospitality you showed our daughter." He handed her a large basket filled to overflowing. "We wish you to accept this as a token of our respect and gratitude."

The Queen unpacked the basket's contents, for the most part simple domestic articles sent by his wife. She appeared to be genuinely delighted by all of them. Reaching behind her, she completed the traditional exchange and handed him her gift, a small ebony carving.

"Let us talk," she said. "Later, I will write to your wife and thank her for her gifts."

When they had conversed for some hours, she said, "You speak the rapid, passionate speech of the prophet and seer."

Smuts smiled and shook his head. He wanted to visit the grove of cycads which his daughter had told him lay behind the Queen's headquarters; he wanted to speak of trees and nature. In mystics and the metaphysical he had no interest.

"Do not deny your gift, Old Master."

"My gift?"

"You have the gift, though you have not used it much. Think, for example of the general, Louis Botha. Would you argue your telepathic bond with him and tell me that the two of you share no more than coffee and *biltong*?"

"What could you know of Botha?"

It was her turn to smile. "I am the Rainmaker, Modjadji, Queen of the Lovedu," she said, as if that were explanation enough.

Standing now, towering over him in breadth and depth, she spoke again. "Watch out for the day-witch, Oubaas," she said. "She will get you in the end."

"And you, Modjadji?" he asked. "Do you fear the day-witch?"

"I fear no one."

He thought about the fact of her approaching suicide, a tradition she would not be able to avoid. "What will she do to me?" he asked.

The Modjadji thought carefully before she spoke. "*Hu lega*," she said at last. "That is her favorite method of causing illness or death. She delights in sending misfortune by means of medicine." She closed her eyes and mounted her warning, ending with the words, ". . . *Hu fa*. You will die."

Smuts heard the pounding of his heart. "What of *Hu dabekulla*, Queen?" he asked at last. "Will I not be able to neutralize the work of the day-witch?"

She sat down heavily, opened her eyes, and leaned against the wall of the hut. "The circle will end when it must end," she said. "You will be ready for it if, when the time comes, you have properly reviewed your life. You have been brought here to learn from me, so listen well—"

"Brought here? I think not. I came because my daughter told me of your cycads," he said. "I wished the honor of meeting you and the joy of seeing them."

"How you came to be here does not matter. That you hear me and act upon what I say does, for it will guide the destiny of our country."

"I am listening," Smuts said. "Though I confess I do not comprehend."

"Comprehension will come," the Queen said. "For now, listen and learn.

"When the day-witch has done her worst and you begin to see your life in memory, you must reenter the stream of your past. There you will find one task which remains undone, for it had to wait until you could whisper in light of the wisdom you have gathered. Tomorrow I will teach you how to do this. For now, you must let me rest," she said. "I am greatly fatigued—"

"I'm getting old, Adam," Smuts said aloud, reentering the present as he crossed the boundary of Irene. Talking to Adam was a pattern developed in his early childhood as the son of a farmer, tending to his family's horses and geese, their goats and cattle. A silent, internal child by nature, he had been happy to be silent, and was mostly so except in the presence of an old farmhand, a shrunken, wrinkled Hottentot as old as forever and aptly named for the oldest man in creation.

Adam was a natural-born philosopher who guided him ever so gently into the set of beliefs which continued to govern his life. Though the Hottentot had likely been dead for sixty or seventy years, it was he to whom Jan Christian Smuts spoke now and always when he had something pressing on his mind. Communing with Adam came as easily to Smuts as communing with nature and with God. If God existed—and as far as Oubaas was concerned He certainly did—then Adam, who had been made in His image, did too.

"A new journey begins, Adam," he said, unlatching the gate that led to home. "I wish you were here to travel by my side."

❖   ❖   ❖

His foot twisted unnaturally, as it had been since the day he had so crudely removed the day-witch's thorn, Smuts moved toward the podium. The unnatural movement set up the searing pain in his leg. He bore the pain with his usual stoicism, telling himself, as he had for over a year, that it would pass.

Over a year, and almost as long since the Nats wrested away power from the United Party, and from him.

Amazing that they still come to hear me, he thought, taking his place with difficulty behind the podium and staring into a sea of close to half a million mostly white faces. Did they understand the irony of unveiling the Voortrekker Monument on Dingaan's Day, he wondered, or were they too entrenched in the Nationalist credos, in their talk of *Die swart gevaar*, the black danger, and *Die kaffer op sy plek*, the nigger in his place, to remember the freedoms that the Voortrekkers sought as they crossed the land?

He had said many times that he considered apartheid to be "a crazy concept, born of prejudice and fear." He would say it today, if he thought for a second that it could make a difference.

He did not say it. Instead, bracing his shoulders and straightening his spine, he drew from Walt Whitman's *Study in the Evolution of Personality*.

"We must look to the future," he began, his expression carefully benign, his voice gentle, his hands quietly at his sides to avoid his long habit of placing one or both of them at the back of his hip, thus putting his body under further strain. Later, he thought, he would rest.

Later.

But he did not rest, not until many months had passed and his body insistently rendered him mostly supine with a heart problem that he could not ignore. Only then did he return again to the Rain-Queen's warning. Bored, determined that he would not write his memoirs in the way of other used-up old men rendered incapable of making new memories, he allowed his family to think that he had fallen into a coma.

Contrary to what Mary Shelley might have believed, it was not merely poets who indulged in waking dreams, he thought, with a rare touch of humor. Then, without further ado, he used the now-well-practiced techniques he had learned from the Rain-Queen. First, he concentrated on becoming conscious of his breathing. When he could feel its movement inside his body, he focused on producing a circle of white light which he moved slowly toward his heart. Feeling its heat, he rode its beam systematically, chronologically, toward his past.

He began with Adam—

Cape Province, 1880

"Nee, Master Jannie. No. You are wrong."

The ten-year-old bristled, then smiled down at the wrinkled little Hottentot. He could never stay angry at Adam; the old man told too many good stories. "I still think the English are the best at everything." He stood at attention, executed a clumsy salute, and shouted, "Long live the King."

"The Scots," Adam said. "They are most courageous people."

"Because the men wear skirts?"

Adam laughed. "*Nee, Kleinbaas,*" he said.

Jannie's body relaxed when he heard the pet name. Once Adam called him Little Master, he was assured of forgiveness. "Why, then, Adam?"

"Because they are truly God's chosen people. One day, when you are old like me, you will look back on your life and see how much the Scots have influenced you."

Pretoria, 1899

"Your name?"

"Winston Spencer Churchill . . . sir."

Smuts examined the young man who had been brought

before him. He looked like a ruffian, disheveled and defiant.

"Commandant Botha informs me that you were captured on a British train."

The young man nodded. Smuts let it pass.

"I am told that you call yourself a journalist, in which case you are correct to be claiming immunity as a non-combatant."

Churchill looked as if he were about to speak. Smuts held up his hand. "I have also been told that you were wearing a pistol, in which case this detention is the least of what you deserve." He paused for a moment. "Tell me Mr.—um—Churchill, for what purpose would a journalist be carrying a pistol?"

"I acquired it for a journey I hope to make to the Drakensberg, sir."

"The Drakensberg?" Smuts raised an eyebrow. "What draws you there?"

"You have read H. Rider Haggard, have you not, sir?" Churchill asked.

This time it was Smuts who nodded.

"Then you are doubtless familiar with his tales of the Zulu warrior, Umslopogaas, and with the Lovedu tribe about which Haggard wrote."

"Of course, but—"

Smuts stopped and watched as Churchill took from his pocket a rolled sheaf of papers. "Here," he said. "If you would be so good as to read this, sir, you will see that I have researched the supposed death of Umslopogaas, the Zulu, as Mr. Haggard described it. As the result of my studies, I have come to believe that it did not happen that way. In fact, I believe that Umslopogaas remains alive. I do not think that even you, sir, would venture into the territory of the Mines of King Solomon without protection."

"You may or may not be a journalist, but you do spin an interesting tale. I will read this," Smuts said. "Take him away."

Upon reading the notes, Smuts persuaded General Joubert to release Winston Spencer Churchill, only to find that the young Englishman had already managed to make good his escape.

Scotland, 1934

"And what do you think of us now, Dr. Smuts?" the Dean of St. Andrew's University asked, balancing a cup of tea in one hand and moving a square of shortbread toward his mouth.

"I would hardly have made my address on freedom here had I not admired your . . . mettle," Smuts replied.

In fact, though he had never let go of his admiration for the British, it consistently amazed and amused Smuts how right Adam had been about the Scots. How daunting, someday, to historians and students of his life and philosophies when they discovered that the two singlemost influential people in his life had been a wizened Hottentot, who taught him that color had naught to do with humanity, and the Modjadji, a Lovedu Rain-Queen . . . descendent of the very same Ayesha immortalized by his friend Churchill's beloved Rider Haggard—

Doornkloof, 1950

Seated in the garden, his loving family attentive to his needs, Smuts longed for the next opportunity to continue the unusual journey which was fast becoming his obsession. In order to wait more patiently, he exchanged pleasantries with his wife.

"What have we learned in this life, do you think?" she asked.

He thought for a moment. He would like to have said that, if he had learned nothing else in what was approaching eight decades of life, he had learned that greatness was to be found in strange small places, in the mouths of farmhands and rainmakers, the deeds of footsoldiers, the written word of philosophers and poets. Instead he answered in the form of a question.

"What might our lives have been without Walt Whitman?" he asked. "Without Shakespeare and Shelley?"

Isie reached for his hand and held it fast.

Who was it, Smuts asked himself, who wrote that the poet ". . . must write as an interpreter of nature, and the legislator of mankind, and consider himself as presiding over the thoughts and manners of future generations; as a being superior to time and place?" When he could not remember, he cursed old age. Surely a man who had learned Greek in six days could remember the source of a quote that had so largely influenced his life.

He quoted Shelley: "Poets are the unacknowledged legislators of the world," he said. Hearing the words out loud, he remembered that they were stolen from Walter Savage Landor, and he felt better.

That night, Smuts appeared to sink into another of his comas—

South East Africa, WWI

Smuts saw himself astride a horse, passing a soldier who had collapsed with an attack of malaria, and he knew he was fighting against General von Lettow-Vorbeck and battling malaria with an endless stream of quinine. He was heading a reconnaissance force, in its first march to M'Buyuni. Outside of wondering by what miraculous means blacks and coloreds avoided malaria, he had not complained, but knowing the discomfort of the disease he jumped from his horse, placed the soldier on his saddle, and walked and talked the enlisted man the rest of the way back to camp.

Behind him his men straightened their shoulders. Softly, they began to sing, chanting to *John Peel*:

"*D'ye ken Jan Smuts when he's after the Hun?*

> *D'ye ken Jan Smuts when he's got them*
> *on the run?*
> *D'ye ken Jan Smuts when he's out with*
> *his gun?*
> *And his horse and his men in the*
> *morning?"*

Surrounded by the enemy, outfoxed and outnumbered, still they sang his praises.

Depositing the soldier with the medics, Smuts isolated himself and invited the council of Adam, who said, "I do not care much for the Zulus, Kleinbaas. They are too free with the *sjambok*. Neither the rhino nor the hippo were created to be made into whips which damage the human beast's body and spirit. As for you, Kleinbaas, you could do worse than use T'Chaka's bull as your weapon."

T'Chaka's bull. Of course! The concept of the horns of a bull, enveloping the enemy by an outflanking movement.

Smuts rallied his forces for a thrust at Moshi, the end of the Tanganyika-Kili railway. There they attacked the enemy with rifle butt and bayonet and emerged victorious.

The next morning, he began his lessons in loathing the Germans. Dawn brought a view of mounds of Askari troops, the dead mixed with the wounded. Upon their bodies lay water bottles which had been filled with raw spirits—and not a sign of the German leaders who had left their wounded, sick and dead for the enemy to take care of.

"*Bwana unkubwa*," the wounded moaned as he bent to speak with them. "Great Master."

Chequers, 1934

"Tell me, sir, did you ever read my notes about Umslopogaas the Zulu?" Churchill asked.

"I did indeed," Smuts answered. "In fact, they so

fascinated me that I hastened to advise General Joubert to secure your release . . . only to find that you had already done so yourself."

Churchill guffawed with such delight that he almost fell off his chair. "Then it appears I foiled your government twice," he said. "I did prove my theory, you know?"

Smuts stopped and watched as Churchill pulled from his desk a second rolled sheaf of papers. "Here," he said. "If you would be so good as to read this, sir, you will learn 'The True Tale of the Final Battle of Umslopogaas the Zulu.'"

Paris, 1919

"Stop here," Smuts ordered his driver. "I need to walk."

Without hesitation, the driver stopped at the Place de la Concorde, causing havoc to the traffic.

The General hardly noticed. Entering the Champs Élysées on foot, he marched on the city's concrete in an effort to still his body's restlessness and his mind's anguish.

"I should not be here," he said. "I am a man of the veld, a specialist in grasses—"

He was en route to Versailles and the signing of the Peace Treaty and should have felt at ease, but all that he saw in his mind's eye was the image of dead and dying soldiers, left behind by the Germans, and the sound of the *sjambok* being used to whip prisoners for the joy of causing pain.

"South Africa must fight the German folly," he said to the Paris sky. "We can do no less."

Baltimore, Maryland, 1930

Smuts rose to address the fifty-four representatives of the League of Nations, whose formation was in largest part due to his own efforts.

". . . I want the disputes of mankind in the future, the troubles that arise and lead to war, to be treated in the family spirit," he said. "Consider that we are at the family table. . . ."

He was, he declared, in favor of a Jewish home in Palestine, as must anyone who, like he, was a lover of all humanity.

On board ship, returning to South Africa and lulled into believing that he had done something real for the world, he learned of the Quota Bill being supported in his absence by his own United Party. The bill, it seemed, named the Jews as undesirable immigrants.

Raging, he returned to devote himself to changing his party's support of what he considered to be an outrageous bill. His opponents mocked him and called him Smutskowitz; a settlement near Haifa, Ramat Jochanan, was named after him in recognition of his support. Unmindful of the former and proud of the latter, he continued to rage. So great was his fury, so inspired his oratory, that in the final vote his party stood unanimously against the bill. He was ". . . supporting a legalistic principle, not a people," he said. "It was a case of justice—"

Doornkloof, September 10, 1950

In early September, Smuts gathered his strength and rallied. He talked about horseback riding again and asked to be driven to the bushveld farm so that he could enjoy the sight of the wheatfields while they were greenest. He was almost done with revisiting his past and knew that he was dying, but he had not yet found that task of which the Modjadji had spoken. Somehow, he must hasten the process.

Hoping that being in the outdoors at this time of the year he loved so much would provide inspiration, he asked to be taken into the garden and left alone. "Do this for me, *Ouma*," he said, using the Afrikaans word for grandmother because that was what she was called by the many who loved her.

Since he seemed to be feeling better, Isie happily did as he had asked. "Rest," she said. "Later our grandchildren will come to visit and we will take photographs. They grow so fast, those young ones."

His wife was hardly out of sight when Smuts again summoned his past. It came to him this time in a whirl of color and sound. As if he were inside a kaleidoscope, he viewed the remaining highlights of his life—

Dining with Roosevelt in Cairo, he says, "We are both Dutchmen. Small surprise we get on splendidly."

Churchill is handing him two oil paintings of the pyramids, done by his own hand. "One will hang in Libertas in Pretoria," Smuts tells his old friend, "the other in my family home."

His seventy-fifth birthday. He is handed a kist made of an old pear tree, found dying in a hamlet of Malmesbury.

Seventy-seven now. As a personal tribute to his longtime friendship with King George V and Queen Mary, Queen Elizabeth and her family visit South Africa. They speak of the food parcels he sent to the palace during the First World War, and of the fact that Queen Victoria addressed Isie as "Dear Ouma." He tells them proudly that von Lettow-Vorbeck, now living in South Africa on a pension he personally had secured for their sometime enemy, addressed her in the same way. Then he shows them the view from the top of Table Mountain and takes an ostrich feather from the Queen's hat to place it jauntily in the band of his best panama. They spend a few days together at the Mont-aux-Source in the Drakensberg—

"It is cold out here," Isie said.

Smuts was silent. Over and over he had surprised his doctors by emerging from his comas, appearing to regain some strength, and slipping away again. He felt bad about deceiving Isie, especially with the end so near, but she would have thought that he had gone mad had he told her the truth.

"Bring me a blanket and leave me here a little longer," he said. "Please."

"A few minutes only, Jannie," she said. "I will bring you back outside tomorrow."

I don't think so, Smuts thought, breathing in the jacaranda blossoms one last time. Then he closed his eyes, this time not to bid his past come to him but to pray that this final journey into his past would bring him the answer he sought—

Eastern Cape, the Municipality of Alice, 1940

Smuts stood on the campus of the University College of Fort Hare, founded by Scottish missionaries on the site of the largest 19th Century frontier fort in the eastern Cape. The fort was, short of the site of the University of Cape Town which fronted Kirstenbosch Gardens and lay on the lower slopes of Table Mountain, the most beautiful site he had ever seen for a place of higher learning.

It was also a perfect site for its originally intended purpose: military defense.

Built on a rocky platform, moated by the winding arc of the Tyume River, Fort Hare had provided the perfect battleground for the British in their fight against Sandile, the Xosa warrior. Sandile was the last Rharhabe king defeated by them in one of the final frontier battles in the 1800s.

Now, the only battle taking place was that of the faculty in its mission to educate the school's one hundred and fifty students. As part of that purpose, they had invited Smuts, once Prime Minister and now Deputy Prime Minister of South Africa and an avowed believer in the right to existence of all men, to speak at the graduation ceremonies.

Smuts thought about the speech he planned to give. What was most on his mind was his campaign for South Africa to declare war on Germany, against the advocacy of the Broederbond who were firmly on the side of National Socialism and of the country's current Prime Minister, Herzog, who at best advocated neutrality. Should he, Smuts, win, Herzog would be forced to resign and Smuts would once again become Prime Minister.

The students gathered and waited respectfully for their honorable guest to mount the podium and begin his speech. As he stood before them, most of them applauded enthusiastically. He held up his hand for silence.

"Thank you for honoring me with this invitation," he began.

In the far reaches of his mind, the Modjadji's words intruded upon his concentration: *"You will find one task which remains undone, for it had to wait until you could whisper in light of the wisdom you have gathered."*

With infinite weariness, he felt the presence of the day-witch guiding Death closer. Help me, Modjadji, he pleaded silently. What is it I am to do?

"Speak again as you did the first time and while you do, look for the man who is called Mandela. When you are done, follow him. Talk to him, and your work will be done."

Trusting that he would somehow be led to the one called Mandela, Smuts gave his speech. When it was over, he searched the faces of the students.

"He is of the land," the Rain-Queen said, taking pity on Smuts. *"Find the place which gives you peace and you will find Mandela."*

Slipping away from the post-graduation party on the pretext of needing a breath of air, Smuts made his way to the University's farmlands which lay behind the fort. He was guided by the light of a small fire and by the unmistakable sweet odor of roasting corn toward a small group of students who stood as he approached.

"Which one of you might be Mr. Mandela?" he asked.

A tall, handsome young man stepped forward. "I am Nelson Mandela, sir. It is an honor to meet you."

"Could we walk and talk?" Smuts asked, knowing suddenly what it was he must say.

"Will you not sit here with us?" Mandela asked.

"What I have to say is for your ears only," Smuts said.

Hearing this, the others said their farewells. When they were out of earshot, Smuts sat down upon a log that had been pulled up to the fire. He accepted a *mielie* and crunched into the sweet golden ear of corn. When he was done, he threw the husk into the fire.

"You will forget that we had this conversation," he said, "but you will never forget its intent. To you, the whole future is a tabula rasa; to me, the next already written in concrete. I will become Prime Minister again and we will fight against the Germans in North Africa. Six years from now, I will be forced to pass the Asiatic Land Tenure Act, restricting the free movement of Indians, and you will feel betrayed. You will become involved in, obsessed by, finding the road to freedom for yourself and your people. There will be many times when you think your cause helpless, times when you will be tempted to give up. Men like John Vorster will take over the government and they will laugh at Jan Christian Smuts for having made the blunder of not hanging them all for treason when he had the chance.

"You must not let them win, Nelson Mandela, for upon your shoulders rests the destiny of our country—"

Doornkloof, September 11, 1950

Surprised and happy to find himself alive this Monday morning, Smuts asked twice to be driven into the countryside, and was. Though the car was not as comfortable as the big Vauxhall he had used in the old days, it was, he thought, a reasonable mode of locomotion now that he could no longer take his long walks alone.

That night, he took his place at the head of the table and ate dinner with an appetite such as he had not felt for some time. Around seven o'clock, he asked his two daughters to accompany him to his room and help him remove his boots.

Feeling suddenly that life was good, he recalled one of his favorite Shakespearean quotes: "Be absolute for death; for either death or life shall be the sweeter." Then he felt himself losing consciousness. One of his daughters was a physician; he knew she would do all she could to no avail. A clot had wedged in his brain.

The day-witch's job was done. And so, at long last, was his.

A HARD DAY FOR MOTHER
William R. Forstchen

Brigadier General Joshua Lawrence Chamberlain, CSA, flinched involuntarily as a shell flickered overhead, airbursting over an artillery limber wagon. Above the thunder of the cannonade the screams of the wounded horses, cut down by the burst, tore into his heart. He spared a quick glance back over his shoulder, watching as a gunner walked down the line of thrashing animals with revolver drawn, and put the bests out of their misery.

Damn war. Loved working artillery but what happened to the horses always bothered me.

"General Chamberlain, are you still with me?"

"Sir?"

He looked back into the cold dark eyes of James Longstreet, "Old Pete," they called him. *Funny, never did know how he got that name. Grand army for nicknames . . . Grumble Jones, Gallant Ashby, and of course Stonewall. Thomas never cared for that one, but still better than Fool Tom, what the boys back at VMI called him. Yankee Josh, that was my name at VMI,* he thought with an inward smile, *professor of rhetoric, philosophy and history with my best friend Thomas Jackson just down the hallway, teaching tactics and artillery.*

Ah, the wonderful days then, he thought wistfully. *Seemed to spend more time on the VMI drillfield than*

*in the classroom . . . watching Tom drill his boys with
the guns, and the battery practice firing, now that was
a delight. Never thought we'd see the day when it would
be real shot and canister shrieking down range, tearing
into boys who were fellow Americans.*

*Then it was more of a game, my playing soldier like
my friend Thomas with battery practice, followed by a
supper in the basement of the Presbyterian Church and
prayer service together afterwards. Jack—a veteran of
Mexico—always seemed to have that cold fire in his eyes
when the guns fired; for me, it was make believe. Make
believe until Manassas when the boys poured double
canister into a Wisconsin regiment at fifty paces. God,
how could we?*

"General, I do hope you are paying attention."

Joshua forced his thoughts to stay focused on Pete.

"Sorry, sir, the heat, just the heat," Joshua offered.

Pete nodded.

"Joshua, if you don't feel up to this . . ." Joshua looked
over at his division commander, John Bell Hood. He
knew that Hood was not really happy about Joshua's
assignment to command a brigade in his division. The
assignment to brigade command had been Jackson's
doing, a request for Joshua's promotion made on his death
bed, a request the Old Man, Robert E. Lee, felt honor
bound to fulfill. For after all, in the hours of turmoil
after Jackson went down at Chancellorsville it was Colonel
Joshua Chamberlain, Stonewall's adjutant, who briefly
commanded Jackson's entire corps, pushing the attack
in until Stuart came up to take over.

Joshua flinched involuntarily at the flash memory of
Jackson lying in the road. Joshua looked down at his
uniform, flecks of dried blood still staining the arms where
he had flung himself over his fallen comrade to protect
him after he had fallen. The new stars of a brigadier
were on his collar, and he wanted to reach up to touch
them but knew that would be too self-conscious an act.

His new brigade had been McIver Law's command, a friend of Hood's, but Law was down with typhoid when the Army of Northern Virginia started its move north and Joshua was slotted in to fill his place. Jackson had trusted him. After all they had been friends for years; it was Joshua who had led Jackson to the Lord and they had prayed together nightly through two long years of war. *But Jackson was gone and I'm the only northern-born man in this army in command of a brigade.* Now, he realized, was the moment of challenge, to prove that he could fight and was not just a favored staff officer who had won position through the dying wish of the legendary and eccentric Jackson.

Joshua stiffened when he realized that Longstreet was staring at him appraisingly. He knew the Hood had been pushing for Joshua to be shunted off to Corps staff, regardless of Jackson's dying wish, and his illness of the last few days might be the excuse.

"Just a touch of sunstroke on the march up here, sir," Joshua added hurriedly. "Never could get used to the sun," and his voice trailed off.

Were they still wondering? Even after two years of hard service he knew he was an outsider, sensing that more than one silently asked why he's in their uniform rather than the blue which waits for them on the other side.

Maine, how I do miss Maine. Guess after all this I'll never be able to go back there again. No, not after this. Funny how fate turns. A professorship at Bowdoin was offered but then came the one from VMI which also provided two hundred a year more. Mother wanted me for the ministry but the fantasy of war, or at least playing at war, was the lure of taking the professorship at the West Point of the South. After those years at VMI how could I go any other way but to throw myself in with the boys I had taught? Slavery aside, Virginia was my home. Like Lee, I could not raise my sword against my adopted state. Then of course there was Jackson, how could I ever bring myself to fight against him? Stood as godfather to his daughter, formed a prayer group with him and so many nights discussing the bible and, of course, the power of artillery.

"General, you know your orders. Now the question is, can you take that hill? This is not an artillery battle, it's a straight-in infantry charge."

Pete looked at him closely, ignoring the nearby burst of a shell that sprayed them with dirt.

"Sir, if any brigade will carry that rocky hill it will be my unit," Joshua snapped as he pointed across the smoke-clad fields to the dark hill rising three quarters of a mile away.

Directly ahead, out in front of the Peach Orchard, Barksdales's Mississippians were going in, a thunderous crescendo of rifle fire greeting their advance.

Longstreet, nose quivering as if smelling the battle, turned away from Chamberlain. Hood, Chamberlain's division commander, looked over at Joshua imploringly, nodding for him to press the argument one more time.

"General Longstreet, sir."

Longstreet looked back, distracted.

"Sir. My brigade forms the rights of this assault. Sir, I implore you, let me maneuver my brigade around that large hill." As he spoke Joshua pointed to the larger cone-shaped hill to the south of the rocky escarpment. "Just thirty minutes more, sir, and we can be on their flank."

Longstreet shook his head angrily.

"Damn all, Chamberlain. Lee himself ordered this attack *en echelon* against their left, not a full maneuver against the flank. There is no time to wait!" With a wave of his gauntlet-clad hand he pointed straight at Little Round Top. "There is your objective, sir, now go and take it!"

Joshua looked over at Hood who lowered his eyes. Drawing himself up in his saddle, Joshua saluted.

"As you order, sir."

Longstreet, without another word, spurred his mount forward. Though ordered by Lee to stay to the rear, the fury of battle was upon him and he rode in the ranks of Barksdale's advance which was swarming up towards the Peach Orchard. Hat off, he urged the men forward and disappeared into the smoke.

"Old Pete, there he goes," Hood sighed, shaking his head, "hope he doesn't get himself killed. Can't lose him now, especially with Jackson gone."

Joshua nodded, saying nothing. That was still too close. *My best friend gone from this side forever. Crossing the river . . . Will I cross as well before this day is done?* he wondered, raising his field glasses to scan the hill one more time. *Still no troops up there. Can't count on that now, we've sprung the attack, should have waited to flank.*

What would old Thomas say about this? Joshua wondered.

"*Two book learning professors,*" Jackson had called us, "*the philosopher and the gunner.*"

"Well, the good Lord willing, Joshua, this will be the end of it," Hood announced. "Maybe after it's over you can cross the line and see that brother of yours. Which corps is he with?"

"My brother Tom? Fifth Corps," Joshua whispered. "Last I heard he was promoted to command a regiment with them."

"Well, that's Third Corps over there," Hood said, pointing towards the Peach Orchard which was wreathed in fire and smoke. "Maybe you won't have to face your kin today."

Joshua said nothing. *What would Mother say? Two of her boys facing each other thus. Never did we raise a hand to each other. When some of the boys down along the docks at Brewer worked Tom over a bit, I was the one who came to his rescue. God, don't let him be over there now, not that.*

"Get a move on, Joshua," Hood announced. "Time to go in. Remember, Robertson's on your left flank. Hang on tight to him, don't let a hole open up or you'll be cut off. Remember, Joshua, you are the extreme right of the line. There's nobody beyond you. If we're going to carry this day, it'll be your brigade that does it. Time your attack to roll in after Robertson hits."

"Yes sir."

Hood leaned over, eyes alight with the fire of battle.

"Joshua, this could be the last day. Take that damn hill and we roll up their line. We can end it here, Joshua. Do you understand me?"

Joshua nodded, attention focused on the hill.

"The fate of our nation might very well rest on your shoulders."

Joshua looked straight into Hood's eyes. Not like him to speak like that. Battlefield rhetoric. *Strange, I taught rhetoric, now I see the power of it, sense it in my soul. Fate of the nation. Which nation?*

"Now take that hill, Joshua, and good luck to you."

Joshua saluted and turning his mount he cantered down the line, weaving his way past the batteries which were turning their fire on the rocky ground below the hill which was his objective. As he drifted through the woods the rumble of fire rolled down along the flank as regiment after regiment stepped off into the assault.

Following a narrow path he emerged into a clearing where his brigade was deployed, the men looking up at him curiously as he trotted past. Their gazes were blank, drawn, exhausted after the ten long hours of marching and countermarching as they maneuvered into the position for the assault. He could he brief snatches of conversation, whispered prayers, jokes, angrily barked commands of sergeants for the men to remain still. Strange voices, deep south, Alabama, almost a different language. The years in Virginia had softened his nasal twang and clipped r's of Maine but it was still there, especially when he got angry, and he knew the men of his new command looked upon him with suspicion.

"Colonel Oates!"

The commander of his right flank regiment, the 44th Alabama, stepped out from the shade of a tree and saluted.

"You lead off, Colonel. We're cutting across the face of that hill up there." He pointed to Big Round Top. "We come down into the valley between the two hills and then assault the Rocky Hill from the south. Now let's move."

Oates saluted again and with a roar of command his regiment was up. With Joshua in the lead, skirmishers sprinting out ahead, they started over the boulder-strewn ground. The going on horseback was tough and Joshua dismounted. Panting hard he scrambled up the slope, a scattering of rifle fire erupting ahead as the skirmishers brushed aside a light screen of Union soldiers.

"My boys, sir," Oates explained, struggling to keep up with Joshua's long-legged stride. "We sent out a detachment for water while waiting for the word to go in. They haven't come back. Every canteen in my regiment is bone dry, sir."

Joshua nodded, pausing for a moment to gain his bearing, pulling out a handkerchief to wipe the sweat from his face period.

Can't flag now. Don't think about the heat. The extreme right. Jackson would like that, out on the flank. The last day, Hood said. The last day of what? The war, the Union, the Confederacy if we fail?

Joshua looked over his shoulder. His men were closing up, red faced, panting hard; a few of them were deathly pale, skin clammy looking, and some were falling out, collapsing silently. *Can't stop for them. Lord don't let me fall, at least not here, on that hill ahead, yes, a bullet rather than the heat, but not here.*

Firing raged down in the valley below. Devil's Den

he had heard someone call it. *Hell in the Devil's Den*, he thought with a smile. The smoke parted for an instant and up on the Rocky Hill he saw a banner. National colors surging along the crest, moving to the south flank. They were deploying to meet him . . . damn. Another flag bobbed into view, one of their new brigade guidons—a Maltese cross in the middle of the triangular pennant—and there was a ripple of fear. Fifth Corps. *God no, not that.*

Water, damn it. We're going to need water if we're going to take that hill. An hour of fighting in this heat will knock a man over as surely as a bullet if he doesn't have water.

"Colonel, pass the word back. If we see a stream or spring, a corporal and two men from each company detailed off to fill canteens. Now let's keep moving."

Going up over the flank of Big Round Top he started down into the valley. The humid heat hung thick under the trees, trapping the swirls of powder smoke drifting down from the Devil's Den to their left. The thunder of battle was washing along behind them as the attack developed from the Peach Orchard, down through the Wheat Field and across Devil's Den. A shrill cry rolled through the woods, the rebel yell, sending a shiver of excitement down his spine. Through a gap in the trees he saw butternut and gray swarming over the boulders of Devil's Den, pushing towards the base of Rocky Hill.

The slope of Big Round Top started to drop away and he could sense more than see the narrow valley ahead and the upward rise of the rocky Hill beyond. Motioning for Oates to continue to file on, he waited as his other regiments came up.

"General Chamberlain, sir."

Joshua looked up to see a sweat-soaked officer, weaving his horse through the trees, ducking low as a shell slapped overhead, bursting in the top of an elm, shearing off branches.

"Here!"

The orderly came up and saluted.

"General Robertson's compliments, sir. He is going in and requests that your left flank support his attack."

"In which direction?"

"Why straight ahead, sir," and the orderly pointed towards the valley and the open west-facing slope of the Rocky Hill.

Joshua studied the ground for a brief instant, watching as the attack pouring out of the Devil's Den started to go to ground as plunging fire rained down from the heights above. The hill might have been empty when they had started but it wasn't now. There was infantry up there, perhaps a brigade. *By heavens, if I had that hill I'd pack it with artillery and hold it till doomsday. Any attack up the open west face of the hill would be suicidal now. It had to come from the south, or better yet the eastern flank.*

He tried to study the ground. *Stuart, where was Stuart when needed?* Rumor was sweeping through the army that the Old Man was building into a rare rage over the absence of the plumed cavalier. *There should be cavalry on our flanks, probing the way, providing recon, rather than launching this attack into thin air.* He cocked his ear, listening to the battle, carefully studying the heights, ignoring the hissing hum of bullets that were plucking through the trees. *Only a brigade? A brigade was enough to hold that place. Robertson and my brigade could storm it all the day long and get nowhere. No, it had to be the flank if there was any hope.*

Fate of the nation. *Well Joshua, looks like you are the judge of that fate with what you do here.*

He took a deep breath and shook his head.

"Sir?"

"Tell General Robertson to please hold his assault and extend his line to the right," Joshua said. "Give me time to get into position. I'm moving to hit them in the rear."

"Sir, General Robertson's orders were quite clear to me," the young major announced. "Though I do not wish to do so, sir, I am forced to remind *you* that General Robertson's date of command supersedes yours, sir, and he is therefore the senior in the field."

A bullet smacked into the tree between them, showering the major with splinters and sap. Joshua remained still, watching the major's eyes as the boy flinched.

"Sir!"

Joshua's attention was turned by a freckle-faced corporal by his side, eyes wide with excitement.

"Go on, son."

"Colonel Oates' compliments, sir. He said he's a-movin' into position and begs to report that a spring has been located. He said, the Colonel said that it's a fair piece away, sir, and he reckons it'll take ten to fifteen minutes to get some of the boys there and back with water."

"Tell the Colonel to hold until I join him and to detail off men to fill canteens before we go in. Have someone pass the word to the other regiments as well."

The boy saluted and ran off.

"I don't think this is the time to wait for water," Robertson's orderly announced coolly.

"I think it is," Joshua snapped, raising his voice loud enough for the men around him to hear. "Jackson took time to see that his men were fed and watered before sending them in to die for their country and by God I'll do the same."

He hesitated for an instant. "Some folks think that I'm a Yankee and can't stand the heat. And you know something, Major, they're right, but on this day I think many a Southern-born boy is feeling it as well. So I want them to have water before they go in. The additional ten minutes might decide this day, Major. Please inform General Robertson that I beg to decline his"—he paused for a moment, carefully choosing his words—"request to use my regiments. We shall assault the Rocky Hill from the south and east on the flank."

He could see that the major was about to offer an objection. *Southerners*, Joshua thought. *Lord how I do love them but at times they can be so damned argumentative.*

"That is all, Major," Joshua snapped. "Now if you will be so kind as to excuse me," he added working in a flourish of Virginian drawl, "I have a battle to fight."

Joshua turned and moving quickly he darted back down the line. As he passed each of his regiments he called for the unit commander to follow him.

It'll take the boy ten, maybe fifteen minutes to find Robertson, Joshua thought. *If Robertson comes over personally that will be another fifteen to twenty minutes, time enough for me to get in and make it an accomplished fact before he can countermand me.*

I should be playing it safe. Follow the letter of my orders, bow to Robertson's request. Fight my brigade well and I'll come through proven in my first command as a general. Secure then.

Joshua shook his head angrily, surprised as a mild curse escaped him. No, that was not Old Tom's way. He wanted brigadiers who fought using their brains and seizing the moment. Any fool can charge, too much of that in this army, in that respect Longstreet was right. He thought of an argument he had had with one of Pete's division commanders, Pickett. The fool dreamed of a grand frontal assault, big Napoleonic charge and the Yankees would run for certain. Something personal in the insult there, that northern-born boys were cowards. *It had almost come to an out and out fight when I defended the mettle of the typical Union soldier. No, up here, defending their home ground, they'll dig in and fight like hell.*

Drifting through the woods, he passed down his line, nodding encouragement, always checking his left, judging the curve of the hill ahead. Seemed to have a spur extending southward then curving a bit to the east. At least he reached the end of his line, the standard of the 44th Alabama hanging limp in the heavy humid air, Oates and his staff gathered beneath it. The other regimental commanders, having followed Joshua down to the end of the line, gathered around expectantly.

"Water?" Joshua asked.

"Detail coming in with it now, sir," Oates announced. Joshua looked over his shoulder and saw a couple of dozen men, burdened down with canteens, coming in from the hill behind them. Eager hands reached out to snatch the precious liquid. He saw squads of men dashing through the woods behind them to resupply his other regiments.

"Right. Now listen carefully. We don't know what's up there. Wish we had time to properly look around, we don't. We can hope their attention is fixed to the front but they'd be fools not to cover this side. We start off with the 4th Alabama on the left of our line."

He looked over at the unit commander, Lieutenant Colonel Scruggs. "Hit straight in on the south. Next the 48th on their flank, then the 47th. Try and break around to the southeast. Forty-fourth and 15th will hold in reserve. Understand?"

The men nodded.

"Get back to your commands. Colonel Scruggs, no need to wait. As soon as you get back to your men, go in."

"Sir, what about Robertson on my left flank? It's already stretched too thin."

"Let them follow you."

"A hole might open."

"Colonel, do you honestly think they'll counterattack? They'd be fools to come down off that hill. Let your flank take care of itself. Now go!"

Scruggs grinned, saluted and, with a whoop of delight, raced back down the line, the other commanders following after him. Joshua looked over at Oates.

"Bit unorthodox, sir," Oates announced dryly. "*En echelon* means coming in after Robertson and hugging his flank."

Joshua knew that Oates was not happy with his new brigadier. Law was an old friend and Joshua was an interloper from another corps.

"Well, Oates, if it fails, you'll have your friend back in command."

Oates was silent for a moment.

"Thanks for waiting for the water, sir. My men were suffering, I hate that."

Joshua nodded, hands clasped behind his back, waiting nervously.

A high quavering scream erupted on the left. Scruggs was going in. Unable to contain himself Joshua stepped forward, motioning for Oates to wait.

He saw Scruggs' line burst through the woods, surging down into the narrow valley, the men charging, rifles held high. They hit the slope of the hill and started up. A wall of smoke blossomed halfway up, men tumbling over, splinters of wood, broken branches swirling upwards. The charge of the 48th came in on their flank, overlapping the line, and the ripple of smoke on the hill extended southward, then to the southeast slope. *So they were wrapped around the flank like a fishhook*, Joshua thought. *Exactly what I'd do.*

The 47th went in next, sweeping past where Joshua stood, the power of the charge sucking him into the vortex of the fighting. Wild, mad, passionate screams erupted around him, the rebel yell corkscrewing down his spine so that his own voice was added as he rushed forward, bounding over boulders, leaping past men falling to his front and either side.

Pausing for a second he looked up the hill. It was impossible to see the other line, concealed now behind a curtain of yellow-gray smoke which was punctuated by flashes of dull red light. The charge was slowing, his own men were hunkering down, crouched behind trees and rocky outcroppings, firing up. Here and there along the line knots of men surged forward, gaining another dozen yards before being beaten down, desperately clinging to their gains or slipping back down the slope.

Joshua paced down the line, urging his men to keep up their fire, shouting encouragement. Men of the 47th started to work their way to the right and, up on the hill, he saw where the wall of fire ended. As the men of the 47th extended their line to the right he saw blue-clad forms dodging through the trees, leaping over rocks, staying low, extending their own line.

Another charge by the 47th went up the slope, this time pushing straight into the Union lines and for an instant he thought they had broken through. A wild melee of hand-to-hand combat erupted and then the gray and butternut surge slipped back down the slope like a tide retreating from a rock-bound coast. Men of three regiments were now intermingled, all of them pouring fire up the slope, surging ahead, falling back, surging ahead yet again.

Damn good fighters up there, Joshua thought. *Not many Union troops would hold against such a bayonet charge.* And then his heart froze. For an instant the smoke parted and he saw the flag, the dark blue banner of Maine, rippling on the skyline as its bearer defiantly waved the colors back and forth. Next to the colors he saw him and knew. How could one not know his own blood, even if it was just a glimpse captured for a second in the mad confusion of war.

Tears filled his eyes, blinding him. He turned away and saw a young tow-haired boy, scalp bleeding from a shot which had creased his brow, raising his rifle up, taking careful aim. Joshua reached out and pushed the rifle up even as the boy squeezed the trigger.

Startled the boy looked up at him. Joshua gulped hard. "You were aiming at my brother," Joshua whispered.

Wide-eyed the boy looked at him and then nodded. "Sorry, sir."

"All right, son, just shoot somewhere else," Joshua replied.

Shoot somewhere else. What old friend from Maine had he just condemned by that? *Let not this cup come to my lips oh Lord,* he thought, *yet by having the cup pass, who else was doomed now instead?*

Joshua looked back up the slope. Tom had always turned to Joshua for approval in all things, the younger seeking the elder. He watched how Tom was handling his regiment. He had chosen his ground well, not on the crest where he'd be silhouetted, halfway down instead, barricaded in behind the boulders. Tom stood up. Joshua held his breath as his brother sprinted along the line, obliviously extending it out, bending it back as the men of the 47th pushed around the flank.

Tom stopped, looking down the slope as if gauging where the next blow would hit and for an instant Joshua wondered if Tom could see him. The smoke closed around them and Tom was lost to view.

The 47th ran forward yet again, the rebel yell echoing, the men going up grimly, pushing hard and then falling back. Forcing himself to concentrate, Joshua gauged the defense. They were on the end of the line here. He stepped back, studying the ground behind him and to his own flank. His own flank. A low stone wall was barely visible fifty maybe seventy-five yards to the right and rear. Suspicious, he grabbed a sergeant passing by with a squad moving to the flank.

"Sergeant, head over to that wall," Joshua ordered.

"Sir, that's the wrong way to the fight."

"Just do it."

The sergeant shrugged, saluted wearily and motioned for his men to follow. The sergeant had barely made it halfway to the wall when a flurry of shots rang out, dropping several of the men in the squad.

Startled, the men of the 47th looked over their shoulders. *So they had a flanking force out to catch us*, Joshua thought. *Good work, Tom.*

Joshua hailed a captain, ordered him to detail his company off to sweep the wall and then sprinted back through the valley and up the slope to where his two reserve regiments waited.

As he reached Oates and Perry of the 15th, Joshua saw Robertson riding up, hat off, swearing at the top of his lungs for Perry and Oates to fall in and support him.

Joshua stepped between his two regimental commanders and Robertson.

"General Chamberlain, just what the hell are you doing leaving me unsupported?" Robertson roared. "Damn all to hell, sir, I order you to detail off your reserve to support my flank as I go in. Thanks to you I've yet to commit for fear of losing my flank."

"Sir, I request that it be the other way around," Chamberlain replied. "I've found their flank; it's in the air."

Again there was a moment of hesitation. It was Tom he was about to do this to.

Robertson looked down at him coldly.

"If General Hood was here," Joshua added, "I think he'd agree."

"Hood is down," Robertson snapped, "I'm in command of the division now."

"Then, sir, I beg you, let us do what General Hood would have wanted. Have you committed your front yet?"

"No damn you, Chamberlain, I couldn't without leaving my right wide open."

"Sir, look," Chamberlain said hurriedly and with the point of his sword he traced out the hill in the dirt, their position and described his plan.

Robertson looked down coldly.

Joshua finished and looked up at Robertson. "Sir, I was at the conference with Hood and Longstreet. It's what Hood wanted all along. We can still do it. But we have to do it now."

Robertson hesitated, then finally nodded.

"Damnation, Chamberlain, this better work or Pete will have your stars and mine."

"Sir, it's a hell of a lot better than trying to charge up that forward slope," Joshua shouted, pointing towards the inferno in front of Little Round Top. "In all this confusion they won't realize we've stripped this part of the line and even if they did they'd be insane to come down off that high ground."

"All right, go."

Joshua saluted and turning he grabbed Oates and Perry. "Follow me!"

At the double Joshua started back down across the valley and seconds later he heard the rhythmic clatter of the two regiments following him, tin cups and half-full canteens banging on hips, shoes and bare feet slapping on rocky ground. Racing behind the 47th Joshua kept his eye on the hill, slowing for a minute as his twin columns swept over the low stone wall where men of the 47th were pushing back the light flanking force. He looked down at a dead Union soldier . . . red felt Maltese cross on his hat, brass letters and numbers 20 & B underneath the cross.

Tom, may God forgive me, Joshua silently prayed. *Was there something in the Bible about this, about two brothers, both driven by honor to face each other as enemies for what they believed was right? Too much now, can't remember.*

Stopping, he motioned for Perry to pivot and go in over the men of the 47th. The charge of the 15th Alabama went up the hill, disappearing into the smoke. The crescendo of fire was deafening. He waited; it had to be timed right. How long have we been hitting them? An hour, two hours? Hard to tell.

The seconds passed, volleys tearing through the woods.

Four regiments now against Tom. Damn, the boy was putting up a hell of a fight. Can't hold much longer now. Have to keep my own reserve together and wait a few more minutes for the 15th to break through or wring the last ounce of fight out of them.

Suddenly he saw men coming back down the hill, a few at first, wounded, but then more, some men backing away, others running. The sight that greeted him was startling and he felt a sweeping pride for his younger brother and the boys who followed him. . . . They were charging by God. Rifles up, screaming like madmen, they were countercharging!

Awed, he watched the wild defiant act and in an instant he knew. They were out of ammunition, none of them were firing as they advanced, they were coming on with the bayonet alone.

"Oates!"

"Here, sir!"

"They're out of ammunition! Now's your time. Charge and take it to the top of the hill!"

With a wild scream Oates leapt forward, sword held high. The men of the 44th, rested, with sixty rounds of ammunition in their cartridge boxes and canteens still half-full broke into a swirling countercharge, advancing like all rebel units do, not in orderly lines but rather as an insane tempest of fury and raw mad courage which had carried their ancestors across a hundred fields of strife.

Up the hill they charge, Joshua at the fore, sword held high. The men of the 20th, carried away by the momentum of charging down the hill, could not stop. The two lines collided, breaking into a maelstrom of hand-to-hand combat. Rifle shots, fired mostly by rebels, were let loose at near point-blank range, dropping dozens of blue-clad defenders.

Joshua continued his charge up the hill, urging his men on as they swarmed over the 20th Maine. Running up the hill the smoke parted for an instant and an officer was before him, pistol raised, aimed straight at Joshua's face.

Time seemed to slow, to distort out. He saw the gaping bore of the Remington .44, finger around the trigger, already starting to draw back, and then the cool steel-gray eye behind the sight. Joshua slowed to a stop, the barrel inches from his face and he looked into the eye, saw a flicker of astonishment and of pain.

"Tom, don't," Joshua sighed, "Not for me, but it would be a hard day for Mother if you do."

The gun dropped, tears clouding Tom's eyes. Joshua reached out and put his hand on his brother's shoulder.

"Stay close to me, Tom." Taking the revolver so Tom would not be mistaken for someone still in the fight, Joshua continued to press up the hill.

Men of the 20th tried to scramble ahead of them, gasping for breath, tongues lolling, features pale and drawn, stamped with the blank stares of exhaustion and despair. Joshua was thankful that the men of the 44th recognized that the men from Maine were finished, played out, the regiment overrun and were simply leaving them behind. They swept past the shattered unit, a few men left behind to gather in the prisoners. The charge continued to swarm up the slope, the men of the 15th having rallied and following in its wake, adding weight to their advance. To his left he saw the ranks of the 47th and 48th advancing, rolling up the units that had been on the 20th Maine's right.

As they neared the crest a ragged volley greeted them. The charge slowed for an instant and then pressed forward, crashing into the rear of the units defending the crest of Little Round Top.

In an instant all semblance of defense broke down, the men of the 44th and 15th swarming up over the battery of guns which were pointing down the will to the west.

All along the crown of the heights a wall of blue broke

and started to pour northward. In the valley of death below, Confederate troops who had fought their way through the Devil's Den were up, cheering hysterically as the regimental flags of the Alabama regiments fluttered on the heights. Like a wall collapsing, the Union line shattered, the breakup rolling down the slope of Little Round Top and on out into the Wheat Field, red Saint Andrew's crosses surging ahead. Joshua paused, taking in the sight, awestruck by what his charge had unleashed.

Some of the men around Joshua struggled to turn one of the field pieces northward and, without bothering to aim, fired a defiant shot towards the Union regiments deployed out along the southern reaches of Cemetery Ridge. He could see men turning, looking up towards the heights crowned with the battle standards of the Army of Northern Virginia. He could sense the panic rippling down the line, striking into the very heart of the Army of the Potomac like an icy blade.

"By God, sir, I've never seen anything like it!"

Joshua turned to see Robertson scrambling over the rocks, his brigade storming forward over the eastern flank of the crest, having marched around behind Joshua's brigade while he had charged up the slope. Robertson's men surged forward, pushing on down into the rear of the Union lines.

"We're already into their supply wagons," Robertson roared. "It's chaos down there. Mad panic. We've cut the Taneytown Road. We'll be across the Baltimore Pike soon, by God! Between them and Washington, Joshua! Washington, sir, we're on out way to Washington!"

Joshua sighed. The heat, the damnable heat, and ever so slowly he sat down, unable to speak.

"Joshua?"

He looked up. It was Tom.

"How are you, Tom?"

"Tolerable, Joshua, tolerable."

"Your men?"

"Every officer dead or wounded. Maybe ten, twenty enlisted men got away. The rest, well, you have the rest."

"They fought like tigers, Tom. You should be proud of them." He hesitated, "I would have been proud to lead them."

"But you didn't, Joshua, you didn't. I did." Tom looked at him with mournful eyes. "Why, Joshua? You should have been with us. Why?"

Joshua was unable to reply. *Why indeed? Do I believe in this cause? In Virginia, yes. But I believe in Maine as well. Believed in the Union and still hate slavery. Yet I brought victory to the South. God, where is the answer to this?*

Tom sat down by his brother's side, gaze fixed on the western horizon. Twilight was settling in, the distant ridgeline of the South Mountains silhouetted by the deep indigo blue of the gathering night. A roll of thunder disturbed them and, looking back to the east and north, he saw flashes of light, as if a summer storm was driving eastward. The pursuit was spreading out, pushing down the Baltimore Pike, Hanover Pike and to Washington beyond. In the valley below all that was left of the old Third Corps and most of the Fifth Corps were being gathered in by their captors.

Word was that Hancock was dead, Meade wounded and captured. Howard was in command. Poor Howard, good Maine man, a Christian warrior, but up to a fighting withdrawal? *The army has no confidence in him, still blames him unfairly for the fiasco at Chancellorsville.* Joshua shook his head at the thought.

Stuart was at last doing something right, coming down out of the north as if by plan, falling on their retreating columns, triggering panic and pushing the pursuit through the night. First and Eleventh Corps had been destroyed on the first day of battle. Third, Fifth, and most of Second on the second day. Only the sixth and

Twelfth were relatively intact but word was coming back that they were now disintegrating into a rabble on the roads heading east as Stuart's boys slashed in out of the darkness. The grand old Army of the Potomac was already fading into history.

A band, tinny and out of tune, was playing "Dixie." He saw a cavalcade of horsemen bearing torches, moving across the open fields, heading up to Cemetery Ridge, a lone figure on a gray horse in the middle, cheers echoing up around them.

"Must be your Lee going forward," Tom sighed.

"He's a good man, Tom, a good Christian."

"So I heard."

Joshua looked over at Tom.

"You want to tell me something, don't you?"

Tom nodded.

"Go on, we could always talk."

"When I was below, seeing about my wounded, Longstreet came up to me, asked if I was your brother."

"And?"

"Told him I was. Longstreet said you were the hero of the battle. You won it with your charge. Won the war as well most likely. Chamberlain's Charge, he said they'd call it. Heard someone else say they were giving you Hood's division to command. Everyone's talking about you, Joshua, saying you could go home, be Governor of Virginia, maybe even a President of the Confederacy some day."

Funny, the thought of afterwards had never occurred to Joshua until now. It was Jackson, his friend whom he had fought for. But Jackson was dead.

"Joshua?"

"Yes, Tom."

"I guess you did good. Maybe some day we'll meet here again, be able to shake hands. Your Alabama boys aren't a bad sort. Once the fighting was done they pitched in to help my wounded, said we were a tough lot and good opponents. Some of them are helping to bury our dead. Strange, you and I, all of us, brothers. We try to kill each other, then weep over out dead together. Strange war.

"Joshua, are you proud of what you did?"

The question startled him. Jackson would have been proud. What happened this day was always his dream—the decisive battle, the one that decides a war, rather than the half victories of the past. *Maybe some day I'll understand this, be able to write about it, but now? Come back here later to think about it all, sort things out, to try and figure out the why of it and the reason fate put me here. The biggest question though ... just where is home after this, which country is mine?*

"A hard day for Mother you said," Tom whispered. "You were right. This will be a hard day for Mother, Joshua. A very hard day when she learns of what you accomplished."

Joshua nodded, unable to reply. Fate of the nation, Hood said. He looked across the summit of Little Round Top and could indeed see that he had shaped the fate of a nation. *Fate put me here, now what shall I do?*

Patting Tom on the shoulder he stood up, looking off to the north. A flash of light erupted, followed long seconds later by a distant rumble. By the glow of the campfire of his headquarters he saw the battle standards taken this day, the flag of the 20th Maine in the center. Drawing himself up to attention he saluted the colors, then turning, disappeared into the night.

Gettysburg, Little Round Top, July 2, 1913

My fellow comrades, soldiers of the South and North. We are gathered here today on this the fiftieth anniversary of the battle that decided the war. The years have drifted by as a dream. I have been haunted my entire life by the memory of so many boys I had once led into battle and those from my home state who stood against us and who shall be forever young. Their honored graves are just below us, resting forever in the shadow of the hill where so many of us gave the last full measure of devotion.

My comrades, I call upon us all to highly resolve that these dead shall not have died in vain.

Little did I expect, never did I dream that my country would call me to one last duty, to hold the exalted office of the Presidency of my adopted country. Yes, my adopted country. For Presidents Lee, Longstreet, Stuart and others were born of the South while I, guided by the Divine Will, was of the North.

If fate had been but slightly different I might very well have worn the honored uniform of blue as my brother did and stood upon this hill in defense of the Union. That thought has haunted me these past fifty years and has shaped all that I have become. I have repeatedly asked of our Creator why was I fated to be here at this, the deciding place of the war.

I think now that I understand. So much that once divided us is in the past. Slavery is dead, ordered so by President Lee. Both nations have learned the need for the power of a central government to be circumscribed by the wishes of the people through their respective states.

We comrades who once struggled to kill now extend to each other the hand of friendship. And I must ask, why should not that clasp of friendship be a permanent bond yet again? I wish now to present to you the inner dream, which first dimly took form, so long ago, when I saw the glorious banners of my brigade take this hill, and beside them, the glorious and unsullied banners of the state that gave me birth . . .

Speech by the President of the Confederate States of America Joshua Lawrence Chamberlain, which paved the way for the Referendum of National Reunification ratified by both Congresses on July 4, 1914. Joshua Chamberlain died four months before the reunification of the North and the South at the age of eighty-three, as a result of wounds received while leading his division on July 8, 1863, during the capture of Washington, D.C.

THE CAPTAIN FROM KIRKBEAN
David M. Weber

Captain Sir John Paul stood on the quarterdeck of
His Majesty's seventy-four-gun ship-of-the-line *Torbay*,
shading his eyes against the Caribbean's brilliant August
sunlight. *Torbay*, the seventy-four *Triumph*, and the
sixty-four *Prince William*, were four days out of Antigua
with a Jamaica-bound convoy, and he lowered his hand
from his eyes to rub thoughtfully at the buttons on his
blue coat's lapel—twelve golden buttons, in groups of
three, indicating a captain with more than three years'
seniority—as he watched the sloop *Lark*'s cutter pull
strongly towards his ship.

The cutter swept around, coming up under *Torbay*'s
lee as the seventy-four lay hove to. The bow man neatly
speared the big ship's main chains with his boathook,
and the officer in the stern leapt for the battens on her
tall side. A lazy swell licked up after him, soaking him
to the waist, but he climbed quickly to the entry port,
nodded to the lieutenant who raised his hat in salute,
and then hurried aft.

"Well, Commander Westman," Captain Paul said dryly.
"I trust whatever brings you here was worth a wetting?"

"I believe so, sir." *Lark*'s captain touched his hat—no
junior dared omit any proper courtesy to Sir John—then
reached inside his coat. "*Lark* sighted a drifting ship's
boat yesterday evening, sir. When I investigated, I

discovered three Frenchmen—one dead officer and two seamen in but little better shape—from the naval brig *Alecto*. She foundered in a squall last week . . . but the officer had this on his person."

He held out a thick packet of papers. Paul took it, glanced at it, then looked up quickly.

"I, ah, felt it best to deliver it to you as soon as possible, sir," Westman said.

"You felt correctly, Commander," Paul replied almost curtly, then beckoned to the officer of the watch. "Lieutenant Chessman, make a signal. All captains are to repair aboard *Torbay* immediately!"

It was sweltering in Sir John's day cabin, despite the open windows, as Captain Forest was shown in. *Prince William*'s commander had had the furthest to come, and he was acutely aware that he was the last captain to arrive . . . and that Captain Paul did not tolerate tardiness. But Sir John said nothing. He didn't even turn. He stood gazing out into the sun dazzle, hands clasped behind him and lost in memory, while his steward offered Forest wine. His fixed gaze saw not the Caribbean's eye-hurting brightness but the seething gray waste of the Channel and surf spouting white on a rocky shore as Sir Edward Hawke's squadron pursued Admiral Conflans into Quiberon Bay.

By most officers' standards, Hawke had been mad to follow an enemy into shoal water in a rising November gale when that enemy had local pilots and he did not. But Hawke had recognized his duty to keep the invasion army gathered round nearby Vannes in Brittany, not England. Confident of his captains and crews, he had driven Conflans' more powerful squadron onto the rocks or up the Vilaine River in an action which had cost the French seven ships of the line and almost three thousand men in return for only two of his own ships.

Quiberon had been the final triumph of what was still

called the "Year of Victories," and Midshipman John Paul of Kirkbean, Scotland, serving in the very ship Captain Sir John Paul now commanded, had seen it all. *Torbay* had been the second ship in Hawke's line, under Captain Augustus Keppel, and young Paul had watched—twelve years old and terrified for his very life—as broadsides roared and a sudden squall sent the sea crashing in through the lee gunports of the French seventy-four *Thésée* and drove her to the bottom in minutes.

Paul would never forget her crew's screams, or his own ship's desperate efforts to save even a few of them from drowning, but more even than that, he remembered the lesson Hawke had taught him that day as he turned to face the captains seated around his table with their wine. Every one of them was better born than he, but John Paul, the son of a Scottish gardener—the boy who'd found a midshipman's berth only because his father had aided the wife of one of Keppel's cousins after a coach accident—was senior to them all.

Which means, he thought wryly, *that it is I who have the honor of placing my entire career in jeopardy by whatever I do or do not decide this day.*

It was ironic that twenty years of other officers' reminders of their superior birth should bring him here. *Under other circumstances, I might well have been on the other side,* he mused. *Traitors or no, at least the rebels believe the measure of a man should be* himself, *not whom he chose as his father!*

But no sign of that thought showed on his face, and his voice was crisp, with no trace of the lowland brogue he'd spent two decades eradicating, as he tapped the papers Westman had brought him and spoke briskly.

"Gentlemen, thanks to Commander Westman"—he nodded to *Lark*'s captain—"we have intercepted copies of correspondence from de Grasse to Washington." The others stiffened, and he smiled thinly. "This copy is numbered '2' and addressed to Commodore de Barras at Newport for his information, and I believe it to be genuine. Which means, gentlemen, that I've decided to revise our present orders somewhat."

"Toss oars!" the coxswain barked, and Captain Paul watched with carefully hidden approval as the dripping blades rose in perfect unison and the bow man hooked onto *Torbay*'s chains. The captain stood, brushing at the dirt stains on his breeches, and then climbed briskly up his ship's side. Pipes wailed, pipeclay drifted from white crossbelts as Marines slapped their muskets, and his first lieutenant removed his hat in salute.

Paul acknowledged the greeting curtly. In point of fact, he approved of Mathias Gaither, *Torbay*'s senior lieutenant, but he had no intention of telling Gaither so. He knew he was widely regarded as a tyrant—a man whose prickly disposition and insatiable desire for glory more than made up for his small stature. And, he admitted, there was justice in that view of him.

The motley human material which crewed any King's ship demanded stern discipline, yet unlike many captains, Paul's discipline was absolutely impartial, and he loathed bullies and officers who played favorites. He was also sparing with the lash, given his belief that flogging could not make a bad man into a good one but could certainly perform the reverse transformation. Yet he had no mercy on *anyone*, officer or seaman, who failed to meet his harshly demanding standards, for he knew the sea and the enemy were even less forgiving than he. And if he sought glory, what of it? For a man of neither birth nor wealth, success in battle was not simply a duty but the only path to advancement, and Paul had seized renown by the throat two years before, off Flamborough Head in HMS *Serapis*, when he sank the American "frigate" *Bonhomme Richard*. The old, converted East Indiaman had fought gallantly, but her ancient guns, rotten hull, and wretched maneuverability had been no match for his own well-found vessel. Her consort, the thirty-six-gun *Alliance*, could have been much more dangerous, but *Alliance*'s captain—a Frenchman named Landais—had been an outright Bedlamite, and Paul had entered port with *Alliance* under British colors.

His knighthood—and *Torbay*—had been his reward for that . . . and now he was risking it all.

He grimaced at the thought and headed aft to pace his scorching quarterdeck. If anything befell the convoy, his decision to order it back to Antigua escorted by a single sloop would ruin him, and he knew it. Worse, the orders he had elected to ignore had come from Sir George Rodney, who was even less noted for tolerating disobedience than Paul himself. But at least he also understood the value of initiative. If events justified Paul's decision, Rodney would forgive him; if they didn't, the admiral would destroy him.

He paused in his pacing and beckoned Gaither to his side.

"Yes, sir?"

"Lieutenant Jansen needs more men. General Cornwallis has supplied ample labor and a battalion to picket each battery, but Jansen needs more gunners. Instruct the Gunner to select a half-dozen gun captains—men with experience using heated shot."

"Yes, sir. I'll see to it at once."

"Thank you." Paul nodded brusquely and resumed his pacing as Gaither summoned a midshipman. He heard the lieutenant giving the lad quiet instructions, but his mind was back on the scene he'd just left ashore.

It was August 25, 1781. His squadron had taken the better part of nine days to reach Chesapeake Bay, but he'd picked up two more of the line along the way, having met the old sixty-gun *Panther* in the Caicos Passage, and the seventy-four *Russel*, bound for New York after repairing damages at Antigua, off the Georgia coast. Jasper Somers, *Russel*'s captain, was barely two months junior to Paul, and he had been less than pleased by the latter's peremptory order to join *Torbay*. Paul hadn't blamed Somers, though that hadn't prevented him from commandeering *Russel* with profound relief. But welcome as her guns were, the ship accompanying her to New York had been even more welcome. HMS *Serapis* had brought him luck once before; perhaps she would do so again.

Something had better do so. He had five of the line, counting *Panther* (which was considerably older than *he* was), plus *Serapis*, the forty-four *Charon* (which he'd found anchored off Yorktown with the small frigates *Guadalupe* and *Fowey* and the tiny sloop *Bonetta*), and Westman's *Lark*. That was all, whereas de Grasse must have *at least* twenty sail of the line. That force could smash Paul's cobbled up command in an hour, and he knew it.

But he also knew General Rochambeau and the rebel Washington were headed south with far more men and artillery than Cornwallis could muster. If de Grasse could command the bay long enough for the Franco-American army to crush Yorktown, the consequences would be catastrophic. Efforts against the rebellion had been botched again and again, and support back home had weakened with each failure. Personally, Paul suspected the colonies were lost whatever happened, and the sooner the Crown admitted it, the better. America wasn't Ireland. There was an entire ocean between Britain and her rebellious colonists, and they couldn't be disarmed with the wilderness pressing so close upon them. Besides, England couldn't possibly field a large enough army to hold them down by force forever.

But personal doubt didn't change the duty of a King's officer. And even if it could have, the war was no longer solely about America. It might have started there, but

England now faced the French, the Dutch, the Spanish. . . . The entire world had taken up arms against Paul's country. One more major defeat might seal not only the fate of North America but of England herself, and Washington, at least, grasped that point thoroughly. He'd wanted the French fleet to support an attack on the main British base at New York, but de Grasse's letters made it clear he could come no further north than the Chesapeake. Apparently Louis XVI's willingness to aid his American "allies" did not extend to uncovering his own Caribbean possessions or convoys.

None of which would make a successful combination against Cornwallis any less of a calamity, and Paul's jaw clenched. He respected Rodney deeply, but the last year had not been Sir George's finest. True, his health was atrocious, but his absorption in the capture of St. Eustatius from the Dutch and his inexplicable refusal to force an engagement in June, following de Grasse's capture of Tobago, had set the stage for the present danger.

Without control of American waters, we can't possibly wear the rebels down, Paul thought grimly, *and if the Frogs can win sea control* here, *they may take control of the Channel, as well.* Holding *it would be another matter, but they only require control long enough to land an army. And the only way to ensure that they can't is to smash their fleet—which means fighting them at every possible opportunity, even at unfavorable odds. Those who will not risk, cannot win. Hawke understood that, and so should Rodney!*

He shook himself. Rodney *did* understand, but he was a sick man who had been given reason to believe de Grasse was bound back to Europe, escorting a major French convoy. That was why he'd elected to return to England himself and sent Sir Samuel Hood to assume command at New York after Admiral Graves' unexpected death, with only fourteen of the line as reinforcements.

But Rodney's intelligence sources had been wrong . . . and Sir John Paul was the senior officer who knew it.

That made it *his* responsibility to act. He could have taken his captured letters to New York, but Hood had strongly endorsed Rodney's estimate of de Grasse's intentions, and he was renowned for his stubbornness. Changing his mind could require days England might no longer have, and so Paul had taken matters into his own hands. He would *compel* Hood to sail for the Chesapeake by taking his own small force there and sending dispatches to announce what he'd done.

Samuel Hood was arrogant, stiff-necked, and contentious, but he was also a fighter who would have no *choice* but to sail south once he learned Paul had committed a mere five of the line to a fight to the death against an entire fleet. If Paul's estimate of de Grasse's intentions proved wrong, he could always be punished later. If it proved correct, Hood's failure to relieve him would be an ineradicable blot on not only his personal honor but that of the Navy itself.

Paul drew a deep breath and walked to the side, looking out at his command. To a landsman, his ships must look small and fragile, isolated from one another as each lay to a pair of anchors, but he saw with a seaman's eye. The mouth of the Chesapeake was ten miles wide, and no squadron this small could cover it all. Yet for all its size, the shallow bay was a dangerous place for deep-draft ships-of-the-line. Paul didn't have to block its entire entrance: only the parts of it de Grasse's heavy ships could use.

That was why *Russel* and *Charon* were anchored between the shoals known as the Middle Ground and the Inner Middle Ground, blocking the channel there, while *Triumph*, *Panther*, *Serapis*, *Prince William*, and *Torbay* blocked the wider channel between the Inner Middle Ground and the shoal called the Tail of the Horseshoe. And because they had anchored on springs—

heavy hawsers led from each ship's capstan out an after gunport and thence to her anchor cable, so that tightening or loosening them pivoted her in place—they could turn to fire full broadsides at any Frenchmen attempting to force the channels.

Unfortunately, there were two other ways into the bay. One, the North Channel, between the Middle Ground and Fisherman's Island at the north side of the entrance, was no great threat. Landing parties and detachments from Cornwallis' army had emplaced twelve of *Prince William's* twenty-four-pounders—and furnaces to heat shot for them—on the island, and the channel was narrow enough for them to command easily.

The southern side of the Bay's entrance was more dangerous. Lynnhaven Roads, inside Cape Henry, was shallow, but it would suffice. Indeed, it was in most ways an ideal anchorage: sheltered by the cape, yet close enough to open water for a fleet to sortie quickly if an enemy approached. But Paul's ships were stretched as thinly as he dared blocking the channels; he couldn't possibly bar Lynnhaven Roads as well.

What he *could* do was place a second battery on the western side of Cape Henry, although Lieutenant Jansen was finding it difficult to mount his guns. Simply ferrying them ashore was hard enough, for the battery consisted of thirty-two-pounders from the seventy-fours. Each gun weighed over two and a half tons, but only their three-thousand-yard range could hope to cover the water between the cape and *Torbay*, and at least Jansen had finally found a place to site them.

I've done all I can, Paul told himself, gazing out at the boats pulling back and forth across the water. *Something must be left to chance in a fight . . . and simply finding us waiting for him should at least make de Grasse cautious. I hope.*

He shook himself as the ship's bell chimed eight times to announce the turn of the forenoon watch. His stomach

growled as the bell reminded it he'd missed breakfast
yet again, and he grinned wryly and took himself below
in search of a meal.

"It would appear you were correct, Sir John," Captain
Somers said quietly, five days later.

He and Paul stood gazing at a chart of the Chesapeake
while *Torbay* creaked softly around them, and Commander
Westman stood to one side. *Fitting that Westman should
be the one to sight de Grasse's approach*, a corner of Paul's
brain mused, but it was a distant thought beside the
strength estimate *Lark* had brought him.

Twenty-eight of the line. *Six times* his strength, and
no sign of Hood. It was one thing to know his duty, he
found; it was quite another to know a desperately unequal
battle which had been only a probability that morning
had become a certainty by evening.

"What d'you expect them to do?" Somers asked, and
Paul rubbed his chin, eyes fixed on the chart in the
candlelight.

"They'll scout first," he said. "For all de Grasse knows,
we're the entire New York squadron. But he won't need
long to determine our actual strength, and I expect he'll
try a quick attack then. He'll have the flood only until
the end of the morning watch; after that, the ebb will
make the channels even shallower."

"Um." It was Somers' turn to rub his chin, then nod.
"I think you're right," he said, and grinned suddenly. "I
was none too pleased when you pressed my ship, Sir
John. Now—"

He shrugged, grinning more broadly, and held out his
hand.

The morning was cool but carried promise of yet
another scorching afternoon as Paul came on deck.
Although the ship had cleared for action before dawn,
he'd taken time for a leisurely breakfast. It hadn't been

easy to sit and eat with obvious calm, but this would be a long day, and he would need all his energy. Even more importantly, *Torbay*'s crew must know he was so confident he'd seen no reason to skip a meal.

If only they knew the truth, he mused, and glanced at the masthead commission pendant to check the wind. Still from the west-southwest. Good. That would make it more difficult for any Frenchman to creep around Cape Henry into Lynnhaven Roads.

He lowered his eyes to the guard boats pulling for their mother ships. The French were scarcely noted for initiative in such matters, but in de Grasse's shoes Paul would certainly have attempted a boat attack, for the French squadron had more than enough men and small craft to swamp his vessels. However unlikely Frenchmen were to make such an attempt, he'd had no option but to guard against the possibility, and he hoped de Grasse would delay long enough for those boat crews to get some rest.

He looked up once more to where Lieutenant Gaither perched in the mizzen crosstrees. Paul would have preferred to be up there himself, but that would have revealed too much anxiety, and so he had to wait while Gaither peered through his telescope. It seemed to take forever, though it could actually have been no more than ten minutes before Gaither started down. He reached the deck quickly, and Paul raised an eyebrow in silent question.

"More than half of them are still hull down to the east-sou'east, sir," Gaither replied, "but a dozen of the line— all two-deckers, I believe—and two frigates are four or five miles east of Cape Henry. As nearly as I can estimate, their course is west-nor'west and they're making good perhaps four knots."

"I see." Paul rubbed his chin. De Grasse's maneuvers showed more caution than he'd dared hope for. He himself would have closed with all the force he had, yet he had to admit that, properly handled, a dozen of the line would more than suffice to destroy his squadron.

Assuming, of course, that the French knew what to do with them.

He squinted up at the cloudless sky. The flood would continue to make for another three hours, during which the rising tide would be available to refloat a ship which touched bottom coming in. In his enemy's place, Paul would have begun the attack the moment the tide began making, but it seemed the French had no desire to *attack*. Their course was for the North Channel, apparently in order to exploit the "unguarded" chink in Paul's defenses rather than risk engaging his outnumbered, anchored ships. Yet it would take them at least three hours just to reach the channel, and when they got there . . .

"Thank you, Mr. Gaither," he said after a moment, and his cold, thin smile made the quarterdeck gunners nudge one another with confident grins. He could be a right bastard, the Captain. He had a tongue that could flay a man like the cat itself, and he used it with a will. But that very sharpness lent his praise even more weight, when he gave it, and the storm or fight that could best him had never been made.

Lieutenant Wallace Hastings of HMS *Russel* and his work parties had labored frantically for six days to build the battery. In fact, he'd never thought they could finish it in time, but people had a way of not disappointing Sir John. Or, at least, of not disappointing him more than *once*. And so now Hastings and his gun crews— each with a core of naval gunners eked out by artillerists from Lord Cornwallis' army—waited as another slow, thunderous broadside rippled down *Russel's* side.

Water seethed as the roundshot slashed into the sea like an avalanche. They landed far short of the thirty-six-gun frigate gliding up the North Channel under topsails and jib, but the Frenchman altered course still further towards the east to give the seventy-four a wider berth. Which just happened to bring him less than six hundred yards from Hastings' gun muzzles.

It had been Sir John's idea to disguise the battery's raw earth with cut greenery. Personally, Hastings had never expected it to work, but it seemed he'd been wrong. More probably, *Russel*'s ostentatious efforts had riveted the French ship's attention, distracting her lookouts from the silent shore under her lee. Whatever the explanation, she was a perfect target for Hastings' gunners. Accustomed to the unsteadiness of a warship's pitching deck, they'd find hitting a ship moving at barely two knots from a rock-steady battery child's play. But Sir John's orders had been specific, and Hastings let the frigate slide past unchallenged, then spoke to the man beside him.

"We'll load in ten minutes, Mr. Gray," he told *Russel*'s gunner, never taking his eyes from the first French seventy-four following in the frigate's wake.

It was impossible for Paul to see what was happening from his position at the extreme southern end of his anchored formation, but the rumble of *Russel*'s broadsides said his plan *seemed* to be working. Now if only—

His steady pacing stopped as fresh thunder grumbled from the north.

The twenty-four-pounder lurched back, spewing flame and a stinking fogbank of smoke. *Russel*'s gunner had spent five minutes laying that gun with finicky precision, and Hastings' eyes glittered as the totally unexpected shot struck below the seventy-four's forechains and sudden consternation raged across the Frenchman's deck. The fools hadn't even cleared their starboard guns for action!

Smoke wisped up as the red-hot shot blasted deep into bone-dry timbers, and panic joined consternation as the French crew realized they were under attack with heated shot. And that the British gunners had estimated their range perfectly.

"Load!" Hastings snapped, and sweating men maneuvered shot cradles carefully, tipping fat, incandescent iron spheres down the guns' bores. Steam hissed as they hit the water-soaked wads protecting the powder charges, and the gun crews moved with purposeful speed, making final adjustments before that sizzling iron could touch their pieces off prematurely. Hand after hand rose along the battery, announcing each gun's readiness, and Hastings inhaled deeply.

"*Fire!*" he barked, and twelve guns bellowed as one.

The French seventy-four *Achille* quivered as more iron crashed into her, and rattling drums sent gun crews dashing from larboard to starboard. They cast off breech ropes, fighting to get their guns into action, but the hidden battery had taken *Achille* utterly by surprise, and men shouted in panic as flames began to lick from the red-hot metal buried in her timbers. Bucket parties tried desperately to douse the fires, but the surprise was too great, time was too short . . . and the British aim was too good. Not one shot had missed, and panic became terror as woodsmoke billowed. The flames that followed were pale in the bright sunlight, but they roared up the ship's tarred rigging like demons, and the horrible shrieks of men on fire, falling from her tops, finished off any discipline she might have clung to.

Officers shouted and beat at men with the flats of their swords, battling to restore order, but it was useless. In less than six minutes, *Achille* went from a taut, efficient warship to a doomed wreck whose terror-crazed crewmen flung themselves desperately into the water even though most had never learned to swim.

Achille's next astern, the sixty-eight *Justice*, managed to clear away her starboard guns, but the battery's earthen rampart easily absorbed her hasty broadside, and then the British guns thundered back. Every naval officer knew no ship could fight a well-sited shore battery, and Hastings smiled savagely as he and his men set out to demonstrate why.

"Captain Somers' compliments, sir, and the enemy have been beaten off!"

The fourteen-year-old midshipman was breathless from his rapid climb up *Torbay's* side, and the seamen in his boat slumped over their oars, gasping after their long, hard pull, but every one of them wore a huge grin, like an echo of the cheers which had gone up from each ship as the boat swept by her.

"The battery burned two of the line, sir—a seventy-four and a sixty-eight," the midshipman went on, "and a third ran hard aground trying to wear ship in the channel. Two more came into *Russel's* range while working their way clear—one of them lost her mizzen— and the frigate was heavily damaged on her way out."

"That's excellent news!" Paul told the panting youngster. "The first lieutenant will detail fresh oarsmen to return you to *Russel*, where you will present my compliments to Captain Somers and Lieutenant Hastings and tell them they have earned both my admiration and my thanks, as have all of their officers and men."

"Aye, aye, sir!" The midshipman's smile seemed to split his face, and Paul waved for Gaither to take him in tow, then turned to gaze out towards the open sea once more.

He'd seen the French straggling back out past the capes, just as he'd seen the smoke of the burned vessels . . . and heard their magazines explode. Whatever else might happen, de Grasse had learned he would not take the Chesapeake cheaply. Yet the French also knew about the northern battery now. They wouldn't try that approach a second time—especially not if the wind backed around to the east.

*No, if they come again, they'll try the south or the
center—or both,* he told himself, turning to watch the
sun slide steadily down the western sky. *And when they
come, they'll come to* fight, *not simply maneuver around
us.*

He gazed out over the water, hands clasped behind
him as the setting sun turned the bay to blood, and sensed
the buzz of excitement and pride which enveloped *Torbay*
and all his other ships. They'd done well, and at small
price—so far—and he wondered how many of them even
began to suspect how that would change with the morrow.

This time he climbed the mainmast himself. He'd
always had a good head for heights, but it had been years
since he'd gone scampering to the tops himself, and he
found himself breathing hard by the time he finally
reached the topmast crosstrees.

A hundred and eighty feet, he thought, recalling the
formula he'd learned so long ago as he glanced down at
the deck, still wrapped in darkness below him. *Eight-
sevenths times the square root of the height above sea
level in feet makes . . . fifteen miles' visibility?* That was
about right, and he hooked a leg around the trestle and
raised his telescope.

His mouth tightened. The wind had, indeed, backed
further around to the east. Now it blew almost due west,
and it appeared de Grasse had made up his mind to
use it. French warships and transports dotted the
brightening sea as far as Paul could see, but what drew
his attention like a lodestone was the double column of
ships-of-the-line: sixteen of them in two unequal lines,
heading straight into the bay on a following wind.

He studied them carefully, making himself accept the
sight, then closed the glass with a snap and reached for
a backstay. Perhaps it was bravado, or perhaps it was
simply the awareness that a fall to his death had become
the least of his worries, but he swung out from the

crosstrees, wrapped his legs around the stay, and slid down it like some midshipman too young and foolish to recognize his own mortality.

He sensed his officers' astonishment as his feet thumped on the planking, though it was still too dark on deck to see their faces. His hands stung from the friction of his descent, and he scrubbed them on his breeches while his steward hurried up with his coat and sword. Then he turned to Lieutenant Gaither with an expression which—if Gaither could see it—would warn him to make no comments on the manner of his descent.

But it wasn't the lieutenant who commented.

"Did y'see that, boyos?" a voice called from the dimness of the ship's waist. "Just full o' high spirits and jollification 'e is!"

Divisional officers hissed in outrage, trying to identify the speaker. But lingering night shielded the culprit, and their failure to find him emboldened another.

"Aye! 'E's a dandy one, right enough! Three cheers fer the Cap'n, lads!"

Paul opened his mouth, eyes flashing, but the first cheer rang out before he could say a word. He leaned on the quarterdeck rail, peering down at the indistinct shapes of gunners naked to the waist in the dew-wet dimness while their wild cheers surged about him like the sea, and all the while sixteen times their firepower sailed toward them through the dawn.

It ended finally, and he cleared his throat. He gazed down at them as the rising sun picked out individual faces at last, and then straightened slowly.

"Well!" he said. "I see *this* ship will never want for wind!" A rumble of laughter went up, and he smiled. But then he let his face sober and nodded towards the east.

"There's more than a dozen Frogs out there," he told them, "and most of 'em will be about our ears in the next hour." There was silence now, broken only by a voice repeating his words down the gratings to the lower gundeck. "It's going to be hot work, lads, but if we let them in, the Army will be like rats in a trap. So we're not *going* to let them in, are we?"

For an instant he thought he'd gone too far, but then a rumbling roar answered him.

"*No!*" it cried, and he nodded.

"Very well, then. Stand to your guns, and be sure of this. This is a King's ship, and so long as she floats, those colors"—he pointed at the ensign fluttering above *Torbay*—"will fly above her!"

The two French lines forged past Cape Henry, and Paul watched their fore and main courses vanish as they reduced to fighting sail. The six ships of the shorter column passed as close to the cape as they dared, bound for Lynnhaven Roads in an obvious bid to sweep up and around the southern end of his line, but the other ten pressed straight up the channel between the Middle Ground and the Tail of the Horseshoe.

He paced slowly up and down his quarterdeck, watching them come, feeling the vise of tension squeeze slowly tighter on his outnumbered men. *Torbay* quivered as Gaither took up a little more tension on the spring, keeping her double-shotted broadside pointed directly at the leading Frenchman, and Paul frowned as he estimated the range.

Two thousand yards, he thought. *Call it another twenty minutes.*

He paused and turned his eyes further south, where the other French column was now coming abeam of Cape Henry.

Any time, now . . .

A brilliant eye winked from the still-shadowed western side of the cape, and the ball howled like a lost soul as it crossed the bow of the massive three-decker leading the French line. A white plume rose from the bay, over five hundred yards beyond her—which meant she was well within reach of Lieutenant Jansen's guns—and then a long, dull rumble swept over the water as two dozen thirty-two-pounders bellowed.

Screaming ironshot tore apart the water around the French ship, and Paul's hands clenched behind him as her foremast thundered down across her deck. She staggered as the foremast dragged her main topgallant mast after it, and a second and third salvo smashed into her even as she returned fire against the half-seen battery. Smoke curled up out of the wreckage as the heated shot went home, or perhaps a coil of tarred cordage or a fold of canvas had fallen across one of her own guns as it fired. It hardly mattered. What mattered was the sudden column of smoke, the tongues of flame . . . and the French squadron's shock.

Despite the distance, it almost seemed Paul could hear the crackling roar of the French ship's flaming agony, and Jansen shifted target. Smoke and long range made the second ship a difficult mark, but her captain was no longer thinking of difficulties the *defenders* might face. His squadron had lost two ships-of-the-line to fire the day before; now a third blazed before his eyes, and he altered course, swinging desperately north to clear the battery.

But in his effort to avoid the guns, he drove his ship bodily onto a mud bank. The impact whipped the mainmast out of her, and the entire line came apart. Choking smoke from the lead ship cut visibility, deadly sparks threatened anyone who drew too close with the same flaming death, and the second ship's grounding made bad worse. If one of them could run aground, then all of them could . . . and what if they did so where those deadly guns could pound them into fiery torches?

It was the result Paul had hoped for, though he'd never dared depend upon it. But even as the southern prong of the French thrust recoiled, the northern column continued to close, and he studied his enemies almost calmly. Did they intend to attempt to pass right through his line? The width of the channel had forced him to anchor his ships far enough apart to make that feasible, but such close action was against the French tradition, and getting there would allow his ships to rake them mercilessly as they approached. On the other hand—

He shook himself and drew his sword, watching the range fall, and the entire ship shivered as her guns ran out on squealing trucks. Each gun held two roundshot— a devastating load which could not be wasted at anything but point-blank range, and he didn't even flinch as the lead ship's bow chasers fired. Iron hummed over the quarterdeck, and he felt the shock and heard the screams as a second shot thudded into *Torbay*'s side and sent lethal hull splinters scything across her lower gundeck. Another salvo from the chasers, and a third. A fourth. The range was down to sixty yards, closing at a hundred feet per minute, and then, at last, his sword slashed the air.

"*Fire!*" Lieutenant Gaither screamed, and whistles shrilled and *Torbay* heaved like a terrified animal as her side erupted in thunder.

"That's the best I can do *here*, Captain," Doctor Lambert said pointedly as he tied the sling. The implication was plain, but Paul ignored it. A French Marine's musket ball had smashed his left forearm, and he feared it would have to come off. But for now the bleeding had mostly stopped, and he had no time for surgeons with three of *Torbay*'s seven lieutenants dead and two more, including Gaither, wounded.

At least Lambert is a decent doctor—not a drunkard like too many of them, he told himself as he waved the man away. The doctor gave him an exasperated look, but he had more than enough to keep him occupied, and he took himself off with a final sniff.

Paul watched him go, then looked along the length of his beautiful, shattered ship. It wasn't like the French to force close action. They preferred to cripple an opponent's rigging with long-range fire, but *these* Frenchmen seemed not to have known that.

Darkness covered the carnage, but Paul knew what was out there. De Grasse's northern column had sailed straight into his fire. Some of its ships had closed to as little as fifty yards—one had actually passed between *Torbay* and *Prince William* before letting go her own anchor—and the furious cannonade had raged for over four hours, like a cyclone of iron bellowing through a stinking, blinding pall of powder smoke. At one point both of *Torbay*'s broadsides had been simultaneously in action with no less than three French ships, and Paul doubted that all of the survivors of his line together could have mustered sufficient intact spars for a single ship.

But we held *the bastards*, he told himself, standing beside the stump of his ship's mizzen. It had gone over the side just as the surviving French finally retreated to lick their wounds, and he made himself look northward, despite a spasm of pain deeper than anything from his shattered arm, to where flames danced in the night beyond *Prince William*. HMS *Serapis* was still afloat, but it was a race now between inrushing water and the fire gnawing towards her magazine, and the boat crews plucking men from the bay looked like ferrymen on the seas of Hell against the glaring backdrop of her destruction.

But she would not go alone. Two French seventy-fours had settled in the main channel, one the victim of *Torbay*'s double-shotted guns, and Paul bared his teeth at them. Their wrecks would do as much to block the channel as his own ships—probably more, given his command's atrocious casualties. *Torbay* had over three hundred dead and wounded out of a crew of six hundred. Neither the wounded's heartbreaking cries nor the mournful clank of her pumps ever stopped, and exhausted repair parties labored to clear away wreckage and plug shot holes. It was even odds whether or not she would be afloat to see the dawn, for she had been the most exposed of all his ships and suffered accordingly.

Prince William was almost as badly battered, and Captain Forest was dead. But his first lieutenant seemed a competent sort, and *Triumph*, despite heavy damage aloft, had suffered far less in her hull, while the ancient *Panther* had gotten off with the least damage of all. If he could only keep *Torbay* afloat, perhaps they could still—

"Sir! Captain! Look!"

The report was scarcely a proper one, but the acting second lieutenant who'd made it had been a thirteen-year-old midshipman that morning. Under the circumstances, Paul decided to overlook its irregularity—especially when he saw the French officer standing in the cutter with a white flag.

"Do you think they want to surrender, sir?" the youngster who'd blurted out the sighting report asked, and Paul surprised himself with a weary laugh.

"Go welcome him aboard, Mr. Christopher," he said gently, "and perhaps we'll see."

Christopher nodded and hurried off, and Paul did his best to straighten the tattered, blood- and smoke-stained coat draped over his shoulders. He would have sent his steward for a fresh one if any had survived the battle . . . and if his steward hadn't been dead.

The French lieutenant looked like a visitor from another world as he stepped onto *Torbay*'s shattered deck. He came aft in his immaculate uniform, shoes catching on splinters, and enemy or no, he could not hide the shock behind his eyes as he saw the huge bloodstains on the deck, the dead and the heap of amputated limbs piled beside the main hatch for later disposal, the dismounted guns and shattered masts.

"Lieutenant de Vaisseau Joubert of the *Ville de Paris*,"

he introduced himself. His graceful, hat-flourishing bow would have done credit to Versailles, but Paul had lost his own hat to another French marksman sometime during the terrible afternoon, and he merely bobbed his head in a curt nod.

"Captain Sir John Paul," he replied. "How may I help you, Monsieur?"

"My admiral 'as sent me to request your surrender, Capitaine."

"Indeed?" Paul looked the young Frenchman up and down. Joubert returned his gaze levelly, then made a small gesture at the broken ship about them.

"You 'ave fought magnificently, Capitaine, but you cannot win. We need break through your defenses at only one point. Once we are be'ind you—" He shrugged delicately. "You 'ave cost us many ships, and you may cost us more. In the end, 'owever, you must lose. Surely you must see that you 'ave done all brave men can do."

"Not yet, Lieutenant," Paul said flatly, drawing himself to his full height, and his eyes glittered with the light of the dying *Serapis*.

"You will not surrender?" Joubert seemed unable to believe it, and Paul barked a laugh.

"Surrender? I have not yet *begin* to fight, Lieutenant! Go back to the *Ville de Paris* and inform your admiral that he will enter this bay only with the permission of the King's Navy!"

"I—" Joubert started, then stopped. "Very well, Capitaine," he said after a moment, his voice very quiet. "I will do as you—"

"Captain! *Captain Paul!*"

Excitement cracked young Christopher's shout into falsetto fragments, and Paul turned with a flash of anger at the undignified interruption. But the midshipman was capering by the shot-splintered rail and pointing across the tattered hammock nettings into the night.

"What's the meaning of—" the captain began, but his

scathing rebuke died as he, too, heard the far-off rumble and strode to Christopher's side.

"See, sir?" the boy demanded, his voice almost pleading. "*Do you see it, sir?*"

"Yes, lad," Paul said quietly, good hand squeezing the youngster's shoulder as fresh, massive broadsides glared and flashed beyond the capes. *My God*, he thought. *Hood not only believed me, he actually attacked at night! And he caught the Frogs just sitting there!*

He watched the horizon for another moment, and then turned back to Joubert.

"I beg your pardon for the interruption, Lieutenant," he said, taking his hand from Christopher's shoulder to wave at the growing fury raging in the blackness of the open sea, "but I think perhaps you'd best return to your own ship now."

Joubert's mouth worked for several seconds, as if searching for words which no longer existed. Then he shook himself and forced his mind to function again.

"Yes, Monsieur," he said, in a voice which was almost normal. "I . . . thank you for your courtesy, and bid you *adieu.*"

"*Adieu*, Monsieur," Paul replied, and then stood watching the lieutenant and his boat disappear into the night.

Other voices had begun to shout—not just aboard *Torbay*, but on *Prince William* and *Panther* and *Triumph* as well—as what was happening registered, but Paul never turned away from the hammock nettings. He gripped them until his hand ached, listening to the thunder, watching the savage lightning, knowing men were screaming and cursing and dying out there in the dark. A night battle. The most confused and terrifying sort possible . . . and one which favored Hood's superbly trained ships' companies heavily.

And then the cheering began. It started aboard *Prince William*, and his heart twisted at how thin it sounded, how many voices were missing. But those which remained were fierce. Fierce with pride . . . and astonishment at their own survival. The cheers leapt from *Prince William* and *Panther* to *Torbay* and *Triumph*, and he knew the same bullthroated huzzahs were rising from *Russel* and *Charon* and the batteries. The deep, surging voices tore the night to pieces, shouting their triumph—*his* triumph—and he drew a deep, shuddering breath.

But then he thrust himself upright and walked to the quarterdeck rail, and the cheers aboard *Torbay* faded slowly into expectant stillness as the men still standing on her shattered decks looked up at their captain.

Sir John Paul gazed back at them, good hand resting on the hilt of his sword, exhausted heart bursting with his pride in them, and cleared his throat.

"All right, you idle buggers!" he snapped. "What d'you think this is—some fine lord's toy yacht? This is a *King's ship*, not a nursery school! Now get your arses back to work!"

VIVE L'AMIRAL
John W. Mina

Admiral Nelson stood on his quarterdeck and brought the spyglass up to his one good eye. It had taken a great deal of practice learning how to adjust it with one hand, but he finally became quite adept and could now focus instantly. As the diminutive sea warrior scanned the horizon, he could barely make out a distant sail.

"That's it, the enemy fleet," he commented, almost to himself. "Give the signal for all ships to form line of battle. And add that I know each man will give his all."

The tall, handsome man standing next to him stood for a moment staring at his close friend, as if wanting to say something. The two looked at each other, then the taller one nodded and replied. "Yes, my admiral. I will make it so."

Nelson watched his friend, the captain of the flagship, as he walked away. There is a good man, he thought. I'm glad I have so many good men. Then he turned his attention back to the fleet he was about to attack. They, too, have so many good men. Thank God there are so many fools commanding them. Now, with His help, I will achieve a great victory. This last thought filled him with the familiar thrill of anticipation he had become addicted to. Each battle, for him, whether it was ship to ship, fleet to fleet, even man to man, was a door to that world of glory. But this time there were other emotions interfering with the purity of his bloodlust. How did this happen, he asked himself. His mind started to drift, pondering the irony of the situation.

A particularly violent heave of the ship jerked the young officer out of his fevered sleep. "Damn, this bloody ship," he gasped. "And damn the swab who named her the *Dolphin*. With all this heaving she should be called the *Swine*."

"Well, well," said a man in a gentle voice with a French accent. He was middle aged, his grey hair balding, with a spectacular white beard that framed an eternal smile. "The little lieutenant is awake and feeling spry enough to curse the ship that saves his life. You are ready for some broth, no?"

"God, no!" Nelson replied. His body was racked with pain and he felt too weak to sit up. "If it is the ship that saves my life, then I curse it doubly. This fever will take me soon, I can feel it. I just wish death would not wait and prolong my agony."

"No, my friend, you will not die. Unless you will it so. These last few days the fever has lessened. But come, you must take some of this. You need your strength."

"You are wrong, doctor. My time is over. But I am not afraid to die."

"*Mon Dieu*, you are stubborn! It is life that you are afraid of. Have you no sense of duty?"

Nelson looked into the surgeon's eyes and detected no deceit. He took a deep breath and spoke. "Very well. I will be a hero and brave every danger." He forced himself to a sitting position and began to sip the soup.

As the weeks went by, the lieutenant slowly recovered his strength. Soon he was able to sit for long periods and looked forward to talking with the doctor. "Tell me, Doctor Dupres," he asked, "what draws you to the sea?"

"Please, we are friends now. You must call me Claude. But as to your question, it is the best way to study the earth and its wealth of life. I am also a natural philosopher and, for an opportunity to sail around the world, even an English ship such the *Dolphin* is acceptable. On this last trip to India I discovered three new species of rat and a subspecies of cobra. But now, like you, I long for my home. I miss my little girl. It has been three years since I have seen her. You, also, must miss your family. Are you married?"

Nelson blushed slightly. "No. I'm not married. I miss my sister, mostly. But Norfolk is very beautiful in the summer."

"If you wish to see beauty, my friend, you must visit me in Paris. Yes, I insist. The first chance you get after you return home, you will come and stay with me. After all, you will need time to recover. Doctor's orders!"

The admiral was brought back from his reverie by the ships moving in place. He felt the light westerly breeze as it cooled his face and smiled. A firm hand gripped his shoulder and he turned to see his friend grinning back at him.

"I am happy to see you smile, Admiral. Your demons have fled, no."

"Yes, Pierre. This light breeze will work in our favor. You were wondering why I gave up the weather gage. It's because I know Collingwood. Old Cuthbert will never attack without the weather gage and, with this small wind, most of his advantage will be lost."

"But can we afford to give him any advantage?"

"We'll soon see, Captain, we'll soon see. All I ask for is a victory, no more. But I would dearly love to see Clara again." Sweet Clara, he thought, and he remembered the first time he saw her.

Nelson walked up the stone path and knocked, tentatively, on the heavy wooden door. He was not prepared for what he saw when it opened. Standing before him was a stunning girl, about five feet tall with bright black eyes and hair to match. He stared at the dark haired vision in front of him, unable to speak.

"*Oui?*" the young girl asked, then noticed his uniform. "Oh, you are English. You must be Lieutenant Nelson."

"No, my dear," came a familiar voice from inside. The doctor came out and hugged his friend. "Look at his shoulders. This is *Capitaine* Nelson! How have you been, *mon ami*? It has been too long. You look very bad. The fever has returned? But I talk too much. Come inside. Clara will bring you some wine."

They went into the house and Claude motioned Nelson to a large, soft chair in a brightly sunlit room overlooking a garden exploding with color.

The Englishman uttered his first words. "You, at least, are looking very well, Claude. Living on land agrees with you."

"You still do not understand, do you? It is not the land, it is the food. I am surprised that anyone can live on the . . . the *merde*, that they serve in the English Navy. Any navy for that matter. Salt beef and pork years old. Years! And the suet! So much fat. For such a brave man you have a very sensitive system. If you do not eat a proper diet you will always be ill. If you live."

"Calm down, Papa," said a sweet voice. Clara had brought the wine and Nelson, once again, stared as if in rapture. She noticed his attention and rewarded him with a smile.

Nelson looked at Clara but addressed Claude. "When you first invited me to your home, you said, 'If you want to see beauty, come to Paris.' I see now that you could not have made a truer statement."

Clara blushed and returned to the kitchen. Nelson followed her with his gaze, then looked at the doctor who was trying to hide his smirk.

Claude held up his glass and offered a toast. "To good friends, and better wine!"

After they both had drained and refilled their glasses he went on. "So, my friend. It has been four years. What have you been doing?"

"I just returned from hell. Actually Honduras. But you're right. The fever returned. It was your words that brought me through once more, Claude. But let me start from the beginning. I was made post-captain back in '79. They gave me a command, a 28-gun merchantman that sailed like a turtle with only three legs. I took her to Quebec and got into some trouble. We captured a poor American fisherman whose only way to feed his family was the pitiful boat we took. I released him with his vessel, but my acting second lieutenant, a man called Hardy, reported me to the admiralty. He was mad about not getting his prize money. I had to endure a court-martial. The only outcome was a reprimand and lecture about following orders by that windbag, Sandwich, but it was humiliating. Then there were a few cruises in the West Indies. I really caused a stir there. I confiscated all the American merchantmen for not paying duties due. Everyone was against me but I couldn't just sit there and watch the corruption. I figured that either I deserved to be sent out of the service or be noticed for what I was doing."

"And which was it? I see you wear your uniform still so you must have been noticed."

"I was noticed indeed! Again I had to face a court-martial. I was cleared of all charges but am being sued by the traders."

"Surely your government will back you. Even thick-headed bureaucrats understand the value of a good officer."

"I don't know, Claude. I don't have the right titles or connections. In my country men are not judged by merit but by bloodline. Again and again I've watched some feather-headed macaroni get a plum command while I got passed over, just because they are landed and titled.

When I was a midshipman there was a saying, 'Aft, the most honor, forward the better man.' I've learned that, in our service at least, it is too often true. The 'officer class' is rarely worthy of the men they command."

"Well, in any case, you are here now and must not think of such things. There are many in my country who feel the same as you about the nobility. There may be changes in the wind but, while you stay with me, there is only friendship and . . ." he smiled wryly and glanced at the kitchen where his daughter had retreated, "Who knows?"

Four months he had spent with the Dupres that summer. Enough time to rejuvenate his emotions, recover his health and, most of all, fall in love. Clara, dear Clara . . .

Captain Pierre Gaspard gestured with disgust at the leading ships in their fleet. "The Spaniards! They are incompetent fools! Look how they blunder. A snake could form a straighter line."

"Exactly, Pierre," the admiral replied. "That is why I put them in the lead. I am using them as bait. Collingwood will not be able to resist the opportunity to engage. And, while the Spaniards are miserable at maneuvering, they mount so many guns that they can't help but do some damage. Don't forget my order for every ship to aim for the hulls. I am counting on them to draw the fire of enough of the English fleet for us to destroy the rest. Then we will help the Spanish to finish their task.

"Even now, Collingwood moves into position," Nelson observed. "Look there. He's splitting his line! It is just as I hoped!" Then he brought up his spyglass and carefully examined the enemy fleet. "The fifth ship in the closer line. I believe it's the *Victory*. That's Hardy's ship." He brought the glass back down and turned to Gaspard.

"Captain," he said speaking imperiously. "When battle is joined, you will make sure we engage the *Victory*."

"*Oui*, Admiral. If it can be done, we will do it."

Nelson brought the glass back up and studied the enemy ship. Hardy, you bastard. Now we will give you a chance for prize money. His thoughts returned to those terrible days back home after that last miserable cruise and how Claude welcomed him back to Paris.

"Nelson, Nelson, my dear friend!" Claude's bear hug was squeezing the air out of the Englishman. "Too many years. Too many years! I have missed you. Please come in."

Nelson welcomed the chair in his weakened state and gratefully accepted a glass of wine. "Thank you. Thank you so much. It is very good to see you. I'm afraid I come not as a guest but as a refugee. There is so much that I must ask of you."

"Bah. There is nothing I would not give you, joyfully! But first I will command you as your doctor. You look like a corpse. Your eyes are red with puffy bags, your skin looks like yellow wax. And you are so thin! First wash, food and rest. And then we will talk."

After he was washed, fed and rested, Nelson felt like a new man. He joined Claude who was sitting in the garden. "Where is . . . ?"

"Clara? Ah, you do not know. It was many years you have been away. She waited, but . . ." He held up his palms, "Life must go on. Two years ago she married my good friend, Jean Prudhomme, a very influential statesman. It is true that he is my age, but he loves Clara very much and has the means to give her a good life. When you are feeling better, I will take you to visit them. I know she will be delighted. And Jean, I think, you will like very much. Now you must tell me how you come to be in this pitiful condition."

"More pitiful now, since I know of Clara's marriage. I wanted to come back sooner, I wanted to ask you for her hand, but I did not wish to return until I was able to support her. I'm afraid my financial situation went from bad to worse. You remember that matter concerning the American traders? Well, they went to court and got a judgment against me for twenty thousand pounds. I appealed to the treasury for support but they keep putting me off. The admiralty was no help either. You remember that fellow, Hardy, that I told you about? The one who reported me for releasing a prize? Well, at the time, we exchanged some words. And besides calling him a rat bugger, I also gave him a poor report. He was, after all, a mediocre officer. Apparently he had some important friends in Parliament and had them speak poorly about me to my superiors. Nothing official, but you know how these things work. A man's merit and character are far less important than his inherited position. I wish the whole lot of them would choke on their scones." He realized his tone had turned bitter and apologized. "Please, Claude, forgive me. I do not wish to burden you."

The doctor was smiling at him. "No need to apologize, my friend. I understand your feelings. Jean, Clara's husband, will enjoy talking to you about this. As I told you, he is a very important man and will likely emerge as a leader in the near future. But we will discuss that later. Tell me more of your troubles."

"There were other financial problems. My fortune, God knows, has grown worse for the service: so much for serving my country. I sat around for three years waiting for a command. I even had to watch that bastard Hardy, my junior, take command of a 64-gun ship-of-the-line; one that was promised to me! Debt started piling up. Then, last month, my dear sister Ann died. There was no longer any reason for me to remain in England. So, with the certainty of debtor's prison looming in my future, I come to you for succor."

Claude looked thoughtful. "I may be able to arrange a loan . . ."

"No. I want no money. I will never pay one shilling of that judgment. I placed my head on the block for the King, for what? I have always felt that it is much better to serve an ungrateful country, than to give up your fame. But I have not even been able to serve. What I need is help establishing myself. I am not returning to England, Claude."

"But what of your career?"

"My career in the English Navy is over. Hardy saw to that. What I hope for now is to be placed in command of a merchantman, or even a privateer. I do prefer a man-o'-war."

The doctor was looking at his garden, watching a praying mantis devour a dragonfly. "Yes. You would be most effective in a warship. You talked about serving an ungrateful country. What about serving a grateful one?"

"France?"

"We war now with the Russians in the Mediterranean. What if I could arrange for you to command, say, a frigate?"

"You could do this?" A thousand thoughts raced through Nelson's head.

"No promises. But, as I said, Jean is very powerful."

The sound of guns brought him back from his reverie. "The Spaniards have opened fire, Admiral."

"Yes, Captain. With so many bloody guns you would think that they should be able to hit something." In the distance he could see the smoke surrounding the huge Spanish battle ships. The rapid pounding booms from their guns were answered by the English bow-chasers.

"Should we give the signal to fire, Admiral?"

Nelson turned the glass toward the line of ships approaching. "No. Not yet. I want to wait until they are fully committed." He could see the tension in Gaspard's face.

"Waiting is always the worst!" the captain said. "The

English have been crushing us for so long. Just once, I would like to be part of a victorious fleet action. The Nile was a nightmare!"

The admiral lowered the spyglass and faced his friend. "Collingwood will soon see that this will be no Nile. We are not anchored and are far from unprepared. No, Pierre. This will be no Nile!"

A gun from the lead enemy ship sounded, followed by a splash and a dull thud. "Forward hull struck above the waterline," came the bosun's shouted report. "No damage. The bounce took most of the kill out of it."

Nelson knew there would be many more, with much greater effect, but was more concerned about his ships carrying out the maneuvers he had organized. That was the key.

A few minutes later he gave the order. "Fly the signal. All ships to fire." Then as an aside to Pierre, "Let ours be the first."

His words were barely out when the roar of the broadside from the *Bucentaure*, his flagship, filled all his hearing while the deck below him shook. "Now we are engaged, Captain. Now all is in the hands of God."

"We are in your hands, Admiral. And we believe in you. We believe that you will win a great victory for *l'Empereur*."

"I am not fighting this battle for *l'Empereur*, Captain. I'm fighting it for the men. Whatever governments do, it is always the men who suffer. These are my men and I will give them a victory."

The mention of the Emperor brought him back to the first time he met Bonaparte.

M. Jean Prudhomme, Minister of the Interior, was in the habit of throwing elaborate dinner parties, and this was no exception. Nelson had just returned from a successful cruise in the Ionian Sea and was looking forward, more than anything else, to holding Clara's vibrant body tonight after all the guests had left. For the last two years now, he had been welcome, even expected, to stay with the Prudhommes whenever he was not at sea. He relished the command that Jean arranged for him, especially since it kept him out of the country during the worst part of the revolution. Nelson's actions against the Russians and the Turks had been victorious and had increased his wealth and fame. But he was most grateful to the Frenchman for the tolerant attitude he had regarding Clara. France was a better place to have an affair than England. Not only did Jean allow Nelson and Clara's indiscretions, he encouraged them. In addition, the minister had taken pride in introducing him to many important people. Nelson had become quite popular and was thriving in the glory. Although the sight in one eye had been lost, his happiness was not diminished.

"Tell me, Captain Nelson," said a rather obese woman dressed in a blue velvet gown and bedecked with a rainbow of thumb-sized jewels. "Is it true that your poor eye was injured fighting off an entire Turkish fleet?" Her enormous breasts managed to violate all the laws of physics by not flying out of her low neckline as she puffed her chest towards him.

"Er, well, yes. I mean no!" He was somewhat distracted by her charms. "I mean I did get wounded in that engagement, but it was hardly an entire fleet. Actually there were only five vessels and three of them were brigs. It is true that we were outgunned by the two frigates but they were, after all, Turks. Their gunnery was atrocious and as for seamanship, well, I was able to put my frigate, *Liberté*, between the enemy frigates and half their shots went into their own ships. Two of the brigs became entangled and missed most of the fight. Then it was just a matter of pounding the frigates until they lost all maneuverability. The first struck her colors in only a short time, her captain proved to be a whining coward, but the other was tenacious. After knocking down all her masts we finally had to board. That's when I got hit. As I charged on to their deck, they let fly with a nine-pounder. Fortunately for me they were still firing round shot and I was missed by the ball which hummed past my ear and knocked my foremast jack on the head, poor fellow. But I caught some red-hot wadding in my eye.

"Once the second frigate surrendered—we had to kill the captain—it was a simple matter to catch and take the brigs."

"Ooh," the woman sighed, impossibly pumping her bust out even more. "Five ships captured by just one! Emil! Come here and meet Captain Nelson!"

Nelson only had to repeat the story three more times, never tiring of the attention, before it was time for dinner to be served. He was seated at the huge dinner table across from a dynamic young artillery officer who was expounding about the prowess of the army.

"Well-trained and disciplined soldiers, given enough supplies and decent commanders, are all you need to win a campaign," the officer proclaimed. "Of course, it must be properly balanced with cavalry and artillery. Is this not so?" He addressed his last question to Nelson.

The naval man finished his wine, then refilled his glass as well as that of his dinner companion. "Well, Major Buonaparte, I do agree that training and discipline are essential to any military endeavor. But you left out sea power. Granted, certain landlocked theaters do not require a navy. But in Europe, at least, the seas are as important as the land."

"That is preposterous!" the major boomed, obviously feeling the effect of the wine. "It is the army that is supreme. There are limited occasions that support from the sea can help. But to imply . . . *Mon Dieu!*" His voice trailed off as his gaze shifted to a fixed point behind Captain Nelson. "Over there, in the red dress," he muttered.

Nelson turned around and saw a voluptuous blond woman talking with one of the ministers. "Yes, indeed," he nodded in agreement. "It seems, Major, that we agree on one topic."

"Is she not the most beautiful vision to grace the earth? Look at that bosom! Surely Helen of Troy has been reincarnated."

"She is exquisite," replied Nelson. "But I must contest your belief that she is the most beautiful."

"Not the most beautiful?" Buonaparte was angry now and his eyes flashed with a violent flame. "And who, Englishman, would you say is finer?"

The captain remained calm and gestured toward Clara, who was seated at the head of the table.

Buonaparte looked to see the wife of their host, then looked back at Nelson and immediately softened his stance. "*Oui, Capitaine*. I understand. I see that you are smitten and will not press my point. One can not profit from arguing beauty with a man who is in love." He raised his glass. "Come, my friend, let us drink to *l'amour*."

"To *l'amour*," Nelson agreed and drained his glass.

That had been back in '94. It wasn't until four years later that he had an opportunity to speak with *l'Empereur* again. Nelson was sailing *Liberté* toward the eastern Mediterranean. He had been cruising south of Greece when he heard about the destruction of the French fleet at the battle of the Nile. He was also given a dispatch with rendezvous coordinates where he was to pick up Buonaparte, now General Napoleon Bonaparte. The general had been stranded in Egypt as a result of the disaster.

"Does anyone on this ship know these waters, Lieutenant Gaspard?"

"Henri St. Jaques, the master's mate. He used to sail on a merchantman that met with black marketeers along this shore. He said to watch out for the shoal at the north end of the bay. Shall I call him, Captain?"

"No, Pierre. Just make sure the helmsman is aware of it. Are the boats ready?"

"*Oui*. The crews are all strong and well armed. I will lead this one?"

"No. I will take it in myself." Not even his first lieutenant knew the purpose of this landing, he thought. They had to get in and out quickly, without the locals knowing. If it became known who was hiding in their little town, they would riot, or worse.

The boats were lowered and, with only the faint glow of the crescent moon, were rowed toward shore. The boats ground gently against the rocky beach without incident. Only a few minutes passed before a hushed voice could be heard.

" 'Allo? Who are you?"

"It is Nelson of the *Liberté*."

"Ah. Thank God! Come, bring your men. We must hurry. The general is hiding in a cellar. Enemy agents know he is in this town and have hired local mercenaries."

They followed the man into the town through a winding maze of narrow streets. "Here," he said, pointing to a deep crack in the side of a building. "General!" he called quietly, "our people have come. It is Nelson."

There was some grunting and soft curses, then a figure emerged from the hole. Nelson realized that it must have been the general, but he was so filthy and wrapped in rags as to be unrecognizable.

"There isn't a moment to be lost," the captain said and led the way back toward the boats.

They made it all the way to the beach before the attack came. A large group of men had waited in ambush, hoping to catch the whole landing party with the general as well. They leaped out of the shadows firing muskets, then screamed and charged, fiercely wielding scimitars. Nelson was struck in the right elbow with a musket ball and went down immediately. The others rallied to his side and managed to beat back the savage but disorganized attackers.

The captain was helped to his feet while one of his men finished tying a tourniquet on his arm. "We must keep moving. There will be more soon. Into the boats!" He stayed in command until they were back on the *Liberté*.

"Take her out to sea, Pierre," he ordered, then collapsed.

When he awoke, he heard someone talking in his cabin. He tried to sit up but there was a severe pain in his arm. Then he realized that he had no right arm. His groaning alerted the others in the cabin that he was conscious.

"I owe you a great debt, Captain," said a somewhat familiar voice. "I also owe you an apology."

"Apology, General?" asked Nelson in a weak voice.

"*Oui*. The first time we met you argued that sea power was important. In my ignorance I disagreed. Since then I have learned of my folly. Even before the Nile defeat I was haunted by your words. Now I see that naval strength is vital. Vital! I must have a strong navy!"

Nelson smiled. "Apology accepted. I wish I could be there to see it."

"Be there? You will be in command! I have followed your record. You are brilliant! The biggest problem in the French navy is that it has only idiots to command it. Villeneuve lost my whole fleet with his bungling."

"General Bonaparte," Nelson said, with an ironic smile. "There is no place in any navy for a one-armed, one-eyed admiral."

"Pah! You are a better man as you are than any whole admiral in the world. This I will not argue. We will build a new fleet, a better one, and you will command it. That's all. Now rest."

Admiral Nelson watched the approaching English ships with a detached air. Seven years, he thought. His fleet had been seven years in the making, and now he believed that it was the best in the world. All his efforts convincing Napoleon to channel some funds into the navy paid off. It was amazing what a difference decent food and supplies made. It's true, the English sailors had more battle experience. But he had personally overseen the training programs and knew his men were up for this task.

"The lead ship is starting to wear, Admiral," said Captain Gaspard as he peered through his glass.

Nelson looked through his own to confirm, then moved his sighting farther forward to check on the Spanish squadron. He could see that they were fully engaged, now, in a ship-to-ship fight. "Look at the *Santissima Trinidad*, Pierre."

The captain also viewed the scene. "My God, Admiral. They are being hammered by three English battleships. See how they fight! All four decks firing both sides. What an action! But how long can they stand it?"

"Not even that great floating fortress will endure long under such combined fire. As you can see, the English have positioned themselves so that at least one ship can rake the *Santissima* at all times. But come. We have our own battle to fight. Are the midshipmen prepared to carry out the special orders?"

"All is in readiness, but the men are reluctant. After all, only a madman would set fire to his own ship and cut down a yardarm during a fight."

The admiral smiled. "Only a madman. Perhaps they are right. But they will carry out the order when it is given? The timing on this is crucial."

"Yes, Admiral. They are your men and would leap out of the rigging if you ordered it."

"Well, let us hope it doesn't come to that." He watched the lead ship of the enemy, the *Leviathan*, turn and start down the French line, vigorously engaging his own lead ship. This continued with the second English ship, then the third. When *Leviathan* was in range, its bow guns opened up on the *Bucentaure*. A few shots struck home, others passed menacingly overhead.

"Now, Captain, give the order!" Nelson screamed.

Within seconds a fire sprung up beneath the foremast and the maintop yard came crashing down. The ship fell off from the wind, opening a large gap in the line. Instantly the *Leviathan* wore again and made straight for the gap, followed by the rest of the English line.

Once the *Leviathan* was committed to its course, Nelson gave the order for the fire to be extinguished. The yard was already cut free and pushed overboard. Now *Bucentaure* and *Leviathan* were about to exchange broadsides. Here's where the real fight begins, he thought. He felt the rippling rumble as his great guns fired in succession. The shock of the enemy's return fire was staggering, tearing great gashes in the deck and throwing up showers of deadly splinters. He saw a promising young midshipman crumple to the floor, a two-foot long, razor-sharp piece of oak protruding from the back of his neck. The headless corpse of a sailor fell out of the rigging and landed at his feet.

But the admiral remained calm, his mind racing to the next series of orders. This is my element, he thought. As long as these men will fight, I will lead them. "Prepare to wear to the larboard. As soon as the third ship, I believe it is the *Vanguard*, passes through, we will close the gap. Have the men on deck lie down when we start, Captain. She will be able to give us a punishing rake across our bow as we turn. But then we will have them. Captain Devereaux must move soon or the trap will not close."

They watched the second ship pass, exchanging broadsides while in range, then the *Vanguard* approached. Nelson gripped the rail, tightly, the knuckles on his left hand turning white. "Get ready . . . , get ready . . . , now!" The deck was a flurry of activity as men ran around hauling halyards and belaying. Then most lay flat on the deck. The *Bucentaure* pointed its bow straight towards the

Vanguard while Admiral Nelson stood there defiantly, braced for the broadside .

There was an enormous blast sending shock waves to the heart of the vessel. But the blast did not come from the *Vanguard*. Nelson looked beyond to see a brilliant conflagration in the middle of the Spanish squadron.

"Dear God! Pierre! It's the *Santissima Trinidad*! She's exploded! The magazine must have caught. And look. The three English ships she was fighting have all been dismasted. This will help us win today but, God, what a price."

The blast was so tremendous that both fleets were stunned and every man stopped what he was doing. There was silence, broken only by the great splashes made by shattered masts and yards falling into the water from the vast height to which they had been exploded. By the time the fighting resumed, the *Vanguard* had missed its chance to rake *Bucentaure*.

Now the flagship was preparing to rake the stern of the *Vanguard* as it moved across her rear. The men on board the English ship realized their position and ran about wildly, trying to change course. Nelson ordered the firing to resume and the men cheered as the enemy's main-topmast came down in a tangle of cloth, wood and rope. Two more broadsides were delivered before the *Vanguard* was out of range, one of which crippled the rudder.

The admiral now turned his attention to the rest of the English line. The fourth English ship had realized the situation and wore to the south, continuing along the rest of the French line, but the three that had gone through were now cut off from the main body. Nelson checked the rear of his line and saw that Captain Devereaux had indeed led the last four ships to the leeward, closing the trap.

The new lead enemy ship had just dealt *Bucentaure* a withering broadside and the admiral felt the jarring from an explosion below decks. One of our guns blew, he thought, then heard a sick cracking sound from the foremast. He stood helpless and watched as it fell. "Clear the wreckage!" he ordered. "Cut it loose. Cut the halyards!" The men worked feverishly but the tangle was too great. His heart sank as Hardy moved up in the *Victory*. He knew they had lost most of their headway. Then he made a decision. "Captain! Helm hard to larboard!"

Pierre looked puzzled and somewhat panicked. "But Admiral, that will put us in the path of the *Victory*."

"Turn, dammit. Now!" he bellowed.

The ship made a sudden lurch to the left and turned into the wind. Please God, prayed Nelson, don't let her miss her stays. The *Bucentaure* hesitated for a moment, then the remaining sails filled and she swung around, heading in the opposite direction of his own line. The two lines were so close now that the new course brought them directly next to the *Victory*.

"Now men, pour it on!" Nelson was screaming and waving his arm, cutlass in hand, as if he was ready to lead a boarding party.

The two ships pounded each other with broadside after broadside. Nelson watched his first lieutenant clutch his chest and fall. Then he noticed that the enemy's rigging was thick with marines shooting muskets. A sharp pain in his right shoulder briefly distracted him, but soon his mind was back on the battle at hand. His other ships had maintained formation and were making use of the disorder he had caused in the British line. A quick glance over his port rail showed that Devereaux was easily handling the three battle ships that had been cut off and would likely be joining the main body soon. Inspection of the Spanish action, however, revealed chaos. Only time would tell there.

Nothing to worry about now except *Victory*. He smiled at his own pun. The heated action continued with his own ship giving at least as much as it was getting. His crew cheered spontaneously as the opponent's mainmast fell lengthwise across her bow, the canvas covering many gun ports.

With redoubled effort, his gun crews worked furiously, firing shot after shot into the enemy ship. Both ships had ceased forward movement now and the *Victory* was drifting toward the French flagship. Incoming musket fire had stopped as all available hands, marines included, were trying to cut away the fallen sails and clear the gunports. Nelson was really enjoying this battle and was only distantly aware of the throbbing pain in his shoulder. Then, as he scanned the English warship, he caught sight of Hardy standing at the stump of the mainmast waving his arms furiously.

"There you are, you bastard," he said quietly to himself. He relished the evident misery of his foe. "We will see how qualified you are to command a ship-of-the-line." He raised his voice once again. "Pierre, sweep the deck with grape and prepare to board."

This time Captain Gaspard did not hesitate. The marines stood ready, muskets and cutlasses in hand, while the starboard gun crews prepared to attack with pikes and boarding axes. Meanwhile, the larboard guns belched out a murderous swarm of grapeshot, doing little damage to the *Victory*, but decimating the men on deck. The ships were now touching at the bows, and lines with grappling hooks were being cast and secured.

"One more round, double load," roared the admiral. "Then we board!"

The last blast was devastating to the English crew and Nelson saw Hardy go down. Then his men swarmed onto the *Victory*, screaming like the possessed. When they reached the enemy deck they fought ferociously, hacking, stabbing, chopping . . . But the men of the *Victory* were not ready to strike their colors. Their fighting was just as savage and the battle was yet to be decided. Nelson made his way forward, intending to join in the fray, when the captain stood in his path.

"Admiral, you are wounded," Gaspard said pointing to Nelson's bloody right shoulder.

"It is nothing, Pierre. Get out of the way, now. I must join the men."

"This is an order I cannot obey. Even if you were not wounded, I would not permit you to board that ship until the colors are struck. You may be the admiral of the fleet, but I am still captain of the *Bucentaure*. Come, now. I will take you to the surgeon."

Nelson started to protest but realized that he was feeling very weak. "Very well. I agree to stay out of the melee. But I will not go below until *Victory* strikes."

"You are stubborn, my friend, but I will grant your wish."

The two officers stood side by side, leaning against the rail, and watched the fighting rage back and forth. Another English ship came up to help *Victory* but was engaged by the *Redoutable* and so *Victory* and *Bucentaure* were left to resolve their own conflict.

A musket ball struck the rail and sent a shower of small splinters into both men's faces. They looked at each other, each thinking the other had been wounded. "This is too warm work to last very long, Pierre."

"Yes, Admiral," replied Gaspard, then noticed how weak and pale Nelson looked. "You are still bleeding badly. If you will not go below then I will bring the surgeon here." Not waiting for a response, the captain hurried away.

Nelson felt his legs buckling under him and had to struggle to keep from losing consciousness. Maybe if I sit on the deck it will be easier to stay awake, he thought but the attempt left him lying on his back. As the light faded from his eyes he thought he heard his men cheering "They've struck! The *Victory* has surrendered! *Vive l'Amiral!*"

Horatio Nelson opened his eyes and saw that he was in his cabin with Captain Gaspard bending over him. "Pierre. Did we . . . ?"

"Victory, Admiral. Five of the English ships escaped, fifteen were taken, six went to the bottom. The Spanish did quite well, actually. As you know, in death, the *Santissima Trinidad* crippled three of the enemy. The rest were fought to a standstill and, with the aid of Captain Devereaux's squadron, managed to capture or drive them all off. All of the escaping ships were from that engagement. Our triumph here was complete. Not one English vessel did we allow to break free. Your plan to cut off their lead ships was totally successful. And your ingenious plan to ram the *Victory* . . ."

"That was no plan, Pierre."

"Shhh, you are very weak. I know that. But the others think anything that worked so perfectly to disrupt the enemy must have been a plan. We will not spoil their enthusiasm. After all, even the great Napoleon benefits from occasional strokes of luck, no?"

At this point the surgeon came in. "Do not make him talk too much, Captain, he has lost a great deal of blood and I do not wish for him to be weakened even further." Then he addressed the admiral. "A musket ball passed through the axilla, the fleshy part of your armpit."

"Well, Doctor," Nelson replied. "At least it is on the right side. I couldn't bear losing my one good arm."

The doctor loosened the bandages and examined the wound. "I'm afraid there is still bleeding inside. A major artery may have been nicked. I would open you up but already you have lost too much blood. All I can do is pack it and hope."

"I'm sure you will do your duty, Doctor." Nelson turned back to Gaspard and smiled. "So the *Victory* has struck. I thought I might have been dreaming."

"Oh yes, Admiral. But I did not accept the surrender."

"Why not? You are the captain. The prize is yours."

"I thought that this is an honor that you have earned. But we will discuss that in a moment. First I must know your orders. As you know, the way is now cleared for the invasion of England. This, *l'Empereur* wishes to do as soon as possible. But many of our ships and most of the prizes are in great need of repair."

"Pierre, listen to me," Nelson pleaded gripping his friend's arm with an air of desperation. "You must anchor. I feel a great blow coming on. All must anchor and batten down."

"I will make it so. Now, if you will stay awake for a few moments I have someone who wishes to see you."

Nelson lay there feeling his strength drain away and realized that he was having trouble breathing. His thoughts turned to Clara. His beautiful Clara. How she would grieve if he didn't return. He also thought about the battle. To triumph was supreme, but did he really want to be instrumental in the invasion of his homeland? What homeland? A homeland that had forsaken him. Ah, well, it didn't matter now. At least Hardy was dead.

"Admiral Nelson."

Pierre's voice brought him back. He opened his eyes and saw two shadowy figures standing over his bed. "Is that you, Pierre?"

"Yes. I have with me the captain of the *Victory* who wishes to surrender his sword to you."

"Hardy? I thought I saw you die."

The other figure spoke. "Not dead, Horatio, I just slipped in some blood. Here," Hardy said in disgust and tossed his sword onto the foot of the bed. "I feel no honor in surrendering to the biggest traitor in English history."

Nelson gasped in a breath and coughed out, "Kiss my ass, Hardy." Then he closed his eyes.

"But Admiral Dumanior, Admiral Nelson gave the order to anchor," Captain Gaspard protested.

"Admiral Nelson is dead, Captain. Now I am in charge of the fleet. We are needed for the invasion of England. Do you think I will let the order of a dead Englishman interfere with the Emperor's plans? Give the signal for all ships to sail."

Pierre gave the order to his surviving lieutenant and noticed that the wind was picking up.

BLOODSTAINED GROUND
Brian M. Thomsen

Sam hated the New York office, but it was better than being penniless and sober or, even worse, lynched in Missouri.

In his youth he had fantasized about the carefree adventures that he would enjoy as an adult, adventures which didn't require a bankroll or public acceptance.

I was a damned fool back then, he mused to himself as he chuckled sardonically, *just like the rest of the whole human race.*

The curmudgeon really had no cause to complain. Things would have been much worse if James Gordon Bennett and the New York *Herald* hadn't bailed him out of the financial catastrophes that had befallen him over the past few years.

Whatever made me think that writing a moderately successful boy's adventure like Tom Sawyer *or* The Prince and the Pauper *ever meant that I was going to be a best-selling novelist, let alone a success? Damn, I was a fool!*

After the disappointing sales of *Life on the Mississippi*, Samuel Clemens had hocked everything to finance the publication of his even more ill-advised fictional endeavor, *The Adventures of Huckleberry Finn*, only to receive the worst reviews in U.S. publishing history and threats on his life had forced him to migrate northward. His wife opted to remain behind and join in with his detractors.

275

I know how to write, or at least I did when I wrote that book, he mused. *Ain't anybody ever read something in dialect before? Huck and Jim don't know grammar the way I do. A simpleton should have seen that.*

Sam took a pull from the bottle of bourbon that he kept on his desk at all times. It was part of his deal with Bennett that a new one would be provided on every third day if the bottle it was replacing was not yet empty. This condition was in place so as to keep the down-on-his-luck columnist in reasonably sober condition at least some of the time so that he would be available to write an occasional column, feature, or whatever else his publishing master desired.

Sam thanked his dubious maker that no one ever bothered to check if the dregs of the old bottles were composed of bourbon or flat sarsaparilla that had been poured in to replace its previously more spirited liquid contents.

No matter how much money he has, he's just another damned fool! Sam thought of Bennett as he drained the bourbon bottle on this its second day of term. *Serves him right for taking pity on a Missouri has-been, or never was, or whatever!*

Bennett had discovered Clemens in the gutter outside of the Water Club and recognized him from a picture that had been run in his very own New York *Herald*. Taking pity on the once promising writer, Bennett offered him a job, ever eager to add a new and exciting, if not controversial, name to his paper's masthead in order to compete with Pulitzer's burgeoning news empire.

Holding the bottle up to the light in order to ascertain its emptiness, Clemens made a mental note to pick up a bottle of sarsaparilla as soon as possible, shrugged, and conceded, *Well, I guess it could be worse.*

The invasive sound of waddling footsteps approaching the writer's semi-private domain afforded him barely enough time to ditch the bottle in the concealed safety of the desk's bottom drawer until its contents were safely restored to the status of not quite empty.

Two seconds later Marshall, Bennett's personally appointed bourbon sergeant at arms, barged into the writer's office with nary a knock nor an apology.

"The President is dead," the Features Editor said matter-of-factly.

Crap! Sam thought to himself, *is this how far I've fallen? Obituary hack?*

As if reading the recalcitrant writer's thought, Marshall quickly corrected the writer's misassumption while placing an envelope on the desk in front of him.

"Don't give me that look," the Features Editor said sternly. "The obit is already done. For some reason Bennett said you should be given enough time to do a proper memorial, and since June 25 is less than two months away what could possibly be a better occasion."

"Huh?" Clemens said, quickly trying to clear his head enough so that he could comprehend his assignment.

Marshall shook his head and put his hands on his hips as if he was straining to keep his temper while talking to a simpleton.

"June 25 is the anniversary of the Little Big Horn," he explained condescendingly. "Bennett thought it would be the perfect opportunity for his favorite has-been author of the American people to sing the praises of the dearly departed president. Remember, he was a friend of this paper and the publisher. So it better be good."

Marshall pivoted and was about to leave when Clemens called after him. "How did he die?"

Marshall stopped at the door, his hand on the knob, ready to close the door behind him. "Sort of ironic. He was killed by an arrow shot by some crazed Indian guide . . . but you don't have to worry about that, no matter how it conveniently lends itself to poetic justice. Make him a legend. Legends don't die."

The Features Editor slammed the door behind him,

as Clemens rolled his eyes at his new assignment. *Just my luck having to make a heroic legend out of the likes of President George Armstrong Custer. It would have been easier if he had just died with the rest of his men at the hands of Black Kettle's warriors.*

Turning his attention to the envelope in front of him, the writer was not surprised to see that it contained a ticket to Washington for what he assumed was to be the Presidential funeral, as well as a hotel reservation slip. *Well, at least it gets me out of the office for a while.*

Clemens was used to traveling on the fly. Stopping at the front office only long enough to wheedle some pocket money as an advance against expenses, and then at his furnished rooms for his traveling bags, he was soon southward bound on the train to the nation's capital.

The train to Washington afforded him time for a nap, a few more drinks and an opportunity to read the obituaries that were already appearing in the New York *Herald*, the New York *World*, and the other rags that passed for newspapers. As the porters brought him a new paper after each stop, per his instructions, Clemens began to piece together the information at hand about the quite unexpected assassination of the nation's highest ranking executive.

Custer had been killed by a half-breed Crow scout by the name of Goes Ahead who had served under him during the northern Plains campaign and had in fact, also survived the massacre at the Little Big Horn by arriving with Reno's men after most of the carnage had already occurred. The thought-to-be-crazed Indian had killed the President with a single arrow during a Sunday afternoon picnic reunion of the Custer gang and their wives. Some of the President's former comrades in arms had arranged for some wild west entertainment of which Goes Ahead was supposed to have been a part. The half-breed had unexpectedly opted to use the President as his target of choice, killing Custer with a single shot, before he himself was killed in a barrage of bullets from the President's entourage.

Most of the papers recalled the President's glory days as the youngest brevet brigadier general in the Union army, the victor against all odds at the Little Big Horn, and the Democratic candidate who defeated Ulysses S. Grant's bid for a third term. The facts of his life were mostly from old presidential press releases, and the summation of the assassination had obviously been sanitized by some White House source.

Clemens immediately noticed that none of the papers covered Custer's lackluster years at West Point where he had earned more demerits than any other cadet to date who still had managed to graduate. Equally absent were mention of his court-martials and suspensions from duty, and the rampant corruption in government that had escalated once he entered the White House. All of these appealing facts were absent.

Well, if it ain't in the papers, Clemens mused, *I guess it's not true,* more than aware of the faults of the man he was now charged with making a legend. *If Grant had won that election or stepped down, things might have been different, but then again, maybe I wouldn't be going to this funeral or exiled from Missouri for that matter.*

The last funeral that had earned as much ink had been Grant's, though the papers had been far from kind. The publishing powerhouses focused on the financial disaster that he had left his family in at the time of death by failing to complete his memoirs, the anarchy and corruption that had pervaded his administration, and the alcoholic exploits of his earlier military career. Clemens even remembered a mention of Custer's testifying against his brother at some trial in New York in the former President's obituaries.

I guess that's what happens when you outlive your popularity, Clemens thought, pausing a moment to write

down the memorable line that had just occurred to him
in hopes of being able to use it later.,

Another drink, Sam read back his notes, *Maybe Custer
was lucky after all, at least as far as newspapers and
history are concerned.*

Clemens was about to try his luck at another nap before
the arrival of the next stop's reading material when the
compartment door was opened by the porter who quickly
ushered in a new traveler.

"I'm sorry, suh, Mr. Clemens, but the train is getting
crowded," the porter apologized.

"That's all right, Armstrong," Clemens replied. "I
understand."

"I hope you don't mind the company," the well-dressed
dandy replied.

"Not at all," Sam answered with a sly grin as he reached
into his pocket and withdrew a cigar, "provided that you
aren't worried about stinking up your fancy duds with
my cigar smoke."

The dandy thought to himself for a moment, weighing
his lack of alternatives, and—much to Sam's chagrin—
declared, "Not a problem," and took a seat across from
the writer.

Resigned to the company, Sam lit the cigar and set
his notes aside.

"Forgive me for being so rude," the dandy said
sheepishly. "I should have introduced myself. My name
is Autie Reed."

Clemens cocked an eyebrow in recognition. *Custer's
nephew who was with him at Little Big Horn; a fortuitous
turn of events.*

"Sam Clemens," the author offered.

Reed brightened. "The author!" he exclaimed. "My!
I just loved *Tom Sawyer!*" Reed quickly softened his
tone as if due to embarrassment, and added with a bit
of melancholy. "Sorry for the outburst, but I guess you
are used to that."

Clemens nodded, wishing that such positive outbursts were more common.

Reed continued. "It's sort of ironic, I guess. I was reading *Tom Sawyer* when I was with my uncle on the Plains, and now I get to meet you on the way to his funeral."

"Sorry for your loss," Clemens said with a perfect touch of false sincerity.

"And the county's," Reed added.

"Of course," Sam replied, hoping that the nephew hadn't noticed that he had rolled his eyes out of reflex after hearing such a stupid platitude.

Reed brightened for a moment and looked up.

"So are you going to write about the funeral?" the nephew said hopefully.

"Something like that."

"Well, I can help you," the nephew replied eagerly. "I know all about my uncle and his heroic exploits. There was never a greater man in the entire history of this great country."

"So I've read," Clemens said guardedly, gesturing towards the newspapers that were strewn about the compartment.

"I was with him at the Little Big Horn when we destroyed Black Kettle's Cheyennes."

"Really," Sam said, taking out his note pad in feigned surprise. "I thought we almost lost that one."

Reed backpedaled slightly. "Well, casualties were high and all, but uncle's plan worked and eventually we routed them." The nephew shrugged, and added, "But I guess you know all about that."

"Maybe," Sam replied slyly, and shrugged in kind. "After all, it was that battle and the notoriety that followed it that led to him being placed on the presidential ballot."

"That was never his intention," Reed said defensively. "He was first and foremost a soldier on a mission, and after that it was simply the will of the people."

. . . and the newspapers and the people who owned them, Sam thought silently, and then said, "But, of course. Why don't you tell me about your recollections of that day?"

"Sure," Reed replied enthusiastically, then asked, "will you use it for whatever you plan on writing?"

"I reckon I might," the author replied, took a new drag from his cigar, and balanced his note pad for easy access.

"Well, it was June 25, 1876, and the whole Custer gang was there."

"The Custer gang?"

"That's what we called ourselves. Uncle Autie—that's what I called him before he became President—Uncle Tom, Uncle Boston, and Uncle Jim, that's Jim Calhoun not Custer. He's my other uncle."

"And yourself," Clemens added, "Autie Reed, the nephew of the great man."

"Right," Reed confirmed, getting on with the story. "The General . . ."

Clemens held up his hand to interrupt, and asked, "General Terry?"

"No," Reed explained, "I guess I should have said the Colonel since that was his current rank."

"Custer?"

"Right."

"His rank was colonel but you called him 'General'?" Reed chuckled.

"I know it sounds funny, but we did," Reed continued to explain. "That was his rank in the Civil War."

"But not during the Plains campaign?"

"No."

"He was a colonel."

Reed smiled. "Lieutenant Colonel," he corrected.

Clemens smiled slyly, and said, "I'm glad we got that straight."

"You just have to take that sort of thing for granted in the Seventh Cavalry. Uncle Autie was special. He commanded respect, no matter what his detractors said."

"Like Sherman, Grant, and Hancock," Clemens offered, citing the names of the most vocal of Custer's enemies.

"Yes," Reed confirmed. "Uncle Autie showed them when he got his turn at the head chair."

Clemens decided to redirect the nephew back at his own firsthand account as the writer himself was more than aware of the mudslinging and accusations that had occurred between Custer and his rivals during the election. "You were saying about June 25?"

"Right," Reed agreed, and continued with his story.

"Well, the entire expedition against the Sioux was under the command of Brigadier General Alfred H. Terry who had placed Colonel Custer in charge of our command over Captain Benteen and Major Marcus Reno."

"They weren't part of the Custer gang?"

"Oh, no. Uncle Autie didn't like them much and the feeling was mutual. The General didn't tolerate incompetence, and they held it against him. That's why it was up to my uncles to take the reins of leadership. Everybody else just had to follow orders."

"The General's orders?"

"Exactly," Reed said emphatically. "Now, on that fateful day our scouts had indicated that there was a large group of hostiles along the Little Big Horn River. The other commanders were easily intimidated by this information and would have opposed my uncle's plan to proceed with his attack no matter what his plan was, so he decided not to tell them."

"Benteen and Reno?"

"Right," Reed confirmed. "Uncle knew that any discussion would lead to opposition, so therefore he proceeded with his plan in a manner that would provide them with no opportunity to get in his way."

Clemens gave a quick smile and a nod as if in agreement to the soundness of Custer's decision.

"We all rode together to that fateful ridge, holding

back the Cheyenne and Sioux who believed that by sheer attrition and greater numbers they would take the day, not realizing that the secondary commands under Benteen and Reno would come around in support. Though we lost close to two hundred men on that bloody ridge, we held on, dispersing their greater numbers with the arrival of the fresh horses and men and succeeded in driving them off until we emerged victorious."

"The casualties were high?"

"Very."

"And Benteen and Reno led their men to the ridge in the nick of time?"

Reed smiled, and said, "Not exactly. Tom and Boston led their commands in the place of Reno and Benteen. Both of those men were delayed, and arrived later, once victory had been secured."

"So your uncles basically took over the command of the other two companies?"

"And it worked," Reed acknowledged, nodding like the spring-balanced head of a tin toy. "Afterwards, the entire gang came together and gave thanks that we weren't part of the initial bloodbath."

"I bet you were thankful that you weren't with the rest of those poor souls on the ridge."

"You can say that again! Boston and Tom had to lag behind so that they could go get Reno and Benteen's men at the proper time, and Uncle Jim kept an eye out for me."

"So, none of you were there during the actual massacre?"

"Hell no! We would have been killed. The General always said that you had to keep the enemy unbalanced. They never expected that a leader would follow his men rather than lead them, so the dumb savages didn't realize that the battle had not yet begun when the massacre had already started. I remember the look on their faces when they saw old Yellow Hair riding towards them, flanked by companies led by Tom and Boston, the hooves of their horses tearing up the recently bloodstained ground. They thought he was back from the dead for vengeance."

"Why did they think that?"

"It was all part of the General's plan," Reed explained conspiratorially. "Summerfield, one of the standard bearers, had grown his hair out like my uncle's. Uncle Autie had him wear one of his fringed jackets as he led the company. Stupid Black Kettle assumed that he was old Yellow Hair."

The more the author reflected on this new revelation that came off so glibly from the tongue of the deceased president's nephew, the more astonished he became. Only his years as an exceptional poker player managed to keep his reaction hidden from his compartment mate.

"Landsakes," Clemens said shaking his head as he reached for a copy of the New York *Herald*, "I wonder how this happened then."

"What?" the nephew replied.

"This picture of your uncle facing down the Indians against overwhelming odds while his men died around him."

"Oh," the nephew replied. "that was Mr. O'Connor's idea."

"Mr. O'Connor?"

"Yes," Reed replied. "He was a friend of my uncle's. He even had the General pose for it right there on the battlefield. He thought that it would more accurately depict the spirit of his heroism."

And the rest is history, Clemens thought, and then said aloud, "Shrewd."

"No one shrewder."

Not wanting to reveal his true feelings to Reed, the author decided to ask one last question before begging fatigue.

"Yep, no one shrewder," Clemens acknowledged. "Too bad that Injun got him on the White House lawn. Did you know him too?"

"Certainly," the nephew replied with a touch of indignation audible in his voice. "Goes Ahead was our scout. He had advised the General, as well as Benteen and Reno that there were too many warriors at the Little Big Horn. That stupid half-breed always held it against Uncle Autie that he didn't heed his warning. If he had, I assure you, history would have been quite different."

And maybe two hundred more men would still be alive today. The author made a mental note.

At the next stop another passenger joined the author and the nephew in the compartment, and, as it was a member of the fairer sex, Reed quickly turned his attention towards her, regaling the young lady with tales of his own heroic exploits during the Plains campaign, thus giving Clemens the opportunity to nap for the rest of the trip southward.

Upon their arrival in the nation's capital, Sam Clemens quickly bid his compartment companions farewell in search of a fresh bottle of bourbon. An eager-to-please bellhop at the hotel where Bennett had arranged a room for him, provided him with more than enough of the spirited liquid from Kentucky to sate his thirst and more, and in no time at all, Clemens had passed out, sleeping through the night and the next day, thus missing the entire funeral that had been the reason for his journey.

Realizing his situation, the author quickly dispatched the still-willing bellhop to round up all of the Washington papers so that he could piece together as many facts (if newspapers reported such things) as were available so that he could bluff his way through this bit of reportage. Thus, have secured his "firsthand research," he quickly set off for a local bar known to be frequented by military men in hopes of adding a little more color to his notes on the President's final passing.

As was the usual case with military men, Clemens soon found himself an outsider in their crowds, and a catalyst of silence to each group he joined. Realizing that socializing with the men in blue was getting him nowhere, he quickly decided to dedicate himself to some serious drinking, and took a place at the bar next to a slovenly soldier whose shoulder bars bore the insignia of a cavalry major.

After asking for a bottle of Kentucky's best, the author was about to start down his latest road to inebriation when he heard the bartender say to the soldier, "If you want another drink, Reno, you're going to have to show me some coin first."

As the semi-conscious major searched through his pockets for the means to prolong his state of panacea, Clemens' not yet fully alcohol addled mind recognized the possible identity of his coin-desperate drinking companion. The author quickly told the bartender, "His drink's on me."

"Thank you, kind sir," the soldier said, his eyes brightening from their formerly half-mast state at the possibility of more drinks to come. "You are a gentleman and a scholar."

"And a fool and a scoundrel," Clemens added.

"Aren't we all," the soldier admitted, "including some of them who are no longer with us."

"Are you Major Marcus Reno formerly of the Seventh Cavalry?" Clemens asked.

"And if I am?" the drunken soldier replied.

"I understand that you were at the Little Big Horn with Custer at his moment of glory."

"I was drunk at the Little Big Horn at that bastard's moment of carnage, and now that he is dead, I don't care who knows it!"

"Shut up, Reno," a voice said from across the room.

Clemens sidled over, and gestured for the soldier to lower his voice.

Reno muttered under his breath. "What are they going to do, court-martial me? I kept my part of the deal. I've been quiet."

"Deal," the author queried, refilling the soldier's glass.

"Custer didn't have me court-martialed for drinking on duty, and I kept Benteen busy while the Custer gang usurped his and my commands," said Reno, taking another drink. "It wasn't that hard to keep him in the dark, and once the body count from the massacre was tallied up, I had little choice but to toe Yellow Hair's party line, and wallow in the blood of my fallen comrades."

Clemens could not help but notice Reno's voice was once again becoming distractingly loud.

"Yes, indeed," he began to boom, "let's drink to the bastard, I mean the General, I mean the President. First in line for the medals and honors, last in line to meet the enemy."

"Shut up, you old drunk!" another voice from the crowd ordered.

"Go to Hell," Reno retorted at the top of his lungs, "and give Custer my best!"

The exertion from his last outburst and effects of prolonged alcohol abuse brought on a coughing fir in the old soldier, and Reno was quickly spitting up blood.

"Someone get a doctor," Clemens shouted.

"Too late for that," Reno said between coughs. "Get O'Connor to write my obituary. He can make a hero out of any old fool."

"O'Connor?" Clemens said out loud, cradling the dying major in his arms until a pair of medics arrived to take him back to the base hospital.

"Sorry for the inconvenience," the officer accompanying the medic team offered, "but you know how old soldiers are, particularly when a comrade of ours has died, let alone one who has meant as much to us as President Custer."

"The General," Clemens said.

"That's what we who served with him called him."

"So you were part of the company at the Little Big Horn?"

"That's right," the officer replied. "Served right next

to that sorry wretch," he added. Gesturing towards the prone body of Reno that was being carried out the door. "It's a damned shame how some men go to pieces."

Clemens put his hand on the officer's shoulder to detain him for just another minute.

"He said something about an O'Connor," the author asked. "Was he part of the Seventh Cavalry on that day of glory?"

"Not really," the officer replied, disentangling himself from Sam and the crowd to follow his medics and Reno, "he was a reporter from the New York *Herald*. He was assigned to follow Custer around."

Clemens returned to his drink and made yet another mental note.

Tomorrow he would have to return to New York and he was pretty sure that he knew what he would find there.

The trip back northward was uneventful, and Sam Clemens was able to enjoy the privacy of his compartment for the entire trip, a situation that he took advantage of with the able assistance of a porter who for the right price had easy access to liquor and ladies in search of companionship. As his expenses were all on the New York *Herald*, he decided to make the most of it while he still could as he had a feeling that his days on Bennett's dole would soon be coming to an end.

His office was as he had left it and he realized that he would not miss it when he had to give it up.

As Marshall, his keeper, was out with a hopefully fatal or at least uncomfortable malady, the writer decided to expedite his own fate, and after a quick trip to the archives with a brief stopover in the personnel department, he gathered up his notes and the one or two belongings that he had kept in his office that he considered worth keeping, and set off for the night club where he knew that his benefactor would be enjoying an expensive cigar and a snifter of fine brandy.

Clemens was told to wait at the bar until Mr. Bennett was made aware of his arrival. The bartender offered him a drink, but he uncharacteristically declined, preferring to have a clear head for the upcoming discussion. After a few minutes the majordomo returned, and escorted him to a private sitting room where James Gordon Bennett, publisher of the New York *Herald* and the New York *World*, waited, cigar in one hand, brandy snifter in the other.

The large man set down his drink on an end table, and stood to greet his employee.

"Sam," he boomed, "this is an unexpected pleasure. How was Washington?"

"Unsettling," Sam replied, avoiding taking the publisher's hand by reaching into his own jacket to extract a cigar.

"How so?" the publisher asked. Sam detected a certain guarded quality in his tone. "Surely, you picked up more than enough material for a suitable memorial for the great man who has passed from the earth."

"I prefer to make my own fiction, thank you."

"Your assignment was to write a suitable memorial for President Custer that we could publish on the anniversary of his victory against all odds at the Little Big Horn."

"Why don't you have O'Connor do it? He was a *Herald* reporter," Clemens said, adding, "Oh, that's right. He's probably too busy being a press secretary and all."

The publisher asked pointedly, "And the point of all this is?"

"Custer was a fraud," Clemens barked, "and you abetted him."

Bennett laughed.

"Custer was a pawn," the publisher corrected, "and I made him. Grant wanted to seek a third term. That was contrary to the interests of a group of very important people. The corruption investigations helped to undermine his administration, but certain sources within the Republican party leaked that they were preparing to nominate Rutherford B. Hayes in his place. No one is more popular than an old war hero, except, perhaps, for a new war hero. Custer was the Democrats' answer since he could suit the bill on both counts, Civil War hero and Indian fighter—at least that was the case after we of the press worked our magic on him."

"Little Big Horn was a fraud!" Clemens insisted.

"No," the publisher corrected, "it was a terrible massacre of innocent white men at the hands of bloodthirsty savages . . . and out of that bloodstained ridge, a living legend was born. We knew the toll the battle would take. That's why we were very careful to put the proper interpretation on the events. Custer had to emerge both a hero and alive. He wouldn't have been much of a candidate if he was dead."

"But what about his men," Clemens countered, "the ones who really died on that ridge?"

"Men die in war," the publisher said matter-of-factly. "No doubt about it. But their deaths served a good cause."

"Your cause," Clemens countered.

"And those of a few of my compatriots," the publisher conceded, "as well as that of Custer, and the American people for that matter. He didn't have greatness thrust upon him. He asked for my help in attaining it. I was willing to assist him so that he could in turn assist me in other areas. Anything to get rid of those damned Republicans."

"Like ousting Grant and his lot."

"Exactly," the publisher agreed, took a drag from his cigar. "But this is water under a bridge. Your job is to further enshrine Custer in history. It is important that the legend outlive the facts."

"Why?" Clemens demanded.

"Custer had a nephew by the name of Autie Reed," Bennett replied. "I think that it would only be fitting that he ride his uncle's coattails to the White House."

"To protect your interests?"

"And those of my friends."

Clemens removed an envelope from inside his jacket, and handed it to the stately older man. "This is my resignation. Have another one of your has-been hacks to spin a tale of fiction befitting a legend. I resign."

"Not a problem," the publisher replied. "There are plenty more where you came from. Get out of here, and remember, men like me control the press. The facts are what we see fit to print."

"The facts are fiction," Clemens replied.

Bennett laughed, and chided the departing author, "Still sells better than anything you've ever written."

Clemens left the exclusive club, and sought out a bar to try to wash away the image of the bloodstained ground and the innocent lives that were lost on the ridges above the Little Big Horn in order to assure the election of a Democrat to the office of the President of the United States of America.

He reckoned it would take him more than a few bottles of Kentucky's best. He hoped that in a few hours he would know exactly how many.

VATI
R.M. Meluch

November 1941

Werner Moelders climbed out of the Horch staff car to face the Air Ministry. A massive building, it was designed to impose, intimidate. It did.

It would not have affected him were he not here without orders.

He had been too angry and desperate to wait, stuck in the frozen Crimea without fuel, without ammo, without airplane parts, without support. He had to make the Reichsmarschall listen to him. Face to face was the only way.

He'd known what he was going to say as he left the Eastern front. Here, now, in front of this 2800-room showpiece of the Reich, he had to wonder if he wasn't being headstrong and stupid. So hot he'd been to get here, the possibility of a charge of desertion hadn't occurred to him.

Brutal weather had closed behind him an icy door. He couldn't run now if he wanted.

Well, he thought cheerfully, that won't be a problem if they shoot me right here for leaving my command without orders.

He squared his angular shoulders and marched in.

Immediately he was ushered through layers of security

without question, as if everyone knew where he wanted to go.

They all knew him on sight. The most decorated man in the Luftwaffe, his picture was in every paper, every magazine, on picture postcards. Handsome. Aryan. Cameras loved him. He was the man who first broke the Red Baron's record. The Knight's Cross at his throat bore oak leaves, swords, and diamonds.

They sent him up the grand stairs through the kind of security gantlet one only passed through to see the Führer.

Oh hell.

Hitler was here. Hadn't expected this.

May as well be ordered shot from the top.

He touched his hat tucked under his arm. It was flat. He'd forgotten to put the spring back in. Fighter pilots regularly pulled the damn thing out. Now he was going to look sloppy for the Führer.

Never fear. The trusty adjutant was always good for making pilots presentable. Had dealt with worse. Was relieved that Moelders was sober. Produced a spring.

Hat looks sharp. Back under the arm. All's well.

Except what was he to say to the Führer?

Before he could rethink, the doors burst open from within. An aide started out, saw Moelders. Eyes big as wall clocks. Turned abruptly back into the room, clicked heels. Announced: "Oberst Werner Moelders."

A perplexed Moelders advanced to his fate. Quick glance round the room. Hitler not here at the moment. Absolutely everyone else was. Tin ties all around. The room was top heavy with Luftwaffe commanders who, like himself, ought to be on the front.

And all gawking at him as if seeing a ghost.

Galland, pretending to cough, growled the explanation in his ear, "The last words spoken in this room were: Get Werner Moelders back here right *now*!"

A vast expanse of uniform full of the Reichsmarschall advanced to meet him. Ice blue eyes raked up and down

the young ace. Goering missed only a beat before he
told Moelders flatly, "Faster next time."

Nobody laughed. It ought to have been funny, and
no one laughed. Something grim was afoot.

Porcine eyes stayed fixed hard on Moelders. Goering
knew full well that Moelders wasn't here in answer to
any summons. That he'd left the Russian front without
orders. Goering prodded with silken menace. "Apparently
you have a report for me."

Moelders' speech, rehearsed all the way here on the
HE 111 from Tscheplinka airport scattered and blundered
out in one lament, "Herr Reichsmarschall, why have you
abandoned me?"

Pupils shrank to pinpoints within the ice chips of irises.
Blue Max quivered under his chins. Goering hissed,
"Udet talked to you!"

Moelders blinked, adrift. "Udet?" That was who was
missing here. Moelders had an earful prepared for Udet
too, the Director General of Equipment. Aircraft
production was a singular joke. "Where is Udet?"

A leaden pause. Someone finally answered, "Dead."

A hitch. A cough. Sorrow muffled in shock. Heard
himself bleat, "How?"

An exchange of eyes. A hesitation.

"It was an accident," said Goering, pointedly. "Test
flying an experimental aircraft."

And there was the reason behind the sudden recall
of everyone to Berlin—to serve as honor guard at the
State funeral for Udet.

Moelders wouldn't let go of it. All anger, confusion,
and demands: How had it happened? What kind of
aircraft? Who was the Erk? Had sabotage been ruled
out? Where was the SS when you actually wanted them?
He wanted a thorough investigation—

Finally catching furtive desperate wave-offs from the
other pilots as if he were coming in for a wheels-up landing.

He shut up.

A door opened. Heels rapped together. *Heils*. Nothing more to be said now. Only listen to Hitler talk of the fallen ace Udet, of the Great War, of sacrifice, duty, honor, destiny.

Once outside among his own kind, Moelders took up his questions again. Where had Udet crashed? How?

"Let it go, Moelders." Galland cupped his hand against the wind to light his cigar. "Just let it lie." Wagged out the match. Turned up his leather collar. "And stay clear of the Fat One. You drilled him whether you know it or not."

"I don't like operating without complete information."

"You'll just have to." Galland clamped his teeth on his cigar. "There are no answers to those questions."

"Someone must know—"

Galland wrenched the cigar from his mouth, spelled it out for him, "There aren't any answers, because they haven't made up that part of the story yet, you dickhead!"

Moelders blinked great eyes like a deer in the crosshairs. Let Galland yell at him:

"It wasn't an accident. It wasn't even in an airplane. It was a free death."

Moelders murmured hollowly, bewildered, "They didn't say."

"And they're not going to. Can't tell the German people the second highest scoring ace of the Great War was so depressed he took his own life."

Blinked quickly. Turned his large eyes up to keep tears trapped. Felt his face crinkle, lips twitch. Meant to sound calm, official. Ought to be used to losing friends by now. Voice betrayed him, bobbled all over, "Did he say *why*?"

"No one's admitting it even happened. But rumor has it there was a note scrawled on his bedboard." Dark eyes gleamed black humor. Smoke jetted from his nostrils. Dark mustache spread with the wry twisting of his lips. "It said something like: Reichsmarschall, why have you abandoned me?"

❖   ❖   ❖

They carried the Old Eagle to rest next to Richthofen in the Invaliden Cemetery under a somber November sky. It was a long procession. Nazi salutes lined the streets on either side, and Moelders and Galland, mismatched bookends, marched a slow goose step alongside the flag-draped coffin on its horse-drawn caisson. Goering brought up the rear.

At the gravesite the Reichsmarschall bid Udet arise to Valhalla. Moelders crossed himself. Knew he'd hear about that one later. And did.

Felt as if he'd just walked over his own grave.

Moelders was taking off his black armband when he had a visitor. Filled the entire doorway. His shadow fell across everything.

Which Hermann is this? Moelders had to wonder. The jolly, magnanimous ace of the first war who wants to be my buddy? Or the demanding, small, tantrum-throwing dictator? And how angry is he?

"I thought I grounded you, Moelders."

It's my buddy. Moelders relaxed. "I haven't been flying fighters," he hedged.

"I'm told every morning you fly over the front in a Feisler Storch."

This had been reported with gushing admiration—how Moelders carried his own radio right up to the front, dove into a fox hole, and directed the fighter attack from where he could provide up-to-the-second information.

Moelders was always a lead-from-the-front sort of man. Greyhound slender, with a deceptively delicate look, he was easy to underestimate. Got airsick. Flew anyway. Always thinking of better ways to do things.

He had been the one to break up the tight, showy, ridiculous, Italian airshow triads that had once been the prescribed formation for fighters in combat. You spent more effort keeping formation than you did watching for the enemy. Moelders spread his fighters out and sent them up in pairs: One to hunt, one to watch both your tails. Fighter and wingman. You didn't even think of flying any other way now. It became the basic fighting unit in the Luftwaffe—and of every other air force that ran up against its deadly-efficient simplicity.

Werner Moelders was the most successful fighter ace there ever was. And didn't get there by stepping on anyone who wasn't the enemy. Too busy teaching his green fighters to survive up there. Men adored him. Called him *Vati*. Daddy. He was twenty-eight.

"You're too valuable to lose, Moelders," Goering chided.

"Going to the front and looking for myself is the only good way to get accurate information from the front to the pilots," Moelders defended his unauthorized flights.

"It's a good way to get yourself *shot*."

"I have to know what I'm sending them into. I won't spend my men like bullets."

"They're not your bullets."

"As a matter of fact, they are. You gave them to me. You made me General of the Fighter Arm."

"Not any more."

Moelders closed his eyes. Here it comes. He is angry after all.

Chummy tone turned to a snarl and then to a bellow, "They all say what a brilliant tactician you are. Since you seem to think you know all about equipment shortages, *you're* the new Luftwaffe Director General of Equipment!"

Udet's job. Eyes flew open. "That kill jar?" Moelders cried.

The Fat One frowned, offended. "You're supposed to thank me."

"For putting me in a position to be frustrated to *death*? Under layers of paper-pushing generals who would rather use aluminum to build termite-proof bunkers in Africa than build *modern* fighter aircraft? I'm still using Stukas in the Crimea!"

"The Führer likes Stukas."

"Retreading obsolete aircraft—and turning them out at a pitiful 375 per month—will lose Germany air superiority within the year."

"The war will be won within the year. We don't need to waste resources developing new types of aircraft. Jeschonnek says 360 aircraft a month is adequate. Anyway, wouldn't it be silly to step up production when we don't have enough pilots who can land an airplane rubber-side down as it is?"

"Then train more pilots! A *lot* more pilots—now! And train them *better*! Because our Chief of Staff is short-sighted, backward-thinking, and flat out wrong—and Udet knew it!"

Goering's voice became a lethal, ironic whisper. "Are you going to kill yourself?"

"I can't," Moelders snapped. "I'm Catholic."

Anger welled to an icy boil. "*I didn't abandon you*, you insolent pup! I'll authorize every stupid thing you ask for! I'll go over the Chief of Staff's head. I'll give you all the rope you want and just see if you don't twist it round your neck and hang yourself with it!"

When General Moelders finally located his new desk, his head was buzzing from too many toasts celebrating his promotion. Galland had come from France for the funeral, so there was champagne aplenty with which to drink his rival completely under the table.

Moelders' brain felt like a barrage balloon within the tiny confines of his skull. And, flying a desk now, there was no oxygen mask to press to his face.

He squinted where the desk had to be, buried under a shambles of notes, specs, requisitions, bids, all left in the chaos of Udet's last desperate days.

Moelders pushed at the papers. They shuffled thunderously.

On top of the heap, a big note shouted at him with huge, over-sized letters in the heavy gouged scrawl of a despairing man:

BUILD FIGHTERS.

April 1944

The Allies had pounded the Pas de Calais to dust, and all but pushed the Luftwaffe off the French map. The constant bombardment had taken out 1500 German locomotives, all the bridges that might carry supplies to German troops on the French coast, and any radar station they weren't going to leave intact to receive false signals.

All was in readiness for Overlord. They waited only on weather and tide.

Then suddenly they found their eyes punched out.

Allied reconnaissance flights stopped coming back. The German antiaircraft gunners must have got very good, because there was nothing in the air that could overtake a swift Mosquito reconnaissance plane at 408 mph. Till now, anyway.

Knew the Germans were moving aircraft back into France because the activity showed up on long-range radar. Couldn't pinpoint the new airfields to bomb them. Flak thick enough to walk on. Not a good development. Someone new had to be in charge of Luftwaffe operations on the Western front.

A glint in the sky over Portsmouth, moving very fast, drew Allied eyes up from the decks of transports where men dragged camouflage netting over rows of tanks.

Mosquito?

No. Wood planes don't glint like that. And even Mosquitos didn't move that fast.

Faster than a Mosquito.

Faster than a V1 rocket.

"It's a UFO."

"It's Superman."

"It's the bloody Hun!"

A shark shape with swept-back wings. A pair of them, like Huns on a free hunt.

Ack-ack opened up on them, but failed to lead off an angle anywhere near to catching them. Had to wonder where the interceptors were. And what happened to bloody radar?

No answers came. Only a lot of worried, muttering brass. The Hun was meant to believe that the invasion force would hit Pas de Calais. Someone wasn't buying it. Not if the Hun was looking for them here in the packed harbors of England's southern coast.

In the void of answers, the name Dieppe echoed over and over.

No one was telling the massed troops that the Hun had come in under radar and climbed to altitude fast as thinking about it. The intruders had hied halfway home before the Mosquito interceptors got airborne.

Radar had been able to clock the fleeing bandits, but there had to be a mistake.

"How fast?"

"Five hundred forty miles per hour."

A dead pause. Said something brilliant: "Can't be."

Looked over the mustered invasion forces of Overlord. "Jets." On the eve of invasion. Too easy to picture 300,000 dead soldiers floating facedown in the churning Channel water. "Hitler's got jets."

Knew this place. Moelders had been here before. His pilots used to eat lunch in the open sunlight, at tables with linen cloths, with vases of cut flowers and bottles of French wine. They had toasted an invasion that never came to pass.

Four years later they expected invasion again. Incoming, this time.

No tables in the sunlight now. His men hid under trees, camouflage netting, and a roof of flak. Fighter planes crouched in blast pens. Erks propped fake trees to hide the long runways needed to heave a jet fighter into the air.

Fortunately the ME 262's low-pressure tires allowed takeoffs from grass, or there would be no disguising the runways at all.

Generalfeldmarschall Hugo Sperrle had retreated from the bombed-out airfields of France. As his final act as General of the Third Air Fleet, he pulled back the last of his fighter groups to Berlin.

Here Moelders begged to be cut free of his desk and sent to the front to put his new aircraft into operations for himself. His record of 101 victories had fallen two and three times over, so the Reichsmarschall let him back into a cockpit.

Moelders' first order as the new General of the Third Air Fleet was to move the Luftwaffe bases back into France. If the railroads and bridges were out, well then *fly* the equipment in, just *get* it in. As for defense, this was German territory. Defend it or lose it. And losing was not an option.

Retreat was not in his nature. Men die in retreat.

He abandoned Sperrle's plush headquarters in the Luxembourg Palace in Paris. His HQ was in Pas de Calais. Where the invasion was said to be coming.

He could not believe how far out of hand the situation had gone. Sperrle should have been put out to pasture years ago. His attacks on England over the past two years had been sporadic at best, and at the wrong target. Sperrle's target had been London.

Bombing civilians ran against conscience, and struck Moelders as poor strategy besides. Should have hit their airfields, their factories, their radar. And he should never have stopped *looking* at England. Sperrle's idea of reconnaissance only went to show how long it had been since that man had ever been in a cockpit.

To a fighter pilot, seeing—seeing *first*—was life.

Moelders knew that the Allies knew what *he* was doing. Even after taking out their reconnaissance flights. "As a cloak of secrecy, we operate like a sieve," muttered in hiding under the snarl of Merlin engines. Allied fighter sweeps were relentless.

Thank God for the V1 sites. Stupid, random weapons to his mind. Good for drawing off vast tonnages of Allied bombs. The Allies did much better shooting V1's out of the air than they did hitting their bases. But let them try. Gave them something to bomb that was not one of Moelders' airfields.

At once he was hauled back to explain to the Führer what he thought he was doing; why was he taking fighter cover away from Berlin; and why were those jets going operational without bomb racks on them?

Aides cringed outside the doors of the Führer's inner sanctum, expecting the young general to reemerge carrying his handsome head under his arm.

Moelders had brought back pictures of English harbors.

Watery blue eyes scanned with incomprehension, amazement. Couldn't understand, would not believe what he was seeing. "Where did you get these?"

"I took them myself."

The Führer stared in the shock of being blind-sided. He'd been advised that the Allies were planning an invasion, but this. This. No one had dared describe this to Adolf Hitler.

Moelders added, "Every harbor looks like that. The buildup along England's southern coast is so big the whole island is tilting."

Hitler had gone white with rage. The bearer of bad news waited.

The voice came very soft, directed inward, "I have long known my generals are not telling me everything they know. What of the north? You didn't take any pictures of Patton's army."

"Too easy. It's almost as if they want us to take pictures of that stuff."

Softly, almost a dare, "And where do you think the attack will come?"

There were 800 miles of coast to defend.

"Mein Führer, I don't care where they think they're coming."

The eyes grew quite round. Forelock drooped across ridged brow. Waited for him to explain that. Better be good.

"I wouldn't cower in my house waiting for a thief to break in. I would storm out and hit him." His finger landed on a picture of Southhampton Harbor crowded with transport ships, their netted decks packed with tanks. "Here."

Hitler rose, vibrating. He gave Moelders his head all right. And threw the reins and everything else he could call to bear in behind him against England.

He wanted the roads of France lined with antiaircraft batteries. Mines. He wanted mines in the Channel. And aircraft. Why was aircraft production at a pitiful 1000 planes a month?

The Owls came in the moonlight, when they could see, in case the Allies jammed their radar. HE 219's were new in the West. Quick, versatile, they had been keeping the Bear at bay on the Eastern front.

The London Blitz had ended three years ago. So when the air raid sirens wailed back to life, one had to assume it was another V1 rocket strike. Either that or another spasmodic terror raid on London. Those seldom came anymore.

The sector controller saw the plots rising over France, over Belgium, over Norway, swarming, and heading toward England. A mass of them. Too many targets.

Scramble, they ordered. Scramble everybody.

But as the raiders crossed the coast, they dropped

bundles of *Dueppel* radar-reflective foil, and they turned.

Allied fighters rose to meet an attack on London that did not come. The Owls veered and struck no deeper than the coastline—the harbors and the coastal airfields of Hawkenge, Manston, Tangmere and Lympne.

All the AA in the world ripped open the skies to give the intruders a 90-mm salute. The guns only fired to 12,000 feet at night so as not to hit friendly fighters.

The enemy bombers were high and the friendly fighters were over London.

As the first wave of bombers retreated, they left some targets burning bright enough for the second wave to see. The second wave did not even need the pathfinder flares to light the way. They skimmed in under the radar, popped up over target and skulked off low over the water.

The British claimed nine intercepts. The Germans counted three losses to groundfire.

But night bombing was never very accurate—almost as accurate as night intercepts—and Moelders wondered if they'd inflicted any real damage.

During the London Blitz, daylight used to bring an end to the bombing. Dawn's first light this day brought an enormous wave of bombers, largest yet. Some of them carried guided bombs, the kind the Luftwaffe sent against ships. The Owls were coming after the troop transports that would carry the invasion forces for Overlord.

Tempests and Spitfires and Mustangs stacked up over the coast to greet them.

A German guided bomb was on a wire, so there was no radar to jam. But the bomber needed a straight run to guide the bomb down by sight.

By God and Supermarine, they were not going to get one.

"Tally ho! Tally ho!" a Tommy called the attack.

"Watch for the fighter cover! Watch for the fighter cover!" the Allied fighters warned each other as they closed in for the kill.

The bombers straightened out for their attack run as if the interceptors were not there. As if they had guardian devils. Something was wrong.

The Hun bomber could not be here alone, even as the controller was reporting no plots overhead.

The Allied fighters craned their necks. Squinted into the sun for fighters. They had to be here.

They came from below like sharks. They looked like sharks with their blunt-point noses and swept-back wings. And they climbed over you before you could twitch, tearing into your crate with 30-mm cannon as they whistled past.

"What the hell are those!"

A barrage of excited voices broke out in Moelders' wake. He cursed himself for going too fast. Got in some strikes, not concentrated enough to bring the kite down. Woke them up though.

"Did you see his tail fin!"

"Did I see—!" A sputter. "I didn't see *shit*!"

"Have a care there, Yank. There *are* ladies on the R/T."

Quick apologies to the dulcet-voiced ground controller and back to yelping after the jets.

There are Huns on this frequency too, Moelders wanted to say. Had told his own squadrons to shut up on the radio. All the voices were English.

"Gotta be the Red Baron himself!"

"He's dead, you clot."

"He's right there and I want him dead!"

Moelders pulled up high and clear to turn for another strike. Looked round for his wingman, Karl.

"Sorry, Yank. This one's mine. See those chevrons? I believe that's a ruddy Hun winco."

It's a ruddy Hun air marshal, if you don't mind. Indignant. Singled out a target. Checked the aft fuel tank. Okay to dive. Pushed the throttle. Stomach flew back into the tail section.

"Here he comes. Here he comes—"

"I got him I got him I—oh hell."

"—There he goes. Shit off a shovel."

No kill. Too fast again. Diving like lightning. Approaching critical .86 mach. No shudder. The sweet fighter will let you kill yourself without warning. Eased back. Glanced back. Nest of them after him. Calling him a coward, bastard, sod.

Fine, Moelders thought as a raging tower of orange flame belching from below told him an Owl had struck something fuel-laden. At least some of the bombers had gotten through while these boys were chasing his scalp. Would not want to explain himself at that debriefing. Weird impulse to instruct them on the priority of targets.

He'd slowed to pull up. Queasy. The hounds were still baying on his tail. Closing now.

"Come back here, you coward! I got you now! I got you!"

You boys do know that I always fly with a wingman . . . ?

"Reg! On your six! On your six!"

Karl's voice: *"Abschuss!"*

Homeward to paint another mark on his wingman's tail fin and review the mission.

Knew the news wasn't all good. His daylight bombers received a proper pasting from the RAF and the USAAF fighters. There were simply too many of them, too eager.

He'd even lost a 262 to a propeller-driven crate. Been sucked into a tail chase with a Spitfire YO-D over Tangmere. Old tactics don't work in a new aircraft.

The pilot did not survive. You can't crawl out against g's in a diving 262.

At least the wreckage had fallen into the water, not into British hands.

The jets should have struck the Allies with terror. There was no terror in a Mustang's heart. They made you feel rather like one of the royal stags at the Reichsjaegerhof. Not something to be feared. Something to be bagged.

Keen. They were all keen. All the young men who

had missed the *Kanalkampf*—the Battle of Britain, they called it on the far side of the Ditch. Those that had been too young. They were jolly eager to get into it now.

The overeager Tommies were good for taking out a few of their American friends. A Mustang had the same angular wings as Tommy's old nemesis, the ME 109E. Of course, Moelders knew he had sent no short-winded 109's against England this time. So he told his Luftwaffe, if it looks like a 109, shoot it.

The next wave was a huge success. Bombers at 30,000 feet without fighter escort. The maiden ops of the Arado 234 jet bomber.

The Arados had scant defensive armament—two guns, rear-firing, the only view an Allied fighter would ever get of them. Didn't have to fire them. No one even came close.

The Arados dropped their babies and came home unmolested. Landed under an umbrella of flak to beat back the Mustangs that dogged them home.

Could have used a dozen more squadrons of them. But it was a miracle he had any. During Moelders' tenure as Director General of Equipment it had been a battle to keep production focused on a few workable designs, while egos thick as enemy groundfire kept threatening to funnel resources off to someone else's pet project.

The first day would prove to be his luckiest. From there he learned just how big and angry a hornets' nest he'd kicked.

Still it had been the right decision. The only decision. What else was there? Wait for the ground troops to come to shore? He shuddered. Wouldn't that have been one of history's colossal blunders? The Allies had to be thinking twice about launching all those men into the water now.

Dieppe. Hoped they remembered Dieppe.

The Allies were quick to bring the battle back to France. Straightaway they rooted out the airfields with the long runways to hit the jets on the ground. Rat-catching, they called it.

Pounding of 88-mm guns announced their coming. And soon the humming of heavy engines.

Viermots. B-17's. Saw them lumbering over the horizon under a Mustang cloud as his 262 surged into the air with racks of 55-mm rockets under either wing. Resist like hell punching the throttle. Felt like a landbound walrus on takeoff.

Became an archangel at altitude.

Even angels blanched at the sight of an oncoming box of B-17's. A fortress of fortresses, bristling with weapons. How to attack it? The top? From underneath? Sides?

They were already here and he had run out of options. *Head on it is.*

Released the safety on the rockets, turned into the attack. Radioed Karl, "Follow me."

"*Vati*, do you know what you're doing?"

Knew full well he didn't. No one had ever attacked a box of *viermots* with a jet before. Making up tactics as he went along.

Closing speed was ungodly. The big bombers loomed. Got huge just like that.

Karl: "*Vati*, where are we going?"

"Don't blink. And when you break, break upward."

Screen full of B-17. Swear he could see the pilot's eyes.

"*Los!*" Rockets away and wrench the column back. Climb!

Vision narrowed into a tunnel. Tunnel to a dot. Grunt against g's. Ease out of the turn.

The tunnel widened. Swallow back nausea. Karl whooping in his ears. "That'll make you forget your wife!"

Not habit-forming. Blink. Swallow hard. Swallow again. Look back where his B-17 hobbled, smoked, dropped from the box.

Waves of boxes behind it dropped bombs on his runway. Prayed his Erk had found a safe place to hide.

Smell of J2 fuel doing loops in his stomach.

Trying to climb high enough to turn and hit again. Anytime you give up speed, there's always a Mustang waiting for you. It was a law of nature.

Lost track of the other half of his *schwarm*. "Fritz, are you here?"

Fritz's voice: "I have eighty-nine of them cornered."

Turned. Raked up a straggling *viermot* with cannon fire.

Then searched for a place to put down.

His alternate airfield looked like the face of the moon.

Had a sudden memory of jabbing a landing on a muddy runway during the Phony War. Gear had stabbed in the soft ground. Done a truly capital nose-over. Do that in a jet, he'd get worse than a stiff back. Jets burned like hell. Like hell itself.

Couldn't really picture himself without skin.

Still reluctant to abandon ship. Ended up landing on a highway. French farmer, sweating rivers, drove them back to their gutted airfield. Erks in black coveralls busy as ants.

Both sides had learned during the *Kanalkampf* that a destroyed airfield does not stay destroyed. Put out the fires. Fill in the holes. Ferry the 262's back to the field and we're in it again.

Fighting more furious than he could ever remember. Losses were staggering.

The objectives of the combatants were the same as they had been that summer of 1940; only reversed. Now, while the Allies needed to gain complete air superiority to cover their invasion force, the Luftwaffe need only survive until autumn when the English Channel grew teeth.

It was the kind of battle you don't know you've won until much later. A thing *not* happening was certain only in retrospect.

The days of spring bled and smoldered and rained together. Worst weather in twenty years.

A day. A Tuesday. Like the rest. The weather was bad early. Skies cleared in patches through the afternoon. More losses. English harbors choking up black clouds from burning oil spills. The Channel water was rough.

Feldmarschall Erwin Rommel telephoned before the line was cut again. He had slipped back to Berlin two days before—by car, as OKW didn't like its commanders to fly. Rommel called because the tides were right, he said. Had a fear of the land battle starting without him. Trusted Moelders to give him a straight, accurate answer.

"No. You're not missing the show," Moelders assured him. "It's still an air war. Try to enjoy your leave. You get few enough of them." Glanced at the date in his diary. Remembered, before he rang off, "Say happy birthday to Lucie." That was June 6.

By November everyone knew there would be no invasion from the West this year. Hitler was calling it a victory, the fatal blow to all their enemies—as if a buildup of forces did not yet threaten on the far side of the Alps, or the Bear's millions weren't pushing back in force, or bombs from Britain did not still rain from the sky every night.

Hitler swore revenge on that warmonger Roosevelt. Wanted to attack America. He wanted 262's on aircraft carriers. Bombs on 262's. Asked Moelders for his suggestions.

"Sue for peace while we still can," Moelders answered.

Blew up. Railed at Moelders for his lack of Nazi ideology. It was his Roman Catholicism that stood in his way. "Rome and Moscow are the same," he reminded him. Demanded Moelders' loyalty. All of it.

Moelders didn't understand. "But you have it, *mein Führer.*"

No. Wanted him to renounce the church.

"Everything of this world is yours," Moelders assured him.

"What is that supposed to mean?"

"I can only render unto Caesar that which is Caesar's and unto God that which is God's."

The Führer reminded Moelders from whom came his Knight's Cross, oak leaves, swords, and diamonds, his rank, his command. Did he want to keep those? Caesar demanded.

Moelders unfastened the Ritterkreuz with all its attendant decorations from his neck, surrendered it on its red, black and white ribbon. "Hail Caesar."

Cigar smoke stung his nostrils. Moelders recognized his visitor even before he stepped into his library, before he spoke: "Where's your tin tie, Moelders?"

Rolled gray eyes up to find Galland standing above his chair in a wreath of cigar smoke. Moelders answered without animation, "I've been sacked."

Galland took in the cozy room—the little girl fallen asleep over a picture book by the hearth, the baby boy clutching *Vati's* pantleg for balance with one wet hand, the other pudgy little hand in his mouth. Moelders had married another pilot's widow back in '41 and had started a family at once. "So this is your new position? Nursemaid?"

Moelders pulled the boy onto the chair with him. "This is Viktor."

Galland lifted a scarred brow at the name. "For your triumph over the Americans?"

"For my brother."

Viktor made gurgling sounds, vaguely wordlike, gazed about with wide, wide eyes. Had 20/10 vision like his father, no doubt.

Moelders smoothed down a wispy cowlick. "I just want to protect them. But I'm three years old again, holding my mother's skirt. My father is dead and my homeland is under the heel of the world. I told her I wanted to be a soldier. It's what I wanted since I can remember wanting anything."

"You don't talk like the man who just saved the Reich."

"Is that what I did? I wanted to save *Germany*. I don't think I saved anything. I prolonged the war. Can tactical brilliance be a strategic blunder?"

"You're babbling, Moelders," Galland said loudly; then, drawing up a chair, in a murmur, "The walls have ears. I know my phone does. They record my calls."

No need to say who "they" were. Moelders nodded.

Galland went on, "When you dropped out of sight, I was afraid you'd . . ." Paused, regarded the children, rephrased, "Had an accident. People do."

Moelders gave a bleak smile. "Remember when all the accidents were real? Spanish roads. Spanish wine. Our *driving*. No one even shooting."

Sleeping beauty stirred by the fire. Sighed back to sleep.

Father's eyes fond, sad. "What's to happen to them? I don't know what I achieved in the West, if anything. The bombs still fall. The Amis aren't going to just sit on that island. What it cost them not to cross—it's too bitter to contemplate. They won't let the Ivans fight it out alone. There are millions of them. With factories we can't touch."

"And a supply line I can't even think about," Galland countered.

"They'll find a way to get into it. We should hold our borders while we still have borders. I can't even imagine how this will end. If the war ever does end, do you think we could manage to have an *election*, again?"

That was the closest to treason Werner Moelders would ever come. A soldier to the core, mutiny was not in him. But apparently he'd had enough of the greatest supreme military commander of all time, too.

"Are you going to run for office?" Galland asked, only half jesting. "They talk about you and Rommel that way. Bad for both your healths, by the way."

"I'm only thirty-one."

"You're older than I'll ever be." Galland was thirty-two.

"I'm not a politician. But having these makes you think." He snugged his little boy close to his side. "I look into the future and all I see is war. The end—there isn't any end. None that I can see."

"Do you want to get back in it?"

Brow lifted. Listless curiosity.

"If you can stand taking orders from me, you can fly for me," said Galland. "The squadron's all aces. I could use another qualified pilot. Tolerably qualified."

Moelders' reaction was not as eager as expected. Gray eyes gazed into space. "You can lose every battle but the last one. Can I have won the battle and in so doing lost the war?"

"What?"

"Slim says I think too much. Is there such a thing?"

"I don't know, hero. Are you going to come fly, or sit here in a flat spin?"

Moelders settled little Viktor into the deep armchair and rose slowly. "I'll fly for you."

War without end. Amen.

But all things end. It came with the drone of Superforts in 1945. A wail of air raid sirens. Ack-ack pounding the night. Search lights raking the darkness.

Moelders' ears pricked like a hound's. Engines. Couldn't see them. Knew the heavy Wright growl.

Viermots. The really big ones. Knew most of them would get through. Damn them, how deep they could strike. Wished Germany had English radar.

Thought of Hitler's voice on the radio earlier in the day, whipping enthusiasm, envisioning a new dawn for the Third Reich.

As this night, over sleeping Dresden, the dawn came early. Brighter than a thousand suns.